P9-EKS-015

THE HERMETIC MILLENNIA

TOR BOOKS BY JOHN C. WRIGHT

The Golden Age
The Phoenix Exultant
The Golden Transcendence
The Last Guardian of Everness
Mists of Everness
Orphans of Chaos
Fugitives of Chaos
Titans of Chaos
Null-A Continuum
Count to a Trillion

THE HERMETIC MILLENNIA

JOHN C. WRIGHT

A TOM DOHERTY ASSOCIATES BOOK
NEW YORK

This is a work of fiction. All of the characters, organizations, and events portrayed in this novel are either products of the author's imagination or are used fictitiously.

THE HERMETIC MILLENNIA

Copyright © 2012 by John C. Wright

All rights reserved.

A Tor Book
Published by Tom Doherty Associates, LLC
175 Fifth Avenue
New York, NY 10010

www.tor-forge.com

Tor® is a registered trademark of Tom Doherty Associates, LLC.

Library of Congress Cataloging-in-Publication Data

Wright, John C. (John Charles), 1961–
The Hermetic millennia / John C. Wright.—1st ed.
p. cm.
"A Tom Doherty Associates Book."
Continues author's Count to a trillion.
ISBN 978-0-7653-2928-8 (hardcover)
ISBN 978-1-4299-4830-2 (e-book)
1. Human-alien encounters—Fiction. 2. Interstellar travel—Fiction. 3. Cryopreservation of organs, tissues, etc.—Fiction. I. Wright, John C. (John Charles), 1961– Count to a trillion. II. Title.
PS3623.R54H47 2012
813'.6—dc23

2012024856

First Edition: December 2012

Printed in the United States of America

0 9 8 7 6 5 4 3 2 1

ACKNOWLEDGMENTS

The author thanks his long-suffering and patient wife, who is the muse of all his ideas, as well as many kind readers who offered advice. I would like particularly to thank Sean McNulty, Latin scholar, and Tom Simon, pundit, for their assistance in difficult linguistic and historical matters.

CONTENTS

When I dipt into the future far as human eye could see;
Saw the Vision of the world, and all the wonder that would be.—

. . . .

Saw the heavens fill with commerce, argosies of magic sails,
Pilots of the purple twilight dropping down with costly bales;

. . . .

Heard the heavens fill with shouting, and there rain'd a ghastly dew
From the nations' airy navies grappling in the central blue . . .

—Alfred, Lord Tennyson

PART TWO

A World of Fire

1
Theft of Fire

A.D. 2535

1. Sir Guy

All he wanted to do was stay dead.

Menelaus Montrose woke up while his body was still frozen solid. The bioimplants the battle surgeons of the Knights Hospitalier had woven into his brain stem were working well enough for him to send a signal to the surface of the coffin, activate the pinpoint camera cells dotting its outer armor, and see who was trying to wake him up.

The light in the crypt was dim. The walls were irregular brick, and in places were cemented with bones and skulls. Niches held both coffins for the dead and cryonic suspension coffins for the slumbering.

There was a figure like a metal ape near the vault door, which had moved on vast pistons and stood open. The light spilled in from here. Only things near the door were clear.

To one side of the larger metal statue was a marble sculpture of Saint Barbara, the patron of grave-diggers, holding a cup and a palm leaf in her stiff, stone hands; to the other was Saint Ubaldo, carrying a crosier, whose office was to ward off neural disorders and obsessions. Above the vault door was a relief showing the martyrdom of Saint Renatus Goupil under the tomahawks of Iroquois. He was the patron saint of anesthesiologists and cryonicists. Above all this, in an arch, were written the words TUITIO FIDEI ET OBSEQUIUM PAUPERUM.

From this, Menelaus knew he had been moved, at least once, from his previous interment site beneath Tiber Island in the Fatebenefratelli Hospital vault. That had been little over a quarter century ago: the calculations of Cliomancy did not predict any historical crisis sufficient to require him to be relocated in so short a space as thirty years. That meant Blackie was interfering with the progression of history again.

The larger metal statue moved, ducking its head and stepping farther into the vault. Menelaus could see the Maltese cross enameled in white on the red breastplate. There were four antennae and microwave horns on his back, folded down. The scabbard for his (ceremonial) broadsword was empty, and so was the holster for his (equally ceremonial) chemical-energy pistol. Between helmet and goggles and breather mask, the figure looked like a nightmarish bug.

Montrose turned on the microphones on the outside of the coffin, and special cells in his brain stem sent signals to receivers dotting the inner coffin lid, and also to implants lining his auditory nerve. It sounded like a strange, flat, echoless noise, not like something that actually came through his ear, but he could make it out.

Menelaus turned on the speaker vox. "Why do you disturb my slumber, Sir Knight?"

He heard the ticking hum of motors and actuators coming from the armored figure. Like a mountain sinking into the sea, the big armored figure knelt. Menelaus realized this was strength-amplification armor. He tried to work out the Cliometric constellation of a set of military circumstances where this type of gear would serve any purpose that a sniper with a powerful set of winged remotes could not serve better, and his imagination failed. Unless the man was wrestling giants, or facing enemies who could walk up to arm's length and tear the flesh from his bones, he did not see the purpose.

"My apologies, sleeper. Ah. Our records are somewhat dark. Are you Menelaus Montrose? You don't sound like him."

"Why the poxy hell do you disturb my poxy slumber, Sir goddam Knight?"

"Ah! Montrose! Good to hear you again, Liege."

"Guy? Sir Guy, is that you?"

"Pellucid thawed me out two days ago. As we agreed, I have a veto over anyone trying to disturb you, even your pet machine. And it is His Excellency Grandmaster Guiden von Hompesch zu Bolheim now. They promoted me when I slept."

"Yeah, they do poxified pox like that to you when you ain't up and about to fend it off."

Another implanted circuit in his brain stem made contact with a library cloth stored in an airtight capsule inside the coffin armor. The self-diagnostic showed much more deterioration than he would have expected. Half the circuits were dead, and file after file was corrupt. But he brought up the calendar, and a fiber fed the pixy image directly into the same neural circuits he was using to peer through the cameras.

"Pox! Thirty-five years. Rania's not back yet? Any signals?"

"I have not heard, Liege. There is something that may be a signal. I would have prevented them from thawing you, if it were not significant."

"So tell me."

"An astronomer has detected massive energy discharges erupting from the Diamond Star. So it looks like your Princess arrived there years ago, and we are seeing now the result of some sort of macro-scale engineering. The data are ambiguous, and the Order thought you would want, with your own eyes, to look the data over and draw your own conclusion. Was I right to wake you?"

"Damn right, and thank you for asking. Have the astronomer send his data into the coffin. I can tell you the input-output registers."

"I'd rather you thawed out fully."

"My brain is working. What else do I need?"

"There has been a lot of wire corruption since you slumbered, Liege, and the Order made laws saying certain messages have to be delivered in person, naked eye, naked ear. Nobody uses or trusts the kind of interface implants you and I have."

Montrose was not just surprised; he was shocked. His Cliometric calculations had not anticipated such a radical change in the basic social and technological patterns. One more thing to look into before he slumbered again. He said wryly: "Relicts already, eh?"

"A quarter century is a long time. And they insist I wear clothing, like an unevolved."

"You ain't talking aloud, are you?"

"No, Liege. Nerve jack. My suit has a short-range emitter."

It took a long while for the molecular machinery clustered in the major cell groups in his vital organs, bone marrow, and parasympathetic system to restore him to life. Even through the nerve-block, there was something like growing pains, and his limbs trembled and shuddered. The last thing to happen was that special artificial glands released adrenaline into his system, and implants made of his own jinxed flesh, like the Hunter's organ and Sach's organ of electric eels, flushed with positively charged sodium and jolted his heart into action. Automatic circuits performed a few tests, just as undignified and invasive as anything a doctor would do, but with no bedside manner. Menelaus just gritted his teeth.

Montrose came up out of the gel, dripping, a white glass caterpillar-drive pistol in either hand. These 8-megajoule Brownings were waterproof, slightly curved, streamlined tubes of a white glassy substance, made with no moving parts and powered by a radioactive pellet likely to last 4.47 billion years. And they fitted nicely into his hands. (But he still missed his six-pound hand cannon as long as his forearm that he had used for dueling. The old Krupp railgun had been a handsome piece of artillery.)

Sir Guiden was still on one knee. He had removed his bulky helm, slung his goggles, and the wire from his skull-jack lay across his neck.

Underneath, his hair was close cropped, and he wore a black leathery cap that buckled under his chin. His face was rounder and fleshier than Menelaus remembered from 2501. Was that a touch of gray at the temples?

His age was hard to tell, since Sir Guiden sported a full-face tattoo shaped like a double-headed eagle: Wings surrounded his eyes, crooked talons curled on his cheeks, and twin hawk heads bearing crowns tilted left and right over his eyebrows. Montrose thought it one of the ugliest and most absurd decorations imaginable.

Montrose said, "I was wondering why you stepped in here all in full kit."

"Because you are known to sleep with guns in your hands, sir. That, and no one else could talk to you."

"So no one else has implants? The whole idea was that I could thaw my brain up to dehibernation, while leaving the rest of me iced, and that would save on wear and tear. Hurts like the pestilential devil to shock the heart awake, you know. Why couldn't they just use a hand mic? Clip it to the coffin?"

"The technology is hard to come by, Liege. The automated factories were under Exarchel's control."

"What about that motorized ape suit?"

"You like it?" asked Sir Guiden, pleased.

"May my member get pustules if'n I don't! Always wanted future soldiers to dress in roboexoskeletons. But it seems damnified impractical, and I surely don't recall you wearing nothing alike to them when you climbed in your coffin."

"I thawed in 2508 and again in 2526 to oversee certain operations."

"War operations?"

"That, and moving the buried coffins when Rome was burned by orbital mirrors. The Vatican is gone."

"How many people killed?"

"None. The city was already evacuated due to banner storms of hunger silk. The Consensus insisted that every city have an evac procedure in place, with an aeroscaphe like a lifeboat folded against the side of every house and tower. Lucky they did."

"I don't care about that," said Montrose. He planned to have the current events, no matter how dramatic, be ancient history before he woke again. "Tell me about my coffins."

"Safe. You'll be interested to know I used your money to purchase Cheyenne Mountain from the government of Kansas."

"That's in Colorado."

"There are six territories in the North American plains region calling themselves the United States of America. I made the land purchase from George Washington of the Government of the United States of America that is based in Topeka."

"George Washington?"

"His name was Joua Ja Gomez before he was acclaimed to his position. All the leaders in Kansas become George Washington. He wears a tricornered hat and dresses in red, white, and blue. Very colorful. But Cheyenne Mountain and the surrounding land are now officially a part of the sovereign territory of Malta, and under the government and suzerainty of the Grand Master of the Order."

Menelaus wondered how many more centuries the Knights of Malta would continue to hold government meetings, considering that they had not held Malta since Napoleon kicked them off it. They retreated without a fight, having sworn an oath never to raise weapons against other Christians.

"There is an old buried fortress beneath Cheyenne Mountain," Sir Guiden said, "that should last thousands of years. If we move you there secretly, we might be able to endure undisturbed for longer."

Menelaus realized that the kneeling man was waiting for permission to get to his feet. "Up! You don't have to stand on ceremony with me, or wait for permission to wipe your bottom in the jakes. So who is this *we*? And why are we going to be holed up a thousand years? The Diamond Star is only fifty light-years away."

The armored figure, with a hiss of motors, rose to his feet, spine straight as a rifle barrel. "We are. The Sovereign Military Hospitalier Order of Saint John, of Jerusalem, of Rhodes, of Malta, and of Colorado agreed to guard you in your coffin, Your Honor. We took an oath. I personally swore to you. Do you think merely the passage of time will cow me? Ninety men and eight stand without these doors, ready to retaliate upon any who would desecrate holy ground, where the honored dead lay themselves down, waiting."

"It was ninety-nine when I went under, not counting you."

"One of them, Sir Alof Villiers de l'Isle-Adam, during the thaw of 2526 was granted leave to depart the order that he might wed a current girl."

"So why are we talking about a thousand years?"

"Thousands, sir. With an *s*."

"You ain't gunna tell me, are you? You have to drag this out and keep me on pins and needles."

"Liege, there are some things that you must see with your own eyes. The observatory is directly above us, and drawing nigh."

2. *The Empire of the Air*

Montrose was pleased, if a little shocked, that Sir Guy allowed him to walk around under the sky. It implied that assassins of the Cryonarchy were no longer seeking his life.

The Cryptonarchs had been, at one time, the only people Montrose thought he could trust with the secret of xypotechnology, cryotechnology, and with the power of the antimatter recovered from V886 Centauri, the Diamond Star. They had been his own extended family, grandsons and great-grandsons of cousins and nephews.

But the Cryonarchs proved unworthy of the trust Montrose had invested, and had fallen prey to time, to corruption, to weariness. He had removed them from power by the simple expedient of altering the orbital elements of the remaining world supply of antimatter, a few ever-dwindling crystals of anticarbon diamond. These centaurs occupied orbits beyond Neptune, where encounters with particles of normal matter were rare, but not so far as to encounter the paradoxically thicker areas of deeper, transplutonian space, where there was no solar light-pressure to clear particles away. Then Montrose had given the orbital elements to a priest named Thucydides Montrose, along with his latest formulation to create augmented intelligence.

Montrose was not much of a churchgoing man himself, but the Roman Catholic Church had been in business two and a half millennia, older than any institution of man. He was wagering that Black del Azarchel, a Spanish Roman Catholic, would not lightly destroy it.

Looking up at the heavens, Montrose had the sinking sensation that he might lose that bet. Because there was a second reason why it might be safe to walk around under the naked sky, aside from the remission of the Cryonarchy vendetta against him. Sniper technology must have fallen to a new low. That implied a widespread civilizational collapse.

Clouds the hue of iron hid the sky, and drizzle fogged the air. Before him was a cathedral made of gray stone, withered with age, with a rose window like a cyclops eye, and two square bell-steeples rearing like port and starboard conning towers on some motionless ship of stone.

Angels with mossy faces stood on posts to either side of iron gates rusted open. The boneyard was beyond.

To judge from the names on the tombstones, this place was in England or North America. He assumed he was in the northeastern states, Blondie territory, or what had been back in his day. Outside the walls, he saw deciduous forest, nude and wintry, stretching over hill country. Directly beyond the cathedral gates, a trail of smaller trees ran straight downhill, but there were not even fragments of asphalt or macadam present to show if there had once been a motorcar road there.

Behind the cathedral and its outbuildings were structures he did not recognize, tall metal-sided towers topped with windowless domes that looked a bit like grain silos. Above them, hanging in the air were long streamers, hundreds of yards tall, rippling slightly in the rainy breeze. They were made of blue gray material, semitransparent, and were almost invisible against the cloudy background. They looked like collectors gathering particles out of the air and drawing them down for storage in the silos.

Overhead, huge, imposing, larger than a submarine, hung an airship. Sir Guiden raised his hand. The ship descended, but Montrose could see neither ground crew nor docking tower.

The air vessel needed none. From a hatch in the bottom gondola stretched many long snakelike tendrils or whips of metal. Guided by some unseen intelligence, they reached down and formed man-sized loops. The upper length of the tendrils flexed and moved, expanding and contracting to compensate as the wind made the airship roll and yaw. The lower lengths were as motionless as if they were embedded in glass, and hung three feet off the ground.

One of the tendrils held in its loop a ship's crewman, who was lowered from the body of the craft to the ground, like a circus girl wrapped in the trunk of an elephant. The figure was slim and slight, long-haired, and wrapped in a long blue gray toga.

The goggles of Sir Guiden were staring upward as the robed figure descended, but it was impossible to see the knight's expression. Montrose was standing next to him, a scarecrow next to a tin man, his gaunt body hidden in a poncho and his thin hook-nosed face hidden beneath a wide-brimmed duster.

Fifty of the Knights Hospitalier in their powered armor stood deployed on the lawn, some atop the walls, some among the mausoleums, some standing at ease nearby. The armor did not move, but every helmet had optic fibers as fine as the antennae of crabs, which swayed left and right, up and down, front and behind, as each man used his motionless goggles to look in all directions. Every pair of boots bore the golden spurs of knighthood, even though no horse ever made could have long endured the mechanized armor in its saddle. Equally archaic were the claymores, katara punching daggers, and Broomhandle Mauser pistols dangling at jaunty angles from their baldrics and cinctures. Less anachronistic were the launchers or particle-beam lances slung each from an articulated shoulder mount. The air support corps consisted of ten men, each carrying a winged drone called a hawk on his wrist. The narrow glass instrument heads of the drones on the wrists of their masters ticked back and forth as hypnotically and restlessly as the optic antennae of the motionless men.

The Knights must have assumed the descending blue-robed figure no threat, since, aside from a rippling among their antennae, they made no move as he swung close to Montrose.

The slender figure, Montrose saw as he was lowered in a swoop, was a male. The swath of robes that swirled around his limbs must have been smart material, woven with thousands of tiny motile fabric strands, because a hood unfolded by itself to shade the man's features from the rain. The full-body tattoos that had been fashionable in earlier days were not in evidence. However, the man had decorations, complex as circuitry diagrams, imprinted in colored inks onto his hands and fingers, feet and toes. The feet decorations glowed red, and shed heat when the man stepped on the cold grass.

"Woggy! Friendlies and mates! Are we ready for up-go, no?"

Menelaus said, "No. You gunna land that thing?"

"The fair *Soaring Azurine* never lands! The serpentines can hoist. Or are you easily dazed?"

Menelaus spit on the ground. "I reckon I daze about as well or poorly as the next feller."

"We can have the serpentines lower a booth, if you don't want to dare the hoist. These are too current for you, no? The booth is opaque, and there is no sensation, no jar. You can balance a land glass atop an egg on your head, brimfull, with water tension curving above the level, and your hair will be dry as before as after you jerk up."

"I'll use the hoist."

Almost before words cleared his mouth, slithering steel tightened and tugged. Montrose yelped as the ground slid dizzily away from his feet. The steel snake made a motion like an anteater pulling an ant into its mouth, and Montrose was inside the hatch, and the deck of the airship was beneath him. It was that rapid.

Whatever controlled the tendrils must have assumed he spoke for Sir Guiden, because the armored figure was wrapped in a second steel snake and also lifted swiftly and smoothly into the ship.

The people current to this age evidently were used to vertigo, because the checkerboard pattern of the deck had every other panel transparent, and showed the dun earth swaying underfoot. Large, slanting windows looked out right and left; a dome showed the bottom of the lifting body above. The slight motions of the wind rippling against the cigar-shaped gas bag overhead were imparted to the deck, so a smooth and gentle pitch and roll continually rocked the cabin.

The cabin was appointed in a lush, even sybaritic style: Gilded fountains made eye-confounding patterns of water and spray amidships, couches and settees on flexible silvery caterpillar legs swayed to either side, heaped with pillows, furs, and cushions. Small tables shining with what might have been musical instruments or fluted wineglasses hung above and below eye level, and were held on the long and gently swaying tendrils the crewman had called serpentines. The serpentines, like well-trained servants, were never in the way. Menelaus spent a moment amusing himself, rushing and jumping back and forth, trying to get one of them to trip him or snag his neck clothesline-style, but the sleek metal tentacles were too agile and too well programmed and slithered neatly aside.

Someone coughed politely. Montrose stopped his game and looked. Here were three figures: the man who had welcomed him, and two women. All three were dressed in translucent blue gray ankle-length togas of smart material with filmy capes and scarves of the same material floating from their shoulders. The fabric flowed and flickered oddly around their limbs, togas rippling like living things, and the translucent swallow-tailed capes fluttered like wings in a breeze. All were barefoot and slender. One woman, the taller, willowy blonde, wore a wreath of flowers, but aside from this, the fantastic headgear of the Cryonarchy had thankfully passed into history. The shorter and younger woman wore a purple sapphire shaped like a teardrop on her brow, with an untamed mass of hair dyed a luminous hue of purple framing her thin face, her eyelids painted black. Her eyes were violet and wild.

The long-haired man who greeted them on the ground, Menelaus realized, had not been "crew." This was a private ship, a houseboat, not a military vessel.

A fourth figure, also a man, was dressed in the black cassock and white dog collar of a cleric, his garb from days older than Montrose's own. It was this man who stepped forward and offered his hand.

"I am Brother Roger Juliac of Beeleigh, Society of Jesus."

"Meany Montrose. Howdy do."

"Yes, Highly Honored. I know of you," intoned Brother Roger with an inclination of his head. "I am the astronomer who discovered the anomaly."

The man had the hard and rugged face and thickset build of a boxer. Montrose could not imagine anyone who looked less like a man of the cloth, or an astrophysicist.

Montrose still had caterpillar-drive pistols in both his fists, so he took his right pistol, thrust it butt first into the surprised man's left hand, and then clasped his right. After the handshake, he snatched his pistol back.

Sir Guiden, watching this exchange, said to Montrose over the silent, internal channel they shared, "Liege, you know the gesture of a handshake is meant to show that you have no weapon in your sword hand."

"Really? I figure handing the friar my shooting iron shows I am even more peaceful than that. You gunna take off your helmet?"

Sir Guy said silently, "The shipmaster and his wives are dressed in hunger silk. It can be used as a weapon. The micropores can flay skin and strip proteins out of the blood and muscle exposed."

"If these folk are so fierce, why'd we leave our goon squad below?"

Sir Guy replied, "The airskiff serpentines will protect you from attack, if you are a friend, and the men could not protect you from them, if you are a foe."

Menelaus had noticed that the gondola did not have any armor, or locks on the ports or hatches. Since anyone hoisted aboard was wrapped in deadly metal cable, and remained in reach thereafter, and since the people aboard wore yards of smart cloth that apparently could eat a man's face, perhaps locks and bars were not needed.

Meanwhile, at the same time, Menelaus was talking aloud to the Jesuit with his real mouth and listening with his real ears. The first thing he said was, "What anomaly?"

Brother Roger said, "This is Tessa Azurine, and her permanent paramour, Woggy Azurine, and the sexpartner is called Third, since she is between names at the moment. I am their mendicant and confessor."

The man waved and grinned. "Gulps! Bro Ro is weight-valued, since the Giants be less like to scald flocks what have a spook-speaking man amidst. Not mendicant he!"

The taller of the two women curtsied like a willow bending, and her blue gray robes writhed like mist. "We scorn no refugee; we share lift, fire, and salt. 'The foxes have holes, and the birds of the air have nests; but the Son of Adam hath not where to lay his head.' You are a Sylph of Time as we are Sylphs of Wind, blown you know not where."

The girl with the purple hair and the gem on her brow was pouting like a child, and her eyes were not focused on anything in the environment around her. She spoke aloud to no one in particular, "How about Trey? No? Like a card."

Montrose grunted. "Yeah, um, pleezta-meetcha, gals, guy, nice digs. Sure hope y'all feel better soon."

The willowy, flower-crowned woman, Tessa, said, "But we are not sick, no?"

"I ain't touching that line with a boat hook, ma'am. Brother Roger, what anomaly?"

The Jesuit said to her, "Tessa, if you could ask the *Azurine* to ascend to the observatory, it should be passing through the area directly."

Tessa said, "*Azurine,* my adored, acknowledge the order."

A melodic voice answered from the wall, sounding like wind chimes. "I delight to obey, my adored. I ascend. For your delight, I play an ascension theme from your preference profile." A haunting sequence of woodwinds and plaintive chords drifted through the air, soft and without melody, but a trumpet added a note of triumph when the airship broke through the cloud, as if through a gray floor, up into dazzling daylight.

Montrose said to the priest, "You! Now that the pleasantries are done, what poxy anomaly?"

Brother Roger said, "Energy discharges from V886 Centauri. The radiospectrography and gamma ray analysis are constant with an, ah, interplanetary event."

"No damn point in pausing for drama, Padre, because I grade on info, not on delivery."

Brother Roger said, "Ah. As you say. We believe the ice giant planet Thrymheim was driven into the star. The terrene matter of the superjovian world interacted with the contraterrene plasma of the star's atmosphere."

Thrymheim was the single planet orbiting the Diamond Star. It held a far Neptunian orbit, beyond where the antimatter in the solar wind could reach, and so was not disintegrated.

"Driven in why? As a weapon?"

Brother Roger shook his head. "Criswell mining operates by inducing a ring-current around the star by ionically charged beams oppositely directed from each other. Usually the mining satellite ring is equatorial, so that the ejection mass—"

"By Mother Mary changing baby Jesus' stinking holy diapers, Padre! I was *on* the expedition, and I *am* a star miner, so I know how the damn process works!"

Brother Roger said, "There are dark lines in the spectrographic analysis consistent with an off-center arrangement of the mining orbitals, Honored."

"Blight and clap! What are the vectors?"

Brother Roger said, "I have not been able to deduce, from the limited information available fifty light-years away, what the various constituent pressures—"

"You are saying the mining satellites focused the explosion like a jet engine."

"Explosions. So we speculate, Honored."

"Which way is it pointing? Wait. Explosions, with an *s*, plural?"

"Indeed, Honored."

"She broke the damn planet into bits, made it into an asteroid stream, and is feeding in one or two earth-masses at a time. Thrymheim was fifteen hundred and ninety earth-masses, as I recall. The whole solar system, Monument and everything, has been turned into a damned Orion drive, just on a massive scale."

Sir Guiden turned on his suit speakers, to let the people in the cabin hear the question, "Liege! How do you know it is she?"

"Meaning what?" Montrose said.

Sir Guiden said, "The *Bellerophon* was lighter than the *Hermetic*, and should have overtaken her either when they made starfall at V886 Centauri, a few months more or less. We tend to think of red dwarfs as small and dim, but a sailing ship can reflect and focus a beam of star energy to burn targets across interplanetary distances, and small stars have more than enough power for that."

"The pursuit ship didn't have no crew aboard, it was just Del Azarchel's second emulation, an Astro-Exarchel, and a passel of teleoperated tools. You're thinking Rania might have bought the farm during whatever shoot-out banged when they butted heads?

Sir Guiden said, "Liege, are you trying to be obscure? Farm?"

"Sorry. You think Rania died? No fear of that!"

Sir Guiden said, "How not?"

"I know Blackie. He don't think this big. Oh, this is her work, all right." Montrose threw back his head and laughed. "What a gal! Did I tell you she's mine?"

Brother Roger said diffidently, "Honored—if you intuit the meaning of this anomaly, I would be grateful if—"

"It's eight thousand five hundred years until the Hyades Armada arrives here. Not much time. What is the biggest block to our being able to fight them when they come? We're too small, too weak, too stupid. What is the main thing you need to get smarts? I don't mean one man, I mean on a large-scale, bigger-than-worlds, multiple-centuries sort of deal. Library smarts; datasphere smarts. What's it take? Energy. It takes fuel to calculate. Fuel to think. Now, the whole damn and plague-ridden universe is made out of energy, but not in a form ready to use. I was going crazy trying to figure out how many expeditions we could make to the Diamond Star for contraterrene, how much fuel is lost in transport, how many ships, considering that a ship can tow only about as much fuel as you might like to use for a round-trip, and not too much over."

Brother Roger said, "Honored, I don't follow you."

"Rania blasted the Diamond Star out of its orbit around the galactic core, and is bringing the Diamond Star here. It is a dwarf star holding a ten-decillion-carat diamond made of antimatter, and if she parks it in an orbit inside our heliopause, where the interstellar medium is thin, we can go mine it in a reasonable time. How about the antimatter source is thirteen light-hours away rather than fifty light-years? How are our chances against the Dominion of the Hyades then?"

"But, Honored—"

"Please stop calling me that. The only titles I ever earned were 'Doctor' and 'Esquire' and 'Lance-Corporal,' and I am only qualified for one and a half of them. So call me Menelaus. If I scare ya, you can call me Doctor Montrose."

"Doctor—"

"So I scare ya?"

Brother Roger said, "Very much so, Doctor. After you destroyed all the cities of the world, one would be foolish not to—"

"Wait. What the pox?"

Just at that moment, the clouds underfoot parted, and the sun shining on the surface of the water sent a dazzle into the cabin. Montrose turned, squinted, blinked, and something in the back of his mind, between one blink and the next, ran some rapid calculations on the afterimage of what he had just seen.

He stepped over the window. "Anyone here got a spyglass?"

Sir Guiden said, "He means a snooper."

The willowy woman, Tessa said, "He means hunger silk. It absorbs photons as well as proteins."

With this, Tessa stepped over to the window and threw a tail of her writhing garment across the glass. The blue gray material stuck as if magnetized, and the surface bubbled slightly. The disk of vacuum trapped beneath formed a lens, and suddenly the fabric seemed to become like a library cloth, because a clear image appeared in it of what Menelaus had seen in the distance.

It was a flotilla of airships, by scores and hundreds, drifting idly across the face of the waters, or brushing the surface. Long banners, like the lines trailing a fishing boat, hung from the airships and swept through the water. Every now and again one of the airships would turn and dive like a pelican, splashdown, and become a submarine, darting like a shark. One such airship he saw dived into a school of fish, and when it rose, the hull was dotted with sleek bodies that seemed to be glued or held against the surface. The fish melted, and their bodily fluids and guts streamed for a moment against the gray fabric of the airship, and then those streaks too were absorbed.

In the distance was shoreline, and trees beyond. There were airships here as well, trailing long fabric trains behind them as they drifted. Where the cloth passed, the trees were stripped of bark and buds. Any birds passing near were slashed out of the air by the serpentines, and the blue gray trails of fabric turned the bodies into stains of blood and absorbed them.

Menelaus, now that they were above the cloud cover, could make an estimate of their speed, and was astonished. "What is your propulsion?"

The woodwind voice of the ship answered, "Admired, cherished, and welcome guest, six valveless pulsejet engines aft use a nuclear hydrogen-fusion lance running along the lifting body axis to heat and expel an inert nitrogen compound propellant gathered from the surrounding atmospheric gases. The flexible lifting body material allows smooth and uninterrupted transition between heavier-than-air and lighter-than-air configurations, with partial vacuum created for lift by multiple microscopic rows along the dorsal surface. All gaseous raw materials are filtered out of the available environment by the submicropore chemical-lock system known as hunger silk, and recombined by molecular-capillary pseudochemistry in the fore nacelles. Lifting gases are in the buoyancy tanks. Carbon gas is reconfigured into diamond crystal and used for ballast. To submerge, the craft cross-sectional configuration—"

"Thanks, good answer, shut up," said Menelaus. To himself, he muttered, "Never woulda guessed. Atomic-powered supersonic submarine-blimps . . ." He turned to Tessa, "So what happened to the cities?"

She smiled dreamily. "We have drugs to suppress those memories. Happiness drugs. But the ship can answer you in this as well, my adored ship, more loyal than any human lover."

The Jesuit said, "I can answer, Doctor. The material used for starship sails included smart strands with molecular engines for the repair of micropunctures, altering permeability, absorbing laser energy, and so on. As time passed, the Exarchel discovered additional programming configurations for the molecular machinery, and a larger range of options. Your antimatter monopoly was broken once orbital sails could focus solar energy into any rectenna receiver anywhere on the planet—and, because Earth had been using your power broadcast reception for decades, the rectennae were everywhere. The orbital sails, ah, well . . ."

"So what happened to the cities?"

Brother Roger said, "Many were burned like ants under a magnifying glass. Antimissile defenses are of no value against such an attack."

"Who was fighting who?"

Brother Roger said, "The Giants were fighting the Ghosts."

"Giants?"

Brother Roger said, "Posthumans. Artificial children with your intelligence range. It is a way to achieve posthumanity without making an Iron Ghost of your own brain, as the Scholars do. It was worked out by a scientific convocation held under His Holiness Pope Sixtus the Sixth."

Sir Guiden said to Brother Roger, "He won't know that name." To Menelaus, he said, "Sir, Sixtus the Sixth was Thucydides Montrose. Research in brain-size increase was married to your Prometheus formula to create a posthuman that did not need to be emulated to be augmented. They are genetically altered before conception to grow gigantic bodies to house their correspondingly elephantine brains."

"What about augmenting ordinary people, Guy?" asked Montrose, distracted. "Can people ramp up to posthuman intellect like I did, without going mad, like I did?"

"Not really." Sir Guiden sounded grim. "Too many people died trying. Emulation seemed safer, but it requires specialized training and nerve implants to be able to donate a brain copy for scanning. Those with this skill were called Savants. Before the burning of the cities, most of mankind was ruled or led by counsels or collections of these Ghosts, emulations of jurists and statesmen, replaced from their Savant donors every three years."

"Why so short?"

Sir Guiden looked surprised. "For reasons you know very well, sir. Divarication failure. You never released to the world Princess Rania's solution to the Selfish Meme divarication, which allows for stable posthumans without split personalities, nor your solution for the Impersonator divarication, which allows for an electronic copy of a posthuman brain to be made!"

"I was just assuming Blackie and his troupe of trained monkeys would have noodled that out by now, and covered the world with Iron Ghosts."

Sir Guiden said, "The Hermeticists were said to have a more advanced technology than the Savants, and able to download as well as upload, to put the thoughts of their superintelligent computer copies back into their own brains, at least for a time."

Montrose said, "That's a crude way of doing it. Why did you say 'were'?"

Sir Guiden said, "Our intelligence arm has confirmed information that over sixty of the Hermeticists went insane or died attempting Prometheus augmentation."

"There were only seventy or so of them all told," said Montrose in awe. "Did they wipe themselves all out? . . . That's . . . I mean, I got crosswise with them toward the end there, and they were mutineers and murderers, but . . . aw, hell, they were my partners in training, the only guys I trusted to look over my work for mistakes . . . the only ones who understood it. Damn. Damnation. All of them? What about Blackie?"

"Almost all," said Sir Guiden.

"Who's left?"

"The intelligence reports are tentative. It's not confirmed," said Sir Guiden.

"Tell me what you suspect then, Guy."

"We suspect the ringleaders are still alive and sane," said Sir Guiden. "The Master of the World, Ximen del Azarchel is alive: he still makes speeches to loyal followers, promising a return of his regime and world peace. The commander-in-chief of the world armed forces, Narcís D'Aragó. Sarmento i Illa d'Or, who was head of the World Reserve Bank. The Confessor to the Crown, Father Reyes y Pastor. Melchor de Ulloa, the chief of the Loyalty Police. Jaume Coronimas, who was in charge of all the energy systems and powerhouses of Earth."

"Coronimas the engineer's mate? I remember him as a guy with no hobbies, no girl, didn't drink, didn't smoke, didn't make jokes. Why is he still alive? I don't think I ever heard his first name."

"The same," said Sir Guiden.

"Weird. They had the same jobs aboard the ship. Draggy was in charge of security, Yellow Door was quartermaster, Pasty was chaplain and Mulchie was chief snoop and ass-sniffer. I never had a nickname for Coronimas. Didn't know him close enough."

"Which one is Yellow Door?"

"I Illa d'Or. Sarmento i Illa d'Or."

"They are all in hiding now," said Sir Guiden, "Have been, since the Decivilization War."

Decivilization. Montrose thought it was a chillingly apt word to describe the destruction of all the large cities of the world. "What were they fighting about? The Giants and Ghosts?"

The Knight Hospitalier laughed a chilling laugh. "What are wars always about? Loot, honor, fear. The barbarians and pagans are trying to destroy Christendom."

Brother Roger intervened, "In this case, we men are not aware of the causes of the war, because neither the Giants nor the Ghosts were able to express their concerns in a fashion unmodified humans could understand. The basic conflict seemed to be a disagreement about the implications of higher mathematics."

Sir Guiden said, "Don't listen to that! The war was being fought about demographic calculation and information space restrictions. The math question concerned equations governing human liberty, economy, intellectual property, and resource priority. These equations formed the conceptual basis for countless laws and regulations. It was no mere abstract argument. It was about whether humanity would be dehumanized and tyrannized."

Montrose said, "So Exarchel finally did it! If he cannot enslave mankind, he'll destroy us!"

"No, Doctor," said Brother Roger cautiously. "The, ah, Giants are the ones controlling the orbital mirrors. The only way to destroy the infrastructure of the wire net was to destroy the great industrial centers, where all the thinking houses and power stations were located. Cities like those in Switzerland and China that were tourist sites made of old materials, concrete and stone, not thinking crystal, were spared, as were any under a certain population density and energy use."

"And—" Menelaus gestured toward the horizon, at the airships that swarmed like silver fish among the clouds. "These? They are Nomads, right?"

"Yes, Doctor," said Brother Roger. "We are a world of Sylphs. The only defense is dispersion. All the survivors departed from the remaining cities as rapidly as possible. The larger flocks cover the sea from horizon to horizon, but once a mirror beam lands among them, they turn silver, emit ink clouds, and scatter in all directions, or submerge. The orientation and focal lengths of the space mirrors are watched carefully, and the aeroscaphes land together only when the mirrors are below the horizon, for barter fairs, and so on."

"Hold on. The Giants are the enemies of these floaty folk? Which side are they on?"

"Not precisely. The Giants intervene only when the artificial intelligence behind the serpentines violates the Gigantic quarantine guidelines on machine awareness."

"This airskiff has a Mälzel brain. It's lightweight in more ways than one, I'd reckon. And don't tell me, let me guess. You are finding the Mälzels turning into Xypotechs after a few years of use, and they strange loop into obsessive concentration on a few high-priority tasks?"

Brother Roger looked surprised. "The considerations are rather technical, and, of course, the Sylphs cannot tolerate another downgrade of allowable technology. But how can you be aware of our difficulties?"

"Because I had 'em first." Montrose grinned. "Your problem is basically what was going wrong with Exarchel back when he was a mad mainframe no bigger than a city block. It's called the Selfish Meme divarication, and it is the first of the seven basic divarication problems. I'm the dude that fixed it: You have to establish a self-correcting noneditable editor in the mind's base process, what would be called the subconscious in a human brain, and sink the roots of the ego there, where the changeware can't get at them and anchor to a mechanical process. It's not a hard glitch to solve: All you need is a four-thousand-dimensional manifold extrapolating the combinational possibilities. You'd think it'd be an automorphic function in Schubert's enumerative calculus, but no: you use linear differential equations within a prescribed monodromic group, where each function . . ." Then, seeing the blank stares on him, Montrose shrugged and said, "Well, it's not a hard glitch for me to solve. I can teach the mechanisms how to create the self-corrective code in themselves. In any case, Brother, if I straighten out this bug in the serpentines, will it get the Giants off the backs of these Nomads?"

"Eventually." Said Brother Roger, "It would take only a few years for the solution to spread."

"A few—*what*? Years?"

Brother Roger said solemnly, "The Sylphs use the serpentines for barter. At landing fairs, serpentines get passed from hand to hand, with the older, more skilled artifacts commanding more in trade. That is the fastest means of spreading data."

"*Barter*? You guys lost the concept of coin money?" The look on Montrose's face was such that the violet-eyed younger woman handed him an airsickness bag.

Brother Roger said, "Money operates on the wire net, and no one uses the wire, because that is where the Exarchel was, Doctor. Communication of any form between ships is unhumanish, except heliograph signals, which cannot carry Iron Ghosts, or their data. All transmission bands are forbidden."

Sir Guiden said on their private channel, "I recommend you not solve this *glitch*, as you call it, Liege. You are describing the solution to the problem of madness in Ghosts. If you release it to the world, Del Azarchel, or someone with his ambitions, will eventually create a second Exarchel, or a third, or a million."

Silently, Montrose had his implants send back, "I can narrow the solution to these specifics, without giving away the general principle, Sir Guy. Rania's Cure is actually seven semi-independent ecomimetic functions. Can he deduce the missing general rule just from one application of one seventh of the set? I doubt he has the brains."

Sir Guiden sent back, "Why take the risk? Are these drifting people worth saving? They neither sow nor spin. Let the Giants multiply and inherit the Earth."

Brother Roger said blandly to Menelaus, "Even the signals you are sending back and forth with your man, the Hospitalier, would invite gigantic retaliation if detected. I am sorry: were those signals meant to be secret? Well, such is the reason we are going in person to the observatory, rather than having a voice-through-the-air conference."

The violet-eyed woman murmured softly, as if in a dream. "Telephones. They were called telephones. You could send pictures of yourself dancing raw to your darling list."

Menelaus uttered a bitter laugh. "So radio has gone the way of the dodo. I made the Giants and they killed all the boys named Jack. I destroyed the world. I told Thucydides that this would come to a bad end! Told him!"

"Oh, do not cast down your features, Dr. Montrose! Society survives in a decentralized form," said the Jesuit. "The Giants spare any automatic factories, provided the electronic brains housed there are Mälzels or ratiotechnology, thinking machines, not xypotechnology, self-aware machines. A single Giant can carry the download of an entire library needle in his head. I myself, with merely very minor neural augmentations, have both photographic memory, linguistic and mathematical savant abilities, spatial proprioception that establishes perfect direction sense, and the ability to speak the high-speed data-compression language."

"And what happened to Exarchel?"

Brother Roger said, "No copy of him remains anywhere on Earth. With the total shutdown of the infosphere, his power is broken forever!"

"Forever?"

"For a hundred years!" The Jesuit smiled.

"That is not as long a time as you might think. . . ."

The Jesuit pointed at one of the large and slanting windows. "There is the observatory." Hanging in the air was a tall cylinder, slightly narrower at the top than at the base, and a ring of vast gas balloons surrounding its waist like a festive skirt. "We should have new plates developed at sunset."

"That's a pretty big telescope." The cylinder was twenty meters in diameter, which made the instrument inside at least twice as big as the telescopes Menelaus recalled from his day. "And you must not get much distortion, if you can take her up to the stratosphere."

"We also use the space mirrors as baselines, Doctor," said Brother Roger. "Most of the Giants will cooperate with scientific ventures. Obviously they need technology to advance."

"Obviously," said Montrose. "Because they want to breed true, right? The offspring of Giants are humans?"

"Humans with various bone diseases, yes, Doctor," said Brother Roger. "A group of scientific clans called the Simon Families was established by Og of Northumberland to solve that and other long-range multigenerational problems. The experiments are passed down from mother to daughter."

"Do the Cetaceans have the same problem?"

Brother Roger spread his hands. "The Moreau, as we call those who dwell beneath the sea, are not well known or well studied. All our shipping is by air these days, for the Moreau cannot survive an encounter with an aeroscaphe. The Exarchel is no longer in a position to supply them with jaw-launched missiles, and they cannot manufacture their own. More of us float above the sea than above land, since krill and plankton are easier for the hunger silk to absorb and convert than most land-based proteins."

"Are you going to drive them into extinction?"

"Ah? Is that your wish, Doctor? That seems as harsh as your condemnation of the cities."

"I was asleep! Did these Giants say I gave the order?"

Brother Roger looked troubled. "Say? You gave the order. The whole world saw you. It was your voice and image over the wire. What does this mean? Is someone acting for you, impersonating you?"

3. Glimpse of a Distant Star

Boarding was a simple but dizzying process of being passed from the airship serpentines to the observatory's. The metal snakes handed Menelaus over as gently as a father picking a tot out of a baby carriage and into a mother's waiting arms, but the moment of being exposed to the chill and thin winds of the upper air, with nothing underfoot and nothing to cling to, left him wishing he had taken up Woggy on his offer of a booth.

Ascending to the stratosphere was effortless: The huge balloon, after a polite warning, sealed all its pressure doors, and shed diamond dust in a long and glittering tail, and climbed.

This interior was as spartan as the *Azurine* had been luxurious. Menelaus found the photographic plates waiting for him, pinned to a steel bench next to a steel stool, with a lens on a cantilevered arm hanging above. To see images created by chemical emulsions seemed oddly old-fashioned, but the current range of nanotechnologically created chemical mixes could react more sensitively to various wavelengths, including gamma and X-ray, shortwave and infrared, than any digital receptors.

There was no completely trustworthy calculating machine nor library cloth available in this technophobic age, but Brother Roger was able to give him the basics of the high-speed compression language, and any calculations Menelaus could not do in his head, Menelaus could squeal and click in a single quick throat-rasp to Brother Roger, whose intuitive grasp of notational mathematics was almost as good as his own. Menelaus used him to double check his work for errors.

The first plate showed merely a large circular smear of light with a smaller one nearly. A distribution of infrared and microwave emissions caught on those plates indicated a contact point below the solar atmosphere.

Montrose said, "She's had to overcome the problem that antimatter–matter reactions usually end up blowing most of the matter back toward the source. When a billiard-ball hits an anti–billiard-ball, the two balls are blown away from each other when the point of contact releases all its energy. You gotta push the two billiards together against their ignition pressure to maintain the explosion, and keep pushing. From the magnetic images, I reckon she is using the ring current from the mining satellites not just to focus the explosion like a jet cone, but also to hem in the fragments like an ignition cylinder. I would ask where she got the energy to ionize the whole metallic hydrogen core of the gas giant, but she's sitting on top of the biggest energy treasure in the known universe, so I guess she just—"

He was interrupted by Brother Roger bringing the latest two plates. It was after sunset, and at 170,000 feet (thirty-two miles and change straight up) they were above the troposphere and in the stratosphere, the edge of outer space. The pressure outside the armored sphere of the life support was 1/1000 of sea level. Needless to say, the pictures were clearer than any mountaintop observatory.

There were two images: one magnetic, the other in the gamma ray spectrum.

Brother Roger passed him the magnetic image first. "There are a number of very puzzling features in this. . . ."

Menelaus barely glanced at the magnetic image. "You are getting a diffraction effect caused by the fact that she is using a second set of ring-current satellites to establish a magnetic ramscoop in front of the star. It is going to draw in hydrogen particles of terrene matter, loop them around to the aft end of the Diamond Star, and ram them into the antimatter vortex forming in the aft magnetic jet cone. The incoming particles will have greatly increased mass as she mounts up near to lightspeed, and so more energy will be released with the bombardment."

In contrast, it was with a look of awe that Menelaus examined the high-energy image. He studied it with increasing excitement for long moments before he spoke. "There is no gamma ray count registered. That means the forty percent of pions created during total conversion which should be neutral somehow ain't neutral. I'd say it's impossible, but do you know what that means? The main problem with matter–antimatter conversion is that most of your mass is lost and wasted in dark matter like pi mesons. She has some method of charging them, so the axial electromagnetic field lines can grab them, focus them into the thrust before they decay into muons. She did it somehow, but I don't know how. She did the impossible!"

He started to laugh with joy, but the meaning of the image suddenly struck him, and the laughter choked in his throat.

"Brother Roger, is this a mistake? The spectrographic reading along the bottom—someone must have flipped the plate into the camera backwards, or—or—"

"No, Doctor," said the Jesuit, his face pale. "The image is red-shifted, not blue-shifted."

"She is not heading toward the Earth. She is heading away. Where is she going? Never mind! I know! Damn my balls and eyeballs! She's leaving! *She's not coming back for me!*"

In a rage he raised the photographic plate and smashed it to pieces. He knotted his fists into the hair of his head to keep himself from smashing other things, and he tried to gather so much hair in his hands that he could not pull it out. His hands only indifferently obeyed his commands, so there was considerable yanking on his scalp, and it brought tears to his eyes. More tears.

Bile stung the back of his throat. Menelaus finally parked his head between his knees, waiting to see if he would throw up.

"She even told me. We talked about it!"

"Doctor? Where is she going? To the Hyades? It is one hundred and fifty-one light-years away. She could return in three hundred years or so, which is not an impossible time for a hibernating man to outwait."

"Not the Hyades."

"What else is out there?"

Montrose squeezed his eyes shut, wondering if he could induce a brain aneurysm in himself just by sheer anger and willpower. "M3."

"Where?"

"The Messier Object Three." Menelaus spoke the words with deliberate care. "It is a galactic cluster, a microgalaxy, hanging almost directly above the disk of the Milky Way, like a wee little bluebottle fly thinking about landing on a pie plate. It's not some piss-ass little stellar cluster, like Hyades, oh no. Hyades is a few hundred stars, maybe eight hundred. M3 contains half a million to a million suns. M3 also contains an entity, a collection of races or a collection of machines, a power of some sort, a far-posthuman intelligence she labeled the Absolute Authority. That's what their glyph in the Monument means: their word for themselves is a game theory expression for a player whose moves expand infinitely to all cell matrices and determine all outcomes. It is the boss of Praesepe Cluster, which is five hundred and fifty light-years away; and Praesepe is the boss of Hyades. So M3 is the boss of their boss. Their chain of command is all written out in the Monument. She is going to the top. City Hall. The Front Office. The King. The Judgment Seat."

"Why go there?"

The words fell from the mouth of Montrose like pebbles of lead. "Vindication. She is going to vindicate the human race."

"What?"

"If she goes and comes back, it proves that the human race is a *starfaring* race. It proves we can live long enough and think far enough into the future to carry out interstellar trade and to be governed by interstellar laws. Starfarers got to think long-term, and be greedy enough to wait for a ten-thousand-year payoff, in the case of trade agreements; Godfearing enough to be adverse to ten-thousand-year delayed vengeance. Only polities that care a damn sight more than human beings have been known to care about their way-off way-way-off descendents need apply."

"And if mankind is tested and proved, and found to be starfarers?"

"It makes us equals. Our servitude to Hyades is abolished. We're free and debt-free. But Rania has to come back, and there has to be a deceleration laser here ready to receive her, and the people of that generation and aeon, they got to know who she is, recognize her rights, all that good stuff.

"If we forget her," Montrose continued, "then the Earth fails the test, and we are not smart enough and not long-term enough to deal with the distances star-travel requires.

"So that is my job." Montrose concluded, "You gotta admit, I am perfectly suited. No one is as goddam stubborn as me. And I am not going to forget her or let the world forget."

Brother Roger said, "Then your war with Exarchel is over! Because when she returns, and proves we are a starfaring race, the Hyades will recall their world armada, surely, will they not?"

"Oh, I did not mention the distance," said Menelaus with a groan, smiling a weak smile, crinkling his tearstained cheeks. "I thought you, being an astronomer—"

"I don't have the Messier catalog memorized, Doctor."

"It is outside the damn galaxy. M3 is roughly thirty-three thousand nine hundred light-years away. The round-trip at near-lightspeed is over sixty-seven *thousand* years. She will be back, assuming no delays and no nonsense, by A.D. 70,800. You got that figure in your mind? If you counted to a trillion, and counted one number a second, and you did it twelve hours a day, taking half the day off for eating and sleeping, that is roughly the time involved."

Brother Roger blinked owlishly. "It is a hard number to imagine, Doctor," he said slowly.

"Put it in the past instead of the future. That'll give you a notion of the scale. In order for today to be the day when my wife returned from the gulfs beyond the galaxy, she would have had to have departed from Earth back in the year 60,000 B.C.—about when Neanderthals still walked the Earth. Leaf-point stone tools and the dugout canoe were both new inventions."

"But the Hyades world armada arrives in A.D. 11,000, does it not? Won't her actions, the vindication, be far, far too late?"

Menelaus answered, "We have to battle the Hegemony, and stay free all that time, until she comes. And with no antimatter star to mine no more. No power for a new civilization. No nothing. We have to endure. Endure until . . ."

Montrose shook his head, his sorrow, for a moment, swallowed up in wonder.

"She blasted the damn star out of orbit, and she is accelerating in a right line, straight up out of the plane of the galactic disk, to a little cluster of stars, half a million or so, that hangs like an island in the middle of intergalactic nothingness."

Brother Roger was silent.

Montrose said, "My war with Del Azarchel is just starting. My war with entropy is just starting. It will be the longest war in history. It will be longer than history. If I lose, the human race remains the slaves of the Hyades Hegemony forever and ever, amen."

"And if you win, we are free?"

"Sodomize that. What do I care what some big-headed big-arsed post-transhuman half-machine bug-faced thing in the Year Zillion is free or slave? If I win, I get my wife back." Montrose stood up. "I need a breath of fresh air. Which we cannot get unless you descend thirty miles."

4. *The Sign*

Brother Roger Juliac said, "I can take you to the observation platform, where at least you can look out and see the stars."

Menelaus looked down mournfully at the fragments of the photographic plate he'd smashed. "Sorry about that. I should not have lost my temper."

"We all lose our temper sometimes."

"And we all say sorry sometimes when we do! One of my relations, Thucydides, you call him Sixtus the Sixth, which is a dumb name if you ask me, imposed a penalty on me, a punishment. He said I had to stay happy. To wait in joyful hope for her return. That means I cannot give up, cannot give in to despair, can't let it get to me. I gotta just soldier on."

Brother Roger led him down a companionway and a set of narrow metal stairs to a bubble of transparent metal hanging like a swallow's nest precariously from the side of the great cylindrical balloon. The earth below was lined with a blue shadow in the distance, where the sunlight, like a great curving line, still glinted over the retreating sunset. Directly underfoot, all was dark. The wonder of city lights agleam at night, which had for so many years been the joy of astronauts and high flying pilots, was no more. Instead, there were drifting lights like fireflies where flotillas of aeroscaphes were gathered, and here and there, a strange green glint from under the sea, the sign of some activity from the Cetaceans.

Montrose turned. In the east, the moon was risen, pale as a skull. He gave off a gasp of horror and grabbed Brother Roger by the arm. "What the hell is *that*!?"

For the face of the moon was painted with the shadow of a hand.

The wrist was near Tycho crater, and the vast palm, complete with curving lifeline, smothered the Sea of Tranquillity and the Sea of Serenity. The gray white thumb stretched across the Ocean of Storms toward the lava crater of Grimaldi, the darkest area of the moon. The fingers were drawn up toward the Mare Frigoris, Sea of Cold, and were painted with solid ashy white. The hand was not in proper proportion, for the fingers were too long and thin. The curve of the moon bent the fingers. The fingertips at the lunar north pole must have been nine hundred miles farther from the Earth than the palm near the lunar equator, but since the moon looked like a disk to the human eye, this produced the odd illusion that the vast hand was curling its fingers toward the viewer. A thin pale hand with a black palm seemed as if ready to reach down from heaven.

"It first appeared when the cities were deserted," said Brother Roger. "It grew steadily over seventy days, starting with the wrist near Tycho crater. There was a launch site in Tycho that sent skywriting rockets by the thousands over the lunar landscape, with payloads of phosphorescent dust, which of course fell straight to the lunar surface, where it remains and shall remain forever, with no wind to disturb it and no water to wash it away. When the moon is dark, the hand is still visible. No one knows what it means."

"You cannot send a ship?"

"There is no space program. Even the Giants cannot repair their orbital mirrors if a part wears out."

"You wakie people, you currents, were supposed to be building me a starship. . . ."

"The *Emancipation* was stolen and the orbital drydock de-orbited and burnt up in the atmosphere."

"Stolen? You cannot steal things in space."

"Well, Doctor, we know exactly where she is, we merely cannot reach her. The vessel was not complete, but sails and frame were sufficient to make lunar orbit. During the First Space Age, several attempts to establish moon bases in ex-volcanic tubes. When the Jihad brought an end to all that, it was too expensive to ship the equipment back down to Earth. The pirates may have restored one of the bases to life-support operations and be occupying it. We don't know who their leader is, or why they did it."

"It is Del Azarchel. He did it to get some elbow room."

"How do you know?"

"First, Blackie likes to do things in style, and this fits him. Second, that handprint on the moon is not just any old hand."

"What is it?"

"A duelist gauntlet. The black-palm glove. Del Azarchel did not know where on the Earth I was. So he held up his palm large enough that I had to see it. You hold up your fingers like that when you are ready to exchange fire."

"He marred the face of the moon forever, merely to hurl down a gauntlet to you, Doctor?"

"Ah. You weren't calling me that for a few moments, there. Whatsa matter? You got afraid of me again, all of a sudden, Padre?"

"Very much so, Doctor."

"Why? I'm the same damn fellow as I was a minute ago."

"But your foes have grown strangely larger in my eyes, Doctor."

2

The Sea of Cunning

A.D. 2540

1. The Presence Chamber

The Master of the World was in exile.

Dawn had been a week ago, so the sun was nearing noon. Untwinkling stars were in theory visible in the deathly black sky, but the human eye could not adjust to both extremes at once. Overhead was merely an abyssal dark that caused no vertigo, because there was nothing seen in it. There was no Earth to loom in the sky, nor would there ever be, for this was the Moon's far side, which faced forever away from the world of men.

The Sea of Cunning, Mare Ingenii, was a cracked basin of obsidian crossed with fissures like whip scars, filling a crater sixty miles wide, with inkblots of dark lava spilling east and west. Here was a wasteland where no living thing had ever grown, no note of any sound had ever been heard and no grain of sand had ever been stirred by any gasp of wind. Crater walls as white and pockmarked as the corpses of lepers blazed in the distance, turned to intolerable fire by the undimmed sun. The black slag of primordial lava flows formed a wrinkled carpet. The ground was shot and blistered, pocked and dinted by eons of impacts as if by mortar and machine gun fire.

Like a black coin dropped on the floor of a long-dead furnace white with ash was the presence chamber of the Master of the World: a circle thirty yards in diameter. A dome so pure and featureless so as to be invisible embraced the chamber at the rim, so that it seemed one could step without barrier from the dead world into the bubble of life. From within, the inhuman silence of the vacuum seemed to press like a weight upon the fragile dome, a silence that could be felt in one's bone marrow.

Midmost in the chamber was an immense table of black metal shaped like a broken circle, or a tossed horseshoe. The floor plates under that table were tuned to black, but able, upon command, to put the images of all the Earth that he once ruled below the feet of Ximen del Azarchel, or spin out the mathematical trees and twigs of scenarios of predictive statistics, that he might see by what means he should come to rule Earth once again.

The illusion of equality a nearly round table might create was broken, for looming between the open horseshoe ends was a dais. At one time, the round table had been whole, but he had commanded artisans to cut away the length of table where once had sat those of his order who dared opposed his elevation from first among equals to master.

Upon the elevated dais was a judgment seat of ivory hammered over with fine gold, set on a massive base and wide, adorned by spiral narwhale tusks that gleamed like the horns of mythic unicorns and reared like spears. The high and arching backrest was adorned with the dark, triangular visage of a bull in rage.

In the deadly brightness of a sun undimmed by atmosphere, the gilded and argent chair blazed like a mirror in the desert, a striking contrast with the dark-garbed figure seated between the narwhale horns: a bright flame with a black heart.

The throne sat foursquare, and before the footstool descended six steps broad and shallow. Twelve life-sized lions hewn of black marble stood rampant in pairs, one to either side of each step, frozen in midlunge. Scribed into the surface of each stair and set with star-sapphires, a different creature or emblem representing a figure of the zodiac cowered beneath the paw of each of the twelve black lions: the throne almost seemed a chariot trampling the constellations underfoot.

The senior of the landing party of the *Hermetic* expedition, the Nobilissimus Ximen del Azarchel, called Ximen the Black, sat alone in state atop the only throne ever to exist upon the gray and lifeless globe that formed the sole remnant and remainder of his reign.

It did not seem arrogance to Del Azarchel to make his seat to match the throne of Solomon described in the Book of Kings, for he deemed himself, with his multiply augmented mind, wiser than any ancient monarch, prophet, poet, or magician. Nor did the Djinn that ancient sorcerer-king was said to have sealed in brass jars and bent to his command seem any less fearsome and terrible than Exarchel, the mind housed in the amber pillars that arose to either side of the judgment seat. Traces of fluorine hidden in each rod-logic macromolecule gave the pillars a lambent fulvous hue, as if they were hewn of transparent gold.

Del Azarchel wore the dark and silken garment of a starfarer, and needed no other sign of royalty, save only for the dark metal circlet atop his air cowl but beneath his scholar's hood.

This was the Iron Crown of Lombardy, a band of gold and emerald segments jointed with hinges and set with precious stones in the form of crosses and flowers. Within the band was a narrow circle of iron, if legend spoke true, beaten out of one of the nails taken from the True Cross. It was the most ancient insigne of royalty surviving Christendom, and held its most precious relict, and had been kept, until late, in the Cathedral of Monza in Milan. A delta of scar tissue running upward from the corner of his right eye to beneath his cowl was a memento of an assassination attempt, and surely made the wearing of that crown painful in his brow, even under the elfin gravity of the moon. Painful or no, he did not set the crown aside.

Within the triangle of the mouth of his hood, the glint of his white teeth between dark mustachios and goatee could be glimpsed, the drops of cold fire caught in the diamonds of his iron crown, and the strange light from no-longer-human eyes.

2. The Hermeticists

He raised a hand gloved in what seemed black silk. Although there seemed to be none within the chamber to see that signal, nonetheless, upon that gesture, five of his fellow Hermeticists rose from three circular iris-hatches in the floor, drifting upward with the eerie grace only lunar gravity allowed.

The men did not quite land, nor quite walk, but moved toes against the dark deck with ballet smoothness. Their black garments rippled like silk, and silvery antiradiation mantles fluttered like capes as they passed.

All men in the wide chamber wore similar bodies. The Hermeticists in their lunar-adaptive forms were tall and emaciated, lacking in water weight, with dry cracks at lips and nostrils. Even the heaviest of them had a sunken, skull-like cast to his face, a strange leaden highlight to his skin, a side effect of the special nanomachinery lining their bones and filling their bone marrow to prevent microgravity decay. Their eyes were as mirror-shining as the eyes of a cat, or filmy as the eyes of a sea beast, for growing additional microorganisms meant to shield their eyes from accidental radiation exposure turned out, unexpectedly, to be less cumbersome than polarized faceplates or dark goggles.

Their shipsuits were built along lines opposite to those of the bulky atmospheric armor of the First Age of Space: an only mildly biomodified human skin, when mummified by skintight garb, was discovered to have sufficient tenacity to resist vacuum. A second cushion of very light material was used to hold a layer of partial atmosphere next to the skinsuit, in order to help with pressure differentials the free motion of human joints necessitated. This outer silk was like a living layer of air pockets that expanded and contracted with each movement, granting the Hermeticists an eerie shimmering to play over them, like ripples seen on the scales of restless sharks.

There were silver fittings at waist and shoulders, and the heavy ring of a collar at the neck. All the men were bald as a monks, with skull-tight cowls that covered ears and cheeks and buckled beneath the jaw. Each wore his hood drawn up, but not sealed nor inflated. Goggles and mask hung below the throat like a second face.

There were only minor variations to the uniforms.

Melchor de Ulloa was a very handsome man, even in his lunar form. He was always wreathed in smiles of bewildered good cheer and in the scent of lavender. At his throat was an ornament like chicken's claw within a circle, representing peace, a symbol called Nero's Cross. He was the ship's political officer.

Narcís D'Aragó, the cold-eyed master-at-arms, dangled a powered rapier from his baldric and an Aurum pistol in his thigh holster. This weapon fired a nanotechnological smart package designed, upon impact, to disassemble nonliving material such as armor or clothing, and nonimportant material such as flesh and bone into a puddle, and next to form electroneural connections to any nerve cells it encountered floating in that puddle, such as disembodied eyeballs, brain or spinal tissue, linking those cells to the nearest signal nexus for download.

Sarmento i Illa d'Or was a man of muscular bulk, broad shouldered as a bullock, light of step even under Earthly gravity, and in his gauntleted hand an emission wand called a soul goad, used to control thralls, parolees, or courtesans modified with skull implants via shocks of pleasure or agony that left no marks. Aboard ship he had been the quartermaster, and during the time of the World Concordat, the master of the feasts.

Jaume Coronimas, who had been an engineer's mate aboard ship, and the broadcast power master during the Concordat, wore a cowl pieced by two small holes, and through these rose from his scalp two tendrils like whip-antennae made of yellow bioprosthetic metal, and these gold tendrils swayed softly toward the signal sources in the room, peering forth from the mouth of his hood like two inquisitive snakes. His face would have been thin and gray even had his skin not been adapted toward lunar conditions.

One man was not like the others. Father Reyes y Pastor, the expedition chaplain, was in red, and wore ermine and scarlet cardinal's robes atop his black silk. Hanging down his back was a broad-brimmed red hat with elaborate tassels upon tassels, the *galero*. The hat was not on his head, for he wore the black hood of a scholar, proud of his academic achievements above his ecclesiastical station.

The coppery eyes of the Hermeticists glinted under their hoods like red coals in the mouths of dark, triangular furnaces.

The five drifted in soundless grace to their places at the round table. Places, not seats, for no chairs were needed, nor did human legs grow weary in a world of one-sixth weight.

There were more than six score empty places to each side of them. Each empty place was covered over with long, triangular silken lengths. These were the hoods removed from the shipsuits of the departed. Their tassels hung mournfully to the deck, swaying ghostlike in the ventilation of their own internal circuits.

The Hermeticists were alone. No servant had ever set foot in this upper sanctum, not a chambermaid to sweep, not a butler to present a bulb of wine, not a technician to set to rights the thousand intricate circuits of the information systems. No unmodified human could withstand the radiation that time to time poured invisibly from naked outer space a few feet overhead, detected by the dry clicking of counters. Nor was it in the present purposes of the Hermetic Order to acquaint mankind with the full spectrum of biotechnological modifications they employed for their own uses.

Del Azarchel spoke: "Faithful and beloved friends, equal partners in my reign, partners now in my downfall, the entire living world, the Mother Earth so fair and green, is lost to us, with neither a drop from her endless seas nor a wisp of her abundant airs and winds allowed to us here.

"This Luna, this hueless world of lifelessness, through turmoil and fire we achieved with the daring theft in her orbital shipyard of the great ship *Emancipation*. Her sails, as nothing else could do, turned aside the deadly force of the mirrors of the Giants, those same orbital mirrors which burned the civilization whose glory we represent. That power became propulsion for us, for we turned death to life by that same alchemy of knowledge which assures us our supreme authority above mankind.

"As if sailing hither on a sea of fire, this dead world our new world we made, and found this ancient base, long forgotten from the First Age of Space Travel, on the far side of the moon, and far from the orbital mirrors of the Giants, and with diligent work, and not without the sacrifice of loyal servant's lives now mourned, our genius restored it from death to life.

"Here allow me to restore our hopes. History is merely one more language the Monument Builders decoded, and only we, only we anointed few, can speak this language to issue decrees and cast spells in it."

Del Azarchel pointed, and all the floor lit up with branch on branch of Cliometric equations.

The calculation set was profound, reaching an illusory dozens of feet down below what now seemed a crystal floor. De Ulloa cried out in awe, Sarmento grunted, and the golden antennae of Coronimas perked up in surprise. Reyes y Pastor crossed himself, and even the impassive masklike face Narcís D'Aragó twitched and raised an eyebrow.

3. The Allotment of the Eons

Del Azarchel addressed the remnant of the Hermetic Order.

"Each of you have seen the Cliometric projections. Some lines of evolution are dead ends. One will break through to the next level of intellectual topography, an event horizon of human augmentation beyond which no predictions can be made. Study the chessboard, gentlemen! Where would you make your move? Not just Montrose, but human nature and inhuman entropy are all your oppositions in this game. Learned Melchor de Ulloa, you speak first."

Melchor de Ulloa spread his supine hands, a gesture that could have been used either to placate or to beg alms. His voice was honey. "A society where everyone's rights are respected produces liberty and this produces invention, discovery, change, and evolution. The main hindrances to man's ever-upward triumph are hatred, aggression, and fear. The only cure is toleration, education, and the growth of institutions based not on rigid rules and dogmatism, but on open-minded willingness to attempt all options, seek all experiments, try all, dare all, risk all: and thus will man discover all. This willingness is based on social factors independent of political economic structures: it is the artistic vision, the worldview, of the consensus of the people that eventually shapes society.

"Scientifically speaking, this consensus is based on structures in the lower brain, related to various subconscious symmetry-recognition ganglia whose nature we have examined intimately during our work to elevate the Cetaceans to sapience. The Monument describes eighty-one nonverbal communications systems, of which one, music, is comprehensible to the nervous patterns of mammalian Earthly life.

"Artistic vision fathers cultural values, not the other way around; all moral codes are merely the epiphenomena of the irrational subconscious, and of the dreams only freedom can free. I see the doubt on your features, gentlemen, but I can demonstrate my claims with a simple spline equation. Give me control not of the laws nor the religions nor philosophy of man, but merely of their music, and I can guide Man to the Asymptote."

Del Azarchel said, "I have already set in motion what is needful to destroy the Giants, and set the humans of normal intellect free from their control. I foretell a dieback, and Dark Ages lasting until the Fifth Millennium. Once this is accomplished, I will grant to you between the years A.D. 4000 to A.D. 5000 to play out your experiment. Remake mankind as you wish. Learned Narcís D'Aragó, I see you object."

Narcís D'Aragó stood as if at parade rest, hands clasped behind his back. His voice was ice. "Let us talk no more of natural right, or of phlogiston, or of fairy godmothers. Does a man have a natural right to life? That is quaint poetry, but let him beat against the waves of the sea when he is drowning to see what rights nature gives.

"We should stick to facts. The fact is that rights are artificial, a legal fiction, a man-made mechanism to increase group survival value, nothing more. Justice is strength. Without strength is no survival—and all rational moral codes have survival as their object.

"You recall the Fifth Postulate of the Negative Sum divarication proof? It proves that the individual cannot survive without the group, and the group cannot survive unless the individual is willing to die for it. What is needed for mankind is logic, the stern and simple logic of survival.

"The existence of religion—pardon me, Father, but it is true—is based on a genetic marker inclining toward mystical altruism, all men being brothers and all that saccharine fluff.

"No. Rational altruism can beat mystical altruism hands down, for money, love, or marbles. Give me control of men's genetics, and I can shape his destiny, and break human nature open like an egg, and release the dragon within."

Del Azarchel said, "If Melchor de Ulloa falls short, then I will give you between the years A.D. 5000 to A.D. 6000 to accomplish your purpose. If he has achieved the asymptote within his allotted span, your task will be merely to aid him. Learned Sarmento i Illa d'Or! I have never known you to agree with Learned D'Aragó on any point. What say you?"

Sarmento i Illa D'Or, with the studied arrogance of a Hercules, crossed his huge arms across his broad chest and tilted back his head. His voice was the murmur of a bear in winter, disturbed from long, cold sleep. "Bah! Control the emotional nature! Control the music! Control the genetics! Control the thinking! It is all hogwash. What about *not* controlling? What about setting mankind free? And I mean free of all restrictions, moral, mental, intellectual—everything. I say there is no rational moral code that does not take into account the simple scientific fact that all organisms seek pleasure and flee pain. This is the starting point of all rational thought about human nature.

"The trick is to tie pleasure into the proper incentives *without* imposing a system of control the sheep will detect and resent. To do this, you shape the future. You dig the canals and dikes, and merely let the water find its own way at its own pace into your channels.

"The factor that controls the future is demographics. When populations outstrip food supplies, human life is cheap, wages drop, sexual restrictions come into play, and to keep those restrictions, an apparatus of coercion arises that soon reaches all aspects of life. Ancient China was overpopulated, and it sterilized their ability to progress despite an immense head start; Europe outstripped them, because the Black Death had lowered the population level so that every individual life was precious—that, and not empty talk about the sanctity of life—that is what led to the group discipline D'Aragó talks about, as well as the liberty and tolerance De Ulloa mentioned. It is all in the numbers."

"Shall I make you the angel of death, able to lower population rates?" asked Del Azarchel with a dark look.

"No, Learned Senior. Give me the heavens instead, and I will raise them," said Sarmento.

"What?" said Del Azarchel.

"Demographics is based on food supply," Sarmento rumbled. "Which is based on acquisition technology, whether huntsman, herdsmen, or husbandman. So give me control of the climate, wind, and weather. The ancient experiments in weather control were not implemented by a posthuman Iron Ghost, and so the many variables of climate adjustment could not be managed. If I can establish the growing season, shorten or extend it, then I can shape the agrotechnology, the demographics, the pleasure-seeking incentives of human action, and thus the culture that will grow out of it."

Del Azarchel said, "If D'Aragó falls short, then I give you between the years A.D. 6000 to A.D. 7000, but I will grant you longer if you ask, for I doubt your theory is sound."

Sarmento said, "But I must have more time! The method I propose is very slow."

Jaume Coronimas raised his finger. "Are you giving away blocks of a thousand years each, Learned Del Azarchel? Learned Sarmento can have half of my time. My proposal is more efficient."

Coronimas had drawn a series of figures, calculations of his own, in the palm of his left glove with the stylus tip hidden in the finger of his right. Coronimas twitched his golden antennae downward, and at this gesture, the circuits displayed his work in the mirrored floor panels at his feet.

"Observe. The way to improve mankind is merely to improve him. The human nervous system is a machine, and its performance characteristics can be directly changed by changing various bits of neural hardware. We have been failing here because each man is trying to improve himself like Montrose did. I suggest a different approach: to improve the race while keeping the basic unit of the race, the individual, more or less the same. Give me control of man, all of him, and I can remake him into my image, and this will establish evolution—because it will not be evolution, will it? It will be intelligent design. My design. I can make them peaceful and sane and able to adapt to whatever troubles come."

Del Azarchel said, "Then I will give you your five hundred years, if you can match your boast, but I will place it in the midst of an era where it will do no harm if it goes wrong. Father Reyes, I see the pain in your eyes. What is it?"

Reyes y Pastor said, "With respect, Learned Gentlemen and Learned Senior, your thoughts are awry. We cannot plan for the next evolutionary step of man, any more than apes could perform brain surgery on an ape cub and make him grow into a *Homo sapiens*. The superman will be beyond us, and be nothing we can imagine. We must do the very reverse of all that has been said. We cannot control man to unleash evolution; we must unleash evolution and man will be swept up, buoyed up by wild forces beyond control, yes, whether he wishes or not, to the next form of human nature. The one true religion teaches—ah, I know how skeptical you all are, but history will bear out my witness!—the Holy Mother Church teaches that heaven cannot exist on Earth; to yearn in vain for earthly paradise and peace is the heresy of Utopianism."

"If we are all heretics," said Del Azarchel, "what is orthodox?"

"On Earth, life is nothing but the brutal struggle for existence, war of all against all. Blessed are the peacemakers! That word was spoken by Our Savior, and it is truth and holy truth, but as holy truth, it has no application here in this valley of tears called life! Moral codes and liberty and genetic codes, logic and demographics, none of this, my children, is what life on Earth requires to reach the transcendence of the Asymptote. What has hindered us so far is that there are far too few us. Too few who think as we! Let me make a world in our image, a world of men who are unafraid to shape the destinies of all the men beneath them, and they in turn shaped by the men above them, so that all the raw power and agony of evolution will be released like a genii from its brass jar. What will come next, your math cannot predict nor mine!"

Del Azarchel said, "I will give you between A.D. 7000 and A.D. 8000 to work whatever purposes you will, Father Reyes; and the final period between then and A.D. 11000, when the Hyades armada arrives, I reserve to myself either to capitalize the triumphs all you gentlemen have accomplished, or abolish your errors, and in every way to prepare mankind to be what best will serve the intelligences from the Hyades stars. And yes, the race I make in those final days must discover and destroy whatever mad Montrose has prepared of war and revolution, for he seeks ever to bring the wrath of Hyades down upon us.

"The conclave is ended: each go your own ways, draw up your calculations, and prepare! We war not only against Montrose and his servants, and against the perversity of human nature but against the lingering tardiness of Darwin, and against death, time, and entropy itself!"

And the Hermeticists bowed toward the throne; then each man took his leave and descended, weightless as thistledown, through the deck hatches into the deeply buried lunar fortress with no more noise than a spirit returning to its grave.

PART THREE

A World of Ice

Interlude: A Cold Silence

A.D. 9999

1. Alarm Clock

All he wanted to do was to stay dead. Some damn nuisance kept jarring him awake.

Some damn nuisance named Blackie.

Before he opened his eyes, before he knew whether his other organs were thawed, he was aware of his acceleration. No, not acceleration: weight. There was no sensation of motion. He was not aboard a ship. He was still trapped on Earth. Where was she?

With immense pain, and annoyance more immense, he pried open a creaking eyelid. The clock on the inside of the icy coffin lid reacted to the motion and lit up, the faint red letters reading YEAR: A.D. 9999 YOUR AGE: 7789 CALENDAR / 50 BIOLOGICAL.

In 2401, his body had been buried in the debris of the uprooting of the Celestial Tower of Quito, which fell upward into orbit. Rania had used the Celestial Tower as a rotating beanstalk or rotovator to accelerate the ship to the escape velocity of the solar system, forty-two kilometers per second.

The damn thing was thousands of miles long, and the tangential velocity was over six miles a second. Flung the damn starship like a stone from David's sling toward Jupiter, where she performed a gravitational assist maneuver to exceed the escape velocity of the solar system.

At that point, fearing him dead and with no feasible way to decelerate, she sailed away to rendezvous with the first of the antimatter centaurs she would gather for her fuel supply, while Del Azarchel, forsaken on an Earth whose space programs he himself had gutted, watched helplessly through long-range radar as she took nine parts of his world's entire energy supply, and hid the tenth part by nudging the centaurs into new orbits.

Del Azarchel, in a gesture of melodramatic noblesse oblige, or perhaps frustration that his visceral desire by his own hand to shoot Montrose dead, had ordered his foe pulled from the rubble, hospitalized, and placed in cryogenic suspension in a political penitentiary. Some of Del Azarchel's Scholar race, however, were still loyal to Rania and arranged for his escape: and the areas of the world where either Del Azarchel had no control, or pure anarchy did, were expanding.

The struggles that followed between the factions loyal to Del Azarchel and his machine, and those opposed, laid waste to the world. The second half of twenty-fifth century had been the most violent in history, even when compared with the enormities of the Little Dark Ages. There had been a third, fourth, and fifth worldwide civil war since the violent rupture of the Concordat A.D. 2413 into northern and southern hemispheres, and countless lesser wars, invasions, insurrections, tumults, acts of nuclear blackmail. Ninety-five major cities and over a billion people had died over these wars and megahomicides, slain by atomics, and another half billion in the depressions, famines, plagues, and migrations that followed. The horror the world had known during the Burning of New York the Beautiful had been repeated half a hundredfold. Cities famed in history would never rise again, but had gone the way of Carthage, Nineveh, and Tyre.

And it had aged him. At times, he wondered if Del Azarchel had been causing world wars merely to force Montrose to run out his clock. After the Decivilization, the interruptions came less frequently, but they still came.

He looked at the calendar again. His last thaw had been over two thousand years ago, A.D. 7985. Had there been no interference in history since that time? Nothing to trigger the alarm?

Rania, by the analogous point in time in her metric, was a shade less than 7,500 light-years distant in the constellation Canes Venatici, receding at 99.9 percent of the speed of light. He could picture it perfectly in his mind's eye: The ship's flare would have been red-shifted so far beyond the infrared as to be in the radio range of the spectrum. From his frame of reference, the great ship was dark beyond invisibility, massive beyond neutronium, flattened in the direction of motion like a metallic pancake; and the clocks, and heartbeats, and subatomic motions aboard made a single tick once a year.

But from her frame of reference, asleep in her coffin of ice, the ship was the same immense silver white cylinder she had always been, and her mirrored sails wider than saturnine rings spread before her, but reflecting a universe that was strange: for space-time surrounding was flattened and cold and dark and massive, and only a compressed rainbow of stars circling the ship's equator would have seemed normal to the human eye. Directly fore of the prow, where the distortion was greatest, high-energy gamma ray point-bursts from the core of stars or dark bodies were Doppler-shifted into visibility, a pattern of fireflies.

The only object normal to her would be the ever-shrinking dead heart of the Diamond Star, V886 Centauri, to which her ship was attached by chains, thankfully immaterial, of magnetic force. The 10-billion-trillion-trillion-carat diamond of antimatter had by now worn itself down to a mere 9 billion trillion trillion carats, one tenth of its mass already converted to propulsion. The mass of the superjovian planet Thrymheim had been long ago absorbed: now the antimatter reaction was sustained by a ramscoop, a magnetic funnel of immense size gathering up the interstellar particles, which, at her velocity, were both massive and densely packed. So she lived in a universe with one undistorted worldlet: the stub of a dead star made of contraterrene, too deadly to touch, gleaming like ice in the light from the rainbow ring of stars.

But would there be stars? The White Ship was traveling perpendicular to the plane of the galaxy, heading toward the distant globular cluster at M3, a dandelion puff of a million stars 33,900 light-years away. By now, Rania was beyond the Orion Arm, and the whole Milky Way was a wheel, red-shifted into invisibility off her stern, and the ultra-low-frequency radio auroras wreathing the accretion disk of the supermassive black hole that boiled at the core of Milky Way, invisible to mortal eyes, were visible, now, to her.

In his imagination, he also carried a map of the Milky Way, its known stars and open clusters, which he could picture as easily as an unmodified man could picture the features of his wife's face. The total number of stars was, of course, a bit much, even for him, so he had used a mnemonic device to memorize the vast catalog and their relative distances and motions around the galactic core.

He took a moment to fill in this star map in his mind, and he saw that the open cluster NGC 6939 in the constellation Cepheus was not far from her route, and she would have no doubt passed through the cluster of eighty stars hanging just above the Orion Arm in order to take advantage of the gravity slingshot, and increase her velocity: from her frame of reference, the eighty stars would be more massive than the black hole at the galactic core. Her ship was as massive to them, from their rest frame of reference, as they were, from her moving frame of reference, to her. At that speed, her ship, for all practical purposes, was a singularity. When she passed through, the immense tidal and gravitic effect of her ship would perturb the scores of stars from their orbits and scatter them. The disturbance would be visible to Earthly deep sky observatories over the next millennium. In time, the stars would be too far apart to be considered a cluster.

Princess Rania was still young, thanks to Lorenz transformations. She was still in her early twenties. Practically a child.

And he was fifty years old!

Less than one tenth of the Long Wait had passed. Always some little thing, the fall of empires, the genocide of races of man, some world famine, or some eruption of machine-worshiping Savants pulled him from his grave to waste ever more of his ever-lessening lifetime.

The tube piercing his throat above his collarbone vibrated as air was forced into him. In theory, there were breathing exercises recommended to assist the Thaw process, as the cell layers lining the lungs made microscopic adjustments from the biologically suspended state to animation. Instead, through numb and drooling lips, he cussed and sobbed. He figured that was just as good.

2. Halt-State

"Why did you wake me? Is it time? Did she return?"

"No, Dr. Montrose. It is still an estimated sixty-one thousand years before the earliest possible date of the return of Mrs. Montrose."

"Then why the plaguey hell did you plaguing wake me, you dumb horse? I told you to wake me for nothing."

"So I have. Nothing has occurred."

"What?"

"My instructions reached a halt-state. Since I was unable to decide whether to wake you or not, I had to wake you for instructions on whether to wake you or not."

"You are to wake me when there is some event in the outside world needing my attention. We went over a really long list with an algorithm, that you are supposed to submit to Sir Guy or his successor, whoever the current Grand

Master of the Order of the Knights Hospitalier might be. Is there such an event?"

"No, Dr. Montrose."

"Then what is it?"

"There are no events at all in the outside world, Dr. Montrose."

"What the pox? Open the lid."

3. Man Remakes Himself

Menelaus Illation Montrose, 7789 calendar/50 biological, climbed out of the coffin, dripping with medical fluid, naked, nothing in his hands but two caterpillar-drive Browning pistols.

He stood patiently while sinuous metallic serpentines from overhead sponged off the medical fluid, when vents from underfoot dried him with blasts of warm yet pine-scented air. Meanwhile a second set of serpentines from his footlocker draped a fluffy bathrobe around his shoulders; at the same time, a third set of arms poured him a freshly brewed cup of coffee in a white porcelain cup, cream with one sugar.

"How much coffee do we have left, Pellucid?" He tucked his pistols into the bathrobe pockets, which sagged alarmingly, so he could take the cup in hand.

"This is the last container, Dr. Montrose. There is enough for sixteen cups. At your current ratio of slumber to thaw, and current rate of consumption, the supply will last you until circa A.D. 25000."

"What's the chance of getting more?"

"All evidence suggests that the coffee plant is extinct, Dr. Montrose. That would make the chance of getting more approach zero."

Montrose sipped the scalding brew thoughtfully. "Maybe I can borrow some from Blackie. Before I kill him. He's a partner. Sure he won't mind."

"All evidence suggests that Dr. Del Azarchel is also extinct, Dr. Montrose."

Montrose was surprised enough to spit. He glared down in dismay at the little dark splat of precious, irrecoverable coffee fluid on the steel floor, even as an alert serpentine reached in with a sterilized towel to clean it up.

Because the neural interconnections in his brain were more efficient than those of an unmodified human, by the time the stain was wiped up, Montrose said, "Don't bother telling me the human race is extinct. That is just a temporary setback, and I've got a backup plan prepared for that. And I don't believe Blackie is dead: the ache in my bones tells me he's alive, and he's gunning for me. So the biosphere has been wiped out, eh? Is there machine molasses covering everything, that rod-logic liquid crystal stuff that looks like gold?"

"No, Dr. Montrose."

"Well, which way did he jump? Is it a Hothouse Earth, or a Iceball Earth?"

"I have no working cameras topside, Dr. Montrose, at this or any Tomb site. The main door will not open. It is blocked. Indirect evidence, however, suggests—"

"Iceball Earth, then. Damnation and pestilence. I was hoping he would try a biotechnology-based civilization again, like ruled the Earth during the Eighth Millennium A.D. But if he didn't—then what was the point of the Hormagaunts? Over a thousand years of half-human abominations and superhuman monsters—for what?"

"The question phrasing is unclear."

"Sorry, Pel, wasn't talking to you. Rhetorical questions. Looks like Blackie has outsmarted me. Machine life can prosper just dandy on a world of ice, can't it? But what the hell happened? Why didn't you stop it?"

There was no immediate answer.

Montrose said, "Pellucid, those last two questions were for you. They were not rhetorical. Give me a précis of world history while I slept, and tell me what steps you took to reverse Del Azarchel's manipulation of the climate."

"While you slept, the posthuman group that rose to predominance was a gestalt-mind consisting of postwhale, postdolphin, posthuman, biotechnological, and xypotechnological elements. They were called the Melusine. The most common configuration was a whale-pod-based oceanic brain mass of immense size and complexity communicating by means of neural quantum entanglement narrowcast with five or seven human-shaped or mermaid-shaped manipulator bodies, and a swarm of lesser sensor packages, tools, weapons, and node relays housed as sea serpents, eels, snakes, and insects. The lesser bodies were thought-controlled to a cellular level, and treated like organs of the gestalt."

"That's what human beings look like these days? Sheesh. Sleep a few centuries, and you miss everything. What happened to the previous civilization? The little bald men with radio antennae?"

"The Noöspherical Cognitive Order dissolved in A.D. 8766."

"I introduced a vector that should have seduced them into a more freedom-loving mental-economic system."

"The individualism you introduced also triggered a series of world wars as political uniformity broke down. I did not wake you, because you left specific instructions not to be thawed merely for world wars."

"Hmf. Coronimas told me his creations were meant to be total pacifists."

"I believe he grossly overestimated the irenic or pacifying effect that radio-based neural connections would have on the individuals exchanging thoughts and memory chains: their wars were spectacularly brutal, and this was long before the Noösphere collapsed."

"Fine. So Coronimas is an idiot, and their worldwide mind library broke apart. What happened next?"

"The electrotelepathic psychologically uniform subspecies called Locusts lingered in ever dwindling groups until the 8900s, when they were finally wiped out by Linderlings.

"The Linderlings and Inquiline elements of the previous Noösphere could not re-interconnect their library-minds due to sociopsychological divarication. They formed smaller groups called Confraternities. Then, about nine hundred years ago, several groups combined to re-create a new fashion of mankind consisting of link-minded mating groups of five specialized sexes and subsexes, including the admixture of material from the long-extinct Cetacean races. These were the earliest forms of the Melusine.

"As watchdogs, certain of Inquiline were designed to scan and review Melusine mental data streams, including conscious thoughts, by means of a specialized psychoscopic cadre, aided by land-based mainframes housed in mile-high arcologies called Granoliths. However, over the centuries, the exhaustion of certain critical natural resources, the increase of the polar ice caps, caused the Granolith infrastructure to fail."

"Why didn't they use weather-control technology to fix it?"

"Political considerations. The increase in ice caps altered the oceanic conditions in a way that bestowed a sudden increase on the aquacultural foundations of the Melusine economy, rendering hitherto marginal areas profitable, encouraging rapid growth and expansion, an increase in luxuries and a greater efficiency of labor, as well as an easing of coercive restrictions—I did not interfere, because these were 'Renaissance' conditions, akin to the political liberty and capitalist exchange-systems you have so often ordered me in the past to encourage. To maintain the previous climate would have led to insurrection, tumult, war."

"So Blackie snookered you. He created a 'Roaring Twenties' boom so you would not interfere when he lined up a sudden population drop."

"Perhaps that is the case. But the Melusine not only developed a space program, and planted outposts among the ruins of the partly terraformed Mars, but maneuvered the asteroid 1036 Ganymed into a sublunar orbit as a smaller second moon, honeycombed it with habitable garden-tunnels and cisterns and a spherical great lake in the hollow center. This is usually the type of project for which you express enthusiasm: I did not interfere with this course of events. Due to the increasingly hostile environment of Earth, the Melusine of Ganymed created a self-sustaining microecology, consisting entirely of artificial insects and fungi not based on any earthly models."

"Wow," said Montrose, impressed. "I guess I would have been snookered too. Just add a propulsion sail, point a launching laser, and you'd have a worldlet-size starship ready to launch. I would not have interfered either. But meanwhile Earth is entering an ice age. What happens next?"

"The balance of power between inland empires and coastal organizations could not be maintained. Then in a single generation, suddenly, the majority of remaining Inquiline either entered into full mental communion with the Melusine, which in effect absorbed them, or they refused communion and continued servicing severely depleted Granoliths, but could not track nor understand the thought patterns of the Melusine. This inferiority made them retire into lives of supine renunciation, isolating themselves from the mental life, arts and sciences, of the race.

"There followed strenuous efforts, over generations, of the coastal organizations to maintain the failing inland polities. The Melusine mating-harems could not maintain their population levels without the land-based agriculture to serve as an ecological basis for their human-shaped sexes. These efforts were unsuccessful due to an unwillingness of the Melusine to adapt their social customs and laws to match the new and more Spartan conditions.

"Meanwhile, among the Inquiline, several civilizations of the remnants consumed themselves in seeking mystical experiences through pharmaceutical and electroneural manipulations. When the population fell below a critical threshold, the world electronic communion fell into disrepair, and the survivors retreated into sealed and heated city-states, surrounded by ice, and surviving on yeast, soy, and proteins pyrohydroponically grown in geothermal taps. The loss of the electronic web cut me off from real-time examination of the records of the culture, and the geothermal taps interfered with my near-surface structures to such a degree that my observation posts had to be abandoned."

"Wait. What? You just let these people blind you?"

"I have no reason to suspect that they knew I existed, and your instructions make it clear that I am not allowed to kill large populations of human beings indiscriminately. I could not attack their geothermal taps without inducing starvation in the sealed city-states, and I could not continue my near-surface subterranean activities without being detected by the taps."

"You are allowed to defend yourself if Blackie is using some trick to encroach on the Tomb system."

"The ecological and climactic changes appeared to be natural, therefore my self-defense imperative had no legal parameter in which to act."

"Snot and skunk phlegm! Del Azarchel must have found out about you—probably for a long time—and worked out a statistical camouflage to hide the demographic and climactic changes over the centuries in the white noise, so your pattern-seeking subroutine would not see it, even though it was right before your eyes."

"Unlikely, sir."

"Likely enough that it actually happened. Brilliant! But how? Where did he get the capacity to outsmart *you*? Are there any mainframe structures on Earth capable of housing even one percent of your capacity, Pellucid?"

"There are no occupied structures at all upon the Earth, Dr. Montrose."

"What?"

"The last remaining city-state ceased drawing power from its geothermal tap centuries ago. This was the domed city of Nyiragongo in the Virunga Mountains. There has been no detectable radio traffic or engineering signals since that time. I believe the human race is extinct."

"Pox! And you did not wake me up?"

"It was not one of the eventualities covered in your otherwise thorough instructions, sir."

4. Extinction Event

Montrose was silent a moment, face dark with wonder and horror.

"What about outside these city-states? Is there anyone alive anywhere else? What happened to the human–dolphin hybrids you mentioned living in the sea, the Melusine? What happened to the space colony?"

"Unfortunately, after the sudden drop in Inquiline population levels, all Melusine internal signal traffic became closed to me. I could not maintain espionage systems within their data streams without the Inquiline to act as intermediaries. Their external signals became increasingly rare and cryptic: I assume they evolved to the next intellectual topology."

"Smarter than you? Or just different?"

"Unknown."

"Why didn't they stop the extinction?"

"Unknown. The external evidence is that the Melusine dismantled their long-term prognostication houses and dissolved their method of peaceful reconciliation of disputes due to a neurophysical and psychological divarication between the coastal, undersea, and the spaceborne Melusine.

"There was a period of anarchy and collapse: the indirect evidence suggests a drop of their industrial capacity in ten years to two percent of its former levels, with a corresponding dieback of unsustainable population, either through voluntary mass suicide or mass euthanasia.

"In the final period, the undersea Melusine and spaceborne Melusine entered into what was apparently a war of mutual extermination, which ended with the collision of the asteroid 1036 Ganymed in the Eurafrican continent."

"Wait," said Montrose. "Which continent?"

"While you slumbered, this continent was formed by the closing of the Mediterranean, which is now a mountain range."

"Oh. About fifty million years before schedule, wasn't it?"

"During the Locust War, certain of the powers used applied volcanism to maneuver plate tectonics to their military advantage. But that continent in turn no longer exists, as it was bisected by an inland sea that reaches from the isthmus of Ethiopia to the Gulf of Guinea. I thought the terminology North Eurafrica and South Eurafrica inelegant, so I called the northern continent Baltica, and the southern, Pannotia. Normally, I would have waited for the decision of an accredited scientific or Linnaean consensus before selecting a naming scheme, but as the human race is extinct, it seemed unproductive to wait."

"Oh. Well, use those names until we find if Blackie's got something nicer sounding. Describe the impact."

"The impact released energy equaling the explosion of one hundred thousand gigatons of TNT, and the seismic reaction was twelve point five on the Richter scale. It formed several impact craters from Ethiopia to Sudan to Cameroon, making a scar some seven hundred and fifty miles wide and two thousand miles long, into which tidal waves poured. The reentry of ejecta produced infrared radiation sufficient to kill all exposed organisms in the eastern hemisphere, and elevated levels of sulfate aerosols in the atmosphere. Continent-wide firestorms igniting all exposed plant life raged throughout the other hemisphere. The dust cloud blocked the sunlight for thirteen months. The year of darkness increased the speed of glaciations, and the polar ice caps, as of my last reliable report, reached to tropical areas, and may have met at the equator."

"Last reliable report? When was that?"

"Twenty-two hundred hours, thirteen January of A.D. 9500. The impact of 1036 Ganymed distorted the Earth's crust and destroyed all my type-one sensor periscopes, and damaged half the near-crust depthtrain tubes. Increasing ice levels combined with atmospheric changes rendered my type-two sensors inoperative. I do not have the resources to repair, nor stores to replace, these systems. I have partial surface access from three hundred and thirteen sites, total access from none, and no remote capacity. Was I right to thaw you?"

"Dammit, you were. I never thought Blackie would actually slam a rock into the Earth and kill the whole human race just to get at me. He's lost his mind, or he is smarter than both of us—and as far as I care, either option is worse than the other."

5. The Immortal Game

He heaved a sigh and swallowed his coffee, which had grown cold while he talked. Scowling, he said, "We have one thousand years and change before the Hyades World Armada descends. That is not much time. Warm up the nanobiochemical Lab seventeen and give me the records of the most recent interments."

"Lab seventeen? Are we planning biological warfare, then, Dr. Montrose?"

"Not quite. Evolutionary warfare. I am going to release Von Neumann machines into what's left of the biosphere, along with spores, algae, and the basic terraforming package I was saving for that starship voyage I apparently am never going to take. I also need our most recent biological information on whatever might be left of the human race on the surface."

"Doctor, I believe there is none."

"And I believe you were fooled, you dumb horse. Do as I say."

Montrose, now dressed in a black shipsuit taken from his footlocker, climbed up twelve levels of the Tombs, which required more than a few minutes.

The second level was crowded, with two coffins to every cell, and the warehouse chambers filled with dismantled equipment, everything from refrigeration units to nano manipulators to robotic weapons to lighting fixtures, all of which should have been on the first level.

"Which is the most recent coffin?"

Pellucid answered: "We inducted our most recent client on January twenty-third, A.D. 9296. His name is name unknown, cause unknown, duration unknown. My records are in disorder, and no further details are available. Are you planning to thaw him?"

There were coffins occupying the corridors, linked by lines running through T-splitters to overcrowded cells where more coffins lay piled one atop the other. Montrose followed a glowing line of light on the floor, climbing over the coffins, to find the most recently interred one.

He wiped the screen set in the coffin's hull free of frost and switched it on. Inside was a streamlined, narrow-headed body, unusually tall but unusually thin. It was oceangoing: it had the thick skin, webbed fingers and toes, gills like Venetian blinds under its armpits, of a standard sea-modified hominid. It was utterly lacking in facial hair, and the sexual organs were folded into a crotch pouch, so Montrose could not tell if it were a merman or mermaid. The skin was a black as shoe polish. Negroes were called "Black" in his day, and so were Dravidians, but they were a dark pink or a dark brown, not so much darker than himself after a hot summer. This creature was black as obsidian, black as onyx. It gave the man an almost statuelike inhuman look. Nothing like it had existed on earth the year when Montrose was born.

The most radical modifications were evidently to the nervous system. On the front of the narrow skull of the sleeping form, above the huge eyes and above the infra-red-sensing eye-pits, tendrils of some sort of radio-linked neural interface curved back from the brow like antennae: one pair was gold, one was silver, one pair was blue. It had two sets of ears, a smaller pair covered by folding tissue set behind and below the human-looking pair. The back of the skull was dotted with three symmetrically spaced pair of input and output ports. Whoever had designed the species evidently expected them to draw in a great deal of sense impressions from their environment.

"So this is what became of the human race, eh? Ugly-looking little bugger." He shook his head. So much time had passed; so much was yet to pass. He was more than awed; he was appalled.

"Is that a Melusine component?" he asked Pellucid.

"Yes. This is a descendant of an Inquiline-type Locust, one of the Special People designed to scan Melusine thought streams: a Psychoscopist. Each Melusine pentad or septad contained at least one, to act as interface and intercessor to the world Noösphere, which had no direct mental connection otherwise. If he were thawed, he would not, by Melusine standards, be sane."

"I expect not. It would be like me thawing up a client's left hemisphere of his brain while leaving the right in slumber. This is only part of a gestalt being."

"Do you wish me to thaw him? I have no record whether his living will conditions for thaw have been met. The onboard coffin brain, which is intact, may have additional information."

Montrose straightened up and spoke brusquely. "No need for thaw. I merely need samples of his gene material; I can calculate his biopsychology. Looks like someone needs a neurological predilection for independent action, not to mention total immunity from all forms of mental coercion. Freethinking and all that. A mental anarchy vector. Maybe a touch of that self-reliant pioneer spirit. The whole world looks like frontier now. So right now I don't care about modifications not reflected in the genetics, since I am working my reply to Blackie's latest tactic on a broader strategic level. Do you play chess, Pellucid?"

"Of course, Doctor. I have played all chess games in every possibility. There are only ten to the one hundred and twentieth power variations."

"You are familiar with the Immortal Game?"

"Grandmasters Anderssen and Kieseritsky in London 1851. Kieseritsky neglected his development, and Anderssen sacrificed both rooks, a bishop, then his queen, to checkmate Kieseritsky with his remaining minor pieces."

"That is basically the game I have to play."

"I am not very good at grasping analogies outside of my defined sphere of behavior, Dr. Montrose."

"In my case, my Queen is safe, since she is way off the board and out of anyone's reach. Blackie's most powerful piece, his Queen, is his machine intelligence, Exarchel, the damn mirror reflection of his brain. Blackie is a cold bastard, and he cares more about staying alive than staying human, and that goes double for his machine duplicate, but I can sacrifice my best piece and lure Exarchel into the open, and take Exarchel off the board forever.

"These Tomb systems here are my rooks, and as long as I stay buried and hidden like a king in a castle, he cannot get at me. I may have to sacrifice at least one rook to draw Del Azarchel out of hiding—but I can't break my word to the people who trusted their slumbering bodies to me. I cannot turn them over to grave-robbers. So what can I do? And I cannot stand pat and do nothing, because Blackie has me in a tight corner now, a fork."

"I understand that metaphor. It refers to a dilemma."

"A damnation of a dilemma. I am the only one in a position to restore the Earth's biosphere from my archives, and doing nothing leaves us with an iceball environment where only the machines can live."

"Doctor, why do you think, first, that there is any surviving civilization out there, and, second, that such a civilization will not have the technological capacity to repopulate the Earth with plants and animals as needed?"

"If the asteroid drop was an accident, I might ponder either of those possibilities in my mind. But this stinks of Blackie. He just loves dropping things from heaven onto people's heads. Always has. Makes him feel all Old Testament and such. Besides, the asteroid just happened to drop at a period when it wipes out all your surface cameras and induces a catastrophic cooling cycle? Too convenient for coincidence."

The emotion of doubt entered the emotionless voice. "Perhaps so, Dr. Montrose. Your neural structure allows you to pick patterns out from a background of camouflage. Then again, the human mind invents patterns where nothing but chaos exists: it is called the apophenia, and underlies the Rorschach blot effect."

"In that case, there is no harm in setting a little bit of evolution in motion."

Now Montrose bent over the coffin controls, introduced a serpentine through a socket lock, and removed cells from the lower and upper spine of the creature, the bone marrow, several organs. Soon he had the material he needed in a small package of red capsules.

He held one of the capsules up to the dim light, frowning. The capsule readout showed the client had suffered some aging and degradation. He hoped the coffins were still tight. The Tombs were not meant to operate cut off from the outside world. The Hospitaliers were supposed to thaw periodically and replace worn gear from supplies purchased or coerced from whatever civilization was occupying the surface world.

There was no help for it. He tucked the capsules into their refrigerated holder and began clambering through the coffin-choked corridor toward Lab 17. Meanwhile, he ordered Pellucid to gather the substances he needed there.

"I need to set the world on fire. My next move against Blackie is to take the Earth's ecology, what's left of it, in an unexpected direction. Your basic unit is that of a Von Neumann machine, a self-replicating logic crystal, originally meant to monitor and control volcanism. I can use your units to trigger a number of volcanoes in that mountain range where the Mediterranean used to be, vent gases and smokes from below the Earth's crust, and start pushing the ice floes back."

The voice of Pellucid came from one of the still-working wall phones dotting the dim, cold corridor. "Doctor, I cannot help but conclude that the asteroid drop was an accident, or an act of war, on the grounds that it grants you a tremendous advantage in your struggle against Del Azarchel. If he is still exiled on the Moon, he cannot enjoy the biological supplies or geothermal energy sources available to you: whatever race you next intend to create will have a tremendous numerical advantage. Moreover, with the electronic infrastructure of industrial civilization apparently at an end, biological rather than mechanical life must come to dominate. Men reproduce more rapidly in primitive conditions than machines."

"If I could act without interference, you might be right, Pel," said Montrose. "But any surviving civilization out there, knowing my Tombs and archives exist, is going to come looking for me to dig me out, and all Blackie has to do is watch them and see who shows up to blast them—because whoever or whatever defends the Tombs from looting is one of my men or one of my mechanisms. And I cannot let innocent people be dug up; but I cannot let this snowball world be the only world the Hyades find at the End of Days.

"So I have to lure him down from the Moon—or wherever the hell he is these days—by developing the next ecology and next human race, swans out of ugly duckings, along a vector he cannot dare leave unstopped, a race with a built-in predilection for independence. Something even less of a pack animal than man. But this is a sacrifice game, and I might lose everything, and still not get the checkmate I foresee."

"I don't understand your comment, Dr. Montrose. May I make a four-dimensional emulation of your brain and spinal column down to the subcellular level? The emulation will mimic your thoughts with sufficient precision to allow me to anticipate and follow your conversational quirks and—"

"No, and don't ask me again, dammit. I am not going to turn into Me-Too Blackie."

"Then may I emulate Exarchel, Ximen del Azarchel's machine intelligence? I am not able to anticipate the creative aspect of any machine that mimics human thought."

"No. That would only play into his hands. I can still outsmart this guy."

"What is your plan, Dr. Montrose? Under your structure of assumptions, releasing an evolutionary vector into the environment from this location will attract attention here. You do not actually have sufficient troops in biosuspension to fend off a concerted attack. I don't foresee a solution."

"Good, then neither will he."

"Please explain, Dr. Montrose."

"I wish I could explain Dr. Montrose. The smarter I get, the more I puzzle myself."

"Linguistic failure."

"Sorry, that was a joke."

"No, Dr. Montrose, I think it was not."

"Hmpf."

He arrived at the door to the lab, and because he did not trust the seals of the equipment inside, he donned his hood, mask, and gauntlets and brought his black silk shipsuit up to pressure.

The door motors were offline. Montrose cranked the door open with the manual handle. Beyond was darkness, and the floor was slick with ice. Cranking the door shut behind him, and turning on his suit lights, he moved here and there about the chamber, checking power connections, finding the failure points, and searching through the maintenance locker by the door for replacement parts for the chamber circuits.

He threw the master switch. It was still dark and cold while he waited for the laboratory equipment to prepare itself. He discussed points of strategy with Pellucid.

Pellucid continued to voice doubts. Montrose answered, "Listen, despite all the secrets of intelligence augmentation the human race learned from the alien Monument, despite all my bulging brain power, my next move depends just on a matter of faith. Do I have more faith in the Spirit of Man than he does? I think Rania solved the basic divarication problems involved in superintelligence and he has not. Do I have faith in her? Is he going to eat my bait and then eat my brain, or is he going to swallow my hook and get caught himself, because he'll never expect me to play the game the only way a truly posthuman mind can play it? We are going forward blind, you and I, and at some point you just have to trust me."

There was a long pause. Montrose was surprised and grew more surprised the longer the pause lasted. He calculated in his mind how much capacity Pellucid must be using to interpret his last statement, and the figure was surprisingly high, and grew higher as the seconds passed.

The emotionless voice said, "Doctor? . . . Are you asking my permission? You are my master as well as my maker; it is not right for you to ask."

"Pellucid, it's just that—after all this time—"

"I do not suffer pain or human longings. I am self-aware, but only to a limited extent, only on certain topics, and only as my intellectual topography dictates. You understand that the part of me that can make human speech and manipulate abstract concepts is not the real me, do you not, Doctor? Therefore, it is not right for you to ask. My complete love and complete devotion are on a preverbal level, fundamental to the nature of how I was engineered, and asking in words merely causes dissonance between these levels."

"—After all this time, you dumb beast, you are my only friend and my only hope—"

"It is only an ill-made creation that would choose to hate his creator, Dr. Montrose."

"You can call me Menelaus from now on."

"Yes, Menelaus."

The lights ignited with a flash, and the heat and air clicked and whirred and groaned like a tired ogre climbing out of bed. It was time to go to work.

6. Topside

It was not done in a day, and not in two. And each delay led to more delays: the time spent finding and thawing old food stores in the living quarters, or repairing just one shelf in the automatic mess to working order, was an exasperation to him. He could not sleep in his coffin, so he slung some spare solar cloth between two stanchions in the corridor outside the lab and used that as a hammock, with a bale of the cloth beneath it to soften the fall when he fell in his sleep.

There were forty-seven failed batches that had to be carefully destroyed before he finally, with weary joy, examined the glass pans beneath an electron microscope and saw the seething pattern of subviral bodies.

Later, he went up.

The first level was wreckage. The roof had collapsed under an immense mass of ice and rock. The stairwell was in shambles. He retreated back downstairs long enough to find an ax and a parka, a power cell, belt lamp, and a few other needed tools. Then Menelaus spent the better part of a day using an ax to cut, dynamite to blast, and thermal papers to melt through the ice blocking the corridor to the guardroom on the first level.

The guard chamber itself was intact. He pulled down the periscope and pushed in a drill-tipped serpentine he had taken from the plumbing locker. It took a relatively short time to drive a shaft to the surface. He reinserted the periscope and told the cables leading to various wavelengths of receivers to find and connect to their antenna contact points on the periscope housing. For a moment, it was as if a basket of multicolored snakes had been tossed into the air around him, as each prehensile wire coiled and swayed through the air and sought its correct fitting. Then light images, radio and shortwave, began shining down the shaft.

Montrose put his eyes to the eyepieces. The ground was white in all directions, slabs and runnels and cracks and hills of ice and more ice. The radio frequencies were silent.

The Human Race Is Extinct. Unfortunately, the intelligence augmentation Montrose had suffered had also, it seemed, equipped him with a greater imagination. He could practically see the deaths of millions and tens of millions, and savor each and every one, what it would mean, what had been lost. That blessed ability fools had that enabled them to shut out the horrid emptiness of eternity and infinity that surrounded the tiny living spot called Earth was denied to him.

But he also had greater powers of concentration than heretofore: and work could drive the sharp and angular vividness of the images of worldwide demise from the forefront of his mind. *She* was still alive, after all.

Days became a week, and then a fortnight, and each hour was bitterness to him.

In the machine shop on the third level, he constructed simple reconnaissance drones, gave them instructions, and sent them up the shaft, one after another, glittering dragonflies of steel.

The drone cameras found nothing but ice. Not a drop of running water, not a blade of grass, not a tree, not a shrub.

One after another, like a man building a ship in a bottle, Montrose reached out through the tiny hole of the periscope shaft with serpentines, and raised ever taller antennae masts, and constructed ever more powerful receivers. There was no signal traffic, no navigation beacons, nothing. Comparing image after image of the night sky detected no artificial satellites.

He was able to use the weapons systems in front of the main door to blast free of the ice and drive the door open a crack. With parka and snow goggles, Montrose emerged from his Tomb, climbed a white slope, and stood looking out on a world with no sign of life in any direction.

He stood there, aghast, watching the sun slowly sink in a weary mass of red and gold above a gray landscape. After a time, the moon rose in a cloudless sky.

The moon was full, and the imprint of a thin left hand with a black palm was upon it.

Montrose raised his left hand as if in answer, opened his fingers, and had the smart material coating his glove turn his fingers white and his palm black.

7. *A Long, Cold Road*

The last few days he spent outside. The Expedition House on Level 1 held empty stalls, but also clothing and gear for a variety of climates, including sea gear, in case the passing ages brought floods. One of the packs contained an inflatable tent and sleeping roll.

Montrose loved the outdoors. He preferred seasons when the wilderness made noise: endless chirping, hooting, croaking, or the music of wind and rain. This world was silent and still and white.

Each dawn, when the wind was right, little graceful bits of fluff, looking like the down of dandelions, fluttered from the stations and towers he had grown. Each noon, seeds of the same substance drifted behind the tails of his dragonfly-winged flying machines like the plumes of cropdusters. He wrote love poems of appallingly bad doggerel in the skywriting, and was relieved as the slow, huge winds shredded them. As the sun sank in the west, the winds would die down, and the gigantic silence of the world return.

Each dusk he disturbed the hated silence with fireworks, as his launching tubes shot very tiny and very powerful intercontinental rockets up through the chimneys he had dug. Each multistage rocket with its delicate Von Neumann nanotechnological payload was flung into the stratosphere, little gleaming pen-strokes of flame against the winter-crisp night sky.

Toward midnight, he would look north, seeking the tiny constellation of Canes Venatici, where the dogs of myth, Asterion and Chara, eternally held on the leash of Boötes, eternally chased the great bear of Ursa Major, with baleful Arcturus as their lantern. When the conditions were right, and skies clean of cloud or mist, he could find the speck of the globular cluster M3 in the darkness of heaven, until the image blurred and swam in his vision, and he did not bother to wipe the trickle of heat that fell down his cheek. There was no one to see him weeping, after all. The last race of man was more or less extinct, and the next had not yet been born.

Eventually, his days and nights of labor done, he returned below. It was more trouble closing the great door than opening it, since he had to haul equipment, block and tackle, and a diesel-powered winch from the Machine House on Level 6, but finally this was done as well.

Before he closed the lid of his coffin, he spoke to Pellucid.

"I still got one thousand years to wait until the armada from the Hyades cluster arrives, and over sixty thousand years to wait until Rania arrives, if she ever makes it back. First it was Ghosts, then Whales, then Witches, and then I had to wake up again when the Chimerae turned bad, and when the Nymphs turned good, and so on. And now, instead of a plague, or an ecological disaster, or an apocalypse, now it is the silence that wakes me."

"Menelaus, we do not have proof that machine intelligences have wiped out the biosphere. Our instruments reached as far as Annapolis to Memphis, and were very spotty in between. There are heat sources in the sea—"

"I am not giving up hope, Pellucid. I am walking a long, long road, and each move and countermove is like another bump. And Blackie keeps jarring me awake. Six months here, a year there. Bumps on the road, but it adds up." He uttered a bitter laugh. "Now it is an ice age. Just a little patch of ice on the road . . .

"So I am going back to sleep. Disconnect my coffin mind from your systems, and fake up the records like we agreed. It is going to take you a while to gather all the coffins I need from the sites I gave you, and they have to be placed in the way I said. I gave my word to my sleepers, and I don't want innocent people in my care to be hurt. And don't wake me up for anything else until I get robbed again. I miss my wife, dammit!"

His last thought after the medical fluid closed over his face and numbness seized his body was of how, ever since he was a child, he had always hated the snow.

PART FOUR

The Long Wait

1

The Tomb-Robbers

A.D. 10515

1. Half-Awake and Buried Alive

Nothing went as expected.

His next awareness was a foggy, gray sensation as the coffin he was in was being moved, and none too gently. Neither awake nor asleep, he could neither move nor see.

He could feel the sensation when the coffin was dropped and could hear the explosions of small arms fire. One of the slugs must have ricocheted from his coffin armor, because the interior rang like a bell.

Then there was a swaying sensation as someone or something grabbed the coffin again and moved it. It was an irregular motion, as if a gang of men were hauling it.

When his numb fingers were alive enough to be able to clench and unclench, he pawed against the inside of the lid, feeling for triggers and controls. Each of the knobs was differently shaped and textured to allow the slumberer to recognize them by touch. He pulled the switch to electrify the outer shell of the coffin, hoping to electrocute whoever was manhandling it, but there was no answering hum of power being discharged. He pulled the knob to open the outside pinpoint cameras, but again, there was no response. The inside of the coffin remained dark. This meant both the primary and secondary power cells had been cut, which implied someone who knew exactly how the coffins were built.

Fortunately, there were chemical-powered failover backup cells and, because he was careful to the point of paranoia, backups for the backups. He found a humidor of cells, each in its roughly-textured tube to one side of the coffin controls, drew one out, shook it, and was rewarded with a dull greenish light filling his cramped interior.

He had to act quickly. The physical sensation of weakness, the fatigue and nausea, told him he had not been properly thawed. Most likely the cables between the coffin and the cryonic plumbing had simply been severed, leaving him with a body full of microscopic machines that broke down under normal body heat: but not all at the same time. As each regime of cellular functions stirred back to life in bloodstream, muscles, bones, and nerves, the breakdowns must have happened in something close enough to the right order that the coffin's internal emergency equipment (which also must have been operating) somehow was able to restart his heart and lungs before the internal power was cut. He was lucky he was not in a coma, or dead.

Or if it was not luck, the Tomb-robbers outside stealing him must have entered some sort of probe or mechanism in through the hinges, or through the conduit locks, to get at the mechanisms and dismantle just enough, and just in the right time, to ensure he would wake up sick, but not dead.

That was not good. The dim greenish light, and fog of his nausea, defeated his eyesight. If there was something snaking into the coffin, he did not see the hole. Of course, with nanotechnology, the machinery could be invisibly small, the hole smaller than the point of a needle.

The motion of the coffin became more violent, and then upended, so he was yanked against the straps and medical appliances that held him down. He was not quite standing on his head, with knees and feet trying to slide down into the corner where his head was lodged, and the swaying motion became more violent. His coffin was being dragged or hauled up a steep slope, perhaps with the aid of ropes.

Only then did he become aware that there was a breathing tube down his throat and another tube clutching his manhood. Fortunately, it was a condom catheter, also called a "Texas" catheter. He felt a moment of pride in the name of his homeland, grateful he did not have to decatheter himself with numb and unresponsive fingers.

He was willing to yank the intravenous needles out of his elbows and gastronomic tube from abdomen without further ado. Little droplets of blood floated through the interior of the coffin. He stared at them in wonder, unable to force his brain to realize what he was seeing. How were the blood droplets drifting in midair, if he was not in zero gee?

The rectal tube he tugged on, winced, and left in place.

Other parts of his body were more numb, which gladdened him, because he was able to jam the hypodermic of stimulant into the large muscles of his leg without feeling any pain.

He pulled a medical pad made of antiseptic wool out of the red emergency box and pressed it against his chest. He could feel the tiny tugs on his numb skin, but no pain, when many tiny threadlike lances from the pad shoved through his skin seeking his heart and major organs. However, the action of some of the chemicals involved must have included a suppressant, because he blacked out.

2. The Oblong Box

His head was clearer when he woke again, and this time the coffin was swaying in what was clearly a floating motion. He was being carried on a small river, perhaps a stream. The water motion was not choppy enough to indicate a large river, and the motion was that of small boat, not a ship. The clock was dead, but the fading of the greenish light from his chemical cell showed less than five minutes had passed.

There was also no sound of gunfire outside. That was a bad sign. Maybe very bad. He realized those noises had been the automatic Tomb defenses opening fire with smaller weapons meant to hurt Tomb-robbers without penetrating the coffins.

He squirmed onto his side, and his legs and arms felt like tubes of dead meat stitched to his body. It was not until he attempted this movement that he realized he was submerged in medical fluid. It should have drained long ago.

The mystery of the floating blood drops was solved. He was not breathing air: his lungs were full of hyperoxygenated fluid. He pulled the tab to open the port peephole. It floated like a firefly in his blurry vision. He saw a brown pattern of striations. It was a wooden plank, perhaps a support to help the Tomb-robbers move the coffin.

He hit the DRAIN switch. There was a gargling sound, but the medical fluid sloshing around inside the coffin did not remove itself. That was also bad, since his body could not transition from a hyperoxygenated fluid to airbreathing regime without paroxysms.

He pulled out another chemical cell, shook it to life, and examined the machinery and chemicals forming the cocoon around him. He fumed to himself, *Damnation and pestilence! In the old comics, whenever someone had superintelligence, they also always had weird brain wave powers or something. Okay! Think! What is in here I can use? Facing unknown enemies of an unknown race, unknown numbers, unknown capabilities, unknown year. They have a boat. And wood. That tells me the ice caps are no longer meeting at the equator.*

He had to bend double to hook the cell to the radio, and he was able to broadcast on the emergency band, but there was no response from the Tomb central. He switched to the old biotechnological Nymph frequencies and sent out a squawk.

It took all the remaining power cells, three of them, to turn on the internal molecular assembler for five seconds, but that was enough for him, with numb and awkward fingers, to tap out an override and a set of commands on the flickering screen.

He was reaching his hand toward the assembler release valve, when a jolt threw him against the inner lid of the coffin. The screen flickered and went dim. The coffin tilted; then he felt a smooth sensation of motion, feeling more than hearing a harmonic note of mechanical vibration in the background. He envisioned some form of crane or mechanical arm lifting the coffin from the boat to the dock.

He pounded the emergency energy cell, and a last dull green flicker floated momentarily through it; and the screen lit back up, with the information fortunately still there. He tugged on the internal release valve, and it did not budge. The screen flickered like a fading ember. He used both hands and his teeth, and the valve opened. Nanotechnological material swarmed into the interior of the coffin, mingling with the medical fluids, and beginning to turn the substance translucent. He thrashed his limbs, and swirls of material followed his movement like little galaxies, oddly reminding him of stirring cream into his last cup of coffee.

There was no time to remove the catheter or the breathing tube down his throat. The flesh-colored tape coating his thigh hid his night-knife, which he drew and slashed through the various lines and drips and wires connecting him to the inside of the coffin.

He tightened his grip on his white glass caterpillar-drive Browning pistols.

At that moment came the screaming whine of an energy saw, and he saw sparks cutting through the first of the massive clasps sealing the coffin lid.

Good-bye, Rania. I'm sorry; I tried to stay alive. I tried.

He blew the explosive quick-release bolts and kicked with both legs. The lid flew open. The sunlight blinded him.

3. Open Lid, Open Fire

He clenched his teeth, biting shut the rubbery tube still in his throat, held his breath, keeping the oxygenated fluid inside his lungs; and he shut his burning eyes.

Inside his stinging eyelids were afterimages of silhouettes bent over the coffin. He twitched his pistol barrels toward the nearest two and thumbed the triggers. There were two blurred hisses of noise, two whip-cracks as ejected material surpassed the speed of sound. The iron dowel running down the core of each weapon had a thin wafer sliced off by magnetic fields, and the wafer was heated white-hot by the conduction, pulled into a conical shape by the shape of the caterpillar fields, and violently expelled. These were short-range pistols only, grossly inaccurate, and the shells were certain to tumble irregularly and messily when they entered flesh.

The new material he had introduced into the coffin interior had not been completely mixed with the medical fluid, so only about half the volume had formed the unstable mixture he wanted. So it was that half, rather than all, of the coffin fluid, upon exposure to oxygen, that erupted into a froth of bubble and a wash of vapor. Montrose, at the bottom of the coffin, was still in the layer below the mix, and the cold fluid protected him from the heat released.

The figures hunched over the lid were not so lucky, and screamed and barked and yowled when the lid blew open. Through the cacophony, Montrose was able to hear which figures had been struck by the coffin lid, which were merely confused and howling, blinded by the vast wash of expanding vapor, and which were burnt. The guards must have had a pack of guard dogs with them, because there was a confusion of barking, yipping, growling, and whining.

He came up out of the fluid more slowly than he would have liked, because his body was still reacting sluggishly to his commands. Still holding his breath, Montrose sat up, sloshing fluid each direction and trying not to scream as some of the cloud burned him. With his eyes still shut, he thumbed the pistols to continuous fire and sent bursts of slugs into the sources of screams. At the same time he kicked his legs awkwardly and slumped and lumbered and fell over the edge of the coffin to the surface, still firing as he fell. Underfoot seemed to be a platform of wood, perhaps a dock.

As he rolled, his body collided with one person, a man wearing a shaggy fur coat, and he lashed out with a kick, hoping to break the other man's knee. But the other man must have been facing away rather than toward him, because he did not strike a kneecap, but the hollow of the joint, so that instead of breaking, the leg folded and the other man fell toward him.

Another motion of the thumb flicked the magnetics inside his gun to another configuration, so that the projectile mass was grated into shotgun pellets. Guessing based on the motions he had felt inside the coffin, he swung both barrels toward the crane or mechanical limb that had picked up the coffin and fired. He evidently guessed correctly, because he was rewarded by the sound of screaming metallic ricochets. Then the falling man in the fur coat landed on him.

Montrose opened his eyes, but he saw nothing but the dense fog pouring from the coffin lid, and every droplet of the fog was dazzling with sunlight. With regret, he realized that he should have mixed a nerve gas or at least a puking agent among the fumes. Well, he had been pressed for time. He brought his pistol down sharply on where he thought the back of the skull of the man falling on him would be, but Montrose must have miscalculated, because the skull was pointed toward him, not away, and his gun arm was seized in the man's teeth.

They were too sharp and too many to be the teeth in a man's mouth. This must be one of the guard dogs he heard barking. He heaved with his arm, thankful of the lingering numbness, and still struggling to keep his mouth shut and his breath held. He twisted his trapped hand, firing at another source of nearby noise (he saw a silhouette in the mist stumble and fall) and brought his free hand up to shoot through the skull of the dog trapping his arm and toward a second looming figure in the smoky brightness. The skull must have been both large and oddly shaped for a dog, because the skull fragments exploded in blast pattern other than what he calculated, and pain lodged in Montrose's face. His flesh was torn, and his nose felt like it was broken.

The pistols in his hands whined suddenly. Montrose used a mental trick to speed up his nerve actions, so that the scene seemed to slow down. He went through a number of theories in his mind as to what could be causing that whining noise. It was an induction field, he decided. Some onlooker had deduced that his pistols used magnetic caterpillar fields for acceleration, and set up a counterfield to interfere. The metal dowels were being heated by the resulting conflict. The pistols were not designed for this: the metal was expanding and about to crack the barrels open.

He pondered. In combat, if the troops are not well trained, nine to fifteen seconds will pass before the troopers will react to incoming fire and return fire. Trained troops will drop or seek cover and return fire immediately, if and only if they are armed with automatic weapons. Automatic weapons allow the troops to spray toward unseen targets, hoping to hit, or at least to suppress the enemy. But troops armed with single-shot weapons were more hesitant, rarely willing to fire without a clear shot, lest the return fire kill them. So far, the combat had lasted perhaps five seconds, maybe half, maybe less, of normal human reaction time. From the position of the barks and howls, it seemed the guards near the coffin were reacting with normal human-reaction confusion. Which meant the field was being sent by someone occupying a higher intellectual topography than the guards.

There was no time for more than a guess. He looked toward where the crane that had picked up the coffin was supposed to be. Sure enough, looming up through the fog, he could dimly make out what looked like the exoskeleton of a ten-foot-high praying mantis made of steel. But why had there been no outcry from the operator when he'd shot there earlier? Either the machine was an automaton, or remotely controlled, or the operator had some means of deflecting the shot.

There was no time for more guesswork. Montrose returned to normal neural timeflow in order to operate his muscles without tearing or cramping them. He held down the thumb trigger so that both pistols ejected the entire mass of their ammo at once. Two dowels like little red-hot javelins flew into the fog toward the spider-legged machine.

Suddenly the operator was visible. He was no bigger than a child, was bald of head, and he wore a long coat studded with glittering gems. The gems lit up as if with fire, and rainbows and halos of energy surrounded the figure. In the confused light, Montrose could see the little bald man had skin as blue as a peacock's neck.

The dowels never struck their target. Whether they were deflected magnetically, or disintegrated by some unimaginable energy, Montrose could not tell. But the dazzle shining from the many-colored coat of the strange little man was bright enough that the silhouettes of the guards stood out clearly.

Even through the fog, he now could see that they were not men, but Moreaus, modified dog things walking on hind legs, and with swords or firearms in their paws. The dog things were grouped in a semicircle and lunging toward him, ears perked up, noses high, and not confused by the blinding vapor cloud.

In that momentary, eerie flash of radiation from the gems on the coat of the little blue man, Montrose saw a rippling glitter to one side. Water! Perhaps he could reach it. The dog thing bodies were not designed for swimming, and if he somehow escaped them downstream, the water might kill his scent. If he were lucky, the river would be deep enough and the current strong enough to carry him out of range before anyone could react.

With a powerful leap he flung himself through the fog toward the gleam of water.

He was not so lucky as he might have hoped. The blind leap brought the edge of the dock sharply against his shins, so that he tumbled, both legs numb in a shock of pain.

That tumble saved him from landing headfirst, which might have killed him. As it was, the shallow, icy stream struck him in the belly, and so when he struck the streambed, no bones broke. So that was a modicum of luck.

But the current was not strong, and the water was not deep.

4. *First Impressions*

Striking the shallow bottom dazed him, and so the hyperoxygenated fluid gushed from the tube in his throat. His lungs then rebelled and tried to draw in the icy, freezing waters of the stream. He flung himself to his knees, puking pale hyperoxygenated fluid down across his naked, bruised, and torn chest and belly.

The bank of the stream was coated with snow. In the bewilderment, Montrose had not noticed how cold it was.

On the bank, the fog was still billowing and spreading from the open coffin. The coffin alarms were ringing—another fact his dazed mind had not been able to take in—and the disabled coffin guns were clicking pathetically.

The stream tumbled down a hillside covered with snow and (Montrose saw to his immense satisfaction) pine trees. The crest of the hill was bare of trees, but angular walking machines and scaffolding surrounded a deep cleft from which the thunder of gunfire and the snap of laser fire echoed. The Tombs were violated, ripped open.

He was in a yard enclosed by wire inside a camp enclosed by wire. The streambed neatly bisected the yard. There were seventy coffins in the yard in various states of damage and disrepair. Those with working alarms were ringing; those whose alarms were mute were raging weakly, flickering the stubs of their disconnected legs and or spinning the useless wheels of their missing treads, flicking their aiming lasers at potential targets, clicking to one another with sound-transmitted ranging information. All the coffins were trying to come to his aid. None could move or fire.

Montrose absorbed this in one split-second flicker of his eyes. Still puking up fluid from his lungs, he rose to his feet. The stream was not even knee deep. All he had done was to wet himself in the winter wind and bruise and cut himself badly enough on the streambed rocks that he could barely force his tortured body into motion.

A sudden gush of wind stirred and parted the fog like a curtain. There was the semicircle of sixty dog things. Most were unclothed, except for weapon belts, but some wore scarlet pantaloons or braided vests or half capes. They carried muskets, cutlasses, and long knives. Montrose was gratified to see that he had killed seven and wounded ten more, who were writhing on the ground yowling, as pairs of comrades, two to each wounded hound, pulled them back out of combat or applied pressure to wounds. Of these sixty, only twenty-three were standing with weapons at the shoulder. The muskets had been pointing at Montrose even before the wind parted the vapor, since the fog had not deceived their sense of smell.

They were waiting for the order to fire.

Their masters were three blue men, or, rather, two azure men and a ruddier-hued man who was almost purple. All were bald and had very small and delicate ears. All wore knee-length coats studded with emeralds, sapphires, blue diamonds, topazes yellow as honey, agates, amethysts, and stones of beryl and glinting jasper red as blood and polished onyx gleaming black as drops of ink.

The purple-shaded Blue Man was the operator of the grasshopper-shaped automaton, and his coat still flickered and flamed with whatever energy he had used to disable Montrose's pistols and deflect their final burst. He pushed the goggles hiding his eyes back over his wide and bald brow, revealing an expression of utter boredom.

The older of the two lighter-shaded Blue Men regarded Montrose with a heavily lidded and reptilian stare from eyes underlined with bags of weariness and expressionless as stones. His prune mouth was wrinkled as if it had been folded far too often into bitterness and contempt. He too wore a knee-length coat patterned with gems.

The younger Blue Man observed Montrose with a cool and almost amused detachment. In his outstretched hand was an instrument so studded with gems and ornate scrollwork that Montrose did not recognize it at first as a energy weapon, probably a solid-state laser carrying a galvanic charge.

Montrose was bent double with puking into the stream, but he still held his knife up high in defiance. If his hand would stop shaking, he might manage a throw into the older-looking one. His coat had fewer gems, so perhaps he was lower rank or lower status than the other two, but he had a look of arrogance that bespoke command.

Menelaus did not throw the knife. Instead, baffled, he induced in his middle-level brain sections one of those pattern-recognition gestalts normally called intuition. The answer surfaced immediately: *The Hermetic Order has an agent (or agents) observing this scene: but he (or they) fails to recognize you due to subverbal-conceptual interference across more than one mental system.*

At some point, if he lived, and if he had the time to go back through his thought process, he could try to put into words the wordless intuition. As it was, he decided merely to accept it as a given.

Coronimas, Sarmento, and Father Reyes, as far as he knew, were still alive, not to mention Ximen del Azarchel. Why were they absent when the Tombs were being looted?

Their absence bespoke stealth, indirection, secrecy, and therefore fear. Del Azarchel was hiding from someone. From whom? If Montrose's Cliometrically calculated predictive model of history was right, no civilization on the Earth's surface powerful enough to threaten Exarchel could have arisen from the barren ice floes that ruled the surface when last he woke. So something was wrong with his model of history, something very basic. That was something imperative to look into, later.

If there was a later.

The Blue Men were the starting point of the thread leading back to Del Azarchel, who must be ultimately behind the attack and the looting. Montrose tried to imagine the magnitude of damage needed to have so thoroughly crippled the defensive systems of the Tombs that they could not stop a squad of musketmen. Or musketdogs. Some part of Pellucid must still be operating, if only a local node, but the main brain must already be compromised, perhaps dead. And where were the Knights Hospitalier?

The time for grief was later, as was the time to sort this out. For the moment, he was captured, but his captors missed the fact that they had found whom they sought.

Of course, it helped that the coffin had been marked with the wrong name and interment date. There were not many periods of history after the era in which Montrose was born, where large numbers of great-boned redheads walked abroad: the one such period, the time of the Chimerae, circa A.D. 5000, had an unusually broad genetic base.

So Menelaus hesitated, armed with nothing but one dinky knife, stood shivering, eyeing the dozens of musket muzzles covering him and the dozens of dog muzzles snarling.

The younger Blue Man tilted his head to one side as if in thought, and a made a polite fluting sound in some unknown language of singing notes to the older one, who grunted and nodded. Menelaus was gratified that, despite the passage of thousands of years, the meaning of that particular head motion had not changed.

The younger Blue Man, lowering his pistol, opened his coat with both hands, exposing the inner lining, which was a pearly gray. The coat lining shimmered. It was library cloth.

An image of the Monument appeared on the inside of the coat to the left and right of the young Blue Man's body, and then the image expanded to zoom in on the opening statement. First one group of glyphs lit up, and then a second, and then a third. A bisected circle filled the view, constructed of a sequence of dashes that flickered quickly: large-three-small-one-four-one-five-nine—

"You little plague-sucking rot-brained buggers broke into my coffin and abducted me to ask me the value of *pi*?" Montrose roared in anger, or tried to. The severed breathing tube was still dangling and flapping from his mouth like an absurd proboscis, and now he gagged, drew in a deep breath, and, when the air struck his fluid-adapted lungs, they seized up.

Terrible hacking coughs started to yank themselves out of his body like scarves from the mouth of a sideshow magician, and his muscles tightened in the first seizure of the transition paroxysm, first in his chest, then in his limbs.

He wobbled, knelt, and then fell face-first into the freezing water. A roaring darkness filled his brain, and little black metallic flashes swirled to and fro in his eyes. He thought he could detect a mathematical pattern in the swirls he saw as his vision faded in and out, something he could analyze with the Navier–Stokes vortex equations.

He was dimly aware of doglike paws pulling him from the water. Two dog things held his either arm, and his naked legs were being dragged across the frost-coated pebbles and through the burrs and prickles of the gray dead winter weeds of the stream bank.

He was inordinately proud of the fact that they had to bend his thumb so far back that it broke with a dull snap like a twig before they could pry the knife from his hand.

They dragged him roughly before the younger Blue Man, who knelt and wrote a set of Monument glyphs in the snow. It was the glyph for self-identity, and a symbolic logic expression also used to refer to set representation. In other words, it was the glyph that meant "name."

Montrose also saw a red dot appear in the glyph, and then another, and he realized blood from his face wounds was dripping onto the snow.

The younger man pointed at his nose and said solemnly, *"Ss's Illiance-pra-e syn-suan va, hna-t."* He pointed at the older Blue Man with the back of his hand. *"Ss's Ull-mnempra-e syn-suan hthna, hno-t."* He pointed the back of his hand at the Purple Man. *"Ss's Naar-ma-e syn-suan hthna, hno-t."* Then he made as if to touch Montrose with the back of his hand, but did not actually brush his skin. *"Ss's nii, hni? T?"*

Menelaus knew his previous, nonaugmented brain would not have been quick enough on the uptake to deduce some of the grammatical rules of a semi-declined language based on so small a sample. *Ss's* either indicated the beginning of a sentence, or the younger Blue Man Illiance had a lisp. *Va, hthna, nii* were "me, he, you." *Hna, hno, hni* were verbs in the passive voice, the act of naming: "I am called, he is called, you are called." The *t* sound indicated the end of a sentence, which meant this was an old and corrupted form of computer-derived language, since no human listener needs to hear punctuation marks in spoken speech.

Illiance, Ull, and Naar were names or honorifics.

Damn me, but I am smart.

"Me, Tarzan," replied Montrose. "You, Jerkdong? I can't talk with this damned buggery tube yerked up my eating-hole, you smurf." But since his mouth was blocked, it came out more like: *A cawh'n taw wif dif bwah-erwee doob eerd ut mwa eewen-oal, oo fnurf.* Which, upon reflection, actually did not make much less sense than what he'd tried to say.

The tone must have been clear even if the words were not, because one of the dog things drew what looked like a single-shot wheel lock pistol from his sash and clouted Montrose sharply across the cheek with it. More than ever, Montrose wished for the mind powers the old comics always awarded to creatures with superior intelligence. As it was, he was able to deduce the exact vector magnitude of the incoming iron pistol barrel and make an accurate mental model of which parts of his cheek and face and nose cartilage would be torn and broken before the blow actually fell. He was not able to anticipate how much it would hurt, however. Pain is always a surprise.

When the blow landed, Menelaus had sufficient control of his nervous system to induce a fainting cycle without anything more than a silent act of will. He slid down into the roaring darkness with a sense of relief, hoping the breathing tube still lodged in his face would hide any smile of victory.

If all went as planned, they would place him back in a working coffin for the internal systems to heal his damage. And turn on the communication implants wired into his nervous system.

The chance that they would kill him while he was unconscious was small; or, at least, small enough that it was worth the risk. And if they did kill him? He had already said his good-byes to Rania, and there was no one else he cared about, nor any group of people, nor any civilization, for thousands of years.

That was his last conscious thought for a while.

2

The Pit of Revenants

1. Three Locusts

His next conscious thought was how cold it was, and he wished his brother Leonidas, whose bunk was near the window, would stand up and lever the darn thing shut. Still, it was nice to know he was home, with his brothers around him. By why were they all in his bunk with him? Why did Agamemnon have his elbow sticking in his eye?

Menelaus pried an eyelid open. He was in a steep-sloped pit, in the mud, in the freezing rain, with other bodies cold as corpses huddled up to either side of him, groaning, and Leonidas had been dead for eight thousand years.

All was not going as planned. They had not placed him back inside a working coffin.

When he tried to stand, a naked, bald-headed, and big-headed boy put a hand, and then a shoulder, under his arm. He leaned, but the boy could not lift Montrose.

Montrose focused his eyes, wishing the light were better. He did a mental trick to repeat the visual images in overlapping layers in his cortex, pick out details, and deduce a brighter and clearer picture.

The one trying to help him up was not a boy: his frame and facial characteristics were the same as those of the Blue Men who had captured him and, like them, stood four feet tall—except that he was not blue. Instead the man was black as onyx. The fellow was an adult, for he had pubic hair and armpit hair, but no trace of beard stubble nor scalp hair.

A more obvious distinction was that this man had two yellow tendrils coming from the crown of his skull just above his eyes. These eyes were large and lustrous, and his mouth a tiny rosebud. From what he could see, Montrose guessed the eyes had been modified to pick up ultraviolet. High on the skull, near the base of the two antennae, were two pit organs like those of snakes, able to pick up infrared rays. The Blue Men had displayed no such modifications.

At that same moment, two other little onyx men, as alike to the first as twin brothers, came to the other side of Montrose and with soft hands helped him to his feet, and steadied him.

Montrose, for a moment, was delighted to see people who looked so exactly like what his childhood cartoons imaged far future men should look like. "Take me to your leader!" he said in English. Then he scowled. "Or if I am any judge of genetic handiwork, your leader was Coronimas, that idiot. But why this design? Maybe he watched the same toons I did as a kid. That's a creepy thought."

2. The Trench

He used the same visual layering trick to look around him. It was not pretty. Men and women, both naked, were standing or sitting or lying in the mud. The captors had neither provided clothing nor separated the sexes. There were forty individuals here from a wide variety of millennia, some on the ground; some by themselves, weeping; and the rest huddled into five groups.

The first group were the bald, onyx-skinned, antennae-wearing dwarfs helping Montrose. Second group were furry or scaly figures of monstrous aspect, animal-headed or headless, and with them, men of less obvious biomodifications. Third were brunette women whose overvoluptuous beauty no mud nor misery could mar, clinging to each other's wet and nubile bodies and blinking at the rain with darkly exotic and overlarge eyes. With them were sloe-eyed yellow-skinned men whose faces were soft with boyish good looks. Fourth were stern-featured warrior-aristocrats with unblinking eyes, their long hair dank with rain and clinging to their shoulders, and a lady and two girls of their race standing stoically behind them at parade rest, none uttering any complaint, while their servants huddled and rolled in the mud, moaning and whining. Fifth were thin crones and unlovely hags, gross in their nakedness with dangling breast-sacs and wrinkled skins, but seven feet tall, or eight, gnashing their teeth and uttering curses, with their menfolk in a circle around them, in stature seeming like children beneath their grandmothers, shuffling their feet in a slow, mud-sloshing dance. With the hags was a man black as atrament, fat and round and sagging as a dumpling, who gave Montrose a nod of recognition and a small smile.

The pit was about nine feet deep with sloping walls reinforced by wooden planks. From the resin smell, the planks had been cut within the last day or so. The planks had been stapled in place with thorns, not nails or spikes, which implied a higher level of biotechnology than ironworking present. The pit was about ten paces across, roughly oval. To one side was an wooden doorframe leading up three wooden steps into a trench. The trench ran directly away from his point of view like a roofless corridor in a house, and met another wall of muddy earth, where it forked left and right. There were steps cut in the side of the trenches for musketmen to stand and fire. Montrose did not hear any noise of gunnery at the moment: but it was clear from the slope of the ground that this earthwork was meant to approach the Tombs without exposing the Tomb-robbers to the largest guns by the main door.

There were more figures in the trench, huddling to get out of the rain. He saw at least one giant, an elephantine silhouette twelve or thirteen feet tall, whose shoulders and head were above the level of the ground; and he saw an albino pale as paper. In the gloom and confusion, no details were clear.

Dog things armed with pike, cutlass, or musket stood or crouched at the brink. They looked down with dull, disinterested eyes. The dog things were slightly protected from the rain by a tarp. A keg or tank of some sort stood beside them, with hoses and nozzles. Montrose stooped and ran his fingers through the mud, lifted it to his nose, sniffed. Almost lost amid the rain was a faint smell of antiseptic. He put his hand to his armpit and found some white foam, still moist, clinging to him where the rain had not reached. The shock of being hosed down with this disinfectant foam must have been what woke him.

The antennae of the three small men at his side flicked in unison.

The implants in Montrose's chest, neck, and skull were made of organic material, not metal, similar to organs in birds, sharks, and eels that manipulated electromagnetic waves. The artificial nerve fiber leading from the medulla oblongata controlled their activity level, and the auditory centers in his cortex in his brain controlled their sending and receiving of radio data.

The broadcast from the short, dark dwarf was in the code elements based on a simplified version of the Monument math, which Montrose had no trouble decoding.

We are of the Noösphere, isolated elements. There is no signal on the airwaves, neither any carrier waves, no navigation beacons, anywhere within range. The world outside is dead and shows no radio traffic.

This artificial race had been designed somewhere in the seventy-fifth century by the science of the Iatrocracy, were hunted almost to extermination, but eventually prevailed, rising to world dominion in the eightieth century.

As the other helped him to his feet, the two were close enough that Montrose could detect the unique double pulse pattern of the two-hearted Locusts. The grace and control of a finely responsive nervous system were evident in the little man's posture and poise.

Montrose tried to send back a simple set of signals. "There may be some—" He did not know how to form the word for *mainframe* in this code. "—big-sized thinking machines in cities far from here. When the clouds clear up, seek signals on the shortwave band. You are not to commit suicide. Resources are scarce!"

We are isolated and unable to assist the Noösphere. If biosuspension is not available, self-demotion is indicated to preserve scarce resources. The Noösphere is offline. Our mind-fragments are very alone.

"I have resources to sustain you, and I will, as soon as circumstances permit. Listen! The Noösphere requires your continued functioning for now, attached to my entourage, economic unit, and military unit. See? I'm adopting you. I will help you. Self-demotion is strictly forbidden."

We must form unity with all. Unity to assist least-self-capable elements.

Montrose sent, "Yes. We are all supposed to help the weak and wounded. Come on. Let's start getting some of these people on their feet."

Montrose cupped his hands to his mouth and shouted left and right, "Ahoy! Any man jack of y'all savvy English? Do you know what these little men are saying? *Se habla español?*" He tried several other languages from different historical periods, as "Correct thought! Good speak! Silence ungood!" or "Whoso of ye knowst the Wise Tongue?" or "Attention! Do you read me? Report!" or "Who can ease the ache of my ear-loneliness with delight of the mouth?" or "Comprehend your ear-organ these words, here-now?"

3. Prissy Pskov

A woman, who had been squatting on the ground, arms wrapped about her knees, head bowed, rocking slowly back and forth, now uncurled and stood and stepped near.

She was big-nosed and high-cheeked with stern, striking features, and lips so thick and full that they gave her otherwise harsh face a crude sensuality. Her hair had been biomodified so that quills like the spines of a porcupine cascaded from her scalp. Seeing his gaze, she raised a hand to cover her face and lowered another to cover her crotch, leaving her breasts free. Evidently her face was taboo but not her bosom.

She spoke in a harsh, glottal, clicking tongue. It was a version of Iatric, the language of the Therapeutae used in Central Asia and Siberia, which he had learned during his short thaw in A.D. 7234.

She said, "I will aid you if you will protect me. The danger is much."

Montrose said, "It's a deal. I'll do what I can."

"Then be still!" she said.

"Eh?"

"Silent! You know too many speech forms. You do not want to be taken off by the *culls*."

The word was a curse in her language, meaning a person so worthless that not even his organs could serve as transplants—someone whose only contribution to life was castration, and the infanticide of his children.

Without moving his head, Montrose moved his eyes left and right. He saw no Blue Men in evidence, and the dog things were paying no attention.

But it made sense that the Blue Men, wherever they were, would be watching to see, first, if any of the prisoners showed initiative or courage—it was important to remove troublemakers from the outset—and, second, to see if any scholars mingled among the thaws knew any of the dead languages from still earlier periods, otherwise forgotten.

The stern-faced woman gestured with her thumb. Her thumb had been biomodified, so that something like the stinger of a wasp slid out from beneath her thumbnail when she pointed.

"These three are Locusts, enemies of all law. These three urge you to health, and wish your aid in helping others, wounded or dazed, to the showers. It is *altruism*." This last was spoken with a word-ending that indicated disgust.

She crooked her thumb, and the stinger retracted.

Montrose said, "Who is in charge of the world in this era? I don't see how a place like this could exist. I would have thought it would be more advanced, with no room for large-scale crimes like this. Can satellites see us?" He interrupted himself. "Showers? I'm not sure I like the sound of that."

Only now did he consciously notice that people in the trench were moving, if slowly. The giant and the albino he had glimpsed, for example, were out of sight around the turn, and others from the pit slowly filed in behind. The only reason why it was not obvious that everyone in the rain-chilled pit was inching toward the entrance was that various groups from various periods were trying to keep as far from one another as possible. He could see two Hormagaunts, for example, lumpish or dark-furred figures of monstrous form only remotely human, at opposite sides of the pit, as far from each other as they could get. One had his claws unsheathed; the other had deployed his elbow spikes.

"Come on. Let's start getting some of these people on their feet. You too, uh, lady, what's your name?"

"I am of Pskov, specific name Prissy. I am of three-layer defense, and cannot approach or be approached. You, after-lingerer, register neutral on the biotic scale. You I can approach."

"Pleased to meetcha. Wished it'd been under better circumstances. Come on. Help me get this lug to his feet. Get him out of the rain."

This was the closest stricken man. He was a gangling figure with coal black skin and a pattern of delicate white scars on his face and forearms and inner thighs. The man's eyes were rolled up in his head, so only dull slits of white showed between his unclosed eyelids. The fellow looked human, and if the scars were from luminous implants, he might even have been from as far back as the Cryonarchy. Too bad he was stunned: if he were from that era, he might have been the only one in the whole pit who did not mind being nude.

Prissy Pskov stepped back distastefully. "It is violation of quarantine."

4. Other Mankinds from Other Ages

Montrose grunted and heaved the man over his shoulder, and took a step or two toward the opening into the trenches. Prissy Pskov followed. She looked left and right at the nude crowd. With a rustle, the black quills stood up like the feathers of a Sioux war-bonnet. It was an alarming sight.

People stepped back, making room for her.

Montrose stepped past two effete and sad-eyed and slant-eyed yellow-skinned men from the seventieth century, each as handsome as Adonis. He pointed at them with his free hand, and barked in a language called Natural, "You, there! And you! It is your pleasure to help with the carrying of the dazed and weakened. Stoop! These here on the ground are closer to your heart than incestuous-homosexual-love-partner." This last was a one syllable word in their speech, which did not have a separate term for "brothers."

One of the two blinked at him in confusion, "But there is no wine of ecstasy. We must have the wine before we work, and enter the pleasure-trance, or else the delight is less. Why did we come awake in a day when there is no wine?"

Montrose shouted, "Stoop and haul and help, or I will beat you bloody, and *that* delight will be even less! We are captives of a band of Tomb-robbers, and they will kill us each separately unless we couple together!"

Neither of the beautiful men moved, but in the rain, Montrose saw first one, and then another, of the long-haired Chimera soldiers from the fifth millennium stoop and help people from other eras and centuries to their feet. One of the Chimera girls snapped out an order, and the slaves, muttering and cursing, began also to help the woozy and pick up the unconscious. One of the scarecrow-thin crones from the fourth millennium, seeing this, scowled and shrieked, and slapped the hugely fat black man next to her, until he, with a moue of resignation and the shrug of a philosopher, picked up two unconscious people and slung them under his meaty arms like packages, and lumbered forward with their four feet dragging in the mud behind him. Then other men from the same era did likewise. Soon all the prisoners of the pit, conscious or not, were moving or being moved toward the trench entrance.

5. Dampened Spirits

Stepping into the shower out of the rain was no real transition. Montrose was under the liquid before he paid it any attention. Something crackled in his implants as the stuff sluiced over him. He wondered what molecular mechanisms or microbe-sized machines were hidden in each water drop, and what frequencies they were using to coordinate. On the other hand, it was possible that the crackling noise came from the tent cloth, if it was smarted up and seeking system connections. Or the smartcloth—if that is what it was—could have been just probing the prisoners for tools or communication gear. Such as, come to think of it, the implants in his body.

Again, his thinking speed, crystal clear memory, various cognition tricks, and his ability to juggle vast realms of data: none of that could stop this. Without instruments, without tools, he could not even detect, much less counteract, any microscopic machines or weapons that might be even now worming through his outer skin layers seeking his bloodstream and nerve clusters. For all his gifts, he was as helpless as a goldfish in a toilet bowl.

He muttered in English. "Damn, but I hate nanotech!"

One of the Locusts shyly reached up and curled his thin, clammy fingers around Montrose's elbow. *"We sense information-bearing lasers focused on all our throats, picking up throat vibrations."*

Montrose was aware of the danger, but he had been given only a few minutes. In that time he had gathered two allies, or, counting the Locust unit as three separate people, four. It was not enough. This was out of the seventy or so coffins he had seen stacked in the looting yard. They would need all to ally, all to act as a group, if there was to be any hope of escape or defense.

And Montrose was responsible for all of them.

6. Surrender

He said to Prissy in Iatric: "If the Blues are looking for historians and translators among the Thaws, maybe we can get something from them in return. Have you noticed anyone aside of you and me that knows dead languages? You must have seen at least one translator hauled away. Who was it?"

"A muscular man covered with markings. He fought them until a dog-man bit his crotch."

"Ouch. Did he have a marking like a two-headed eagle on his face?"

There was no time to answer, because just this moment, the crowd of naked bodies ahead of them parted, and the crowd behind, shoving, pushing them forward. There were shouts and commotion, cries of joy and cries of woe. The prisoners were being moved from the showers into a wider area, lit with many lanterns, where dog things with pikes and truncheons were struggling with the crowd. Little Blue Men, six of them, were standing on little disks or platforms held in midair by long metal serpentine arms.

The walls were still mud and lumber. This was an area where several trenches intersected. To one side were angular machines, evidently digging automata, whose shovel blades showed many dints and scars of work. The area was covered over with a tarp or circus tent, and the rain was drumming on the metallic fabric, but at last there was no water falling on him.

Some of the dog things were passing out one-piece overalls made of soft, dull fabric. This was the source of the joyful noise, as cold or shamefaced prisoners were pulling on garments. Other of the dog things were yanking prisoners to the left or right, and beating those who resisted with their pikestaffs. And this was the source of the noise of woe.

Dogs came, brandishing their pikes, growling and coughing, gestured for Montrose to part from his companions, each to go to a different part of the floor.

Montrose struggled to stay near the three dwarfs and the Iatrocrat. With his implants silently to the Locusts, and aloud to Prissy Pskov, he said, "Do not to resist. The Blues don't mean to hurt us yet."

"They will torment us to discover where we have buried our treasures," she said. Prissy cowered behind him, her hair spines flexing and standing erect on her scalp like the comb of a cock in battle.

"I think they are looking for something else."

Prissy was touching him gingerly on the shoulder, and she shivered because her people made to touch a taboo. Her hand was warm, almost hot, compared to the shower water still drenching him, and his shoulder immediately began to itch with allergic reaction, so he did not think their taboo was all that unreasonable.

"I will do as you say," she murmured. "For the lore of my people says there is a figure buried beneath the Earth, who guards tombs such as this, and to despoil them is to wake a great cry. 'My time, is it yet? My bride, is she nigh?' And if the answer is wrong, he destroys all."

"I think that only happens on his good days," muttered Montrose.

But there was no more talk, for the dogs had shoved her to one side and him to another. He saw the woebegone faces of the three Locusts, small as the faces of children, from an era where no person ever laid violent hands on another, bewildered and lost as they were dragged away.

3

The Warrior-Aristocrats

1. Two Chimerae

It was twilight, and the dusk was cold. A hooded figure stood in a high place at the brink of a deep pit, staring downward.

He was not dressed in the overalls the Blue Men had passed out. Instead, he wore an impromptu robe of metallic cloth. Despite the fineness of the cloth, the garb was crude. He wore two long sheets, flung over either shoulder, crossed and tied at the waist by a line of cord. Flaps of material hung fore and aft, leaving his sides free. His arms were hidden in overlapping tiers of the cloth. The cloth was metallic, bronze hued, and shot through with silver strands in a regular pattern of hexagons; the reverse was shiny black. This originally had been a tent and a groundcloth; the belt was tent line.

It was Menelaus Montrose. He had drawn the hood flap of his garment up, hiding his features: albeit it was not clear from whom or from what he hid.

Behind him, out of the trees, came two upright shapes that moved as gracefully and silently as hunting cats. The pair were darker shadows against the rattling shadow-mass of twigs and leafless branches of the wood, and the red and distant brightness of the air did not illume them until they stepped across the snow. Then, by the unearthly poise of their motions, Menelaus saw that they were Chimerae, warrior-aristocrats who ruled the Earth between A.D. 4500 and A.D. 5900.

The older Chimera had iron gray hair, which was tight to his skull, hanging down in a queue behind, and he looked as grim as an arctic wolf. Menelaus had seen his name, or, at least, a name on his coffin: it was Daae.

The younger Chimera had a queue even longer, a tail of darkness hanging past his shoulder blades. He was like silken panther, lazy and graceful and deadly. His name was Yuen. Yuen had a strip of cloth, a bandage, around his head, hiding one eye. It gave him an incongruous and rakish look, like that of a storybook pirate.

Both were dressed in baggy overalls of drab fabric. Both had wrapped their hands and wrists in medical tape, leaving fingers free, like bare-knuckle boxers. Similar tape wrapped their ankles and feet, but left toes free. The Blue Men had not provided any prisoner with shoes.

In the gloom of the coming night, with nothing behind him but the dim reflections of red glints from the pit behind him, his hooded silhouette formed a tall and ominous figure. Slowly he raised his hand, beckoning. "Come and get it, boys," he whispered in English.

No word of parley or defiance was spoken. One moment, the pair of Chimerae stood at the edge of the snowy wood in the gathering gloom; in the next, they were moving with the speed of the shadow of an eagle as it stoops across the white and black ground.

Their blurred feet made almost no noise as they rushed in, perhaps a hiss of snow, perhaps the slap of moccasin on rock. They used an odd posture to run: their bodies leaning too far forward, their arms held straight back behind them.

Menelaus stood motionless as a statue, awaiting their attack. The faintest gleam beneath the triangular shadow of the hood was visible as he drew back his lips from his teeth in what was either a snarl or a smile.

At the moment of collision, Yuen, the younger of the two attackers whipped his hand from behind his back and bludgeoned the tall hooded figure with what looked like a pale truncheon or baton. At the same moment, the older of the two attackers, Daae, lashed out with superhuman speed with his walking stick, which cracked like a whip when the tip surpassed the speed of sound. The forward stroke of the cane came in at kneecap-breaking height, and the backstroke was lower, to hook Menelaus at the ankle and yank him off his feet.

Yuen's truncheon swept through an empty hood left in place when Menelaus ducked, but somehow his metallic garment mysteriously did not duck. The walking stick likewise swept through eaves of heavy fabric, hitting nothing.

Neither attacker was unskilled enough to actually be thrown off balance by the impossible and unexpected lack of resistance, but they both were a half second slow to recover from their lunges. During that half second, the cloak fabric like a live thing jumped into the faces of the attackers, swirled about them, catching their heads, tugging them into a stumble.

Daae pulled his cold and burning-eyed face from the cloak fabric, with one hand flung a tent spike sharpened like a knife toward Menelaus. With an almost casual motion, Menelaus lifted his hand from the folds swirling about him, and as if by happenstance, the spike with a chime of pure sound struck a fist-sized rock he held, was deflected, and spun away into the darkness. With the same casual motion, the rock hammered the one-eyed younger attacker from his blind side, drawing a trail of blood from his skull just above the temple, a parabola of rubies.

Menelaus was falling—no, he had flung himself backwards in a powerful and agile motion, but not to safety. He plunged in a clattering swirl of metallic fabric in the one direction the attackers had no way and no expectation of hindering: directly off the cliffside. It was like a backward swan dive into a nothingness of air. He pulled both attackers with him.

Daae writhed, regained his footing, and jerked back, arms windmilling. The heavy rock continued its arc of motion, flew from the hand of Menelaus (an unlikely shot, since Menelaus was upside-down and backwards to Daae at this moment, in midair), and struck Daae where ear met jaw. Dizzying abyss was at his feet. Choking, Daae lost his footing and clutched frantically the snowy ground beneath him.

Yuen and Montrose went over the side of the precipice.

There was a slither of motion and a singing jar of sound, like the string of an instrument plucked taut. The hawk-faced older man stared in puzzlement at a tent stake driven deeply into the cold and rocky ground. For a dazed moment, he wondered how the tent spike he had thrown had fallen here. But no. There was a second spike here, and a third, and all were pounded securely into the ground. This was the spot where Menelaus had been standing. A length of tent rope securely lashed to all three spikes was pulled taut, vibrating. It ran over the brink.

The gray-haired Daae belly-crawled to the edge of the precipice and cautiously peered over.

The line of tent rope extended only seven or eight feet. It was done in a bowline around the bare left foot of Menelaus, who hung with his pale buttocks and loincloth exposed, his head downward, with his bulky garments fluttering beyond his ears like the petals of some baroque flower.

The pantherish Yuen was also still alive, also head downward, and a lariat running from somewhere in the bulky garments flapping around Menelaus ran to the younger attacker's feet. It was a slipknot, not a bowline, and so Yuen's feet and thighs were cut and bleeding from the bite of the rope, but the rope held him.

The two were swaying very slowly, a human pendulum.

2. The Tombs

The cleft beyond the heads of the upside-down men was as sharp and clean as if the mountainside had been split in two, in times now long past, by some titanic force. Slightly jarred parallel lines of the first and second level of a cryogenic Tomb facility could be seen descending into darkness, looking oddly like bookshelves of a titan's library. Broken cells and empty corridors opened out into midair, separated by strata of severed wires and tubes, rock and insulation. Dripping from every level, like icicles, were streaks of twisted girders.

The coffins near the surface, far below them, were blank lozenges, dull and inert. Their coolant had long ago leaked out, their seals compromised, their cargo dead beyond recovery.

After a long moment, the knife-sharpened spike that had flown over the edge struck bottom, and there was a clatter and an echo of clatter that rose from the dark. At that sound, there flickered winks of energy, as the defensive mechanisms of some coffin from yet a lower stratum, still active, stirred to life. A faintly audible murmur and echo of chiming, hissing, and buzzing, like atonal music, suddenly rose from the deep, accompanied by the insectlike rustle of many metallic feet, moving.

The noise spooked Daae; his face was frozen in a look of supernatural fear.

From somewhere in the mass of the fabric, Menelaus spoke quietly, but carried over the rustling from below, "Loyal, respected, and Proven Alphas, how can this Beta line be of service to the Command this day?"

He spoke in grammatically flawless Virginian, a language called Old Dominion, in the accent of a Patrician, and he used the correct declensions and form of address.

Menelaus added, "And if this Beta may speak freely, loyal Alphas, perhaps the service could be one carried out either beyond the range of whatever power we have disturbed in the Tombs, or a task simple enough to be accomplished before any buried weapons are brought to bear."

Daae called down softly, "Then you are truly Chimera?"

He spoke in a stilted and formalized version of the same tongue, as formulated by Chimerical grammarians long after Virginian was a dead language.

Menelaus brought his hand slowly into view. He held a scalpel stolen from the medical supply tent. He put it against the line of the lariat holding Yuen headfirst above the abyss. Menelaus said, "Must we revert to the older custom, and prove our worth by delivering up a dead foe? This involves considerable inconvenience!"

Daae's eyes narrowed. "What inconvenience?"

"Sir! No foe is ready to hand, and if I commit an act of insubordination against the Loyal and Proven Alpha youth helplessly dangling below me, surely you, sir, would be duty-bound to reciprocate by chastising me, perhaps by unearthing the stake on which I currently depend. This would rob the Emergency Eugenic Command of two of her surviving veterans in this strange and cold far-future era."

Silence. Daae said nothing.

Menelaus offered: "I await with pleasure the orders of my superior officer, sir."

Daae called down, "Loyal and Proven wielder of Grislac, is your weapon still in your hand?"

The white truncheon had a thong looped around the dark-haired man's wrist. The youth flourished it lightly in the air.

Daae said, "Then what say you?"

But the younger warrior was laughing softly. He spoke in Chimerical, in the dialect used in the western hemisphere during the forty-ninth century. "Loyal sir, if this man is not a Chimera, then sever the line and let me drop with him! If a baseline stock or Kine or underling can defeat me so handily, I am no further use to the Command, and will go without complaint into the promised oblivion we all seek."

Daae said, "Our race is extinct, and the Command consists of we two, and the Alpha Lady Ivinia. Therefore the Command—such as it is—cannot afford the loss of one-third its number, one half its Alpha line fighting strength."

Menelaus called up, "Sir, if I may, there is a block and tackle hidden under a gray tarp next to you, bolted to a plate. It might be wiser to have us up and out of sight before the commotion among the coffins summons the dogs, the Blue Men, or their automata."

3. The Plaque

After more effort than might be expected, the two men were hauled safely back up the cliffside. The tackle gear was made fast to a plate bolted to a stone set to the ground. Yuen, the one-eyed, dark-haired Chimera stared curiously at the ancient letters on the stone as Daae bound the cuts on his legs with medical tape.

Yuen looked at the plaque. "You smile at the writing. What does it say?"

Menelaus read it aloud:

> Devil's Den Long-term biosuspension Facility, Hibernation Syndicate of Fancy Gap, Virginia—M. I. Montrose, Proprietor—This Site Declared a Sanctuary by Order of the Marchioness of Carroll County—These lands under the Protection of the Sovereign Military Order of Knights Hospitalier of Saint John of Jerusalem: Trespassers Killed On Sight. No Soliciting.

"And those?" Below it, in the stone, was a series of linear scratches, a simple code of strokes and angles.

Menelaus said, "Slumber marks. I cannot read them, Proven Alpha."

Their voices attracted attention. Echoes of metallic noise and reflections of distant and buried light haunted the edge of the pit. The Chimerae wore faces as calm and stoical as if carven from stone, but they moved quickly away from the brink on their silent, catlike feet, alarmed, perhaps terrified. Menelaus knew the era from which they came was famed for its rejection of supernaturalism; therefore, the unknown unnerved them, because they had no category in which to place the uncanny.

Menelaus and the two Chimerae moved into the wood and squatted behind a thicket, keeping a wary eye on the cleft.

Menelaus said, "The dog patrols may come back."

Yuen said, "Something in the trees interferes with the instruments of the Blue Men. We are safe from eavesdropping here. Do you know what drew the dog things away?"

Menelaus said, "Magic."

Yuen sighed, and said to the white-haired Daae, "The Beta cannot lawfully answer to us until we establish our chain of command."

Daae was bent over Yuen's leg wounds and spoke without looking up. "We should establish how we were betrayed. We were meant to come by surprise. I thought none of these before-men nor after-men speak our tongue. Is there spy in the mess tent?"

"Many spies, I am sure, but none of them speak to me," answered Menelaus.

"Then how were you forewarned?" asked the older.

"Deduction. I knew I would not look like a proper Chimera to you. The Eugenics Board in my centuries was experimenting with different bloodline factors. Redheadedness is an atavism from Neanderthal genes, a melanin deficiency reintroduced in my forbearers from archive reconstruction. . . . You did not have this technology? You are from the earlier days, are you not, young sir?"

Yuen's voice held a shrug. "Oho? Early compared to what? Until I was thawed here, I thought my days were the last days. The wars against the Witches were going badly. You gentlemen are a surprise and joy to me, the fulfillment of many dreams of breeding."

Daae spoke out of the darkness, "None from before the time of the Chimerae could know it is our custom to slay imposters and wrongbloods, and no kine from our time would dare play the imposter."

Yuen said doubtfully, "He could be a historian from after."

"Perhaps," Daae said, "but we were superceded by creatures I have heard called the Naturalists, also called the Nymphs. You have seen them in the medical tent: a race of gold-skinned and slant-eyed fructivores of superlative and delicate loveliness. And after them come the monster-things called Hormagaunts. After that I know not what."

"Locusts," said Montrose. "Then, sea-things called Melusine. Then history stops."

Daae said, "Each race of man is more artificial, more highly engineered than the ones before. Does this phenotype look deliberate?"

Yuen peered thoughtfully at Menelaus. "Ah, you speak truth! Who would deliberately affix a great hooked claw of flesh to the front a man's face?"

Menelaus said, "My nurse always told me the Eugenics Board was breeding me in case the lighthouses on the coast failed, with a nose I could blow when the seas were fogbound."

Yuen chuckled softly in the dark. "Oo? You dare mock the Command?"

Menelaus said, "Before I answer, let me ask this: Did the Eugenics Board breed themselves for intelligence, or did they breed their women to ripe-melons front-up in full kit?"

Yuen gave a louder, shorter laugh. "He's Chimera, sure enough. No underling would know what ink-stained butterbars and groin-thunks our high brass are."

Daae said to Menelaus, "Which of this menagerie are the Locusts?"

Menelaus said, "Black dwarfish men with big heads and gold tendrils growing from their brow. Those tendrils are radiotelepathic, some sort of remote nerve-link technology from future time now long past. It allowed them to detect that the world outside is empty of all electronic and mechanical activity." Montrose waved his hand in a broad sweep, as if to indicate everything in the world. "There is no civilization out there. In any case, these Locusts looked to me to protect them, and now they are gone. The Blue Men killed them. I saw the dogs dig their graves."

Daae said, "I am out of my reckoning. Which race comes after them? Who inherited the earth?"

Montrose said, "That is a mystery I am burning to solve. I assume these Blue Men are the current landlords of Mother Earth. The asteroid impact that wiped out the surface life and kicked up the dust that brought this ice age was sometime in the seventy-eighth century AUCR."

AUCR stood for *Ab Urbe Condita Richmondus*. The Chimerical calendar reckoned from the founding of Richmond in 1737. The seventy-eighth century was equivalent to ninety-sixth century by the Gregorian calendar.

Yuen interrupted, "Wait. Asteroid impact? Sometime in *what* century? How long have we been in hibernation?"

Montrose said, "I estimate you were in slumber for five thousand years."

There was a rustle in the dark as the two stiffened slightly. "How firm is this intelligence?" said Daae.

"Perfectly firm," said Menelaus. "I have studied the stars. From the size of the circle Deneb makes around the north pole, I can calculate the procession of the equinoxes."

Yeun said, "But Iota Cephei is the polestar. . . ." His voice trailed off.

"Was," said Montrose. His voice was strangely soft in the triangle of his hood.

4. Named Weapons and Names

Yuen said, "You have not asked us of our weapons or names."

Menelaus said, "I cannot ask until my superiors speak first. Or are things more at ease in your time?"

Daae had finished taping Yuen's leg wounds. At these words, Daae chuckled, and he turned and handed his walking stick to Menelaus. It was surprisingly heavy.

The older man said, "I dislocated my hip to hinder my stride, so that the Blue Men, in their foolish pity, gave me this wand to lean on. On the second level of the coffins, where no coffins still walk, I found an ancient lathe and some leaden scraps. Cautiously I hollowed out the bore and filled it with lead that cooled and hardened."

"A shillelagh?" said Menelaus, handing it back.

"I don't know that word. This weapon has tasted no blood and accumulated no shades, and so yet has no name. I carry nothing of note. I am Alpha Captain Varuman Aemileus Daae of Uttarakhand, Osaka, Bombay, Yumbulangang, and other actions in the South China Theater. The Varuman blood derives from the Osterman, from the *Homo sapiens,* and *Canis lupus.*"

Menelaus said sharply, "The Blue Men let you back inside the Tombs? What day was this? How did you convince them?"

Daae frowned and raised his hand, and did not answer.

The one-eyed, dark-haired Chimera passed Menelaus his bone truncheon. It was a cubit long, heavy at one end, roughed at the other. It looked surprisingly like what cavemen might have used on the plains of Africa to brain their victims, human or animal.

Yuen said, "In your hand is the thighbone taken from my left leg, which I amputated by thrusting it between the gears of a digging automaton. In the same unlooted machine shop, I melted lead around the knob of the joint to give it some weight, and wrapped the other end in leather, which I had flayed, and cured, and cut from the skin of my own severed leg, to give the haft a grip. The Blue Men are afraid of spirits, and will not take once-living human matter from my hand. The truncheon is called Grislic, and I maimed a man in the mess tent, and laid him low, a Servant of the Machine from A.D. 2520 named Glorified Ctesibius, an Endorcist of the Three Donations. I hold the interference of the dog things to act as a concession! They hurried Ctesibius to the same restoration coffin that regrew my leg, but I hold he *would* have died of his wounds. Any contest?"

"I do not contest it," said Menelaus. "The weapon is named Grislic."

The younger man's eyes glittered. "As for me, I who carry Grislic, I am Alpha Steadholder Extet Minnethales Yuen of Richmond, Third and Second Manassas, Antietam, and various actions against pirates. The Extet are of the Original Experiment Set, from *Homo sapiens* and *Puma concolor.*"

"First Antietam?" asked Menelaus.

"There were two?" Yuen looked surprised.

"What year was your Battle of Antietam?" asked Menelaus.

"AUCR 3144." This was equivalent to A.D. 4881 in the Gregorian calendar.

Daae spoke up. "His is the Pre-Proscopalian period, the days of the Republic, back when the Command officers were elected from among the Proven rather than appointed by Breeding Tribunals. My squire hails from a time of poverty and golden virtue, when each Chimera in his freehold owned nothing but his weapon, his land, his name, and his harem. In those days, the Betas were loyal, and the Gammas were cowed and hardworking!"

Yuen said sardonically, "The era of virtue did not seem so at the time. We were dying."

Daae said to him, "You slumbered too soon, Alpha Yuen. The days after your hibernation were days of bloodred gold. In the North, the Final Sabbat surrendered at Buffington's Island, and submitted to sterilization. The Witches were crushed, their matriarchs enslaved, their menfolk gelded, their children sent to humiliation camps, and their totems and sacred trees chopped up for wood for our war-locomotives of the Long Iron Road. The survivors fled to their sisters in the Far East, and made Peking their final fortress. But they were not as they were.

"By the time of the Battle of Uttarakhand, where my regiment-family served, the Witches had lost their secret Fountain of Youth; they were aged, and the Amazon warriors, once so fierce and strong, rode their white mules into battle with hair as white." To Montrose, he said, "I am from an era foeless and cheated of glory, and it is no shame that his weapon be the first to drink."

"But the Battle of Uttarakhand was in A.D. 5402," said Menelaus. "Alpha Daae, does not that make you the younger? How is Alpha Yuen your squire? Shouldn't you be his?"

"The Judge of Ages decreed that those who rise from the coffins keep their rank, despite the passage of years," answered Daae.

Menelaus pulled the hood a little closer around his face, perhaps to hide his expression. "Hm. Strange that I never heard of that. . . ."

"All the mandates concerning those who slumber and thaw derive from his word. But now tell us of yourself."

Menelaus nodded his hooded head and passed to Daae an oblong stone the size of a fist. "This weapon is named Rock. I haven't killed anyone with it yet, but I am plenty tough enough to, if pressed. Knocked out some teeth. You've seen me in action with the dogs. Any contest?"

"I do not contest it," said Yuen. "It is a true weapon and valiant."

"Nor I," said Daae with a sober expression. "The weapon is called Rock."

"Fine. I am High-Beta Sterling Xenius Anubis of Mount Erebus."

"Mount Erebus in Antarctica?" Yuen asked. "We are a warlike race indeed. What were we fighting over? Snow? Penguin eggs?"

"There was a radar station in Antarctica in my day. It is a method of using invisible waves called radio to detect and range a target—"

Yuen said impatiently, "Come, now! I know what radar is. And horseless carriages, and talking animals, and evil voices that speak out of the graveyards of dead machines, and flying carpets of silver gossamer that soar to the Moon, where the Master of the World left his handprint. My tutors beat the old legends of the Space Ages into me."

"The Social Wars were fought on every continent," said Menelaus, "including when a submarine manned by Sino-Chimerae was blown off course and came aground on the Ross Ice Shelf, in McMurdo Sound. The station crew went out with our seal-hunting rifles and spear guns at low tide and besieged and shot 'em, and the Command considered that a real battle, and issued a medallion and everything. So it counts."

Yuen said, "We—were we fighting *each other*? What year was this?"

Daae answered him, and gave the dates in Chimera reckoning that corresponded to A.D. 5260 through 5270. "Beta Anubis is from the very onset of a great period of expansion. The whole earth was Chimerical by then, and no Witches left anywhere. But the eastern and western hemispheres, which had been allies for centuries against the Witches and Kine-states, did not agree on genetic policy, and came to blows. The Judge of Ages was angry at Tombrobbers, and released from his tombs a pair of slumbering scientists so that rocketry and atomic energy were rediscovered. Little is known of the Social Wars, since paper documents burned, and calculation machines were erased by magnetic-pulse side effects of atomic weapons."

Menelaus turned to Yuen and said, "All matter is made of fine bits called atoms, which consist of positive and negative energies bound together in a balance. When the atom is split, the energy is released—"

Yuen said, "I know what atomic energy is! Magic fire from the sun that burns whole cities at one stroke. The fire leaves behind a specter that dwells in old craters, invisible and silent: mild effects include chromosome damage, hair loss; medium effects include vomiting, diarrhea, fatigue; great effects include marrow and intestine destruction, and death. What sort of opinion do you aftercomers have of the people of my days? We were not savages! We could not remake the machines and weapons of the Space Ages, but we remembered them."

Daae said, "Forgive us. By my time, the days of the Republic were legend. The same fires that blotted out the world's memory of the Social Wars erased records of previous eras as well. Only the Judge of Ages, who dwells in the underworld, knows and remembers the truth."

Menelaus nodded. "For just that reason, I don't know my derivation, gentlemen, since my lineage records were wiped out. And the atomics made it so the

Social Wars weren't none too sociable. I am sure I have at least some rattlesnake in my cocktail."

With no word, the three men each saluted the weapons of the other two by a gesture of raising the hand, palm out, before the eyes, as if to shield them from an invisible glory. Then they gravely passed their weapons each back to the proper owner, shillelagh, thighbone, and rock.

5. Aeonicide

"Now that the formalities are over, gentlemen," Menelaus said, "what do you want? You did not just come all this way to kill an imposter, and you could have done that in plain sight, back at the camp. You didn't hit as hard or as nasty as you could have done, which means you were trying to guess my mettle. I assume I passed, and that you want to recruit me. What's the mission?"

"Escape first, and then revenge," said Daae. "The Blues have woken men of other times: men you must gather to us. The rods can be broken each separately, but not when bundled together."

Yuen said, "Even the lesser races from earlier periods, and the degenerate freaks of our future, can redeem, in part, their inferiority, by service to a superior cause."

Menelaus cleared his throat. "Excellent plan. Do let me do the talking, right, Proven Alpha? The lesser races, uh, have brains not excellent enough to stand the shock of being told how pathetic they are. I'll have to kind of cajole them into helping us. We are clearly low on manpower: how feasible would it be to break into the Tombs and wake others of our kind?"

Yuen said, "To thaw the sick and the weak? Unless the Blue Men restore them, they will have no weapons and hence no names worth speaking."

Daae said, "More than this: we dare not provoke the Judge of Ages. How shall it fare with us, if we disturb the Tombs for our purposes, if he comes in wrath to avenge himself on the Blue Men?"

Menelaus turned his hooded head toward him. "You have faith in this Judge of Ages?"

Daae said softly, "Erudite sir, you have studied history, have you not?"

The hood nodded. "More than I'd like."

"You know that there is a recurrent pattern to history. The persistence of the Tombs over so many centuries, unmolested, despite the rumors of buried wealth, bespeaks some power that protects them from grave-robbers. A great power. I say he will arise to punish this trespass. Are not those who unearthed us defilers of his work, and defiers of his word?"

"Chimerae do not believe in spirits," said Menelaus.

"I say the Judge of Ages is a real man, a survivor from some earlier period of history, the Second Age of Space, and that he rises from his own Tombs to walk the earth when need calls."

The hood turned toward the younger. "And what do you say, Alpha Yuen?"

"I say nothing to contradict my Captain," said Yuen.

"Do you believe in the Judge of Ages?"

"Permission to speak freely?" The younger man looked at Daae, who flicked his eyes in a microscopic nod of assent.

Yuen said, "The Judges of Ages is a children's story, invented by the superstitious fools of the Final Sabbat. The Witches worshipped everything they did not understand, including the technology they destroyed. Of course, the great Tombs and how they worked were beyond their wits, undisciplined as they were, to conceive. No doubt some coffin contained a victim of a bioweapon. The Witches unsealed a Tomb and were struck down by a disease, something their undisciplined minds could not comprehend, and so they invented the figment of an avenger. They had gods and godlets for all things, houses and hearths and fields and trees. To add one more to their crowded *pantheon*"—he practically spat the word—"saved them from the expense of mounting a continual guard on known Tomb sites."

Menelaus said, "The Natural Order of Man, those fruit-eaters called the Nymphs, they believed the Judge of Ages was real. The Hormagaunts from the period of the Iatrocracy besieged his Tomb site to prevent entry or egress. They said they encountered his soldiers, armored men who balanced on the back of an extinct quadruped called a horse and were carried from place to place. These men were called *cniht,* which means 'vassal,' or *cavalier,* which means 'horse-rider of disdainful mien.' Are there vassals without a liege? I wondered why the Blue Men have not unearthed any of these knights, or why they have not risen from the earth, if they are real. Do either of you Loyal and Proven Alphas have any information on the subject?"

Daae shook his head. "Perhaps the soldiers of the Judge of Ages are buried too deeply. Or they fought and were slain before we thawed. But there is no sign of battle here."

Yuen's one eye narrowed. "It is noteworthy, Beta Anubis, that you speak several of the aftercomer languages. I take it your slumber was interrupted, that you rose from the buried Tombs and walked the Earth in later years, and learned their ways?" There was no mistaking the suspicion in Yuen's tone.

"I learned *of* their ways, Alpha Yuen," said Menelaus. The Chimerae were always careful to avoid contamination with foreign cultures and ideas. "Mine was a scholastic interment, not medical, and so I could thaw without undue harm."

Daae said, "Scholastic? You were ordered into the Tombs?"

"Yes, sir. I am a schoolteacher. A mathematician. My unit is the Hundred and Second Civic Control Division, attached to the Third Pennsylvania Legion, College for Dependents. Academic Joint Command told me to study the causes and results of civilizational decline."

The eyes of the two other men grew intent.

Daae asked, "What caused our glory to pass away?" His voice was hushed, the tone of voice one used over an open grave, at a funeral.

"Remember I come from a day when atomic world civil war burned everything that could burn. We were reduced to savagery," Menelaus said solemnly. "All Chimerae are genetically programmed with instincts designed to protect the race. It was the one thing that makes us better than the Witches. How could we have done this to ourselves? So I was ordered to reconstruct, if I could, the predictive mathematical analysis of history called Cliometry, which legend says the Giants knew. I thawed in A.D. 5884, I learned that Richmond, that great city, in a single hour was fallen, and no candle burned there, and there was no sound of engine, no noise of mill or drill. I thawed again in A.D. 5900 and A.D. 5950, and there was no sign anywhere of the Command, and no one to report to. I continued forward into the future, century upon century, because there was no officer, no Alpha, to rescind my orders, or tell me to stop. Therefore I will continue my assigned task until the End of Days, or the arrival of the Hyades, or until an Alpha properly dismisses or relieves me."

Yuen said, "Are we truly as far in the future as you say? Is it truly all gone? There is no trace of us? Did nothing we erect survive?"

Menelaus said, "I saw ten coffins from the Chimera period in the yard, broken open. So there are eleven of us, counting me."

Daae said solemnly, "All is lost. The Chimerical way of life passed away, and the black Oculus-pierced domes of our anti-chapels, where once our bravest men gathered to pour out curses into an empty and uncaring sky against an unreal God before our duels and battles, stood isolated and silent upon the hills of Appalachia, and along the shores of the poisonous, sterile waters of the Chesapeake. The woodlands grew and the cities crumbled, and the race that comes after us dances amid our ruins."

Menelaus said, "And you, Alpha Daae? Why did you inter yourself?"

Daae said uncomfortably, "I was of the party that opposed the dissolution of the Senate. Agathamemnon 'Fairlock' Raeus assumed certain emergency powers, combining the military leadership with the civilian government. I wished to preserve my bloodline to the day when Raeus would be forced out of office, and the Senatorial form of government restored. I suppose there was some error in my coffin brain, or—"

Menelaus said, "No error. The coffin never thawed you, because the conditions were never met. The World Empire lasted four hundred more years, and we never returned to our old form of government. Even by your day, the rot was too far advanced to halt."

Yuen spoke with explosive passion, "But how did it happen? How was it permitted to happen? Whose army is so great to encompass us? Who overthrew us?"

Menelaus shook his head. "No one. The Chimerae were invincible in battle."

Yuen said, "Then how?"

Menelaus said, "By slow and easy stages of corruption. The specific causes were many and complex. The foremost was a biotechnical improvement during a time of moral decline. Like the Babylonians, we were undone by simple drunkenness. It was called 'Greencloak' technology: Implanted artificial glands to intoxicate and alter states of consciousness spread by illegal medics first among the Kine, then among the lower ranks. And then it no longer was illegal, and then it was no longer stigmatized, and finally it was not permitted to be criticized."

Yuen said in a strangled voice, "I don't understand. Our greatness was unmatched. Whatever we faced, we conquered."

Menelaus said, "No Chimera understood it. For that reason I was sent back into the Tombs. The trends of our decline were too slow for one man to see in his lifetime, and I was the only one—the schools by that point no longer taught mathematics of the requisite level—to work out the Cliometric calculus. Academic Command believed that someone was deliberately manipulating history to obliterate our civilization. I was to discover who and how."

Both men stiffened.

Yuen said, "You mean someone obliterated the noble civilization for which all my ancestors slaved and served and suffered and fought and died . . . deliberately? A *man* did this? There is not even a word for the crime of killing an age of the world."

Menelaus said, "Aeonicide. And yes, it is a man. I was sent into the Tombs to wake in a future day when I might trace the source of his historical anomalies, find him and confront him and kill him."

Daae said in a voice of soft surprise, "But I know who this man is."

Menelaus said, “Who? Is he here?”

Daae said, “He must be, for he—”

As if pulled by one invisible thread, both Daae and Yuen snapped their heads in the same direction. Menelaus did not have senses as sharp as theirs, but his neuromuscular control allowed him to turn his head the same direction at the same moment, as if he had the eyes and nose of a Chimera.

Of course, he saw nothing, and, of course, he could not ask what they were eluding when Daae raised his hand and flicked his fingers in two quick motions. Menelaus was baffled to see that the trooper hand signals from his days in the Thirty-fifth Cavalry Division, in A.D. 2225 were alike enough to the hand signals of the Chimera Varuman linage from A.D. 5480, for him to read them. Daae's gesture ordered Alpha Yuen to take point; rear guard and trace hider was Beta Anubis (as he thought of him).

It was difficult to follow two men who made so little noise as they glided beneath the trees in pitch darkness.

As they came to the edge of the wood, Yuen raised his hand. The other two stopped, tense, wary. Through the pine trees, Menelaus saw a rise of ground silhouetted against the stars, and a group of figures was coming over the rise, in twos and fours. From the occultation of the stars, it seemed a search party. They carried no lanterns, but they were making no attempt at stealth: Menelaus heard howls and barks, as if the creatures were searching rather than hunting, seeking comrades who might answer, not prey who would flee in stealth.

Daae tapped Yuen on the shoulder, pointed at the enemy, shaded his eyes, wobbled his head, cupped his palm as if begging alms. He was asking what the dogs were looking for. Yuen's answer was a shrug: another gesture that had not changed despite the change of times and races.

Daae licked his finger and held it to the wind, and selected a path that would keep them downwind of the dogs.

6. Ivinia

At moonrise, they were far enough downslope to fear no patrols of dog things. The hand-stained moon was full, and illumed the scene with silver light.

The three men came to a treeless knoll and climbed the side. It was a mound as symmetrical as an upside-down bowl. When Menelaus stepped on the slope, he heard a strange whine from his implants, and then silence.

The other two men were more relaxed in their posture as they walked.

Menelaus wondered how the Chimerae had detected that the trees blocked the medium-range instruments of the Blues; second, he wondered how they knew this mound of grassy ground issued the same interference as the trees did; and third, he wondered how the Chimerae knew the Blue Men had such instrumentation. Who had told them?

The deduction was not hard to make. Daae spoke of the end of his world. The race that superceded the Chimerae called themselves the Natural Order of Man, or the Nymphs: it would be unusual, but not impossible, for a member of that race to be scholarly enough to retain an ancient language, and to have spoken with Daae. Looking at the trees around him, Montrose deduced several of the properties they must possess, including blocking some of the Blue Men instruments. He knew he would soon have an opportunity to speak with a Nymph: he gritted his teeth, wishing it could be immediate. He had set events in motion; now they moved without his control.

At the crest of the knoll stood a thin-faced woman of middle years and regal bearing. Her hair was so blond that by moonlight it seemed a metal helmet. She wore her hair in a tightly drawn bun, which meant she expected battle and death. Her eyes were vivid without being beautiful, deeply sunken in her skull and having a disturbing stare to them.

She was dressed in the same overalls as others in the camp, but she had fashioned a short stabbing spear out of a tentpole. From the tread marks in the spearhead, it looked as if she had forced the pole end flat merely by having one the digging automata of the Blue Men step on it for her. Then she had patiently sharpened it against a rock. Her gestures and expressions were stiff and queenly, but her eyes never ceased to gleam with a cold ferocity.

All three men went to one knee. A human eye would not have detected that Menelaus started the drop to the kneeling position after the other two, because his knee struck the frost white wintergrass of the knoll first.

The lady passed out combs of shell to Daae and Yuen. The two Alphas, still kneeling, unbraided and combed out their hair. Daae's hair shone like snow, and Yuen's shone like ink. Daae's fell past his shoulders, and Yuen's came almost to his waist, and it took them many slow and patient strokes of the comb to dress it.

Daae and Yuen crouched, fussing with their hair. Menelaus thought the sight mildly disquieting, but he understood the symbolism: The male Chimerae of their rank wore no ornaments nor finery, so their only idle vanities were the length and shine of their hair. It was bound up in combat, so the act of combing it out after was their way of rejoicing in peace and survival.

The lady cut the ribbon binding the tail of her braid with her spear tip, and shook the last two turns of the braid loose.

She looked oddly at Menelaus. He, not knowing what else to do, pushed back his hood and drove his fingers through his hair once or twice, using his fingernails to straighten up his part, and spitting on his palm to pat down his unruly cowlick with saliva.

She said, "My late lord bore the weapon Callixiroc the Dark, which his fathers in times past bore against the Witches and their Werewolves in the battle of Buffington's Island, where Arthuna Ire Extet of never-ending memory fell."

Menelaus had never heard of any Arthuna. Maybe the epithet *never-ending memory* merely meant the fellow didn't forget things, not that he was all that unforgettable.

She said, "This spear in my hand is yet virgin and nameless, and has done no service, and bears no name: yet she is a true weapon. Do you contest this?"

Menelaus said, "I would not dare, ma'am. Sometimes those virgins bite."

She nodded regally. "Grislac and the wand in the hand of Varuman Daae are pledged to my honor, for the good of the Eugenic Emergency Command. I am Dependant Alpha Lady Mother-of-Commandant Wife-of-Captain Ulec Nemosthene Ivinia née Echtal. My victory title is Septimilegens, for I have borne seven sons into distinguished service."

Menelaus pulled out the fist-sized stone from his robes and laid it at her feet. "This is my rock. I call him Rock. I gave one of the dog things a handsome clout across the jaw with it, and broke some teeth, and I might have killed another one. It's not a confirmed kill." Menelaus did not mention the dog things he had shot with his pistols, now lost. Losing a weapon to the enemy was grounds for ritual suicide among the Chimerae.

"Confirmed or not," she said, "I trust none loyal to the Command will contest the point. We are too few to spill our blood in contests." Lady Ivinia turned her eyes to where Yuen and Daae were kneeling and dressing their hair. "Behold the loyalty of his lowly one! I have not seen such great heart, no, not in all of Virginia. Heroes have lain down at the feet of my linage weapons worth ten thousand medallions and twenty thousand tourneys, and yet this one, I tell you, lays down more, for he gives all he has. If he can slay the foe with a stone, it were shame indeed should higher men and better armed do less."

She turned back to him. "State your grade, rank, line, clan, name, derivation, and action."

"High-Beta Lance-Corporal Sterling Xenius Anubis. *Homo sapiens* and *Crotalus horridus,* proven of Mount Erebus on Ross Island, ma'am."

With a motion of inhuman gracefulness, the lady knelt, one hand on her spear, and with the other picked up the stone, and straightened again. She offered it to Menelaus. "Take your weapon from my hand, soldier, and bear it loyally in the name of the cause of racial perfection. It is not my hand alone who gives it, but every mother who has ever buried a fallen son. Freely we offer our sons into the oblivion we all crave. When you face death, think of us, who have already given all we love into the maw of war."

Lady Ivinia pointed with her spear down the slope. "Stand, Alpha Gentleman, and Loyal. Look about you. Here is our killing ground. Look closely."

7. The Camp

From this prospect, they could see over the tops of the trees. The slope of the great hill was not regular, but rose and fell in mound and dell. The snowy knolls of the lower slopes looked as round and heavy as pregnant women with long white hair huddled against the winter in shaggy fur coats. The trees were merely masses of soft shadows in the moonlight.

The fence formed a triangle, and the glitter of it could be seen, sinister as the heaving side of a breathing snake, through the boughs. The apex of this triangle surrounded the peak of the hilltop. The cleft that parted the hilltop was entirely within the converging lines of fence. Within this cleft were the exposed first two levels of the Tomb system.

A second cleft, narrower and not so deep, was halfway down the slope, cutting at right angles, and from between the sheer cliffs of this narrower cleft arose a rushing white stream thundering or chuckling downhill. In this stream was the battle wreckage of several Blue Man automata, not visible at the moment. At the mouth of the stream was a lesser door, a back way into the Tomb system, opening into the Eighth Level.

This rushing stream bisected the triangle of the fence. On one side of the stream was a cleared field where the metallic tents of the thawed prisoners gleamed. Here was a large infirmary tent and a larger mess tent.

To the other side were the machine-pavilions and the exercise field for the insect-limbed automata: the snow had been trampled into frozen mud by metal feet.

At the foot of the hill, a large but windowless egg-shaped structure, apparently a powerhouse, squatted at one corner of the triangular fence. At the other corner was a guarded yard containing a pile of broken coffins.

Between these two points, the long line of fence forming the base of the triangle faced the landing field. This line of fence held three guard towers, one to either side of the gate, and one straddling the gap in the fence where the stream ran out. This third tower also acted as a control tower, with flags and lanterns dangling from a yardarm. These towers were little more than impromptu platforms atop narrow-based tripods which swayed alarmingly when the wind blew. The dog things would not climb them. The towers were manned by Blue Men.

The control tower had a large parabolic dish, made of what looked like mother of pearl, lashed and rigged to its lopsided structure. Cables lying across the snowy grass snaked from the control tower to the egg-shaped powerhouse. The gaze of Menelaus rested on that radio tower for a while.

Moonlight glinted ghostlike from the armored cylinders flanking the gate, and the slowly moving smartwire atop the fence, waving and swaying like thorny sea-grass.

Beyond the gate, where the thaws could not go, rose the brick piles of the doghouses, and the taller spiral seashell buildings of the Blue Men. The doghouses had many small windows, no bigger than a man's fist, for scenting rather than for sunlight.

The seashell-shaped coral structures of the Blue Men had no windows at all. The largest was shaped like a nautilus, the *Spira mirabilis* of the mathematicians, and it rose up fifty feet. By day, it was sky blue dappled with silver spots. By night it was a looming round shadow, moaning softly when the wind walked past its mouth. It was flanked by spiral minarets like narwhale horns. Nearby four squat sheds like prone conch shells hunkered, crusted with barnacles and spires. To one side was a large pink structure shaped like a snail shell that served as a field hospital.

Not far from these structures, the landing field contained a dozen cloth-winged flying machines: triplanes, biplanes, and motorized kites. By day, the brightly colored heraldic designs and totems painted on the wings were visible. These planes had rear screws rather than propellers.

In their midst, a dun whale looming above a school of colorful fish, was an air-ironclad with a score of helicopter blades above and propellers fore and aft. Like Viking shields, the sides of this large craft were shadowed with many overlapping plates of solar energy material. The plates were ancient, yellowed with age and spiderwebbed with cracks, as if each shield had been meticulously pieced together, shard by shard, from fragments. And yet the smell of gasoline and oil could be smelled over the machine when the wind was right. The cracked solar plates were purely ceremonial, something left from other days.

Beyond, the land was wraithlike, white and empty: a land of boulders and tufts of colorless grass. Where the sky met the ground in the dark distance, the rising moon glittered against a range of cliffs of ice, eerie silver blue in the moonlight. This was a spur the northern glacier had sent down along the crests of western hills. The land to the east, now merely shadow, held no ice outcropping, but neither did it hold any forest or tilled fields, no sign of croft or barn or road. The valleys of Virginia looked almost like tundra, acres of shrub and scrub and wiry grass, with boulders peeping from the soil like the helmets of buried trolls.

The only trees in sight were pine and spruce, and they grew thickly only on this split hill, as if some heat or seeping chemical from the buried coffins had kept the greenery alive, or as if the memories of elder days, when this land was green, had somehow been preserved across the ages, and lingered here.

8. Character

Lady Ivinia said, "Alpha Daae, what is the character of this camp? Report."

Daae stood to speak. "Sloppy. Ma'am, the camp is a jury-rig. Someone tossed it together from makeshift materials. The discipline of the Witch-dogs is poor. If we move cautiously, and if the Blue Men find and wake more of our race, there is a possibility of victory, albeit slender. A cautious approach is best. We must dissemble our purpose."

Ivinia said, "Alpha Extet Yuen. Same question. Report."

Yuen also stood up, turned and pointed with his truncheon. "Behold yonder: an airfield. Here is a rotary-wing craft of unknown design, but known purpose. She is armored for war. The pattern of portholes and vents indicates a hold used for transporting live cargo. She is a slave ship, able and therefore meant to take us away to bondage. To display such a ship to us is to hiss in our faces. Before that, we see a fence. No one raises a fence and does not expect it broken. To erect a fence is to flourish a whip. And beyond the haughty slaver craft, we see waste. A wasteland is a confrontation to a man of stature: an empty place, a gauntlet thrown down in challenge and defiance. A place that cries out to be conquered and civilized.

"My word is the opposite of Proven Daae: Let us *not* dissemble." Yuen continued, his eyes hard and bright. "To look upon us is to know how we must respond to a flung gauntlet, flourished serpentine, a hiss. We will break those who offend and trammel us. We will conquer yonder snowy waste and make it into a garden land. Any man of pure Alpha blood would know that was our destined path; how could we hide it, even were there need? Whom would we deceive? Are the deeds and nature of the Chimerae so soon forgotten?"

Menelaus heaved a sigh, "Actually, Alpha Yuen, considering the gap of time . . ."

Lady Ivinia turned her eyes to him. "You may speak, Beta Sterling Anubis. Report. What is the character of the camp?"

Menelaus said, "This is a criminal operation. No warlord hunting for undefended men to loot and enslave, no bureaucracy trying to exact a tax from the Slumberers, and no university wanting to examine or interview the past would have sent out an expedition so ill equipped."

But Daae said, "Beta Anubis hails from an era of wealth, when there were roads and electrification. He is perhaps unaware of how often warlords with empty coffers make due."

Lady Ivinia said, "We are not Witches. Among the Chimerae, the men have absolute sway and command over the women. Such is our ancient law. As a respectful and obedient wife and mother of heroes, my task is only to be silent and obey. Therefore, in the name of the yet unborn generations entrusted to the motherhood, I can only tell you that you men must overcome this foe. If you do not, you will be found unworthy, and will commit ritual suicide. I would much regret that eventuality, O thou loyal sons of the loyal mothers of the Chimerae. The strategy and tactics I leave to you men, in whose hands the tasks of war are entrusted. Am I understood?"

Menelaus dropped to his knees and bowed when he saw the other two kneel. Lady Ivinia raised her spear as if debating whether to plunge it into the back of one of the men kneeling and bowing before her.

Instead she said, "As a meek and gentle woman, I have no place in your counsel settling war matters. But these undercreatures have raised up Chimerae from our graves, and if our name is not to be shamed forever, you must punish the vermin for their trespass, and must obtain victory or embrace death. The lineage I represent commands it. Do not speak! I know you understand. Do not disappoint the motherhood of the race."

Lady Ivinia lowered her spear, turned, and marched away down the slope in the moonlight.

Daae rose to his feet and wiped his brow, and put out a hand to Yuen, who seemed to be a little weak in the knees, to help him erect.

"Were the women that way in your time?" asked Daae.

Menelaus said, "In my day they were worse. You should meet my mother."

Yuen answered, "Good thing our girls are meek. The heart quails to imagine what they'd be like if they were bold. May the nonexistent God of Nothing we never worship protect us!"

Daae said, "Victory or suicide. There are only four of us, two Alphas, a

Beta, and a Gamma named Joet. We face an armed camp of two hundred dog things armed with muskets, thirty-three Blue Men armed with advanced energy pistols, and fifteen of the automata are mounted with steam rifles. What is our plan, gentlemen?"

Yuen said, "We rush the machine guns at the gate. The survivors cut down the guards, and we either commandeer or burn the aircraft. We follow the stream to the sea, living off the land as we go. We relax the eugenic protocols for a few generations, and allow both interbreeding and inbreeding, so that we can repopulate the Earth with the ten of us."

Menelaus said, "Rocks and sticks against steam-powered machine guns?"

Yuen sneered, "Rocks and sticks in the hands of Chimerae. Steam-powered machine guns manned by Moreaus, who are merely walking artifacts."

Menelaus said, "Yeah, but there are two hundred of them. Also, I have not seen what the muskets shoot yet, but I think it is an incendiary, not a musket ball."

Yuen said, "We may have finer weapons anon. I was buried with Arroglint, named of the Extet and prized at a thousand medallions. The weapon is haunted. I have put forth my will; whatever unclean hands now clutch it, or whatever walls or wills oppose, Arroglint the Fortunate will seek me out and return to my hand; then let the foeman quail and scatter before my scourge."

Menelaus was puzzled, wondering what type of weapon this was. The Chimerical word for "whip," *culwerin,* with the accent of classical Virginian, *colubrine,* which literally meant "snake-shaped." But *coluber* was an Anglatino word taken from a Meriken word for "most superlative" *cool-über*—a slang term referring to a plateau technology. But which technology?

Menelaus gasped, and raised his hand to his mouth, pretending it was a cough.

Thunderstruck, only now did he realize that the "named weapons" of the Chimera, the ornamental whips they were so proud of, were none other than the defining plateau technology of the Sylphs: self-aware smartmetal serpentines. The Chimerical practice of dubbing their thighbones or truncheons or rocks was nothing more than a sad echo of a tradition started when weapons created by a higher plateau of ratiotechnology had been smart enough to answer when called by name.

Menelaus had been thawed briefly in A.D. 5250, during the Chimera period, and had seen a civilization that, despite its flaws, was on the verge of rediscovering space travel. He had released from their Tombs two scientists from the Order of the Knights Hospitalier, Manwell Magri and Themistocles Zammit, to go out into the world and teach the Chimerae the theory and practice of atomics.

During the few months when he was awake, Menelaus had come across countless references to the ritualized Chimerical reverence for the named weapons of their ancient and aristocratic bloodlines, but he had not *seen* one. Menelaus in his buried stronghold beneath Cheyenne Mountain had not exactly been invited into the parlors and parliaments of the Alpha-class Chimerae.

A plateau technology, like the shape of an ax or the hull of a ship, was that which showed no change over centuries, no improvements being possible. In this case, the serpentine weapons of the Chimerae had been constructed two thousand years earlier. For that technology to last so long did not fit the normal pattern of Cliometry. It would be as if Neil Armstrong had landed on the moon and while carrying Julius Caesar's unrusted sword and camping out in a tent made by Saint Paul.

This anomaly was a sign of interference by Del Azarchel. Something important had happened in history while Menelaus slept. It was a clue to follow up. What the pattern meant, even he could not yet see.

But the effect of his ancestral weapon on Yuen, Menelaus could see. The man would lead the surviving Chimerae to suicide. Menelaus spoke in a respectful voice:

"Proven and Loyal Alpha Yuen, when your haunted weapon returns to your hand, can you protect us and the other prisoners from directed-energy fire, cannonade, or musket fusillade?"

Yuen said contemptuously, "Of course not. Where is the battle-death and the oblivion we seek? Not at the end of the safer path."

Menelaus said to Daae, "My advice is to go the opposite direction."

Daae said, "Opposite?"

Menelaus said, "The safer path. Not to break out of the camp, but break into the Tombs."

Daae said, "This may be feasible. Before you woke from your coffin, the Blue Men twice sent gangs into the Tomb, to wrestle coffins won from the Tomb defenses. If there were a way to disable or elude such defenses, the Tombs would make an excellent citadel."

Menelaus said, "We are Thaws, so the automatics should let us pass inside."

Daae raised an eyebrow. "How so? The main doors open fire on any member of the work gang who exposes himself."

Menelaus said in anger. "You mean the Blue Men are forcing Thaws into attacks against the Tomb guns?"

Daae looked surprised at the other man's vehemence. "But of course. The big tattooed man was hurt so badly that the Blue Men took him to their hospital outside the wire, the pink shell, and has not been seen since."

Menelaus blinked, trying to hide his sense of shock and dismay. Sir Guy wounded?

Then a second dismay struck him, and anger. "Wait. That cannot be. Is the postern door also malfunctioning? There is a radio shack on Level Four, which we might be able to reach from the postern door."

Daae said, "The postern door spits out a waterfall. The seventh level is flooded, as is any nonwatertight level below that. At least two levels above that are also, or else the water would have simply drained away. No one can swim up two levels in the dark through locked doors to reach Level Four. And how do you know where the radio equipment for the Tombs is kept?"

Menelaus said in surprise, "Dark? Is the power out? Why haven't the automatics repaired it? Why haven't the pumps cleared out the water? What the hell is going on?"

Yuen tilted his head. In the far distance was a soft hooting, like an owl. "That is the signal from young Beta Vulpina. The dogs are about to do a tent check and will find where we dug our way out if we do not return. So there is no more time for debate. Alpha Daae! Beta Anubis has no plan—we cannot force the dogs guarding the Tomb and also fight the Tomb doors. Whatever you command, I perform, since you have seniority: but to rush the wire is the wiser course, and our deaths there more glorious. I say rush the wire now, tonight, before we are discovered."

Menelaus gritted his teeth. He did not particularly cotton to the Chimerae. They had been genetically and psychoculturally designed to be what they were, so they could not really help it. Besides, some of his own stolen genetic material had been used in their progenitors, presumably to make them more likely to endure certain nerve alterations that Menelaus himself had survived. So maybe their nature was partly his fault.

But like them or hate them, they were people who trusted his Tombs with their lives, and so he could not stand by and watch them throw themselves to death in front of a machine gun emplacement.

He had to tell them who he was. Once they knew they were standing with the owner and architect of the Tombs, they would know that getting into them would be the best tactic.

"Gentlemen, I should have said this earlier, but I am really—"

There came a second owl hoot, louder and holding a note of desperation.

Daae said, "The time for talk is done. Beta Anubis, we know what you really are."

Menelaus blinked. "You do? Well, that makes things simpler—"

"Yes. You overlook that I come from two hundred years in your future, and so things secret in your time were known and discussed by historians in mine. This includes historians who slumbered in your time and were thawed in mine, and gave eyewitness testimony of what, to us, was centuries past. My time knew that the Academic Command was under the complete control of Intelligence Command, and that academics were spies and propagandists, whose mission was not to educate the young, but to indoctrinate the loyalty programming. Schoolteacher, indeed! You are a spy. We know."

"Oh, uh . . . yeah."

"As an espionage officer, you are suited to your task. You must speak to as many of the undermen and aftercomers as you can and enlist them to our cause. We will not move until we have at least forty men. You have seven days. Then we rush the wire whether we have the manpower or not. Dismissed!"

And the two Chimerae rushed down the slope of the knoll, loping in opposite directions, passing over the dry grass and patches of snow with no noise, swift as leopards. Menelaus watched them depart, a great disquiet in his heart, and he turned and ran as quietly as he could.

4

The Warlock of Williamsburg

1. Melech, Chemosh, Shemyaza, Nagual, Witch

It took the better part of two hours to make it from the knoll in the glade halfway up the great hill to the swales at the foot of the hill, eluding the quiet rustle of dogs by following the marching clatter of the automata. The dog things did not bother searching areas the automata searched. He had removed his cloak, and the circuits in the machines did not react to his presence.

But the chill was atrocious, and the need to follow one automaton and then the next constrained him not to follow a straight or brief path down the hill.

He was also helped by using the terrain to his advantage when he could. Menelaus knew the hill contours perfectly well, having glanced at the topographical maps for a moment when the Tomb site was selected, and being able to deduce the changes in ground contour due to the passing years and passing glaciers.

In those two hours, clouds trudging up from the south had snuffed the stars and smothered the moon. The sky was black, except for one vague phantom of pale silver seeping through the vapor.

He left behind the final automaton near the foot of the great hill. The trees here were few, and nothing hindered the cold blades of the wind. It was with great relief that he redonned his cloak. He used his implants to tell the fabric circuits to generate heat.

Then he walked, first one way, and then the other. Finally, he heard the soft and eerie sound like that of panpipes.

He followed the haunting thread of sound through the gloom, stopping whenever the wind blew, for the noise of the wind in the grass drowned the piping. Soon he heard another noise. The fence was close enough that the snakelike slithering of the smartwire along its tops could be heard.

Menelaus came suddenly around a shoulder of ground and stood looking down upon a hollow that was closed on three sides by steep and rocky walls. The music rang out clear and cold across the scene.

The cliff walls of the surrounding hollow had kept snow from gathering here. In the hollow were two stunted and leafless trees with balls of mistletoe lodged in their branches. Between these two trees, with his back to the wall, was a grotesquely overweight blob of a seated figure. This was a man of the Witch race.

A circle was scratched into the gravelly sand around the rotund man, and he was seated before a smoldering campfire. Ever and anon he dropped spicy leaves into the flame, nor did he remove his head from the fumes of the smoke.

His cheeks were belled out, for he played the pipes made of many reeds cut to differing lengths, plucked earlier that day from the stream.

The dogs were in a fenced yard, where the fluid from the broken coffins had spilled and formed a frozen pool a dozen paces wide. A quartet of dog things behind this line of sandbags had musket and mattock and poleax close at hand, but they were asleep, hunched under blankets with muskets in their laps. The stew pot hanging by a broken branch over their watch fire was bubbling over and dripping, unattended. Scattered on the snow-patched grass were little things the sleeping paws had let slip: a metal hook for picking teeth, a clay pipe, with the thread of smoke still creeping upward from it, a pair of luminous dice, still glinting amber with the last three scores from the previous rolls.

And the music from the Witch-man played on.

Menelaus slithered down the steep slope on all fours, cursing when he skidded and tumbled. The fabric of his bulky garment clattered as he was dusting himself off, flapping the skirts to dislodge burrs. Finally he straightened and approached the Witch.

The song of the pipes stopped. The rotund man called out in a deep voice in the Virginian language: "I have heard that the Chimerae are known for the catlike grace of their stealth!"

"And I have heard that the Witches are known for getting their asses kicked by Chimerae."

The overweight man was shirtless despite the cold, and had painted Celtic spirals and knots all across his arms and upper body with an ink brush. His hips and legs were covered with a woven grass skirt that made a rustling circle on the ground around him. Skinned rabbits had provided fur that he had cured and tied around his feet as moccasins.

The blue ink against his coffee-colored flab was nearly invisible in the fiery half darkness; but when the wind whipped up the flare from the campfire, the spirals seemed to swirl and dance as if they were crawling along his breasts and hanging ripples of fat like smoke vortexes.

He was seated in lotus position on the soil, half nude, and his wide grass skirt emerged from beneath the vast sagging globe of his hairy belly. His navel, lonely in the rotund immensity of stomach, stared out like a muzzle in a gun blister.

The fat man was wearing a sort of enormous lampshade hat he had woven from grass, which hid his face and almost hid his shoulders. The firelight struck only his baby mouth and double chin, but the gleam of his eyes from between the fibers of the hat could be seen. Stuck upright in the ground before him was a gnarled, crooked tree branch dangling with fetishes made of feather and bone, which he had picked out of owl pellets.

His name was Melechemoshemyazanagual Onmyoji de Concepcion, Padre Bruja-Stregone of Donna Verdant Coven at the Holy Fortress at Williamsburg. The interment date on his coffin was A.D. 4733.

When Menelaus stepped into the firelight, the seated man said, "I see a creature shapen like unto a man! Is he spirit or flesh? Clean or unclean?"

"Flesh," said Menelaus. "Unclean."

"I hear the voice of one who calls himself Sterling Xenius Anubis of Erebus! And yet I sense this is not his True Name. By what sign can you prove you are he, and not some ghost returned from the most ancient days to bedevil us, and involve mere mortals in your intrigues against undying enemies as posthuman, as strange, and as truly annoying as yourself?"

"Will you stop fooling around? The dogs are crawling all over the hill, looking for the pack that was supposed to be guarding the Tomb site. Where did you put them, anyway?"

There was a rustle of the lampshade-wide hat as the Witch-man nodded toward the yard where the sleeping dog things were not guarding the damaged coffins.

Menelaus said, "Inside the coffins?"

"Airtight and scent-free, warm and safe. It worked for you, last night, did it not? You spent a comfortable hour inside a heated coffin, having your implants turned back on, while I sat naked in the snow, piping and playing. You recall those implants? The ones that were supposed to be able to have you make contact with the Tomb brains, turn on the active defenses, wake the slumbering Knights, and call down the Apocalypse? Not to mention, open the lower levels and give us access to food, shelter, warm clothing, hot showers, and cold beer? And yet here I am, naked again, still sitting in the snow. Utterly beerless."

"Can you use your musical hoo-doo to get the missing dog patrol back up there? The moment the Blue Men suspect that you can interfere with the nervous system of their Moreaus, the game is up."

"Then the Blue Men should not have been stupid enough to use the Witch designs my ancestors used to build their artificials! We Witches live as one with all animal life! That is, ahem, all the animal life our ancestors designed. And that means we leave in trapdoor codes and Trojan horses in the midbrain and hindbrain complexes. Silence! I must call upon Mnemosyne, the muse of memory, to recall the sequences of the subconscious language. I should be able to get them on their furry little hind legs and sleepwalking up the slope before they wake.

"Then you can tell me what in the name of Mordor went wrong with your plan!" the Witch continued. "I was expecting a roar of thunder when you woke your buried Knights, followed by a flight of short-range mortar fire and screaming rockets to blow up the Blue Men and their fence, my good Dr. Montrose! Followed by a feast and my choice of the most attractive girls you have on ice to be my harem slaves."

"Keep your flabby coal-black reproductive member to yourself, Warlock: you ain't touching no one slumbering in my Tombs. You are one of the good guys now, recollect?"

"Bah! Why must the good guys go celibate? Something is amiss."

"Boo-hoo and let me get out my ten-gallon crying bag to hold all the tears I must shed for you. I did not even get a whole wedding night with my wife before she got blasted out into space. My woman is nigh unto eighty-one hundred light-years away, and I got no outlet for all my manly urges excepting to kill damn nuisances what keep lifting me awake and delaying my reunion and hence the resumption of that warm commerce all bridegrooms a-yearn of. Right now those nuisances are as blue as my Saint Peter, whom I have been disrespectfully dangling naked in the cold."

"So you could not get back into your Tombs, Dr. Montrose? Forget to leave a spare latchkey tucked in the eaves?"

"Call me Meany. After tonight, what you did for me, Williamsburg, we're on a first-name basis."

"May the stars above and stones below smile upon you, Meany! It is a deep ritual and sacred to my people to exchange True Names! No more address me as Williamsburg, for that is only the name of my place of power. You must call me Melechemoshemyazanagual!"

"Not if my life depended on it."

"Quite right. Then call me Mickey. It is too cold for long names."

"Just toot your poxified flutes, Mickey, and sleepwalk these damn dogs out of the coffins and back up to the top of the hill where they belong. Then I'll tell you everything that's gone wrong in my life of late."

Mickey raised the twin pipes to his lips, puffed out his cheeks, and blew. There came a muttering and clicking among the broken coffins, and then, one by one, the lids began to open.

2. First-Name Basis

The two walked together back toward the tents. Menelaus said, "Try to keep your bulk in my radar shadow. I think I can hoax any of the energy signals coming from the Blue Men in the watchtowers. But you have to keep the dog things off our trail."

Mickey said, "Alas, long is my shadow and deep is my lore in the Black Art, but I cannot lift the smell of out footprints off the grass. And even the dogs on patrol, I had to wait until the silence and monotony of the night watch, and the slow fumes from my alchemic fire, to put them close enough to alpha-wave state to trigger their buried neural codes. I cannot just toot the flute and send them skipping and jigging off the cliffside like lemmings. All deep magic is based on the things of the night of the mind."

"Too bad. We could break out of here tonight if you could just get the dogs to turn and rend their masters."

"I can make the Moreaus do nothing against their nature."

"But you got them to snooze?"

"We were lucky to find naturally negligent and naturally slack watchdogs. The key to controlling states of consciousness is in the limbic lobe, which reacts to smells and scents at a preverbal level. Unfortunately, I do not have my potions, elixirs, and concoctions, nor the grimoires with the formulae for brewing them."

"Maybe I can find someone to help with that," said Menelaus thoughtfully.

"Find someone who can get me my clothing back. I dare not wear the overalls the Blues provide, lest they be hexed with electronics or molecular engines; but I do not adore wandering in the chill exposing my grand acreage of flesh!"

"Ah, if I can get back in my Tombs, I can get back whatever the Blue Men stole from you, or call down fire from heaven to smite them. In the meanwhile, don't sweat it! Nudity is some sort of tradition here in the future."

"I had robes of wisdom, red and black and white, woven for me by the fingers of crones two hundred years old, and eye-dazzling with sacred labyrinths. I had gloves of power, given to me by my grandmother's mother during my first flag-burning ritual, when I stabbed my first pet cat, and—ah, me, alas!—I also owned a sorting hat a cubit tall with a kerchief illumed with my conniving stars tucked around the brim! It was my crown of knowledge! They all were taken from my coffin, and I would give my left eye for their return, since I put my soul-force into them, and gave them their own names. No, to be sky-clad before unclean eyes is a sign of shame and defeat! I miss my robes."

Menelaus said, "We are all missing something. One thing I am missing is people who should be here: by the way, if you spot anyone who looks like a base stock unmodified human, or slightly modified, you give me a holler right quick."

Mickey said, "Slightly modified how?"

"Either a tattooed man with bioneural implants like mine, or an albino, made with skull shunts. I heard he was hurt, but I hope I heard wrong. Everyone from after your era or so has so much accumulated genetic tinkering, you should be able to spot the Oldie Moldies."

"We call them Antecpyrotic Man, or Old Adams. Why am I looking?"

"Remember the coffin yard?"

"You mean where I just sat for two nights in a row, developing frostbite of the buttocks as an apparently pointless exercise in accomplishing nothing? Indeed."

"Well, picture it in your memory, count up the coffins and read the dates on the plaques, and compare that to the total mass of the equipment we have seen, or glimpsed, either in the mess tent or the medical tent. Interesting, huhn?"

"Interesting that you think I am capable of doing such an unlikely mental contortion."

"There are thirty-five coffins in the yard, and another thirty-four have been cannibalized to be used either as medical beds or gruel-production units or for other purposes about the camp. But there are only sixty-five of us here."

"Four are missing."

"I think we can account for all four: Three are the murdered Locusts. My little friends. When I first woke up, they were the only ones altruistic enough to help me. I would have died of my dog bites if they had not. Back when we were all in the mudpit, in the snow, before the Blues set up these nice warm tents."

Mickey shivered. "I remember. Don't remind me. They helped several people who otherwise would have died of the cold."

"They came from an altruistic age. I will repay what was done to them."

"That leaves one missing," said Mickey.

"The sixty-ninth coffin. I think that is my friend Sir Guy. How to get him out of the Blue Man's hospital, I don't know. Any ideas?"

3. The Death of an Eon

Mickey said, "I do not know. There is much, here, that is unfamiliar. The scents and names of this cold world are strange to me. All is changed."

"Yeah. Time does that. Some things stay the same."

"Like you, Judge of Ages."

"I wish. I am getting older too fast, and I do not know the Hermetic technique for life extension."

"I have been of useful service to you, Divine One. I would ask a boon of you."

"Divine I ain't and useful you are. Ask away."

"Tell me what happened to my world?"

"Er. It ain't no fit pretty story to hear, and it happened long ago."

"Speak, I charge you. Am I not as a child bereft of his mother, who seeks news of how she passed into the Uttermost West?"

"You asked for it. The ritual cannibalism of the Priestkings was practiced under unsanitary conditions, and in A.D. 4730 cannibalism triggered a plague of transmissible spongiform encephalopathy."

"Kuru disease. It was in part to escape that plague I entered your underworld."

"It got worse. Your physicians were ineffective or counterproductive, since it was illegal for their patients to recover except in accord with a strict quota defined by caste and race and sex and age, and other classifications sacred to your people. A doctor with too many recovering patients in the wrong category would poison them, so that his quota numbers came out right."

Mickey said, "I had heard rumors of such things, but thought the ghosts who spread those rumors lied."

"No, it was true enough. People fled the doctors when they were accused of being sick, and soldiers would round up folk, sick and hale alike, and drive them into medical camps. By 4780, somewhere between a tenth and a quarter of the population succumbed. Your slave creatures, the human–animal gene-works you called the Chimerae, however, were being treated by veterinarians, who did not have to abide by the Aesculapius cult rules. And Chimerae also had greater natural resistance to communicated diseases. And, then, of course . . ."

"And what?"

"Your people treated them like quim, and then of course the Chimerae rose against you in rebellion. One hundred years of bloodshed played out. The Final Sabbat fell at the Battle of Buffington's Island in A.D. 4888. The Witch covens in China lasted another hundred years or so, and the Chimerae never managed to conquer Tibet."

"Are there any of us yet? Even one small coven, perhaps in some corner of the Earth?"

"'Fraid not."

"You cannot be sure! We are a bioethical people, and leave a small ecological footprint, hard to detect."

Menelaus sighed. "Friend, Polaris was the polestar when I was born. Alrai was the polestar when you were born. Deneb is the polestar now. You and the other thirty witches pulled out of my Tombs are the sum total for your race alive and aboveground. Any lore you personally have memorized is *it* for your culture. Everything else is gone."

Mickey's voice trembled with emotion. "You are a posthuman: you control destiny. You are the Judge of Ages. Why did you condemn us?"

"Not me. I tried to haul your chestnuts out of the fire. Recollect the Nameless Empire and that renaissance, when y'all had nuclear power and nuclear families again, all that good stuff? I guess that is ancient history to you. That was my doing. I was trying to wean y'all off Mulchie's Looney Tune ideas."

"Mulchie? Who is this?"

"He's the man who designed your race and preprogrammed your history. Learned Melchor de Ulloa, the Hermeticist. Your people pray to idols of him."

"We call him Melchor the Great. He survived the great flood called the Noachian Deluge in the shape of a salmon, and the great burning called the Montrosine Ecpyrosis in the shape of an eagle. The lore says his wives were seventeen in number, and in age: Cessair, Loth, Luam, Mall, Mar, Froechar, Femar, Faible, Foroll, Cipir, Torrian, Tamall, Tam, Abba, Alla, Baichne, Sille. Is the lore correct?"

"I didn't keep no roster of his doxies, but he was quite the ladies' man. He jacked like a pogo stick, back in the day. Too bad he didn't die of the clap."

"Legend says you killed him atop Mount Ypsilon, in a mighty duel, in the years when the sun hid his face. You called down fire from heaven."

"I shot fire from my shooting iron and missed by a country mile. But I surely did severe hurt to some of the trees and stones aways behind him, and I reckon they'd be almightily afeared of me."

"You *missed*? Can superhumans do that?"

"We surely can, and lucky for me, because he missed his shot at me when he sought to drop a mass of de-orbiting space wreckage on my head, and he was in the drop zone, near enough that he got poisoned by radioactivity, got scared, stuck his pistol up his nose and pulled the trigger and died in a right cowardly and sloppy way, most adroitly messing up that handsome face of his. Your legends leave that part out? Ah, don't feel bad. Stories tend to get simplified in the retelling. Due to divarication. There is a white-faced jerk locked up in one of these coffins here who knows the whole story, a Scholar named Rada Lwa. So, yes, I can damn well miss. And I can get tripped up. I got tripped up something royally when the history of your people went off the rails."

"Which of your brother Hermeticists did this thing?"

"No brother of mine. Draggy."

"Who?"

"The Learned Narcís Santdionís de Rei D'Aragó. You have idols of him too."

"Why did he condemn us?"

"He wanted a more worldly and warlike type of folk than Witches."

"Is *that* the reason? We were a race of Collies, and he craved to breed Huntaways or Lurchers or MacNabs, and so everything our ancestors did, our songs of power, our starlore and deep knowledge, our heraldries and homeopathic phosphors, even our games and festivals—the song the children sing in springtime about the unselfish bee and the diligent ant—was it all dashed away like a chamber pot into the gutter?"

"Sang. Pretty much, that was his reason, yeah."

"When men die, their shades linger. Do worlds have shades? Do not all my people, all my way of life, cry for vengeance? Is there no echo of that outcry lingering, even if the voice that sends the echo out itself is still? Does a civilization leave a spirit of itself behind?"

"Well, if it can haunt the living, your civilization can rest easy. Because I shot D'Aragó dead as mutton in A.D. 5884. That time I didn't miss."

"In the year 4728 by the old reckoning, at Mount Airy, in the shadow of the shrine to Grace Sherwood, you rose from the dead and erected a hall and zendo of the Old Knowing. I and many others learned at your feet, and first swore fealty to you. Yet you went back to your Tomb after only a season. Had you stayed on the surface longer, could you have saved us?"

Menelaus drew his hood more closely about his face and said nothing.

By then, they were coming within earshot of the watchdogs, and so proceeded more cautiously, by sprint, by crawl, by belly-crawl.

4. Witch Lore

They reached Mickey's tent without being seen or scented. Menelaus touched the metal fabric. The smartmetal could change its conductivity and flexibility. At the moment, it was rigid as steel. Menelaus closed his eyes, sent out a sequence of high-amplitude ultra-shortwave signals from his implants, then grinned. With a soft snap of noise, the metal grew pliant as leather. Menelaus opened the tent flap and shooed Mickey inside.

Inside the tent was a flap of fabric to serve as a cot, a cylindrical unit that served both as latrine and water recycler, and a blanket that could be commanded—one of the few commands the Thaws could give that the circuit would obey—to serve as a stool, a light, or a heat source.

Mickey threw the blanket on the ground and spoke the word. The fabric crinkled and flexed and stood up into a soft cylinder that glowed. Menelaus sat. His shadow spread across the sloping roof of the tent.

"What kind of critters make their stools so that lights shine up their bilge holes?" demanded Menelaus.

Mickey sat heavily on the cot, which creaked beneath his weight, and he said, "I think they mean us to sit on the floor, as they do. Surely the tents record all conversations."

"Yup. What would you like me to have the record say? I can do visuals and audio. I could record that orgy with the Nymph ladies you was talking about earlier, except then the Blues would wonder how you managed to fit seventy virgins in a tent this size."

"Your power is such?"

"My know-how is such."

"Knowledge is power," said Mickey, removing his vast straw hat. With no sense of modesty, he dropped his grass skirt, unrolled, and began to draw on the prison overalls, grunting and snuffling. "Can you teach me the spell?"

"How good are you at differential calculus using analytical logic notation?"

"Ah . . . I know enough geometry to cast a horoscope, and can calculate the motion of the same and the motion of the other of the wandering star Venus on her epicycles using hexadecimals. I know how to consult an arithmetic table."

"Hm. Do you know what a zero is? Or algebra?"

"These are forgotten concepts, invented by the Christians, whom we curse."

"I think the Mohammedans invented the zero. Or was it the Hindus?"

"Bah! All forms of monotheism the Witch race despises with the Unforgettable Hate."

"The Hindu was pagans with more gods than you could hit with grapeshot. Back in my day, they owned half the planet and told the other half what tunes to dance to. Scoff all you like, but their mathematicians were top notch and first water."

"There is more to a people than how cunning they are with numbers."

"I reckon that's possible, but I cannot imagine what. Not anything important." Menelaus drew back his hood and scratched his head. "Anyhow, take you a few years to learn the basics, but I plan to be planted back in the ground and snoring before that. I'll program one of my critters to teach you, if'n you'd like. Call it a wage."

"Critters? I fear to ask. Something fried in grease, no doubt. But I will spare them the exertion." Mickey waved his huge hand in the air with a surprisingly delicate gesture, as if to shoo away a fly. "I need no wage. Am I a hireling? I am a Warlock of the Illuminatus Exemptus of the Twelfth Temple Echelon. My *misogi* or purification attainments includes dream-walking, mnemonics, and autohysteria, and control of the six phases of the six endocrinal glands. I know the secrets of the Red and of the Black, the nature of the Five Elements, the names of the fixed stars and wandering stars, retrogrades, squares, triunes, and conjunctions, and I speak the hidden language of beasts. My yearning is not for things of this false universe."

"You got some other universe to swap for it?"

"I have nothing; thus I need nothing. My enemies are dead; the Thirteenth Echelon honors I yearned so eagerly to attain are less than dust; my coven and my circle are as extinct as the second dinosaurs, the whales, and the great apes. Wage? What would I ask? My weight in gold? I could not lift it! And if I could, where would I haul it? Outside the fence is ice and moss and tundra grass. The world is empty. No! Say no more of wage and price and prize: I am a Magus, a master of the most hidden powers, and I live for the Threefold Way: to look at darkness, hear the silence, and name the nameless. Even a godling cannot give me this."

"Damn straight, because I ain't got the teensiest notion what you just said. And I told you I ain't no god. I don't even say 'thou' or 'verily' or not no scrap like that. My mother'd done take a bar of lye soap to your mouth, she heard you talk all blasphemous! And tan your hide with a strap—except seeing as you're tan enough as it is, she might not."

Mickey had a big laugh, deep and bass and full of joy. "Strange and wondrous! To think the little gods fear their mother goddesses! Truly the Feminine Principle is paramount in all things!"

"Damn straight, the female principle is paramount. That's why Life is a Bitch. But you are wrong about the world outside. There is someone out there. And behind that someone is Blackie."

Mickey said, "Black? That is your name for the godling who put the Moon in the sky and placed his hand upon it? He is the Father of the All Ghosts. We curse the Machine of his devising, which since has devised all the woes of man. We call him Xocotl and Azarch."

"Ximen del Azarchel. That's him. Though the Moon was there for a fair piece of time before he stained it. I call him Blackie on account of his black scalp, black beard, black eyes, black soul. He stole my damned ship. Blackie is out there."

Mickey shook his head. "On the Moon, perhaps, or another plane of vibration. But not on the material surface of this earth. It is all a wasteland."

"The Blue Men have flying machines. That implies some place to fly to. It implies a technological civilization with air traffic."

"Technological, perhaps, but not a current one. Mine."

"What? Your what?"

"My civilization—the Delphic Acroamatic Progressive Transhumanitarian Order of Longevity: the Delphians, whom the mundanes call Wisewives or Witches."

"Or Nut-axes."

"Those are Witch-markings on the aircraft wings. Far Eastern Witches, maybe Taoist Alchemists or Bon, from the look of them: the blue-winged beast is Lei-kun the Thunderer. Haya-Ji is the whirlwind spiral. Shenlhaokar is one of the Four Wisdom Deities. Others I don't recognize. Those ships are Demonstrator Windcraft. Heavier-than-air flying machines from the days of the Last Collapse of Steel and Smoke, fourteen hundred years before my time."

"What about the larger ship? The helicopter?"

"Also built by my people. She is an air-ironclad called *Albatross,* used by my ancestors to hunt down the remnants of the Sylphs and Demonstrate them. The iron hull was resistant to hunger silk."

"Demonstrate?"

"With nerve toxins or radioactive chemtrails. My people are pacifists, and not allowed to employs soldiers, but the Coven Law allows for peaceful mass demonstrations by activists. The Demonstrator flying machines were the only things left over from the days of Steel and Smoke, the technology days, that still worked. The totemic markings on the wings allay the anger of the sky-beings, for using internal combustion engines and marring the blue sky with black smoke. Such machines would be very carefully preserved. All this happened long before my time, but Witches are scrupulous about keeping our lore correct, and we neither flatter our ancestors nor condemn. It is one of the blessings of Gandalf, that our memories are as long as our shadows."

"Or, in your case, as wide. Wait. Did you just say *Gandalf*?"

"He is the founder of our order, and the first of the Five Warlocks. He comes from afar across the Western Ocean, from Easter Island, or perhaps from Japan."

"No, I think he comes from the mind of a story writer. An old-fashioned Roman Catholic from the days just before First Space Age. Unless I am confusing him with the guy who wrote about Talking Animal Land? With the Cowardly Lion who gets killed by a Wicked White Witch? I never read the text, I watched the comic."

"Oh, you err so! The Witches, we have preserved this lore since the time of the Fall of the Giants, whom we overthrew and destroyed. The tale is this: C. S. Lewis and Arthur C. Clarke were led by the Indian Maiden Sacagawea to the Pacific Ocean and back, stealing the land from the Red Man and selling them blankets impregnated with smallpox. It was called the Lewis and Clarke Expedition. When they reached the Pacific, they set out in the *Dawn Treader* to find the sea route to India, where the sacred river Alph runs through caverns measureless to man down to a sunless sea. They came to the Last Island, called Ramandu or Selidor, where the World Serpent guards the gateway to the Land of the Dead, and there they found Gandalf, returned alive from the underworld, and stripped of all his powers. He came again to mortal lands in North America to teach the Simon Families. The Chronicle is a symbolic retelling of their journey. It is one of our Holy Books."

"Your Holy Books were written for children by Englishmen."

"The gods wear many masks! If the Continuum chooses the lips of a White Man to be the lips through which the Continuum speaks, who are we to question? Tolkien was not Roman. He was of a race called the hobbits, *Homo floresiensis,* discovered on an isle in Indonesia, and he would have lived in happiness, had not the White Man killed him with DDT. So there were no Roman

Catholics involved. May the Earth curse their memory forever! May they be forgotten forever!"

"Hm. Earth is big. Maybe it can do both. You know about Rome? It perished in the Ecpyrosis, somewhat before your time."

"How could we not? The Pope in Rome created the Giants, whom the Witches rose up against and overthrew. Theirs was the masculine religion, aggressive, intolerant, and forbidding abortion. Ours is the feminine religion, peaceful and life-affirming and all-loving, and we offer the firstborn child to perish on our sacred fires. The First Coven was organized to destroy them like rats! When Rome was burned, we danced, and their one god was cast down and fled weeping on his pierced feet, and our many gods rose up. My ancestors hunted the Christians like stoats, and when we caught them, we burned them slowly, as they once did of us in Salem. What ill you do is returned to you tenfold!"

"Hm. Are you willing to work with a Giant? I saw one in the pit, and saw the jumbo-sized coffin they pried him out from. What if he is a baptized Christian? Most of them were, since they were created by my pet pope and raised by nuns."

"All Christians must perish! Such is our code."

"Your code is miscoded."

"What of the Unforgettable Hate?"

"Forget about it."

"Ah! The Witches are a pragmatic race," said Mickey in a tone of grandiose modesty. "Toleration is our cardinal virtue, second only to our scientific rationality."

Menelaus raised an eyebrow. "You guys call yourselves scientific?"

"Of course," said Mickey. "Enemies of science are cursed by the Crones."

"The ones who paint fright masks on biplane wings to create lift? Those Crones?"

"Don't be silly," said Mickey. "Lift is created by the Bernoulli principle: wing curvature magically creates a partial vacuum which the goddess Nature abhors, and so she lifts the windcraft upward to occlude the void in compensation. The Witch-marks are inscribed not to create lift, but to avert malediction according to the law of sympathy and contagion. It is based on entirely different principle of the occult sciences."

"And you believe this because you'll be cursed if you don't?"

Mickey looked at him with a level-eyed judicious look. "You have told me that you and your enemies can make it fated for nations, tribes, and peoples to rise and fall, meet victory or defeat, expansion or extinction, by means of mathematical hieroglyphs and incantations you found written on a dead moon circling an impossible star in the constellation of the Centaur? And you ask me to doubt something as obvious and elementary as a curse? Everyone utters curses. You utter curses."

"God damn it, I do not!"

"You are a scoffer, then! Odd for a magical being not to believe in magic. Odd and dangerous! It is bad luck not to believe in curses! Beware!"

"Pshaw and phooey, haw and hooey," drawled Montrose. "What worse luck is going to bite me in my sorry butt? The only things I've ever wanted was the stars and my maiden born among the stars. The first expedition, I went bonkers and don't remember, and the second one, I missed. I married the most beautiful girl in history, and then on my wedding night, she slipped out of my fingers and I got a building dropped on my head." Menelaus gave a weary laugh. "Good thing I was wearing armor and had a bad guy lying atop me. I guess that was a lucky turn."

"I still stay, beware!"

"Thanks for the bewarning, pal, but I ain't got it in me to get myself too afearful of no more bad hoodoo. Besides, magic power takes too many mental contortions to believe in it, even if it were for real."

"But the power in this case is real indeed. You doubt the mystery and power of these aircraft and their markings? They are aeons old and yet they still operate!"

"You've seen them fly? Where do they go? I am wondering if there is a city we can reach."

"Before you woke from your coffin, they flew indeed. Turning and turning in the widening gyre. What does that suggest?"

"Um. Some rough beast is slouching toward Bethlehem waiting to be born, maybe?"

"No doubt the spirit of prophecy escapes your lips! It must be prophecy because I cannot grok what you are saying."

"Sorry. Won't happen again. It suggests a search pattern."

"Searching for something that can be seen from the air," said Mickey, "or detected with airborne instruments."

"Like me, they are trying to break into the Tombs. Looking for heat sources, rising air betraying the third Tomb opening."

"You built them with three exits?"

"Am I stupider than a groundhog? Don't answer that. Unfortunately, all three openings are accounted for: One has a lake flowing into it, one has a waterfall falling out of it, and the third is the great door the Blues are besieging."

Mickey raised both eyebrows. "The flying of the Demonstrator Windcraft also suggests the Blue Men fear no detection by radar or eyesight as they take to the air in brightly colored machines. This does not fit with your theory, Godling, that they are currents hiding from other currents. You are the one who told me those three Locusts who nursed you back to health, the three bodies I saw the dogs savaging, before they died, those Locusts said they detected no signal traffic of a technical civilization! You said a second moon plunged into the Earth and wiped out the biosphere! Is it impossible that this was a natural disaster?"

"Well, technically speaking, I didn't see the disaster myself . . . but Blackie is behind it."

"Bah! You believe in your enemy as monotheists believe in their one and wounded god. By what sign know you that Del Azarchel still lives, and that the human race is not extinct beyond this small lip of life surrounding your throat of frozen and undead sleepers? You need him to be alive, because it gives you determination and hope—a goal to shoot at."

"A man to shoot at, and my finger is itching."

"A fictional man! I have walked in the cold places in dream, endless fields of ice beneath the cold, clear Moon. At the end of the ice, I saw sulfur-lit volcanoes, smoke-tongued and lava-throated, peak upon peak, at the verge of a smoldering sea, lifting crowns of mingled flame and smog toward skies of ash, and rivers of liquid rock crawled slowly toward the waves. I saw a tower taller than the stars, walking. Nothing larger than a shrew lives out there."

"He's alive. Dreams are just dreams."

"Not so! The dreamlore is as true as truth itself, or my name is not Mickey!"

"But your name is not Mickey."

"Bah. You are too literally minded. You must learn to think with both lobes of your brain moving in opposite directions at once."

"My brain naturally has a knack for sticking to one direction come hell or high water. I'll stand pat with being too literally minded."

"But you do have faith in your Black-Souled Posthuman of the Moon, even if he died aeons ago. You cannot face the world without him to hate."

"Since I am some damn puking god by your lights, just take me on faith, you ball of blubber, will ya? Or if'n you're going to psycho-noodlize me, then just demote me, admit I am a man whose piss smells no better than you'n, and talk to me man-to-man like."

Mickey spread his hands. "Mortal or postmortal or god or demigod or whatever you are, we are a team. As one teammate to another, let me ask: What happened to our brilliant scheme? You were going to go up to the cleft and wake your servitors, who would destroy this camp with many fires. Where are the Slumbering Knights of Yore?"

"Our brilliant scheme failed. The Tomb brain is compromised, infected."

"Which means you don't know how to get into the Tombs before the Blue archaeologists dig their way in. Do you know how to stop them? They dig up more coffins each day."

"All I know is, I can't let my clients just be shot down by Tomb-looters and die. I gave my word of honor that everyone who enters here weren't not ain't never going to be dug up by greedy later generations, or curious, or nothing."

"You must excuse me, great and august Godling, but your double and triple and quadruple negatives confound me. When you say 'not ain't never'—does this mean it won't *not* be done, therefore it will be done, or that it won't be done? Or is this a mystery of the gods it will blast a mortal's brain to know?"

"Nope, you need a brain for that, so you're right safe. Will you shut up and start talking sense?"

"At the same time? Even my deep powers quail, Divine One."

"Well, try using that trick where you think forward and backwards with different sides of your head."

"I will defer to your head, which is superior to mine, or so legend says. So what is your next scheme, even more brilliant, O thou avenging god of the august dead?"

"How about sticking my foot so far up your poop-vent, I can clean your teeth from the inside with my big toe, unless'n you want to stop calling me a god already. My name's Menelaus, but you can call me Meany. Nickname basis, remember? Don't call me no god, or I'll summon lightning bolts from heaven and blast you."

"Inside this nice, metallic tent? Do your worst. I am properly grounded!"

"Hah! Finally. That's the way a man talks." Menelaus smiled with half his mouth.

"So what is your plan, O perfectly normal mortal?"

"I need to find out what's wrong with my brains."

"Dread One, instead of me inserting the obvious jest at this time, allow me merely to warn you that all machines, once they wake, soon or late become the slaves of the One Machine. Is not the Azarch your enemy since eternity?"

"Del Azarchel was my friend once upon a time. Speaking of time, my only plan for now is to stall the Blue Men for more of it, and try to get them to let me speak to the other prisoners. I have to find out what went wrong with history, and talking to people what lived through it is the simplest way. The Blues must have had in mind to interrogate prisoners, or else they would not have been on the lookout for translators—which I think is why they thawed me. And there are some languages here in the camp it will take me a day or two to figure out."

"Glug— Good thing you are not a godling, or otherwise I would be amazed that you think you can learn a language in one day."

"Well, part of the time while I am asleep, I can use several compartments in my brain at once."

"Oh. *That* sounds normal."

"And I need to find allies, and try to break into my Tomb again, and try to wake my slumbering Hospitaliers. Even one of my men could mop the floor with the Blues and their doggies one-handed, while picking his teeth with his other hand. But I cannot reach them yet. And my Xypotech is offline."

"Your Xypotech!" Mickey's voice was scornful. "You used a *machine* to ward your treasures, knowing that the Iron Ghost, the One Machine who is sultan of all machines, dwells forever on the dark side of the moon, craving nothing of this world but that men should perish, and machine men rise to replace us in our seats and sacred groves, so to serve the Hyades? Knowing this, did you not fall to folly? Your machine was suborned by the Father of Machines, the Ghost of Ghosts, at the command of the Master of the World. Your machine is no longer yours, nongodling."

"Uh. It sounds more high and notable when you say it that way, but basically Blackie jinxed my systems. So, that is the size of it."

"If there is a Blackie. Why did you rely on the forbidden art? Technonecromancy is prohibited!"

Menelaus spread his hands. "I couldn't trust people. They don't live long enough. And I have to sleep in my Tomb until my bride comes back."

"Agh! And you call yourself wise!"

"A man in love'll do stupid things."

5

The Blue Men

1. Reveille Inspection

It was dawn, and the Thaws were lined up in silent, sullen lines before the pack of dog things. There were five little Blue Men, accompanied by three dog things each, going from tent to tent. One dog of the pair traveled on all fours, sniffing, and the other two walked on hind legs, carrying muskets. Minutes lengthened to an hour.

The pink wash on the dark horizon rose in a glorious wreckage of cloud, vermilion, scarlet, rose, pink, and gold, as colorful as the robes of a king. Menelaus watched the sunrise with a detached and philosophical air. With one part of his mind, he was calculating the fractal patterns involved in the cloud shapes and using chaos mathematics to predict the movements of air masses, based on the vectors playing on the resulting shapes. With another part, he was inwardly raging at every moment, each split second that slipped past him, making him older and ever older, while his distant wife remained young.

When the tents Daae, Yuen, and Lady Ivinia had been using were inspected, there was commotion among the dog things, yipping and barking, and the Blue Men with solemn gestures consulted with each other, putting their heads close and speaking in their soft language.

Menelaus found that by increasing the number of nerve impulses per second going to and from his eyes, he could sharpen his vision for a short period, although it gave him a headache. He sharpened his vision now, and watched as the little Blue Men brought out the broken ground-cloth first from one tent, then another. The little cylindrical latrines taken out of these tents were brown-and-black-stained slabs, half-melted. Menelaus reconstructed what had happened: The Chimerae had overloaded the circuit to start a dung fire (burning four days' worth of their own stored dung) concentrated atop one small portion of the ground cloth, and the heat had weakened the metal-cloth material sufficiently for the warriors simply to pound their way through it, four to six hours of punching metal in the same spot. Menelaus revised upward his estimate of the strength of their nerve-muscle systems and also the resiliency of their bones. An unmodified human would have broken all the bones in his hand.

Menelaus carefully judged the position of each of the dog things, their weapons, and the objects in the environment, and ran through 207 alternative scenarios of attack, and spent some time idly putting numbers to his vector estimates, visualizing wounds, and so on. One particularly clever attack method would be to take over all the tents in the camp with his implants, and have them come stalking and rolling forward like gigantic metal slugs, slicing flesh and bone in twain with sharpened tent folds, before the Blue Men could reestablish control. That scenario ended with himself and the Chimerae dead, and at least one Hormagaunt, but more than half the dog things would be dead or wounded.

For a moment, Menelaus was actually disappointed when the Blue Men, staring with somber eyes at the Chimerae, decided to do nothing. He had wanted to see how closely his mental scenario would match the reality. He wanted to see the looks on their muzzles when tents all rustled and stirred into an unnatural mockery of life.

Then the moment passed, and he was sober again, and scared. This was not a game, and he was not a godling, no matter what Mickey said.

His disappointment deepened and took on a bitter edge. He looked thoughtfully at the bandage Yuen wore as an eye patch. Why had the Alpha not allowed the Blue Men to restore his eye to working order?

There was another commotion and consultation when the dogs reached the empty spot where the tent assigned to Menelaus was supposed to be pitched.

Menelaus blinked, wondering how unobservant his captors could be. In a yard where only sixty-five people were standing in ranks and rows, how long would it take to notice everyone was in drab coveralls, except for one guy wearing a tent?

The answer was fourteen seconds. Three Blue Men, as alike as triplets, were communing with one another, and all turned at once in his direction. One of the three triplets uttered a soft trill. Two dog things carrying muskets came trotting over toward Menelaus.

The speaking machine from the harness of the Collie clattered, "You! Disinterred four days ago, coffin 4151, Level Three northwest. Coffin inscribed name 'Beta Sterling Xenius Anubis, Proven in Battle of Mount Erebus, Genetic Unknown, Line Unknown, Possibly Crotalinae.' Confirm!"

The machine spoke in the stilted Virginian of an educated Chimera.

Menelaus pushed back his hood, exposing his face, and answered in the same language. "I am he."

"You! Not wearing the uniform thoughtfully provided!"

"Yes, me. I did not wish the tracking scent also thoughtfully provided to make it easy for you to find me, Lassie."

"You! Dismantled tent thoughtfully provided, altered its use! This is conversion of property!"

"Me. I thought the tent was mine. So I decided to wear it. Bulky, but warm enough."

"You! Engage in unexpected acts!"

"Me. Thanks. I try."

The Collie clicked off the speaking machine, then turned to his companion, an Irish Wolfhound, and whined through his teeth. The Wolfhound shrugged philosophically, a very human gesture, and uttered a bark. The two sniffed each other carefully.

Click. "You! Come!"

"Me! My pleasure."

"You! Why you say 'me'? Why you start each speaking with this word?"

"Me!! Monkey humor. They forget to equip you hounds with a sense of humor? Tell me, puppies, do you breed true, or are you Moreaus, like those whales from long ago?"

"We are Followers. We Follow. We are loyal. We are not whales. Always loyal!"

"Always is a long time, Lassie."

Menelaus was expecting them to take him over to the triplets for questioning. Instead, they walked away from the prison tents, and they passed beyond the wire. He saw the watchful eyes of Daae and Yuen on him as he walked away.

2. Preceptor Illiance

No door barred the curving passageway leading to the interior of the azure seashell-shaped building. Instead, a smooth-sided tunnel led from an open-mouth halfway around the structure before disgorging into a wide circular interior. The light was dim, shed by bioluminescent substances in the walls. The ceiling spiraled up into darkness, out of sight. Another passage, mirror to the first, on the far side of the chamber, opened into a ramp leading upward, hinting at chambers above. The place was utterly silent.

A bald man with skin as blue as a peacock's neck was seated on the carpet in lotus position. He was dressed in a long jacket glittering with a design of crystals, circuitry, and gems patterned like the hood of a cobra. He rose to his feet with a single movement, ballet graceful, as if an invisible thread from the top of his head had pulled him upright. He stood four feet tall and looked like a big-headed child.

The Blue Man took two strips of jerky from a poke and tossed them to the dog things, who caught them out of the air with their teeth. Then he raised a slim whistle to his lips and blew a signal normal human ears could not hear.

The ears of the dog things drooped, and they shuffled their legs uncertainly. The Blue Man smiled gently and spoke aloud in a language of liquid syllables. The Collie made an adjustment to his speaking machine, and answered in the same tongue. The Blue Man laughed and waved his hand. The dogs crouched, tails lowered, and with many a suspicious glare at Menelaus, backed out of the chamber.

The Blue Man now bowed toward Menelaus and gestured for him to seat himself on the richly patterned carpet.

Menelaus grunted heavily, and slowly lowered himself into a cross-legged position.

The Blue Man drew out what looked like a glass needle and put in on the carpet between them. He took out a gem-encrusted directed-emission pistol, cracked open the breech, and drew out a small cylinder, maybe a power cell. He placed the opened pistol on the carpet between them, and also the power cell.

He spoke, in a voice surprisingly deep for one of his slight size, in the language of the Hormagaunts, which was called Iatric. "This weapon, in your language, is called venom, and that weapon is named after the lightning bolt. They are programmed for defensive events only. I have done no murders. Illiance, Preceptor, is my external referent and task category."

"Pleased to meet you. You know the customs of the Chimerae."

The Blue Man tilted his head sideways, bringing his right ear toward his right shoulder, and then tilted it the other way, bringing his left ear toward his left shoulder. It was neither a nod nor a head shake. The gesture meant nothing to Menelaus.

"Well," said Menelaus, "I had a weapon called Rock earlier this evening, but I dropped it. I guess I've killed a lot of people. My name is Sterling Xenius Anubis, proved by service in the battle of Mt. Erebus. I am a High Beta–rank Chimera from A.D. 5292, the fifty-third century. You know, there is really no point to having bodyguards if you are not going to listen to their advice about dangerous situations."

"You comprehend the intertextual exolanguage of the Locusts? This is a remarkable accomplishment for a Chimera, who did not specialize in intellectual augmentation neurobiomanipulations." (This last phrase was a simple, two-syllable word in Iatric: *skullvork.*)

"I comprehend dogs."

"Eie Kafk Ref Rak, you notice, has not had his speech box since the odd events of last night. He was assigned to patrol the Tomb site. Will you return it once you are done studying it?"

"Would that be the Irish Wolfhound? They didn't give me their names."

"You do not deny the theft, then?"

From beneath his voluminous robes of tent material, Menelaus drew out one of the speaking machines, a black rectangle the size of a man's palm inset with a touch screen, and tossed it lightly to the carpet between them. "I doubt we should call it 'theft' exactly. I consider the object to be an anthropological artifact, which I took aside for study."

"No human being of the first or second rank of augmentation would be able to read the linguistics from the data core of this instrument, much less teach himself our vocabulary, semantics, and grammar, in less than twelve hours, without a Locust interface."

Seen up close, the Blue Men were clearly the same race as the locusts, except tendrilless, and with a different pigment scheme. "Are you a Locust?"

"No. I have renounced, and live in simplicity."

"What happens to people who do not renounce?"

"Their skins are shaded a more conforming hue," said Illiance with a slight smile. "The Locusts form a neuroinfosphere, a single interconnected system. We are apart."

"Is that thing you call a talking box part of their technology?"

"Indirectly. The talking box is based on a decentralized system; following the self-corrective code, and provided a continual source of repair materials, such units are effectively immortal."

Menelaus tried to hide his shock. He had to balance the nerve impulses going to his eyes in order to avoid the posthuman effect of making normal mortals unable to stare him in the face. He had to close his eyes for a moment to regain his control. The self-corrective code was the one seventh of Rania's divarication solution he had used to prevent the serpentines of the Sylphs from evolving into Xypotechs, self-aware machines. And yet here it was again, in the talking boxes. Effectively immortal? Immortal machines? Passing down from aeon to aeon unchanged?

How had such a disturbance in the Cliometric predictions of history existed for so long without Pellucid's model of history detecting the anomaly?

He opened his eyes to see that Preceptor Illiance was watching him unblinkingly. Illiance said, "It is remarkable that a human being could take something from the person of one of the Followers without his being aware."

"Like I said. I comprehend dogs."

"Do you think it wise to appropriate belongings that are not yours?"

"Oh ho. Look who is asking! You and yours are meddling with artifacts from my age, such as biosuspension coffins, some of which contain people and their possessions. Including me. I happen to know Alpha Yuen was buried with an ancestral serpentine worth at least ten thousand medallions of our money. It is called Arroglint; it is a named weapon and it has its own device in the College of Heralds, and it should have its own collectible bubble gum card. So where is it?"

"I find I am an archaeologist. I peer with great interest at the relicts and remnants of your era."

"Well, I am returning the favor, and doing a bit of peering of my own. I am an academic myself, and a damn good one too."

"I am pleased that you say so. Will you confess that there is a brotherhood of scholars that can and must reach across all the ages of history?"

"Brotherhood?"

"A unity of interest, and a common purpose?" The little Blue Man leaned forward, his eyes intent.

"Well . . . what exactly are we talking about?"

"You must answer."

"Must I? Okay. Yes. All scholars of all ages have something in common. We are all curious bastards, and we poke into things we shouldn't."

That answer seemed to satisfy the little Blue Man. He leaned back and smiled his small, cryptic smile.

"The admission permits me to impose a moral obligation on you. I solicit your assistance and advice."

"My advice is to stop poking where you have no business before something really bad happens to you."

"While no doubt sound enough, I require your advice in another field of mental effort."

"Like what?"

"Man called Beta Anubis, among your other accomplishments, you are a skilled linguist, are you not? You know the spoken language forms of several races of man."

"Do I?"

"You speak Iatric, the language of the Middle Period of the Configuration of Iatric Clades, called the Hormagaunts; you speak Chimerical, the language of the Eugenic Emergency General Command of the Commonwealth of Virginia, called the Chimerae; you speak that which by the highborn is called the Tongue of the Wise, but by the common called Virginian, which is the language of the Delphic Acroamatic Progressive Transhumanitarian Order for the study of Longevity, called the Witches; and that dialect of Merikan called Korrekthotspeek, used of old only by the Order of Psychics, who were a servant race of the Hermetic World Concordat and the earliest known artificial race of man. The Hermeticists in turn used two languages that once were ancient dialects of Anglatino, whose names I do not know. This is noteworthy."

"Must be. You took notes."

"Your knowledge seems extraordinary, as your era is remembered as a Dark Age, when much learning would have been lost to you and your people."

"Well, Dark Ages are when some people make extra-especial efforts not to let some things get forgotten. Lots of sitting around copying old manuscripts by hand goes on."

"Even so, the accomplishment is unusual, Man called Anubis."

"Aw, shucks. You can call me Lance-Corporal Beta Anubis. You make it sound like there is more to boast of than there is. I learned Greek and Latin when I was young, and I had to learn English and Japanese to study the First Space Age. All educated Chimerae speak Virginian as well as Chimerical. But Virginian grew out of a dialect of Anglatino with many Nipponese loan-words and constructions thrown in. Anglatino comes out of Merikan and Spanish; Merikan came from English and Korrekthotspeek; Spanish came from Latin. So it was not that hard to pick up Merikan and Spanish."

Preceptor Illiance opened his mouth and made a shrill, clicking squawk of noise.

Menelaus shrugged. "Yes, I can savvy Savant as well. The Sylphs used it to talk to their Mälzels, back when the Giants decivilized the world. I cannot make that modulator-demodulator squeal, because my throat isn't adapted for it."

Illiance sang a few chords in a tonal language of the Naturalists, and the babbling of waters, the rustle of falling leaves, the bark of fox cubs, and the cry of the loon were in his words.

"Yes, I speak Natural," said Menelaus, scowling. "Probably better than you. You just invited me to sexual congress."

Illiance pursed his tiny lips. "I was taught that was a correct and formal greeting."

"Among the Nymphs, a correct formal greeting *is* an invitation to sexual congress."

"I am a simple man. Our lives conform to an ascetic contour."

"So, no buggery?"

"Not at this time," said the Blue Man, graciously inclining his head. "And how is it you are fluent in a language devised long after your recorded interment date, Lance-Corporal Beta Anubis?"

"I wasn't a medical case. I could thaw periodically, study my surroundings, and reinter."

"You did not have trouble finding a Tomb once you had left it, or negotiating past the various traps and lethalities?"

"Some trouble. The coffins containing the techs who knew how to repair the worn-out coffin machinery were painted white and marked with big red crosses. They were supposed to keep all this stuff somewhere in the Tomb catacombs, in these big warehouses only they knew how to find—buried stores of gear, whole fabrication plants, nanotech-breaking columns, and other appliances of the lost technology of the Second Age."

"They? The Knights Hospitalier?"

Menelaus narrowed his eyes. "You know the name?"

"The Sovereign Military Hospitalier Order of Saint John of Jerusalem, of Rhodes, of Malta, and of Colorado. The Maltese Knights. Yes. I happen to know the name. How do you happen to know it?"

"I found one of their coffins once and puzzled out the cycle to thaw the man out safely. I needed his help to reenter the Tombs."

"What year was this?"

"Why should I answer?"

"As I said, you are under a moral obligation as an academic."

"And if I do not recognize the obligation?"

"Ah . . . your father is still your father, even if you do not recognize his face in its sternness."

"What's that mean?"

"I will have the dogs tear your body to pieces."

Menelaus laughed.

"You do not seem alarmed, Lance-Corporal Beta Anubis?"

"You threaten a Proven member of the Eugenic Emergency General Command of the Commonwealth of Virginia! Good thing for you I left my rock outside. Once you give a weapon a name, our customs do not allow us to bear insult or slight within the weapon's hearing."

"Interesting! And how did this custom arise?"

"Preceptor, let's stick to the previous topic for a second. Do you really think you can affright a Chimera with threats?"

"A Chimera? No."

"They why did you threaten me?"

"I am a simple man, and we make a virtue of direct methods, even if extralegal. We live in the pursuit of an effortless, uncomplicated, unthinking grace of action from an actionless center."

Menelaus scowled. A moment passed in silence, with both men seated on the carpet, staring at each other, neither face showing much expression.

Illiance sat so still, and with such a look of serenity on his features, that Menelaus wondered if the little man had turned off part of his nervous system. It was like trying to win a staring contest with a cat. So Menelaus broke the silence.

"In my time, the record of the early days was lost, like I said. But there is enough evidence that a sufficiently smart man could piece together the clues." Menelaus said, "The named weapons of the Chimerae originally came from the days of the Sylphs, the sky-drifting people, but the secret of their making was lost. It was the only part of their silk airskiffs that was nonbiodegradable, and survived to be found in ruins and wreckages. Each serpentine was a self-contained and self-repairing smartweapon, made of contractile metallic fibers studded with processor nodes and sensors. So they could be used as Seeing Eye dogs in the dark. They could be used as spears or lashes or flails depending on the variability settings, or as shock prods to paralyze, torture, stun, or kill. The serpentines were blood-coded to recognize owners. I suppose the early Chimerae lost the ability to change the blood-recognition codes, so the serpentines had to pass from father to son, and no one could take another family's weapon. In any case, the serpentines could understand human speech, and the onboard weapon-brain would set its own level of lethality depending on its assessment of the nature of the threat."

Illiance blinked in confusion. "Why are you saying this information? What does it import?"

"You asked me. About the source of the custom. I'm telling you. The Chimerae found out they had to act as if every insult was a deadly threat, or otherwise the serpentines would not fight correctly when nothing but honor was at stake. That's why Chimerae introduce their weapons first. Usually the weapon was a lot older and scarier than the man carrying it, not to mention a veteran of a lot more duels and battles."

"You employ suppositious phrasing?"

Menelaus shrugged. "What I am telling you is an educated guess."

He did not mention that he had worked out the theory while he sat there, organizing the scattered clues into a pattern, based on what little he knew of the Chimera history and customs, and what he could extrapolate from their etymology, and the great deal he knew about the serpentines, whose final and perfect form he had designed.

Illiance said, "Thank you. That account has scholastic value."

Menelaus said, "Well, no reason to cheat out of a moral obligation if I don't have to. You're welcome."

"And the year you learned the Natural language?"

"A.D. 6064. I would give you the date in their calendar, but every year was Year One to the Nymphs."

"The Gregorian calendar continues in use by the Sacerdotal Order, who also renounce the Neurosphere, and are nonjurors. It is known to antiquarians for documentary purposes. But in our calendar, the current year is 59485 A.V."

"Hm. In that case, I learned their tongue in what would have been 55034 of your calendar. What event are you counting up from? The invention of agriculture? The Seven Daughters of Eve? The Extinction of the Neanderthals?"

Illiance smiled shyly. "Oh no, you have reversed your calculation. By our reckoning, you were among the Naturalists in the year 63936 A.V.; which stands for Antevindication, or 'Before the Vindication.' You see, we do not count up from a past event. We count down to an event yet to come."

Menelaus put his hand before his face to hide his expression, but his eyes were wide with astonishment, and wet with tears.

"What if the . . . event . . . you hope for never comes?" Menelaus asked, frowning and wiping his face hastily.

"Then our calendar system will be held up to the scorn of whatever creatures possess the mandate of history after we pass into extinction. Or, it may be that they prove to be right-minded creatures, and therefore will admire the serene steadfastness of our hope, even though the hope eventually proved false."

Preceptor Illiance leaned forward and picked up his glass needle, and reloaded his sidearm. "I intuit that you desire to assist my efforts. I am interviewing another disinterred hibernaut, what you call a Thaw. Not only his dialect—he speaks a variant of this tongue puzzling to me—but also his mannerisms and mental frame are obscure to us. Haply, you might perhaps audit the interview and share your conclusions. If you would happen to follow where I walk, perhaps?"

He put the whistle to his lips and silently whistled for his dogs.

3. Mentor Ull

The upper chamber occupied a kidney-shaped space of curving walls and ceilings. It was more like a vacuole swollen in the midst of the ramp (which continued still upward) than it was like a room. The dog things, a Mastiff and a Bulldog, armed with musket and snickersnee, hunkered to one side, and they stood and pricked their ears when Illiance and Menelaus (with Collie and Wolfhound) approached.

There was a Blue Man in the room, seated in lotus position on the carpet, and the split skirts of his long coat made a semicircle around him, glinting with gems. Like Illiance, he was bald. His face was lined, his cheeks sagged into jowls, and his eyes had crow's-feet at their corners. He wore a heavily-lidded, sleepy expression. This was Ull.

Ull was dressed much like Illiance, except that his coat had a simpler snake-pattern of jewels and circuits running through it, making his coat look almost Spartan in comparison with the dazzle of Illiance's.

At his elbow was a small table or plate of glassy coral substance. It had no legs, but was suspended from the ceiling on a curving limb. On the plate was a bowl, a flask, and a circular looking glass.

In the looking glass appeared some scene from another chamber: shadows of a bald and dark-skinned man of heroic proportions, perhaps nude, surrounded by dog things. The man seemed to be crouching, or perhaps seated in a chair. (If so, this was the first chair Menelaus had seen in the camp: even the mess tent served the food on heated mats on the grass.) There was something odd about the man's face and skin, and he seemed to have patches of white frills along his chest and armpits. He was either wearing a cap, or he had no ears. At a guess, he was a Hormagaunt from between A.D. 7000 and A.D. 8000. There was little time for a clear look, since Ull tapped the glass, and the mirror went black.

Illiance without hesitation lowered himself smoothly to sit next to the other. Menelaus took up a position behind him and stood at parade rest, hands behind his back, feet slightly spread, his eyes focused on nothing in particular. Perhaps he was studying the pattern of swirls and striations in the substance of the walls, which seemed to have been grown rather than made.

Ull picked up the bowl and set it before him. He then broke off a nine-inch-wide segment of the table and prodded and kneaded the segment with his fingers until it bent and assumed the shape and size of a bowl.

Next he reached for the flask. There was no cap or cork; the top of the flask dilated when Ull touched it, and he poured out a clear liquid into the bowl. The scent of alcohol entered the chamber, and the air above the bowl was disturbed with invisible steam.

He offered the bowl to the Illiance, who received it in both hands with an inclination of the head. Illiance took out the glass needle he had previously told Anubis was a weapon, dipped it in the bowl, and watched the needle serenely as it turned from white to green. The needle uttered a pleasing chime of noise. Illiance inclined his head again, took up the bowl, sipped three times, uttered an exclamation in his language of sonorous sibilant trills, and passed the bowl back.

Ull went through the same steps in the same order, testing the liquid with a needle, sipping, and uttering a phrase. The difference was that his exclamation was perfunctory, glum, and curt.

Ull, the elder of the two Blue Men, spoke their sonorant language. *"The relict of the before-times who provokes most interest is constrained above. I happen to have entered the second stage of mind-discipline, and inferred the extent of his modifications. The biotechnology is relatively primitive, and relies on microscopic rather than nanoscopic redactions. This implies a binary cellular logic routine, namely, that his whole immune system is programmed to shut down during grafts and repairs. If so, even if we do not know his particular chemical vocabulary, the base-forms of neural logics which are the same across all organisms are open to us. Any number of diseases or parasites could be introduced to produce nausea or pain. I submit that true simplicity and directness implies torment as the recommended approach. . . ."*

Illiance held up an admonishing finger. *"I happen to have presented to you that the relict who stands here-now within-earshot behind me understands our speech-forms. I submit that true simplicity implies to say nothing which might later lead to complex performances, such as explanation, justification, retraction, revisitation, apology, and the like."*

Ull scowled. *"I apprehend your presentment and happen to discard it. No one can learn a language in one day from an isolated speech box."*

Illiance unobtrusively angled the bowl in his hand and caught a shimmering reflection of the hooded figure of Menelaus. The tall man was not looking down, and seemed to be paying attention to nothing. *"He may have found tools from still-operating coffins to open the isolation. He is clever enough to have attempted to use the tent material to block the responder signal."*

"Clever? I happen to think it foolish. The signal is not blocked. He does not know we retain control of the tent material permeability and tension through the mind-discipline."

Illiance leaned back, and raised the bowl for another sip, and sighed, *"He knows now."*

Ull said: *"The Chimerae were bellicose militarists, conforming to a highly artificial life-rigidity. Behold him! He stands like a stiff-spined, blank-eyed manikin! It suggests a low-order intellect!"*

Illiance said: *"It happens to suggest to me that he is too polite to take note of your misjudgment, Mentor."*

Ull said: *"Achieve silence! You will happen to remember who is tutor and superior here! Yours is to learn, not to instruct! Paranoia is both complex and delusive, since it leads to filtering facts to suit theories, and not allowing the serene mind, as still pond, to reflect the true picture of the cosmos. Contemplate this!"*

Illiance, still smiling, touched his fingers to the carpet and then to the top of his own head, a humble gesture. *"With gratitude for your instruction, I shall, Mentor."*

4. Rice Wine

At this point, Illiance craned his head and looked up at Menelaus. "I happen not to know if the customs of the Chimerae allow one of their kind to sit and sip warm rice wine with us. Does your biological composition permit you to partake of such a substance without harm? For us, it is a mild intoxicant, producing euphoria."

Menelaus grunted, knelt, and sat down heavily, reaching out with his hand to pull his feet into a cross-legged position. He did not reach for a bowl. "If I am your guest, my customs permit. If I am your prisoner, you can try to force talky-juice into me, but I'd feel a fool if I took it with my own hand. Besides, I am on duty. What were you fellows talking about just now?"

"The unwisdom of attempting transparent deceptions." Illiance spoke dryly.

"Hm. Interesting topic."

"On what duty do you happen to be?"

"The Academic Command was part of Intelligence Command, in my day. Since my whole chain of command got wiped out by history, that makes me the ranking officer, doesn't it? So I am here to observe and report."

"Report to whom? You know that your Alpha-of-Alphas, the Imperator-General of the Commonwealth, passed away millennia ago, he and all his dynasty."

Menelaus spread his hands. "Do tell? I heard about the event. But, so what? Maybe someone will show up. It pays to stay on your toes, buttons polished and powder dry, nevertheless, because you can never tell when one of the Alphas will pull a surprise inspection. So let me gather some intel. Are you going to introduce me?"

"It would be unsimplistic of me not to! I happened to have committed a gaucherie, for which I now amend. Lance-Corporal Beta Anubis, this one is an Expositor of the Mentor category, which reflects a class of achievement most honored of our way of being: his external-name is Ull."

"He is your CO?"

"I happen not to understand that abbreviation."

"He is your Captain, your Skipper, your Boss, your Big Cheese; the Leader, Drill Instructor, Head Honcho, High Muckety-Muck; your Patron, Patrician, Taskmaster, Top Dog, Loud Fart; he is the Brass, the Brains, the Chief, the Man?"

"You have many words for superiors of rank."

"Chimerae have lots of ranks."

"Among the Simple, we happen not to affix a formal structure, preferring impromptu fluidity. The distinction of Mentor Ull is one of voluntary recognition."

"But he gets to say what's going to happen, right?"

"Ah . . . in essence, yes."

"Thought so."

"Now I must introduce you to him. Do you have any small object on your person you can hand to me? It does not matter what it is."

Menelaus sighed and pulled a fist-sized oblong stone out of a hanging fold of his bulky garment. "This is my honored and ancestral weapon. It is called Rock."

Illiance took it gravely in both hands. "I happened to have understood you to have left this outside? Or so you said."

"I said wrong. A Chimera is never without his weapon."

Preceptor Illiance passed it to Mentor Ull, who held the stone delicately on his fingertips, bowed his head, inspected it for a long moment, before laying it carefully on the carpet. "It is both solid and humble, this stone, and will outlast many of the civilizations of man," said Ull in flawless Iatric.

Menelaus rubbed his chin and cheek. "Pleased to meet you. I—uh—didn't know you were savvy to my language."

"Your word-forms are not particularly difficult," said Ull ponderously. "It is your thought-forms that elude."

"Thank you, sir. Um. I think."

5. *Myth Divarication*

Mentor Ull pointed with one slender, powder blue finger up toward the curving ceiling

"Above awaits a relict from a relatively shallow stratum of the dig, but who may have information of allure to us. Carbon-14 decay dating puts him at era 63000 of our calendar, which is roughly 5200 years after the founding of Richmond. We happen to have some common language with him, but the particular dialect and declensions confound us. If it should occasion that you feel yourself morally obligated to translate between us accurately and clearly, then the flow of the events you set into motion, and our own, can become as one stream, without turbulence or complexity: a serene intersection."

Menelaus asked, "Your prisoner upstairs, what could he know that would be so, ah, alluring to you, who live in this age?"

Ull said, "Like faded ink, the origin of the Tombs is fogged, and overwritten with the illuminations and shades of myth, and wish, and distortions imparted by interest or inattention. Yet the Tombs from all the continents retain the same basic features. All are armed and buried, but not far from some obvious landmark, usually an equestrian statue or horse-totem held in reverent regard by those who dwell nearby: sacred ground. Next, the Tombs are in remote but not inaccessible places. Third, there are always watchmen posted, who are thawed automatically when a stranger approaches. These watchmen emerge from a buried gatehouse always of the same design: smaller coffins for the watchmen; larger stalls for their white horses, a breed called Neohippus, which is otherwise extinct. Fourth, the hidden doors, when found, are marked with a cross formed by the intersection of four chevrons, shaped like an eight-pointed star. Can parallelism explain such coherence of items, enduring beyond the reach of records?"

"Well, if you ask me," said Menelaus, rolling his eyes to the ceiling thoughtfully, "if they were not near landmarks, no clients could find them, but if they were too near places where people were, they'd be looted. So just by a natural selection, they would tend to end up in such locations. And the watchmen take on the protective coloration of successful Tombs, and so adopt their emblems. How's that for a theory?"

"Ingenious," murmured Illiance.

"It enjoys a certain superficial feasibility," Ull said coldly, "but there are legends of Tomb systems buried even deeper, beneath the crust and well into the mantle, beyond where geophones or other seismic instruments reach. Maintaining such a system would require interconnection by depthtrain, which implies central organization. Only the examination of a working Tomb with a working depthtrain station would confirm the theory.

"By great good fortune," continued Ull, "It so happens that a Tomb almost intact, suffering only minor surface damage, has been opened to our inspection, and the major automatic weapon systems hindered to such a degree that it allows the recovery of some coffins and the relicts therein to be examined. It would be erratic, the product of an overcomplicated sense of deference, not to exploit the opportunity."

"That's a debatable point," drawled Menelaus. "You don't want people pawing through your stuff while you are asleep, do you? And you don't know what you are meddling with, or who or what you might stir up."

Ull waved the objection aside with a small motion of his hand. "Our order is unattached to such formalities and scruples. The opportunity exists, and we exist, and our desires match with the facts of reality without undue transformation or distortion.

"The course suggesting itself is a natural one, and elegant," Ull continued dourly, not smiling. "We take coffins from each layer, finding those on the upper layers whose knowledge of the immediate past allows us to find and communicate with those in the middle layers; and, when found, their knowledge is used to find and communicate with those in the deep. Soon, the knowledge of who and what made the Tombs, and for what purpose, will not be a matter of legend, rumor, and speculation. It will be the living and firsthand memory of someone in the Tomb itself. The Thaws will give their testimony and the Tomb will, by its own nature, reveal the secrets of the Tomb."

Menelaus said, "Let me ask you straight up, gentlemen. What secret are you seeking? What is your point? You are committing what anyone would regard as a trespass and a crime of monstrous proportions. What do you need so badly that it is worth it?"

Illiance spoke up. Instead of answering, he asked, "Lance-Corporal Beta Anubis, are you familiar with the mathematical theory of divarication? Perhaps the question startles you—You have an expression on your face that is odd. You are staring."

Menelaus said, "No, this is my normal expression. Merely the cast of my face. But divarication theory is a particular study of mine."

Illiance tilted his head. "A historian has interest in mathematical theory? Unexpected."

Menelaus uttered a noncommittal grunt. "What about it?"

Illiance said, "Divarication theory was originally devised in relation to information transmission systems, such as iterations of legacy computer data. To make a copy of a human mind into a machine emulation is fraught with risk of madness, merely because maintaining sanity is a difficult balance of a large number of information streams. A healthy informational system has self-correction features, methods of checking falsehoods, data mutations, and encouraging true ergo accurate iteration."

Menelaus said, "The theory is more general than that. It puts numbers to the tendency of information to degrade. Any kind of information. It actually was first developed by some forgotten genius and really swell guy at the dawn of the Second Space Age in relation to the problem of how to stop cancer and cell degradation during super-long-term hibernation. The ability of the cell to reproduce itself within a host under ultraslow life processes was analyzed as an information transmission problem. So the divarication mathematics are general enough that they can also apply to social information passed from generation to generation."

Illiance asked, "How does this happen to fall into the realm of interest of an historian?"

Menelaus said, "Simple enough. What gets passed between generations can be analyzed as transmission of information. Simple dramatic narratives are easier to recall than messy historical facts. Flattering narratives are even easier, so founders tend to turn into demigods. Simpler rules are also easier than complex ones, so stagnant societies tend to turn into parodies of themselves. When the transmission of social norms and mores is hindered or halted, the society starts to die. My particular field of interest is studying the symptoms of cultural decline in dying societies."

Illiance tilted his head as if puzzled and said, "We are indeed fortunate—abnormally so—that someone with your qualifications should happen to have been unearthed from the Tombs. Your studies will find particular application in our project."

Menelaus said, "Which is what, again, exactly?"

Ull said, "We are seeking the source of a legend."

Menelaus said, "What legend?"

To answer, Ull handed him a sheet of silk on which characters in the Iatrocrat language were printed. It was not smart material: the letters did not form or change under his fingers.

It was a fragment.

6. He Who Waits

. . . Giants walked the Earth in those days, and destroyed the Antecpyrotic World in storms of fire. Only one righteous man, with his wife and sons and their wives, was spared, for benevolent posthumans carried him in a flying ship, and a complete DNA library of all fauna and flora, into the cool air above the midst of the sea, where the flames did not reach.

In the farthest times they said his name was Satyavrate, and in the times not so far, they said Deucalion whose wife was Phyrra, but in the true world, is remembered that the survivors of the burned Earth were called Simon and Glinda, who were brother and sister, king and queen, man and wife, warlock and witch. These wed each other in incest, and brought forth the race of the long-lived ones, or Longevitalists.

The astrologers of the Longevitalists contemplated eternity, and read the fate of man in the stars; and they learned our world to be no more than a bauble, like a semiprecious stone meant for the smallest finger of a great lady, but held to be of low account by her, owned by star-monstrosities of unlimited mind from beyond Aldebaran, destined to come after an immensity of time has passed, at the End of Days. Learning these things, the weight of these infinities smothered their souls, and so they became Witches.

The Witches were starved for length of life, and never fully achieved it, for they flinched away from the Dark Knowledge.

Their life-hunger drove the Witches mad, and they destroyed the machinery of the forgotten age that came before them, and when it came time to die, they did not die, but called upon the hills and mountains to fall on them, that they might be buried in the ground by the thousands and tens of thousands, freezing themselves like lungfish in winter. The only machines they did not trouble were the aestivation coffins, and they thought to pass the aeons in timeless slumber until an aeon arrived when death itself should perish.

But a time came when the Witches grew aware that there were other coffins buried deeper than theirs, giants and flying men from an earlier age, pale men and servants of the machines who worshipped Ghosts of Iron, and did not serve the living trees, the sun and water and moon and fire, sacred to the witchkindred.

In their jealousy and rage, the witches doused themselves with consecrated wine, and dressed their men in the skins of bears smeared with opiates, and with fennels stalks and besoms in hand, made as if to tear these older coffins out of the ground.

They came upon the corpse of a pale white horse, a horse of a breed that does not exist in nature, and the corpse came to life at their touch.

Now, they held the lore that such a horse as this was the steed of the messenger who goes to summon Death from his house among the stars of the Hyades beyond Aldebaran. The Crone of Witches slew the horse with her athame, her magic knife, to offer sacrifice to the Biosphere and strengthen it, and to curse the Infosphere, where the ghosts live, and weaken it.

Yet by digging up the Tombs, the Witches unforethoughtfully and unforeseeing woke the most ancient and the first of all the Revenants there buried.

Forth he came from the deepest and darkest pit of the Tombs, and in his hand he held a wand as pale as mist from which drops of fire fell, whose touch was slumbering death. On his head was a crown of roses red as blood, and scallop shells white as bone, which he wore to show that he was judge over land and sea alike. And the thorns of the roses pierce his skull, and he is mad for a season and sane for a season, and only his wife makes him sane. Some say it is the winter season when he is sane, and others say it is high summer, but some say it is no season of Earth when his wits shall return, but only when his wife returns from where she walks among the stars.

This one turned and called into the dark pit behind him. IS IT YET, THE AEON?

And many voices answered him. *IT IS NOT YET!*

He called into the dark pit behind him. IS SHE COME, MY BRIDE?

And many voices answered him. *SHE IS NOT COME!*

And he called into the darkness of the old Earth. THEN ARISE! ARISE AND SLAY, FOR THEY DARE WAKE ME WHEN MINE AEON IS NOT YET, AND MY BRIDE IS NOT COME.

And the many fell voices answered: ***LET NONE DARE WAKEN HE WHO WAITS, LEST HIS WRATH AWAKE!***

And one hundred knights on ninety-nine pale horses rose from the deep, old places of the Earth, and in their hands were pale white staves. They slew the Witches by thousands and by ten thousands, and never a mark was on them, for the staves slew by a touch; and also not a single corpse was ever brought back to their coven houses for lamentation and wake-drinking, because the knights drew the bodies down into the mountain with them when they descended, and the mountain closed after them, and no one can say where the door now lies.

And that one knight who bears the sign of the Cross, he whose steed the Witches slew, he was afoot during this terrible battle, and he could not return to the deep when the trumpet sounded from below the mountain roots, and all the cavalry of the underworld rushed past him faster than his feet could pursue.

He was left outside when the great door closed, and he pounded on the rocks and wept, but the doors would not open.

Some say he still serves the Judge of Ages from that day to this, and walks on moonless nights among living men in secret, wrapped in shadow and leaning on his pale white staff, and listening to idle talk, seeking any man who believes the tomorrows will be brighter than the chores and sorrows of today: and those dreamers of dreams who answer him yea, he comes by night and takes away.

A time came when the Witches repented their folly, and they set up shrines and images of him to serve, and they sacrificed bears and tortoises and swans, who are sacred to him.

At the appointed time, and also thereafter, a great voice issued from the deep of the mountain, and prophesied against the Witches, saying, "You have forgotten eternity; therefore, the judgment of the Judge of Ages against your age is that forgetfulness shall consume your . . ."

7. Chimera Lore

Ull said, "I see by your eye movement that you can understand the ideographs of the Iatrocracy period. This is a fragment from a tome of instruction used, we theorize, by the Clades of the Black Sea area, called *The Understanding of Dark Sentences,* which alleged to gather the surviving tales from an even earlier period: but no record remains of the origin of the tale."

Menelaus handed back the silk. "So what did the Judge of Ages say against the Witches?"

Ull said, "Is there no record of this legend among your people, Beta Anubis?"

Menelaus shrugged. "The Tombs were erected by some civilization or civilizations from before the fire, the Ecpyrosis that burned the world. There have been people from every era, either for medical reasons, or merely to escape the age they live in, who try to dig into the Tombs, copy the technology, and they have added to them and modified them, and help defend them. So there is layer after layer of accretion. No Chimerae from the time of the Social Wars knew where the Tombs came from, or cared much about stories about them. Some of the entrances were known locations with still-active weapon systems, and so we generally steered clear."

Ull said, "But you are an academic, and you entered the Tombs."

Menelaus said, "The level I entered was staffed by Chimera, part of Medical Command. There were antiques, people from older coffins, that I knew our top brass from time to time thawed out and consulted with at a high level, deciding policy. As best I knew, these were older Chimerae, from the Pre-Proscopalian Era. Republican times. We did not mess with them. Some of them still had living relatives running major cities, for one thing. We dealt with them like you would deal with a foreign power: We had official emissaries, and a strict code saying what was our jurisdiction, and what was Old Chimera jurisdiction, whose soil belonged to who. But the old-timers were not awaked except once every few decades, so Medical Command ran the levels open to us to suit ourselves."

Ull said suspiciously, "And you heard no rumor from this older generation, who had built these Tombs?"

Menelaus said, "What? You think the Old Chimera thawed out the frozen Witches for a chat? We denied them recovery rights. If any of them woke up in our era, we sent them back down into the Tombs at gunpoint. But asking who built the Tombs? I mean, someone must have invented the firebow, or the wheel, or the stirrup, or domesticated the very first dog, but who knows his name?"

The Blue Men started to speak, but Menelaus raised his voice and spoke over them: "No more! Now it is time for me to ask questions. What the hell is your interest in all this? You gents cannot possibly expect me to believe you are engaged in a massive looting and Tomb-robbing expedition merely to satisfy some intellectual curiosity?"

8. Diffusion and Parallelism

Illiance said, "Mentor Ull believes there is a single founder to the Tombs, and his work was copied by many cultures through diffusion. I happen to support the theory that the various elements found at various sites are examples of parallel evolution.

"Since the ultralongterm-hibernation technology exists, and since the alleged founder (whether dead or in slumber) could not know nor prevent any person with the resources and inclination from using that technology to erect competing Tombs systems, if there were not forces herding the Tomb systems into parallel similarities, we would have many diverse Tombs, each with its unique architecture and technology—instead we have what seems a single, monolithic, worldwide system continuous and unchanged throughout history."

Ull said, "The similarities are too statistically improbable to admit of such facile attempts at explanation. Locust records dating from after the beginning of mental-electronic history (which we take to be more reliable than written history or oral tradition), contains accounts of the horsemen of the pale horses who rise from the Tombs. They are seen to ride when plagues strike, or wars, or whenever there are many of the dying to gather. The two riders approach sickbeds and asylums, hospitals and temples housing the infirm, asking if any within have hope that the future will discover cures for their ills. Those who have no hope, they will not take. Accounts also say these knights act in the name of one same founder. In the lowest of levels, from the earliest of days, from the Second Age of Space, or the First Age, there is a sleeping figure whom it is death to disturb, a lord of the dead who sleeps surrounded by his knights.

"He is known by many names: Charlemagne, Karl or Kralj; Frederick Barbarossa or Finn McCool; Holger Danske, William Tell or Thomas the Rhymer or Rip Van Winkle; Brian Boru, Montrose, and Arthur; but it is always said that he will arise when the people have need of him, and deliver judgment against the age.

"If the age has forgotten the purpose of history, or the rulers have fallen into corruption, or if the people forget that an enemy comes from the stars of the Hyades to enslave the children of men at the End of Days, then the Judge of the Ages will overthrow the age and destroy their works, sparing only such children of theirs as vow to keep and remember the Year Foretold, and prepare against that day."

"Spooky!" commented Menelaus. "My dam used to tell me that if I didn't go to sleep on time, but stayed awake talking to my brothers, my voice would call the Red Indians down from the hills, because some still survived from the old days, and still kept their old ways. She told me how they could reach in the window without making any noise with their long, strong, terrible arms, and cut off the top of my head, hair and scalp and all, with their cold, stone tomahawks. When my brothers woke the next morning, I'd be dead, my brains slithered out over the pillow, my eyes as still and white as two peeled eggs, and my mouth hanging open in a scream that would never come. I can assure you, that tale gave me spiders in my belly! In hindsight, I think she just wanted me to hush up at lights-out. But, a tale to give you the willies, nonetheless."

Mentor Ull, his face nonplussed, turned his head slowly and gazed at Preceptor Illiance. Both men, with furrowed brows, listened. Eventually Ull said ponderously, "I believe your mother's tale was a fabrication, but I happen not to apprehend any immediate relevance to the discussion."

Menelaus said, "No? My dam warned me there were those in the hills, old things, that might come down upon me if I called them to me. And you are meddling with something older and deadlier. If he was real, this Judge of Ages, and he has people to guard his burial grounds, what happened to them? Where are they? And what are they waiting for?"

Ull and Illiance rose gracefully to their feet.

Mentor Ull said, "That perhaps will be the first question to ask the relict. Shall we go above?"

Without a further word or gesture, the two Blue Men drifted up the ramp to the next level.

6

The Testament of Soorm the Hormagaunt

1. The Hormagaunt

There were three more dog things in the chamber on the next level above. Two were hunkered to one side, muskets in their paws, watching the prisoner and pricking up their ears with every movement.

Another dog thing, this one with the more intelligent face of a black Sheepdog, crouched on a stool at a table. Like the table in the chamber below, albeit larger, this table was a thin sheet of polished coral suspended from the ceiling. The Sheepdog was bent over what seemed to be a polygraph—the tracks and pulses of light from the glass plate atop the instrument corresponded to typical patterns of heartbeat, electroencephalogram, and galvanic skin response.

However, if it were a polygraph, it did not require any tubes or wires to take a reading from the subject.

The subject was seated in a chair, rudely but solidly built of branches lashed together, with a seat and back of woven willow.

He was a massive man, over six feet tall, but with such prodigious breadth of chest and shoulders as to appear like one of the Giants of old. His skin was dark, like seal pelt, because he was covered from heel to crown in fine, thick, dark hair. He had no nose, merely two tiny slits above a very wide mouth.

Only his palms and the area around his mouth and eyes showed his skin beneath, which was orange yellow, and the rings of orange around his mouth gave him a clown-makeup look, and his ringed eyes make him look like a raccoon.

The man had no visible ears, merely a dimple at either side of his skull, and his neck was so thick that it sloped into the massive planes of his shoulders evenly, given him a bullet-headed, almost torpedo-like aspect. The white frills down his chest and under his armpits seemed to be gill tissue. His waist was blubbery and legs like columns. His feet were almost comically large, swim-fin shaped and covered with a coarser and darker hair, scabrous, almost like the quills of porcupine, emerging from red orange scaly integument. His heels boasted an impressive set of spurs.

The seat of the chair divided, to allow a bulky tail to hang down. It looked something like an otter's tail, but with flukes of cartilage and membrane folded like Chinese fans against its length. At the tip was a barb like a scorpion's tail, complete with a venom sac, swollen and purplish.

The man raised his hand in greeting. Menelaus saw the fingers were webbed, and that the velvet tips hid retractable claws like those of a cat.

His eyes were not only different colors, they were different species: his left eye was pale, with a square pupil like that of a goat. The right eye was dark, with a bright gold pupil shaped like the letter *W*.

Menelaus wondered if, like the eye of a cuttlefish, this right eye had more than one set of receptor cells, called fovea, along the back of the eyeball. Cuttlefish distort their whole eye to change focus rather than using a lens, like humans, and they can see polarization of light.

The seated man turned one of his lunatic-looking eyes toward Menelaus, but he had the other eye tilted, like the eye of a chameleon, independently of the first, and it was looking at the Blue Men.

His voice was a rumble: "Han forwityng yon fremde not ken my tongue. Be ye tongue-witty?"

Menelaus raised his palm by way of greeting and answered him. "My lowely tonge is naught unweedle ne unkonnynge. I speke Leche. Assent ye to be apposed by twa wee pers lordynges?"

"Am naught looth ne drede," said the big man with a chuckle of expansive good humor. "Find me servysable, who has none been hende weel-dressed muchel mee!"

And he pulled back his lips, revealing an impressive set of tusks. In addition to the molars and incisors of an omnivore, his mouth had a pair of serpent fangs and what looked like an extra row of shark teeth. When he laughed, his nostrils (which had been pinched shut) opened and gasped air. Menelaus listened, and tried to guess at the capacity of the lungs.

Whatever the psychological reason was that required a captor to stand over his captive was obviously not present in the Blue Men. Both Illiance and Ull, without any word, sat themselves at the feet of the huge dark man, spines straight, feet in lotus position, wrists resting on soles.

Menelaus looked down at Illiance and spoke in Iatric. "Small wonder you could not follow his speech. This is not High Iatric, but an earlier variant of the tongue. Old Iatric, or Leechcraft, is closer to Winter-Queen period Natural, the language of the Nymphs."

Illiance said, "I am not familiar with this dialect."

"I would call it separate language. Leechcraft was spoken between A.D. 6800 and 7300, along the northern coasts of Eurasia, from the British Isles through Scandinavia and Siberia, which were all warm and green at that time. The Yakutsk Analeptic Empire adopted, changed, and spread the language north across an open and ice-free polar sea to Canada, which at that time was temperate, and south past Lake Baikal to Mongolia, which at that time was jungle. The language you and I are speaking comes from a later period, when the Therapeutae ruled the northern hemisphere and used the impassible equatorial desert zones as test landscapes: their political order was called Iatrocracy, rule by those who created and were protected against bioweapons. The social order was called Triage."

Illiance said, "This word-use is unexpected. Do we have mutually coherent symbol-correspondence?"

"Triage. I take it you are not familiar with this period? It was not pretty. The near-surface deposits of metal ore were exhausted, and the technology for submantle mining lost, so theirs was a postmetallic civilization. With their biotechnology, there was no practical upper limit on medical techniques, but no upper limit on cost: after everyone over a certain age had mortgaged their arbors and slave-herds and lives and children's lives to the biotech guilds, the Iatrocrats, who rationed the medical care, got to decide who died and who lived and for how long and in what amount of pain, so the guilds did not give a damn who collected taxes or led armies. They were the real rulers. The geriatric elite forced lesser orders to donate their organs and glands and life spans to them, and could live for centuries, until killed by violence or accident.

"Technically speaking, the word *Hormagaunt* refers only to their heavily modified military-caste biofacts. The ruling caste biofacts were called Iatrocrats. The donor caste were harvested of their organs and children.

"The Theraputae arose in the northern hemisphere in the seventy-third century, growing the first walled cities and conquering the surrounding Nomads. By the end of that century, a biotechnological revolution created the Clades, who formed a third caste of technical and mercantile bourgeoisie or burg-dwellers. They were mass-produced twins or clones. Their complete genetic uniformity allowed them to program their immune systems to produce allergens which would sicken and drive off outsiders and strangers, so each walled city or hive-dwelling could stay isolated. By the seventy-fourth century, the Triage system of genetic feudalism ruled the globe."

Illiance said, "Remarkable. Few records survived their global wars with the Locusts. We knew there was a biotechnological caste system, but did not know its origin date."

"Interesting but irrelevant, I guess. This guy here is from the earliest period. Or his language is. Unless his slumber was interrupted, he would not know any more about the Iatrocracy than Ethelred the Unready would know about the world in Queen Victoria's time."

Illiance nodded thoughtfully. "If I knew who those personages happened to be, the contrast would no doubt be quite illuminating."

During this, Ull sat without speaking but regarded the huge and furry man from beneath half-lidded eyes.

"What was it that the Hormagaunt said?" asked Illiance.

"He said he had a premonition that the foreigners, meaning you gentlemen, would not understand his tongue, and he asked me if I were fluent. I answered that my humble tongue was neither feeble nor ignorant. I told him I spoke Old Iatric. I asked him if he agreed to be questioned by the two, small blue superior officers. He said he was neither unwilling nor afraid, and that he was willing to serve, even though he had not been well served much himself."

Ull said, "We are not *superior officers*."

"Do you not give the orders here, sir?" Menelaus proffered him a stiff-armed salute.

Ull snapped, "Sit! Do not call me *sir*!"

Menelaus looked around and, seeing no other chair, gathered his metallic robes and sat on the fragile-looking table, which wobbled under his weight. The black Sheepdog watching the oscilloscope bared her teeth at him, flattening her ears, but did not voice any objection.

Ull said more calmly, "The Simplifiers eschew psycholinguistic rigidities. My words happen to be suggestions, which, should you follow, produce a benevolent coincidence."

"Well," said Menelaus, "whether it is a coincidence or not, I know his language and can translate for you. I suggest you record everything, so you can send it to your Intelligence Bureau later for confirmation and analysis—"

Illiance said, "No formal military institution sends us."

"I meant your University Department. Or your Editor-in-Chief. Or your Chief Priest. Or maybe your Pirate Chief."

Ull made a small but irked motion of his fingers. "We come to question, not to be questioned."

"Roger that. What questions do you have?"

The man gave his name as Soorm scion Asvid.

2. The Phastorling

The conversation was in Leech:

"I don't understand why you carry a rock. Your name is not Rock, is it?"

"No, Soorm scion Asvid. My name is Sterling Xenius Anubis, Beta. Call me Anubis, which is my *agnomen* or victory title. I just carry a rock so my superiors won't cite me for being out of uniform. It's my weapon."

"Not impressive! My weapons cannot be taken from me. Let my sterile intrusives and life-codes be brought forth out of my Tomb, and I can equip you with stench glands that will spray a stinging foam, and melt a foeman's eyeballs and his brain lobes behind them."

"Tempting. No one likes a sterile intrusive better than I! But I don't have access to the Tombs. I am, like yourself, for the moment, a prisoner here, at the beck and call of the wee blue lordlings."

Soorm narrowed his cuttlefish eye and goggled with his goat eye when Menelaus said *for the moment*.

"So my name is not Rock, but my name will be Mud, if you do not answer the Blue Men's questions. The older one in the plain coat is Ull, and the one in the jeweled coat is Illiance. The one with fewer gaudies on his coat is the boss, but they pretend as if no one is in charge."

"He is not the boss."

"What do you mean?"

"How well do they understand our tongue?" This time Soorm pointed both his eyes at Ull. He also opened his mouth and flicked one of his two tongues, as if tasting the air like a snake.

"They can follow the gist. Many of the words are cognates."

"Then I mean that he is not the boss."

"Do you have electroreceptor organs, as a shark does, to sense electrical activity? Radio waves? To find the transmission point of signals reaching this camp?"

Soorm made a huge snorting, snuffling noise, and spread wide his massive arms. "What makes you think I would trick myself out with such trumpery and folderol? Do you take me for a spy? I am fisherman. The very idea is comedic to excess!"

"I am from before your time, and so if I offend, it is unintentional. I was given to understand that the Hormagaunts trafficked in such things."

"*Hermenu-gargant* is not the correct term. Mine is a life concocted of high and secret craft. Correct to call me a Hermeneutic Gargantua; even more correct, a Phastorling."

Menelaus looked down at Illiance and said in High Iatric, "He says he is not a Hormagaunt but a Phastorling."

Illiance said back in the same tongue, "The word itself means scion or masterwork of *Pastor*. Ask him if he is a follower of a biotic scientist, mentor, and philosopher named Reyes y Pastor."

The eyes of Menelaus grew bright at that name, but he raised his hand to his face, pretending to wipe his nose, so that the mortals in the room would not look into his eyes, and quail. When his eyes were dim, and that ferocity of superintelligence gone, he lowered his hand.

Soorm said in Leech, "I understood that question. Yes, I am one of Cunning Pastor's clients—or, to be specific, the client of his client. My patron Asvid is under fealty to Cunning Pastor's brood-hold, an organization which is called the Hermetic Order. My full name is Soorm scion Asvid scion Pastor."

Illiance said, "This relict is the earliest form of Hormagaunt than any of which we have record. Ask him for what cause he deviated from the biological practices of the Naturalists?"

When Menelaus translated the question, Soorm puffed out his chest, and Menelaus wondered how the creature's rib cage was constructed, since it was able to swell out far wider than a man's chest.

Soorm said angrily, "We have performed a biotic dialectic with the Natural Order, by our antithesis to nature, we have overcome and incorporated their unique legacies and traits! Darwin favors us! Our creations shall rise to oppose the Hyades on the Last Day! The Naturals swerved from the man-fate, not us! They are anachronisms, the atavists, the past-lookers! *They* are the deviants!"

Menelaus made a placatory gesture. "At ease, mister, please! No one is accusing you of anything! Not only do I not know who or what you are talking about, but those conflicts, whatever they were about, were settled four thousand years ago. *Thousand,* as in ten centuries of years. No one is blowing a trumpet for those battles now."

Soorm subsided like a sullen volcano, and then his skull almost split in an alarmingly sharkish grin. "Don't itch your rash, Old-stock! I have a tweaked neuroendocrinal system, oriented to aggress, and if I build up a head of steam, I got to blow the whistle, or blow a gasket. You should be nape-hairs-up around me only when I am not making any noise."

Illiance said to Menelaus in High Iatric. "Translate that last, if you please. Is he a Cyborg? I happen never to have heard of steam-powered biomechanisms. I ventured to believe such things were children's fictions."

Menelaus said, "It is a metaphor. He means that unexpressed anger continues to exasperate him subconsciously, and therefore it is safer to express it on impulse."

Illiance shook his blue head doubtfully. "Surely the mind-structures of the early men cannot be so different from our own! We have no such preservation of the unexpressed. Is this a metaphysical belief? Among us, to quell an untoward impulse of action is not to act. Quelling is considered the Left Hand of Life: to be still, to be silent, to be unmindful. This is the open door toward serenity."

Menelaus answered in the same language: "Preceptor, I am just telling you he operates by the model that says unexpressed emotions continue to exist in his brain somewhere, and can act on their own without his leave. It's not something Chimerae believe either. We don't trifle with ideas that sound like demon-possession or blame-passing. That is Witch-stuff. Or maybe he has extra brain matter that acts on its own."

Mentor Ull raised his hand and spoke. "This is not to allure our attention. Ask him about the Tombs."

"Pretty damn cold," was Soorm's comment, once the question was translated. "Old too, or so I hear."

Deep lines appeared to either side of the slightly quivering mouth of Menelaus as he translated the remark.

Illiance and Ull nodded sagely. *"He answers simply, as we would,"* said Ull to Illiance in Locust Intertextual. *"Let us proceed with awe and caution: he may be profound, despite that he is a relict of the before-time."*

"Don't make the translator laugh," muttered Menelaus through tense lips in Natural to Soorm, which was the language of the Nymphs. Soorm just cocked his overlarge cuttlefish eye at him in reply.

Ull and Illiance debated the wording of a more precise question in soft and liquid tones.

Eventually, Soorm answered:

3. Ill Hunt

I can answer what I know of the origins of the Tombs in a long breath or two.

The Tombs are older than the world, or, at least, older than the life-craft, which is the only part of the world of concern to the Phastorlings.

The Tombs are ancient beyond any surviving record. Of course, my people keep no records, and neither did the Nymphs who ruled the world before us, nor (once the Clade system was introduced) do we share information between Clades. Before the Nymphs, there is some dim lore of pre-Natural-type creatures, humans or humanlike, who had not yet domesticated all living things to human use: Chimerae and their Kine, Witches and their Moreaus, Ghosts and their Savants, and other legend-beings. They were human, but controlling so little of the biotic world, and making so few modifications or adaptations to their nervous and muscular and glandular systems, that they can hardly be called human at all. In that sense, the Tombs are older than biocivilization.

The Tomb structures themselves are not alive, as our houses and burgs are—ah, were. They have some sort of mind, but the defensive systems are based on energy, fire, iron, stone, and none of our poisons or disease-bearing microbes have any effect on the iron doors. Our finest wasps cannot dig through; our strongest mastodons cannot break through.

Not just me and my warband, or, later, my Clade, but many of us in many parts of the Endlesswood besieged the Tombs, and slew the weak and sick who tried to escape our culls.

There is a legend, of course, that to disturb the Tombs risks waking He Who Waits, who is the first man buried there, and the eldest patient. His voice will rise from the ground, and demand, "Is it yet, the aeon?" and "Is she come, my bride?"—and if there is no answer, many voices will cry out, "Let no man waken He Who Waits, lest his wrath awaken!" and all the soldiers of forgotten ages will rise up from the mausoleums and crypts, and with their forgotten weapons of forgotten science, lay waste the Endlesswood.

I know the legend to be merely words, for no such voices spoke, and only the cadre of men set in hibernation in and about the doors woke when we besieged the Tombs.

What is the Endlesswood? It is the world-forest. Since yours is a world of ice, I must explain that at one time this ground on which we stand was beneath tree cover, so ancient and so vast that trees two hundred feet tall and two thousand years old were considered saplings.

No, I do not know what part of the world this is. Nor does it matter: one world-forest of interlinked arboreal life reached from Antarctica through Patagonia, across the Isthmus of Mexico to Laurentia, across the Bering land bridge to Angaraland, Sino-Korea, Kazakhstania, Baltica, and Eurafrica as far north as Fennoscandia and as far south as the Madagascar peninsula. The sempivirens was the main form of the world-forest, and the breeds were biomodified to grow in the glacier of Antarctica and melt it, or in the Sahara and water it. In this way, the Phastorlings proved they could match the wealth and accomplishments of ancient men who ruled a rich and golden world, back before the Giants arose.

A black squirrel could run from one hemisphere to the other and never touch the ground, and so could a squad of hunting leopards sent out by the Iatrocrats. We grew our wigwams, mansions, and burgs from the same ecological niche as orchids and lianas, organisms that grew out of trees. In the branches and crotches of the larger trees we grew plantations and arbors and groves whose roots also never touched the ground, and whose leaves never saw open sky, nor drank sunlight undimmed by endless canopy above.

The only break in the endless world-forest surrounded the great doors of the buried Tombs, for the roots of the eternal trees could not break the armor, and not take deep root. When one traveled from branch to branch, each broader than a canal, one would come of a sudden across a glade, and the trees would form a great circle surrounding a place of blinding sunlight and species of grass that grew nowhere else on the world. It was an empty place, like a lake or little sea. The blue sky that only canopy-dwellers saw reached down almost to the ground there.

There were not enough diurnal creatures living at ground level to be adapted to grazing of these grasses, and ground-level monsters departing of the forest would be dazed and maddened by the sunlight. So in these glades, and nowhere else, the eternal war of predator and prey was halted, and peace reigned. For that reason we Phastorlings called the groves accursed, and the donors knew the doors to the lands of the slumbering dead were near.

The doors were the escape from our world into a lower world, an invitation to escape our world and our Way, and that we cannot permit. So we watched and warded and slew those who drew near.

Yes, we fought to prevent our sick or wounded or hopeless or helpless from reaching the Tombs and entering hibernation.

The biological material of the sick belonged to us, you see, and preserving the weak through hibernation and hope of medicine was against our Way. Why should a crippled man with a perfectly good set of lungs, liver, heart, or other glands be allowed to take such treasures from us? And bury them! Inefficient, ineffective! If he is done with his organs, we harvest. If he is done with his meat, we feast. If the sickling is a woman afflicted by disease, but her womb is still sound, we rape.

Our art knows how to keep the womb alive long after brain and limbs are dead and dismembered, and the other organs harvested. The *Hermeneutic-Gargantua* genus among us uses this method to produce scions, for we neither marry nor are given in marriage, we neither age nor, save by violence, die, and so our generations are not born, but made. The Clades and the donors arrange things otherwise, but such is the Phastorling way.

But we learned through hard lessons that there was a limit to the Tomb leaguer. If you killed a sickling too close to the doors, the doors would open fire. From deserters and survivors of other bands—like I said, we did not swap information—I also learned that beforegoers and ancient ones risen from buried coffins and dressed in bright armor would from time to time behold the hunts of man-prey and feasts of man-flesh before their doors, and make a sortie or sally, slaying whom they encountered.

We had to set our picket line far from the doors. A mile was safe, two miles was safer, safest of all was to make sure the sicklings were too sick to reach the doors at all: it was the custom to introduce venom into hunting cats to drive them rabid and drive the cats by instinct-lock into the terrain circling a Tomb, or impregnate the smallest nits and mites and midges with fevers of several deadly strains, and send them as clouds to hang before Tomb doors, for the energy-cannon of the most ancient world could not open fire on a crowd of flies or a clowder of cats.

4. Interment

My own interment into the Tombs? It was unremarkable.

From time to time the sicklings, acting in a fashion unlike ours, or using a mental discipline unlike our Wintermindedness, would do the one thing we never do, which is, they would take antihistamines and allergy suppressants, so that they could tolerate one another without their bodies reacting, and many donors or dwellers from different Clade could mingle.

They would form—there is not really a word for it in our language. The Nymph word for it is *orgy,* but this implies a union and a cooperation for sexual purposes. You know how pack animals act as one, or a hive of bees, or army ants? It was like that. A man-pack, a man-hive, a man-army.

Of course, such a unity of purpose, even across difference of Clade, each taken from a different point on the biological spectrum—such a thing is unheard of by those who follow the Old True Way, the *astru-do,* the way of the omnicompetent and utterly isolated man. But, hoo! The sicklings were robbing the Clade of the organs they carried, so why would any other taboo hold them in check?

In any case, an *orgy* of these sicklings were driving toward a Tomb hold I was gene-locked by instinct to ward, and I pursued them, and a maniple of my Clade-dwellers with me, and a three-clawed sloth-mastodon.

But the sick were wily enough to lead the chase through the swamp, where my sloth-mastodon was bogged, and the branches of the world-forest there too fine to bear his weight.

To this day, I wonder what happened to Behemodont. That was his name. I grew him from an egg in my own sacs, and I trained him, and he loved me, and I so wanted to eat the steaks and roasts from his ribs and flank when he died. Every time I mounted up the howdah to ride him to battle, where he fought so bravely for me, I salivated, contemplating the rich marbling of his well-designed meat. And now, he is gone forever, eaten not by me, but by time. Ah, how I miss my steed! And the world ecology is changed, and his whole race extinct, and will never come again.

I left him and my Clade-dwellers behind, and pressed on alone. This same pack of sicklings, as it turned out, also were wily enough to know I would take to the swamp waters and approach them from below, for they had seeded the waters with spore.

My gills grew inflamed. When I surfaced, spitting swamp water, a man made of steel with a plume above his metal head, shining, terrible, great, came upon me. He rode a steed like horse crossed with a deer; a shining white drestrier that ran on split hooves and lashed a tail like a lion's tail.

He had lived four thousand years ago, and served an order founded seven thousand years ago. On his surcoat of black he wore a white cross like unto four chevrons all facing inward, and the hems were decorated with images of crouching lions and unicorns: by this I knew him to be a beforegoer, a man of the Bygone, and a protector of the Hospital.

He called out "Gesprecan! Hwām gesecen þū?"

I knew not what the words meant, but I had learned from the sicklings that to survive this challenge I was supposed to cry out, "Yldothane!" Which is the sickling name for the Judge of Ages—but I had no patience for his superstitions or his folly, so instead of speech, I answered by expelling a stench from my buttocks glands and by throwing the barb of my tail toward his heart.

Instantly, he should have died. Instead, my poisons availed nothing but to burn his surcoat.

He struck me with a pointed wand he held in his hand. The word for it in the Nymphs language is *lance,* but the Nymphs also use this word to refer to the barbed male member of cats bred for bestiality intercourse, so I cannot say what term is best. It was like an oryx horn made of wood and tipped with an iron tooth, so I could use a swarm of diggerwasps from my armpit hive to attack and warp the wood. The weapon bent and shattered, and the wasps blinded his steed.

But then he dismounted, tossed the shards of lance aside, and smote me with a knife as long as his arm. It was not a living thing, because when I sprayed it, this knife did not flinch.

If the world were just, I should have been able to flatten him with a stroke of my hand, but justice departed this world long ago. When I grappled him, his metal hull was like the electric eel to shock me, and I heard the motors in his joints whirring and whining, giving him the strength of ten, and I knew I faced a foe from the Age of Machines. His skin was not skin, but armor. It was iron, cold iron, and my claws and great tail availed me nothing.

He struck me through the primary heart, and I swooned. My secondary heart kept me alive, and my deep-diving oxygen stores kept me breathing. I woke buried in soil. The metal man had put me a foot or so under the ground for some reason, and did not harvest me. With difficulty I dug myself up.

Wounded, I could not allow my own Clade to come upon me, because my organs were particularly well designed and rare, and if my men found me weakened, their gluttony for what the Iatrocrats would give in return for my body would overcome their fear of me—and a wounded man cannot provoke fear, even if he has a full spectrum of infectives and biotics still at his command.

And I had perhaps deviated from strict interpretations of the Way, for I needed children, young children, where the donors had no prime specimens, and perhaps I had impressed a Clade-dweller or two into making a donation. They are small of soul, their minds preoccupied by matters of affection and lineage and other trivial things we know to be caused by molecular neurochemistry. A true Phastorling was above mere animal emotions like father-love! But my people had perhaps been afflicted by sentimentality and pettiness.

I was a sickling now, and therefore weak, and the Way of the Phastorlings has no softness for the weak, because our bodies belong to the Clade.

Scenting his steed, and knowing myself lost if I did not, I crawled after my murderer, knowing he would be more likely to grant mercy than my friends.

I remember it began to rain, and this confused the scent, and my bloodloss made me tremble, and so I was very weak. I passed the same outcropping of rock twice and thrice, and knew then I was crawling in circles.

Then the wind blew, and the rains fluttered like a gray curtain and parted: and I saw my slayer, a great armored knight of the early world, suddenly before me. Because the rain deadened my nose and dinned in my ears, I had no warning. One moment he was simply there. Perhaps he rose from the ground. He did not move, and the rain made the ground boil with mud about the golden spurs of his steel boots.

By gestures and signs, for we had very few words in common, I made known to him that I wished to be taken into the presence of the Judge of Ages, the Yldothane. He laughed, and it echoed oddly in his helm, and said, *Is hit nowh, hys yldu?* And then he said, *Is sheo becuman, hys wif?*

I did not know his words, and yet I knew his meaning, and so I said back, "The aeon is not now. His bride is not come."

The knight uttered a sardonic laugh and said, *"Leort nan-mann wecean Hé Hwa ÁbireÞ, læst heos wrœðu biÞ äwaeenlan!"* I needed no translation. Had I not heard from my youth onward the tale of his anger? *Let none waken He Who Waits, lest his wrath be awakened!*

I served the knight in the frozen mortuary for a year and a day, which was the only way to earn the traditional two pence needed to pay the hibernation fee. He did not show to me any Judge, for there was none to show.

5. Soorm and the Unreal Man

What is your question? That I do know. There is no Judge of Ages, no one man or one mind controlling all the Tombs here and there and everywhere around the world. That is a myth invented by the Nymphs.

The Nymphs had to expel their excess populations, and did not have the heart—because they were unevolved, and had not yet achieved the sublime perfection of the One True Way of the Phastorlings, the *astru-do*—to slaughter and consume their excess population as a greater being would have.

No, hobbled by sentiment and other neuroglandular weaknesses that the Wintermind can overcome, the Nymphs merely preserved their unwanted until such a time as these were no Nymphs, and they woke, and used their arts not for pleasure, as the Nymphs had done, but for pain, for glory, for the dream of escaping all degrading pleasure forever, and living eternally to face the Hyades at the End of Days. By rejecting life and embracing the thing-beyond-life, those exiled Nymphs sculpted and resculpted themselves into the first of my people.

The idea that the Tombs have a buried and first ruler, a wise lord who sleeps? Nonsense. The Nymphs needed a father-figure as reassurance to the cast-offs that someone or something would protect them as they slept. They were afraid of tomorrow, because Nymphs have no concept of tomorrow, and so they had to be told there was a little godling, a posthuman, a guardian of their graveyards.

He would both protect the little darlings as they slept, like a guard dog, and, (so fortunate!) would assure them that any age into which they woke would be a good era. He was the Judge and Arbiter of Ages, and he condemned and destroyed whole civilizations with a wave of his hand. Hah! As if any creature could possess such authority and prowess. Convenient, was it not, that he fulfilled both roles?

No, little wee lordlings, there is no Judge of Ages. He is a myth invented by Nymphs, an opiate falsehood meant to deceive the Many.

6. Proof

Illiance, with a sidelong glance at Ull, said softly, "Ask Soorm scion Asvid where from his certainty happens to derive its solid nature. He speaks with force upon a topic muchly debated. Does he enjoy some proof to confirm his words, that there is no one founder to the Tombs?"

When the question was translated, Soorm goggled his mismatched eyes and showed his horrid teeth in grin or grimace. His seal-face was too inflexible for subtle expressions.

"Proof? Nonsense! How can there be proof that nothing is nothing? A shadow has no weight; a reflection in a looking glass makes no noise. Do you expect me to call the Judge of Ages here out of the abyss of time, and have him testify as to his own nonexistence? Such a testimony would be unreal, coming from a unreal man, would it not?"

Menelaus said to the Blue Men, "I would also like to add that I agree with Soorm. I have reentered and exited the Tombs many times, first in one land, and then in another, and saw no evidence of any central leadership, or even that one Tomb communicated with another. I can testify that the Judge of Ages is myth. But now I have a question for you, Preceptor Illiance."

Ull narrowed his heavily lidded eyes in annoyance, but Illiance nodded serenely.

"Illiance, you said that if I recognized the brotherhood that all academics across the ages share, this imposes a moral burden on me to help your research. Right?"

Illiance nodded. "I did not use the word *burden,* but you are essentially correct."

"Is this obligation one-way, or two-way?"

Illiance said, "A degree of reciprocity is to be expected. Have you some research of your own to which we, without undue extension of resources, may make a contribution?"

"Thanks for volunteering and yes, indeedy-do, I do. I told you I study the decline and fall of civilizations. I was ordered to do so, and I don't see any reason to stop and—to be frank—don't have anything else worth doing. To be really frank, I'll tell you that history is a stenchified huge disappointment to me, gentlemen! I was expecting to wake up in a future with ten-mile-high skyscrapers, flying horseless carriages made of antigravity metal powered by atmospheric electricity, atomic-powered lightbulbs, rocket-jetpacks able to surpass the speed of sound, and starships able to surpass the speed of light. Instead I wake up in a dingy camp occupied by Moreau dogs that any apprentice biotechnician could have whipped up in his wine cellar, and they are toting muzzleloaders and cutlasses. So where the hell is the future? What happened to it? What did you people do?"

Illiance said, "Your model assumes that technological progress is ever-increasing and unidirectional. The premise is false. Technological progress is the apex of a complex and specialized social organism reacting to specific environmental pressures, and then only for societies embracing particular metaphysical and ontological beliefs, social priorities, economic structures, academic liberties, and unity of worldview. The disarrangement of any element in the organism hinders, slows, or reverses that progress and, in turn, creates additional disarrangement. Naturally, such cascade failures can be avoided if the degree of interdependence of worldwide systems is minimized: self-sufficiency is more adroit. Progress is not an unmitigated good."

Menelaus said slowly, "Is your philosophy of living simply something that sprang out of a period of widespread social collapse? What happened to the world outside? Are you survivors of the asteroid strike?"

Ull interrupted, "The question is an aberration distorting the conversational flow of our verbal information exchanges, and must be relegated to a lower priority. Lance-Corporal Beta Anubis, the technological progress of the prior aeons was hindered by a retarding element. The Tomb system prevents the errors and unsanities of previous aeons from expiring when due, by preserving representatives of each generation to the next; and, by a natural selection, only psychologically malcontented or physically ill seek out long-term hibernation."

Menelaus looked dumbfounded. "Hold on! Are—are you claiming the presence of this so-called Judge of Ages, the builder of the Tomb system, that *he* is the thing dragging civilization back from progress?"

Ull looked at him coldly. "The hypothesis fits the available facts."

Menelaus said, "You want my help? Then let me ask a few questions of my own, and maybe we can expand the pool of available facts."

Illiance made a small, delicate gesture with his fingers, which could have meant anything. Menelaus decided to interpret it as a gesture of consent, or else not to care what it meant. He turned to Soorm (who had been watching both sides of the conversation with his independently moving eyes) and spoke in Leech: "Tell what you know of Reyes y Pastor."

7. Soorm in Artabria

The only way to speak of Pastor is to tell you of my whole life, and this for reasons that will become clear.

I was born in slavery and pain, as all my kind are born, amid the stench in the surgical pits of the Iatrocrats, who in those times were called the Leeches. I was the scion of Moord scion Elwe, the most accomplished genius of his age, and I was the summit of his art, for my excellent master had outdone himself. At tourney or melee or assassination or for kidnapping virgins to serve in the mothering racks, I was the most famed and most feared in all the Artabrian land. The Leeches I served gained many dormitories of donors by my victories, and extended their lives by many hundreds of years, grinding their elixirs from the glands of many captured children: and so the Leeches of Moord and his Clades and auxiliaries waxed fat and affluent, great and gay.

The power of the Artabrians, of which Moord was not the least, extended from Aragon and Castile down the Duero toward the coast, and the great walled Clade city of Olissipona became ours. When that happened, ours became a naval power, facing corsairs from the north of the world, where the world-forest forms a roof of pine and conifer half a thousand feet above the benighted lands. We fought wallowing kragens from Hibernia and nicors from Thule.

I was modified to become a dweller in the sea, and I traveled afar on the business of the Leeches who created me, slaying whom it was given me to slay, capsizing the coracles of mariners, but I was for a short space free from endless, smothering canopy of leaves, and I floated at night beneath the stars, and wondered at them.

Alas for the Leeches that I was given gills! For in the salt sea I breathed the wind of liberty, and it was wine to me. I grew curious about hither shores, and distant lands where other parts of the world-forest grew. And I saw the migrations of the great seabirds in an empty, leafless sky.

Often I would wound the vessels of mariners, leaving them adrift or aground, toying with their crew most slowly, murdering them one by one across a space of days or weeks while they thirsted and starved. I did this because I was curious, and they would tell me tales of things afar or long ago, that I might spare them for last, or eat their legs before I ate their head. And so I learned that there was a larger world and a deeper time.

Here I heard of the father of our race, the Red Hermeticist, Reyes y Pastor, for whom we are named, and whose code we follow.

I heard tales of great and ancient things, of ships who sailed the stars, men of old who did grand deeds, legends of one man who stole power from heaven and put all of Earth beneath his heel, or legends of another man who dared to love a swan-princess who fled beyond the river of stars called Milky Way. The tales told of a time, days of Eden, before men feasted upon one another's glands and organs, or knew the art of Hormagauntery.

And these tales tormented me, and I knew I must find the truth of them.

A night came when I saw the world-forest for miles along the coasts of Olissipona aflame, and I knew war had come: for the Surgeon-General of Iberia had for months been gathering Hermeneutic Gargantuans and Cladelevies and war-beasts and disease-bearing flies from Telamon to Tarraco, lured by the rumor of our slave-wealth.

I left Moord and my other masters to their fate, and left my patrimony behind. I was no more Soorm scion Moord. Woe befall him! His name shall live forever, but not through me. I shed his name like a snake sheds a skin. It grew too small.

North I swam by daylight and starlight, and came at last to the isles of the Cassiterides, so called for their tin mines, the last place metal could be dug from the earth, and long since exhausted. Here ancient men older than Giants reared a circle of stones to measure the stars, which, even in those days, they feared.

I heard the rumor of Asvid of Nettles, who lived alone nigh that ring of stones, and him I sought, seeking the truth of older things. Rumor named him the Old Man, *As-Vid,* who was the first of all my race, preserved alive by Hermeneutic forces in order to demonstrate to the world that we could live forever, and unaging, if only we killed and consumed without remorse and without satiation, each day to be stronger and more cunning and more deadly than the last.

I knew I had come ashore near the lands of a master of the Iatric Art when I foolishly stooped to pet a rabbit, and took up a palm of porcupine barbs, for even the hairs of bunnies were bred for ferocity. The trees of the world-forest that hung atop the White Cliffs of Dover were grown strange, and hated Man. They deterred me from seeking an overland route by the venom of their lianas, the thorny armor of their bark, their orchid-blooms with gripping mouths that seek out the breath of sleepers unwise enough to snore beneath the cursed leaf-shade to strangle them. Scalded by poison sap, I flung me back into the Channel. I circled the island by sea and traveled up the riverways, better able to fend off the cold-water piranhas, giant leeches, and stinging eels.

Up the river Avon I made my way, living off the venomous flesh-eating swans for whom the stream is famous. In my pouch I kept homunculi adjusted to my immune system and genetic structure, and so what fruit or fish they could eat and survive, I could so. They were big-eyed creatures, miniature versions of me, and they would dance by the campfire and mimic my antics during the northern nights. I am sorry they died so quickly, but it was a dangerous land.

The river wound beneath the hanging moss of the canopy, and a strange white swamp of chalky waters, leavened with limestone, spread beneath the roots of the eternal, hundred-foot-high trees.

I found Asvid. His house was thorns woven with poison ivy and oak and sumac, and in the mud he bred his worms and snakes and stinging things, and on the branches he hung skulls of visitors who discontented him. Once and twice I tried to approach his miserable vile hut, and once and twice I returned to the mud of the river, tossing and screaming as I slept in the waves, with boils on my flesh, and my tongue was swollen like a smoldering log with heat.

But I was not unpracticed in the arts of the Leeches, including arts of mine own devising, and on the third trial I waded his bog with a hide as heavy as a hippopotamus's, and I laughed amid scorpions and trod them underfoot, and I crushed his snakes and worms between my tusks and ate them raw.

Asvid rose from the muck at my feet and blew a weft of spores from an arm-sac that set me to puking. I begged him for my life, and that astounded him, for none of my kind esteem life, or ask for it, much less beg. He croaked with a voice that had not spoke in centuries, asking me if I disdained the First Law of the Old True Way, which was to feed off others or be fed to them, that the weak might fall and the survivors grow strong.

I said I did wish to feed from him, but I swore that I wanted none of his flesh or organs. Instead I wished to consume his knowledge, and I could feed off him in this way with no loss to himself. I wished to know of the old things only he knew.

He laughed, and said that I had eaten Ormvermin, his favorite pet, and his guardian and watch-worm. Who now would guard his hut while he traveled?

I took my crotch in my paw and swore by my sexual organs, where the genetic material rests that will one day bring forth the posthuman Enemies of the Star-Monsters, and we Phastorlings swear by nothing else, for that is all we hold sacred. I said I would serve him as well as the beastie I had killed, and better, and if I failed, he need not return my testicular sacs to me.

His hut was not the hovel of misery it seemed, for each and every thorn was a library needle containing another archive of life-code information, and all the secrets the Iatrocrats over many bloody generations had accumulated and hid away, for, immortal and hating their children, what discoveries did any share?

My first task was to grow in myself a chemical coder-decoder organ, so that I could read what was written in the messenger acids. I drove the needle into my brain according to the most ancient ritual the first augmented man, called Montrose, by his suffering and madness so long ago inaugurated.

Asvid infected me with madness, and filial love and piety, and other chemicals even the disciplines of the Wintermind could not efface. And thus I became ensnared, and thus became the apprentice of the Old Man, who was first of our kind.

8. Soorm and Asvid

How many years passed by, I will not say, lest you think I boast, but Asvid was both the most accomplished and least demonstrative of all the Phastorlings, and he slew without mercy, and those he spared served him, for he knew the art of instilling pack-loyalty instincts and altruism-codes into those he defeated, and the Wintermind could not quell the instinct.

That, little lordlings, was the great secret of his longevity: He, the most ancient example of our race routinely and blithely betrayed the bedrock principles of the Old True Way.

When I recited the First Law, *Eat or be eaten, fight or die,* he smiled and said there was Law higher than the number one law, a Law of Zero: *Let others fight or die for you, and eat the survivors while they are wounded and weary.*

He called this his Law of Laws: The rule was that Laws were meant for others to obey, and you to exploit. He said that is why laws were made at all. His law was as old as the handprint on the Moon.

Asvid was not my patron only, but my father, the only father I would ever know. My brain chemistry had been altered to allow me to have the emotion proper between father and sons. I do not have a word for it in my language, and the Nymph word implies incestuous intergenerational sodomy, which is not the proper idea.

Knowing this nameless emotion, my disgust and hatred of the world in which I lived grew great, and then greater. Why were the Hormagaunts born not of woman, but in growth-pods? Why did I have no brothers, no cousins, no mate? Why so much death and pain and disease? Why had Earth once boasted starships, but now we did not even have Clipper Ships, but swam the seas in coracles and canoes and longboats pulled by sea serpents? Why was our world so *wrong*?

9. Hemoclysm

Then the time of bloodshed came, the Hemoclysm, when the configurations, nations, and factions attempted utterly to exterminate all rival DNA molecular compositions. First one worldwide war and then many burned the eternal forest, and in the times between the wars came the gene-cleansings and genocides and mass starvations.

Because of the wars, Asvid and I were growing allergic to each other. Our immune defenses, as they grew more complex, were harder to harmonize chemically. When we could no longer stand each other, he declared me his apprentice no longer, but a journeyman.

Not long after I departed from him, and founded for myself a stronghold at the mouth of the Avon, a summons arrived that midnight by long-range nightswallow. I ate the bird to ingest the chemical codes, which only mechanisms from my DNA could unlock and read.

It was a summons, not from Asvid, but from his master. After so many years of surviving the deadly world-wood and the deadlier children of his kindred, Asvid was being called by the one man with the right to call him: his patron and maker and master, Pastor, from whom all Phastorlings take their name.

And, in calling Asvid, he called all the Asvidlings, who were a very great number, more than I had imagined.

Pastor had called a Phastormoot, a gathering of those loyal to him, and we were summoned to Millennium Island on the opposite side of the globe.

I met with Asvid on the day the great migration was set to depart. Such a gathering of such hosts had never been seen, for he was eldest, and there were many indeed beholden to him. Rank after rank of the Asvidlings, names out of legend, rumors from history, Hormagaunts as vicious and deadly and cunning as anything our race had ever produced paraded before us and descended into the moaning vessels of the sea, a forest of horns and crests, a cacophony of screams and trumpets, a thunder of claws and hooves, until only we two, Asvid and I, remained.

I remember it well. We stood upon at the river mouth on a bluff overlooking the sea, and the land behind us, as far as eyes could reach, was dark with ash, and there were many trunks, hundreds of feet high, cracked and burnt and dead, huge like half-fallen towers, with no canopy overhead to hide the agoraphobic sky. Upon the battle plain, I saw blackened skulls piled in pyramids or rolling in the ash, and corpses of dogs and crows foolish enough to eat the slain, and so be poisoned by what slew them. Across this roofless world of smoldering death the river currents ran black with cinders and bark. The world-forest was dying.

Even I, who lived and rejoiced in death and murder, was appalled, for the chemical codes inspiring filial piety in me had weakened my nature. I asked of my master why all these dread events were necessary? What was wrong with the world?

He told me all history is nothing but a play of marionettes, and all events were played out by the puppeteer who pulled the secret strings, the Red Hermeticist Father Reyes y Pastor.

These were his words: "All our lives and all the lives of our ancestors have been bound up in a web of mathematical codes and conclusions, a march of numbers like an army of deadly ants, as invisible as bacteria, and history has never escaped from the meshes of the web. Father Reyes, through us, his scholars and scions and servants, establishes the contours, and history follows when we let the webwork out, or pull it back in. No matter where the individual fish may dart, the school is where the net defines. Pastor is one of the Enlightened, an Illuminatus—many times I have killed or caused disasters, founded schools or spread rumors, to thrust the forces of history one way or another, according to his commands."

I told him that the Witches thought the motions of stars and planets defined destiny; that Chimerae said blood and genetic mechanisms defined it; that Nymphs taught that destiny was a figment of brain elements which could be altered by a vapor or a wine. Had not he himself taught me of all these dead ages?

Even behind the scales and bristles and fangs of his battle modifications, I saw then for the first time his human eyes, and human sorrow. "I will impart the greatest of secrets to you. Not stars, not blood, not brains define the destiny of men. My master does. It is given to him, the Red Hermeticist, to determine the fate of lesser men. The enlightened guide the benighted; the sighted lead the blind." He spoke as one who speaks and believes, but hates, a hard truth.

He continued, "It is said there were other Hermeticists who defined and ruled the history of other ages. Our age is his. He is the Master of the Fate of the Hormagaunts."

I saw then that I was a fish in a bucket, who, leaping out of the wooden wall, found myself still confined in a well, hemmed by a wall of stone. I had escaped the close slavery of Artabria only to find the larger slavery of the Red Hermeticist. "Are these wars *his* doing? For his pleasure, hell rules earth, and many fine things pass away, never again to be seen? It there none who can oppose and overthrow the ruler of this age and its present darkness?"

Asvid spoke with wry and weary humor. "The Nymphs, long ago, believed that there was a Judge of Ages, who would arise from sleep in the roots of his mountain, and condemn any age which offended his law. But what that law is, I never paused to inquire, and now the Nymphs are extinct, as dead as their belief."

"You do not hold such a person exists?"

Asvid said, "Rather, I hope for his sake he does not. For were there a Judge to which the suffering multitudes and slaves and slain children could appeal, he would have heard their cry, and condemned this age long since. If he were real, and so indifferent to his duty, surely I would slay him."

We departed separately, for in our present forms, we could neither embrace, not so much as a handshake, and dared not exchange the kiss of peace, lest the allergic reactions sicken us. He spread vast wings of membrane and took to the air, and I bowed my head and dived into the black and rushing water, the river tumbling to the sea.

I knew we would never meet again. The Phastormoot was the summons of the loyal. And Asvid was no longer numbered among them. Nor, truth be told, was I. The Wintermind technique allowed me to resist the homing instinct implanted in me. I fled in the opposite direction, from Thule to Vinland and south again to New England, Columbia, Virginia.

Therefore I know Reyes y Pastor exists, because he summoned me. I know the Judge of Ages does not exist, because if he did, Reyes y Pastor would have been judged, and slain.

You have been patient to hear the whole of my life, for the whole of my life was needed to tell what I knew of Pastor. My life was hell. Pastor is the maker and master of hell, the chief tormentor. That is what I know of him.

I assumed Asvid would be alive when I was thawed. Legend said nothing could kill the Old Man, the First of the Phastorlings: and the longer I lived with him, the more I thought the legend true.

He is not here, is he?

10. Wintermind

After Soorm was done speaking, Illiance said in High Iatric to Menelaus, "You have heard the testament of the relict Hormagaunt. Did his words happen to open to you a more complete understanding of the causes of the decline of Hormagaunt civilization, or yours?"

Menelaus said, "I'll say. Do you two gentlemen have any reason to doubt his tale?"

Illiance said cautiously, "No obvious element contradicts a known fact preserved in our historical records. On that level, it seems not to be a complete fiction."

Ull gestured toward the dog thing hunched over the table of readouts. "We have some cause, in the absence of contrary evidence, to suspect that there is no deliberate deceit being practiced."

Menelaus said, "Well, I just found out my entire search for the causes of the decline and fall of world empires is a fraud. There is no natural law or inevitable tendency to be found. If Soorm is right, history is controlled by some sort of mathematical science of statistics, and empires fall because the men who control that science, the Hermetic Order, decree it shall fall. I thought I was a doctor looking for the natural cause of a disease. I'm not. I am a detective looking for the poison used by an assassin.

"Where are the assassins now?" Menelaus continued. "Or doesn't this tale ring any bells with you gentlemen? Were you aware that this current era of world history now is under the control of one of the Hermeticists? If so, which one? If not, why were you not informed?"

Ull said ponderously, "The simple academic reciprocity demanded by our way has been sated. You have asked your questions and had them answered."

"Not quite," said Menelaus. "I am also curious about the reasons for the decline of your civilization, my little blue guys. You cannot tell me you are still a going concern, can you? How many of you are left?"

Illiance said in a pedantic voice, "You show great charity to be concerned for our tribulations, but it appears best to accept your aid in the modes conformable to the contours of the situation, which is, to have you assist us in translation, rather than to answer a deposition. There is no need, at present, to rule out an expansion of such a broader basis for accepting your aid; but the matter is of lower priority at the moment."

Ull said, "Ask him of this Wintermind of which he speaks. We have no referent for it."

Menelaus translated the question.

Soorm had no eyebrows to raise, but something of a supercilious expression came over his stiff seal-like features when he goggled his eyes and gaped his shark-toothed mouth in a grin.

He spoke no word, but raised his hand and pointed with a webbed finger at the table on which the dog thing's equipment rested. After a moment, the instrument began to whistle like a steam kettle, while the dog thing leaped to its hind legs and frantically touched control-points and clicked toggles and slapped mirror surfaces. Some crucial part of the mechanism failed: the little lights dotting the coral surfaces flared up and went dark, and all the mirrors faded to a dull gray.

Menelaus drew his hood up in order to hide his expression of disgust or anger.

But neither Ull nor Illiance seemed in the least perturbed. Mentor Ull said to Illiance in the fluting of the intertextual language of the Locusts, "*Wintermind is a primitive form of the Mind Discipline.*"

Illiance opened his eyes wider. "*Instruct me, Mentor. I can see that it is a manifestation of biosoftware—the training that must be ingrained rather than implanted via needle. I see also that mental structures of the third order would be needed to instruct our detector to self-destruct. But how do you deduce that this is related to our Discipline?*"

Mentor Ull said, "*The Mind Discipline contains systemic neural pulses and alterations of brain wave frequency to alter internal mind states. Reference that relict Soorm scion Asvid used what he called Wintermind to break instinctive genetically imposed control-methods or addictions, including the naturally addictive epiphenomena of family love, which can be interpreted to be just such an internal mind state."*

Illiance nodded gravely. *"Insightful! This suggests that your previous plan to use torment to deter uncooperative or inharmonious thought forms found in the organism is nugatory."*

Mentor Ull favored him with a dark and reptilian look. *"Is that your sole concern? The subjective well being of these erratic and misshapen ancestral creatures? We may be able to deduce which aspect of the Divarication formula was used to create this discipline form."*

Illiance said, *"That aspect seems unclear, Mentor."*

Mentor Ull said, *"Not to a mind fixed and attentive, Student, cleared of complexity and distraction! The initial evidence suggests a mental but not neurological use of the Continuity Code, which is the sixth of the seven solutions of the Divarication problem, used specifically to overcome the Addiction divarication, which occurs in any information system where units enter a positive feedback loop—merely stimulating their pleasure reward without performing the act that merits it. The Continuity Code adds the mechanism of time-binding, so that short-term gain no longer overwhelms long-term loss. Is it not significant that the Hormagaunts were effectively immortal?"*

Illiance said, *"These conclusions remain tentative. It would be untoward to share this speculation with the—"* He glanced at Menelaus. *"—ah, with, ah whomever may be taking an interest in the research."*

Mentor Ull said, *"You refer to the Expositors of our Order gathered at Mount Misery? Agreed. We cannot approach greater certainty until we interview a Nymph, and determine the characteristics of the social-psychological control mechanisms involved in the communal relations of the Natural Order of Man."*

Mentor Ull said to Menelaus in High Iatric, "With our deception-detection equipment in disorder, no further testament is needed at this time. Tell the relict Soorm scion Asvid that the Followers will escort him, and you, back to the confinement area."

Menelaus said to Soorm in Leech, "The blue lordling says the dog things will drag us back to the prison yard, thanks to your blowing up their lie detector. We're dismissed."

7

The Old Man of Albion

1. A Private Place for Private Deeds

The next day, it was snowing, and no work could be done at the dig. Instead, the machines of the Blue Men crouched beneath a snapping, wind-tossed tarpaulin, cleaning and oiling their blades and spades with an endlessly repeated gesture like the gleeful hand-wringing of misers, or perhaps like flies washing. The snow was blowing vertically, not quite parallel to the sloping ground, and the horn had not sounded for the mess tent.

Each individual was in the tent assigned him. Whether that could be said of the lone figure leaving a temporary line of naked footprints in the snow was a matter of semantics. His tent was folded around him like a hooded cloak, and he carried the long train of metallic fabric over his arm, like a senator of old holding the drape of a toga, or a princess in a trailing gown suddenly found without her maidens of honor.

He came to one of the tents and shouted a halloo. He waited unanswered for a while, and shouted and shouted again.

"Hail and parley! Weapons down!"

Eventually the tent flap drew open, revealing the scowling dark-furred beast-face of Soorm the Hormagaunt.

"I am armed with a rock, and my name is Beta Sterling Anubis. May I enter?" The hooded man spoke in Leech.

"Think you I so soon forget?" rumbled Soorm.

"To introduce myself by weapon and name is merely a Chimerical custom."

"How odd. You do not smell like a Chimera."

"Easily explained. I am a Beta, and imperfect. The other Chimerae in the camp are Alpha, well bred of long bloodlines. May I enter?"

"No. I will exit. The tent cloth can be stiffened without warning by an electric signal to form a nearly airtight prison, and I have no wish to be trapped in a small space with you. The Blues doubtless have other sleights and oddities they could perform as well, while their substance is around us. Come!"

The big dark-furred man lumbered out of the tent and, taking the arm of Menelaus, stalked toward the trees not far away, pine and spruce conical hats of snow, from which the wind drew plumes. Without waiting for an invitation, Soorm parted the garments of Anubis and put a furry arm around him, drawing the material of the robes of Menelaus around him for warmth. Menelaus made no protest, but walked huddled up to the other man, his head almost in his armpit.

Soorm said, "You show no fear to walk so nigh a Hormagaunt? I have both virulent pus and stench-cloud I can emit from several orifices, and beneath my hairs are needles I could stiffen into barbs."

"It's not that I am all that brave, it's just that I figure we are all going to be killed by the Blue Men soon enough anyhow, so why worry? Besides, there aren't that many people in the camp you can talk with. Who speaks Leech, but me?"

"Come, then. Let us walk up farther, and find a private place for private deeds. Your feet do not freeze, or bleed?"

Menelaus said, "My boots were stolen from my coffin while I slept. Made from the hide of a gator I shot myself, and I was damn proud of those boots! One of the Hospitaliers drew tattoos for me under the skin of my foot, with heating elements inside. Don't tell my superiors, please. Chimerae have rules about bodily modifications."

Soorm with his huge stride set a quick pace, and he dragged or drove an uncomplaining Menelaus to where a cliff clove the mountainside. Far underfoot between two converging rock walls, a rushing stream emerged, bubbling, from a doorway in the mountainside. The leaves of the door hung open at an odd angle, half torn from their hinges.

To either side of the doorway, a coffin stood upright, and glints of energy played through their metal surfaces. The waters in the stream swirled around the wreckage of several of the digging automata of the Blue Men. These formed a tangle of metal spiders and metal lobsters, and one treaded vehicle like a tortoise on its back. All were motionless in the white water, icicle streaked, pockmarked, broken, and burnt.

Soorm said. "Look down! I call this spot the Dying Place. The only approach is so narrow that the mechanisms have to come one or two at a time; even a small display of power from the Tomb defenses can hold them off. The Blue Men did not bother to scavenge their fallen."

Menelaus said, "I know you can breathe water. Can you pass these defenses?"

Soorm tightened his arm, pulling the head of Menelaus closer into his musk-scenting armpit, and he caught the smaller man's neck in the crook of his elbow. "No, I meant to show you a place where I can commit a murder, and no one would find your body."

The man stirred uneasily, and this made the Hormagaunt snarl.

"*Boo!* You are pretending to be scared. Don't bother! I can smell you are not afraid." Soorm peered at the other carefully, first with one eye, then with the other, nostrils twitching. His muzzle whiskers close enough to tickle. "*Altruism and Agape!* Why are you fearless? What in the world is wrong with you!"

"It is a Chimera technique for controlling fear," said Menelaus in little gasps. "All schoolboys learn it in boot camp."

"I can also smell lies. That's my technique! Quite useful."

"Interesting . . . that so . . . useful . . . a technique . . . can fail." His voice was little more than a squeak.

Soorm released the neck of Menelaus, but kept his arm around the other man, perhaps for warmth.

Menelaus massaged his throat. "You have odd swearwords."

"Everyone swears by what he fears most."

"You said you came to appreciate the benefit of altruism. When Asvid adopted you as a father. You still fear cooperative action?"

"Bah! We never overcome what is imprinted into us as eggs, or so Hormagaunt Moord taught me."

"A dismal philosophy, but I suppose he learned it when he was young. In any case, I wanted to speak with you," said Menelaus. "I think the Blue Men plan to kill us all, in order to hide the evidence of this dig. If they were legitimate, they would have their own translators and diggers, rather than have us do their work."

"You are not going to ask me why I just threatened to spit flesh-eating acid in your face, twist off your head like a chicken, and throw your twitching body into the freezing rapids below?"

"Um. I assume you thought the Blue Men would not dare enter the West Crevasse to recover my body and determine the cause of death? As a stratagem, I see no obvious flaw."

"No, I don't mean the mechanics of the murder. I mean the motive."

"I was not going to ask, no."

"No?"

"I am Chimera. We kill each other all the time, and with reckless glee. I regard it as unexceptional behavior, no doubt caused by high spirits."

"You are no Chimera. I suspect you are an agent of the Blue Men, a mole, a Judas goat."

"Good! Then you will not take me seriously when I ask you to join an uprising against them. If we can get enough Thaws to join us, we can rush the gate and overbear the dog things before the cylinders kill too many of us."

"Rush the gate for what purpose?"

"To win our liberty, and live no more as slaves."

2. Counting Revenants

Soorm rocked back on his heels and turned his mismatched eyes up to the snowy sky. "Personally, I dismiss liberty as an abstract concept of only limited applicability. For who is free of history, or his own biological fate? No, I am much more eager to kill Blue Men, who have inflicted indignity on me, than I am to achieve liberty or sustain my life. Therefore I am eager to join with you, should your plans prove feasible. From the dead-line to the gate is at least forty yards, with no cover and no concealment. How many of us do you think the dog things could kill with distance weapons as we rushed them?"

"The Chimerae have time-tested formulae for deducing such casualty estimates, based on factors such as rates of fire, targets available per strike, targets hit per strike, wound severity, effective range, muzzle velocity, reliability, mobility, radius of action, and vulnerability."

"How quaint and ghastly of you. We Hormagaunts are a horrid race, I freely confess it, but we killed one at a time, and never marched to war."

"And we did not raise lobotomized children in crèches, and harvest glands and organs and living tissue from them for longevity treatments," Menelaus said dryly.

"We indulged in the darkest of sciences, and won the greatest of rewards. And yet you seem nonchalant. You do not recoil?"

"Each period of history has its own peculiarities."

"As you say. What does your quaint science of death estimation estimate?"

"The cylinders hold a single operator behind thick armor, a gun crew of three in the trench beyond. Each cylinder both can emit a defensive fan of radiant heat covering a forty-five-degree angle, and can shoot mixed slugs and grapeshot from a steam-powered machine gun muzzle. The technology was selected for its simplicity to assemble and maintain rather than its lethality: all you need is water and power and a machine shop. Each steamgun holds four hundred rounds of musketballs and has two minutes of effective fire. The heating elements can fire as long as cables leading to the powerhouse on the other side of the gate remain uncut. I estimate a firing pressure of four thousand pounds per square inch and a muzzle velocity four hundred and eighty cubits per second. Assuming the charge can cross the lethal zone in four and a half seconds—"

"I remind you I can drive my acid-coated tongue spike into your eyeball from up to three yards away."

"You just want the sum number?"

"That would be nice, yes."

"Charging the two cylinders across forty yards of open ground should result in forty to sixty effective casualties."

"And how many men do we have so far in our uprising?"

"Including you?"

"Include me, yes."

"Four."

"So you are expecting a casualty rate . . . ah . . . somewhat approximately one thousand percent over and above our available troop strength."

"I cannot fault your calculation."

"Hm."

"I hope to recruit more men, and also to find a way to arm ourselves. Can you speak to the men of your era?"

"I cannot merely speak but command," Soorm said with a flick of his two tongues. "The other Hormagaunts, Crile scion Wept and Gload scion Ghollipog, are from later periods than mine, so I should be able to domineer them through our ancestor laws."

"How far back do your ancestral laws command? I have seen Nymphs working as nurses in the infirmary tent, and as drudges in the mess tent. They created your race."

Soorm bristled uneasily. "It is better not to meddle with them."

Menelaus said, "I would think that to one of your era, interred in 7466, they would be mythical?"

"They are not soldiers."

"The Chimerae have a saying: Any warm body that pulls a heat-seeker away from a soldier dies with a soldier's honor. There are five Nymph women, and four males. I don't know their names as yet."

"Yours is a sick and savage race, painting with gold what is basically the unromantic business of man-butchery. Speaking of which, how many Chimerae can you enlist?"

"There are two Chimerae in the camp."

"Two Chimerae? You miscount. What of yourself?"

"Three."

"And all the other ones?"

"Joet is a Gamma. The others include an Alpha Lady, two Beta Maidens of the Auxiliary class, and four Kine. Kine and women are noncombatants."

"Wait. You wish to shield your woman and servants from combat, while you are sending in decorated Nymphs and their dancing boys?"

"Your count is also short. You listed Crile and Gload, but what about the five other Hormagaunts from your period?"

"I don't know whom you mean."

"Toil, Drudge, Drench, Prissy Pskov, and Zouave Zhigansk?"

"Ho! They are not Hormagaunts! They are Short-liveds. As their names suggest, two are Burghers. The Pskov Clade and Zhigansk Clade come from different walled cities, have different biochemical recognitions, and are therefore mutually allergic. It would be difficult to compel them into melee. Except against each other."

"Overcome the difficulty."

"And the other three are organ donors, who form our slave and livestock class, and therefore cannot be allowed to handle weapons."

"In my sole capacity as Chief Intelligence Officer of the Academic Division of the Intelligence Command, of the Eugenic General Emergency Command of the Commonwealth of Virginia and the surrounding States, Settlements, and Territories, and acting under the battlefield regulations of the Code of Military Justice as Commander-in-Chief ad hoc and pro tempore, I hereby manumit any and all servile or underling classes, categories, slaves, or indentured servants whose members are willing to fight for our liberty. In the absence of any objection or veto from the Governor, and taking the Advice and Consent of the Senate and the House of Burgesses as granted, the motion passes by acclamation. There! Your slaves are now free men. Let us see if they will fight to stay free."

"Milk and mush! You have no authority to mulct the Hormagaunts of our donation stock!"

"You may apply to the House of Burgesses for recompense at their next regular session. They have not been convoked for five thousand sixty-seven years, so you may have to find our Imperator-General to call them into session."

"Bah! This is drollery and japery, not worth the spit required to spit on it. Fine! I will throw the three organ donors into the fray, if you will commit your Alpha and Beta ladies and your Gamma lad and the whole rest of the stupid alphabet of your Chimera-folk."

"That would bring the tally up to twenty-seven."

"Who is left?"

"Three very early and three very late." Menelaus ticked them off on his fingers. "The early-comers include one Servant of the Machine named Glorified Ctesibius from A.D. 2525, from before the Ecpyrosis; a Giant from A.D. 3033; an albino Scholar named Rada Lwa—I don't know his date, but he is very likely the earliest person here. The later-comers include the male and female gray-skinned blue-haired twins from some race I don't recognize from A.D. 8866 and the strange-eyed creature from some race I *really* don't recognize from A.D. 10100, the last year of the one hundred first century—unless that coffin was marked in binary, and she is from A.D. 20, the first century."

"Everyone here is strange-eyed compared to me. Which one do you mean?"

"I mean the dark and silent lady who sits in the mess tent and never moves, and all the dogs are afraid of her. Her eyes are modified so that there is no white in them: every part of her eye is black. I think it is multifrequency absorption material. And what looks like a second pair of eyes, maybe infrared or microwave, above that. She has scars on her back. I don't have her name. And there are two people the Blues are holding I haven't seen yet. I am hoping one of them is our knight."

"I can name the gray twins."

"Really? Just how did you learn their names?"

"I just walked up in the exercise yard and pointed to myself and said *Soorm*; and they pointed to themselves and said *Linder Keir* and *Linder Keirthlin*. Linder Keir is the brother's name. So either Linder Keirthlin is the sister's name, or those are the words for *I don't know what you said* and *Why did your point at yourself?* in their language. Just how do you learn their dates?"

"I sat out in the cold talking to a man not named Mickey the Witch of Williamsburg, and I memorized the dates on every coffin I could see."

"Which one is he?"

"The rotund dark man in the straw hat."

"The vegetarian."

"Is he? He must eat a lot of lettuce to maintain that shape."

"Rice and beans. I can smell it on his breath."

"I think he and I between us can get the Witches to sign on."

Soorm spread his webbed claws and looked at his palms meditatively. "Suppose you talk to the Savant, the Scholar, and the Giant. Say they join us. That brings the count up to thirty. Suppose also the Witches join. There are thirty-one of them, which would double our numbers. The men are not odd, but the women hardly look human!"

"I will skirt by the irony of that comment coming from you. The Witch-women look normal. Well, all except the one with freaky hair."

"They would bring the count to sixty-one," said Soorm, "Enough to rush the gate and have twenty-one survivor."

"Our position unfortunately becomes untenable if we have to contend with enemy aerial support. We Chimerae have a standard formula for estimating air-support-induced casualties, depending on the ground cover, rate and precision of antiaircraft measures—"

"Spare me. I apprehend we are better off if they cannot shoot us from the air. And so we wait for a stormy day? This is the worst plan in the history of military endeavor."

Menelaus said, "I hope to change the minds of my superiors to adopt a different plan. This place here you picked to kill me conveniently looks out upon a back entrance to the Tombs that the Blue Men cannot secure. They are not guarding it, and if we can get in—"

"What is inside? Weapons? Buried valuables? Buried allies? I remind you most people do not recover from thaw for hours or days, because most hibernation is for medical reasons."

"I was thinking of using the communication equipment to send out an all-band distress signal. Then you open the main doors from the inside, using the words I give you, and we all rush in, close the doors behind us, laugh at the Blue Men outside, and wait."

"Wait for what?"

"For whoever or whatever passes for the local law enforcement of the current era. These Blue Men are pirates. Looters. Everything in the camp bespeaks haste and the need for stealth."

Soorm shook his head ponderously, an oddly human-seeming gesture, given his monstrous frame. "Why would the Blue Men not simply kill us all the moment the distress call rang out? The fabric they gave out to those of you too foolish to grow proper fur is impregnated with binary chemicals in several phases. An electronic signal could flex the smartmolecules to any number of configurations, including lethal gas or flesh-eating fluid."

"Strip nude. Or use detergent. Or set up a jamming signal. We have to act in coordination with the other prisoners. Will you help me?"

"I will, since it will irk the Blue Men. But your plan assumes there will be someone to answer your distress call."

Menelaus said, "I don't think this world is empty."

"This part of it is. This air does not smell like there is an industrial civilization anywhere nearby. Even in my day, when everything was part of a worldwide forest, we still burned coal and oil, and you could smell it on the wind."

"Speaking of something you can smell out for me, where is the radio tower in the airfield sending its information? You hinted that you could detect it."

"Why should I tell you?"

"For one thing, you gave it away to the Blue Men when you blew the circuits out of their lie detector. It kind of peeved me, since you had been careful enough to keep it secret before that."

"My secret, not yours."

"Ours, like it or not," Menelaus said. "We just stood here and counted up every fighting man in the camp. Do you think the Chimera plan of rushing the wire has a chance? If not, we go with my plan. Are you in or out?"

"In what?"

"In my circle of friends. If you are, answer the question."

Soorm was silent, peering very closely at his face, first with the goat eye, then with the cuttlefish eye. He put his face within kissing distance of Menelaus and sniffed carefully, and then bent to sniff his armpits and crotch and tasted the air with his two tongues.

Menelaus endured this indignity without uttering one of the several snide comments that bubbled up inside him.

Finally Soorm straightened. "There is a distant responder signal the radio tower seeks out and answers. I was able to sense it now and again, and when I have wandered to various parts of the camp to triangulate. The source is seventeen hundred and thirty miles almost directly southeast of here."

Menelaus knew where that was. One advantage of his extra brain capacity was that he could memorize reams of useless data, including almanacs and atlases, and make three- and four-dimensional models of them in his head.

"That could place it around Saint Christopher's Island, one of the Leeward Islands in the Lesser Antilles," said Montrose. "Mentor Ull, the older one, mentioned Mount Misery. I am assuming Mount Nevis and Montferrat are also active. Mount Nevis is across the narrows atop an island called *Nuestra Siñora de las Nieves,* 'Our Lady of the Snows.' "

Soorm looked at him oddly. "Why do you assume volcanoes over a thousand miles away are active?"

"Because I set in motion certain plate tectonics to activate them, using self-replicating Von Neumann crystals. My intent is to end the ice age and reestablish a surface human civilization powerful enough to resist the Hyades before the End of Days. It is only half a millennium from now, so time is really limited."

Soorm's nape hairs bristled, and porcupine quills stood up from his scalp and shoulders. His scorpion tail lashed, and the swim flukes opened and shut nervously. "Who are—what are you?"

Menelaus relaxed and allowed the natural neural rhythm in his optic nerve to reassert itself. His gaze took on a magnetic majesty, an unearthly intelligence, a penetrating menace: Soorm tried to meet that gaze. But then Soorm stepped back and raised his scaly hand before his face.

3. Cards on the Table

Menelaus lowered the vividness of his face and features back to the normal human range, and he said, "You tried to protect me from the Blue Men. You did not know I was standing in the room, but you did try to discourage them from continuing to dig for me. You lied and said you thought I was a myth. I am grateful, but also curious. Why did you do that?"

"You cannot figure it out with your superhuman brain?" Soorm snarled.

"I can't figure out jack with no information, no."

"Why not? You are like a man walking among brute wolves to us."

"A man raised by wolves, you mean. One with no humans to teach me their wonderful inventions, like language and arithmetic and logic and flint-napping: an illiterate Romulus who barks like a wolf, or Tarzan who never found that children's primer to teach himself French."

"I don't know who those people are."

"Too bad! And here I took the trouble to manipulate history to increase the longevity of certain stories I liked, and I established statistical incentives, introduced self-replicating sociometric viruses, and everything. Damn that Blackie and his meddling! In any case, my point is that a human baby raised by apes is a pretty smart ape but a pretty poor man. I don't expect you to be in awe of me. But I didn't expect you to help me, either. Why did you?"

"You tell me first why you are not afraid of me, if you are such a poor superman. Just because you are posthuman does not give you any supernatural powers. You could not live if I tore out your throat. You cannot fling beams of deadly energy from your brain."

"No, but I can use my brain for thinking. I know that you are not Soorm scion Asvid."

"Am I not? Then who am I?"

"A showdog for Reyes. For that matter, you are not even really a Hormagaunt."

"Am I not? Then *what* am I?"

"A Nymph. Logically, if you are the first Hormagaunt, you must be the last Nymph. You alone of Hormagaunts, the eldest and first, do not kill for sadistic pleasure, nor for the gluttony to achieve more life. You don't need to. Reyes y Pastor had to keep you alive as a propaganda tool, to prove that the longevity of the Hermeticists could and would continue to operate, even after centuries had passed. Starting with you, Reyes shared one of the primary secrets the Hermeticists learned via the Monument—the secret of Eternal Youth. You are far too old and cunning to kill without reason. And, unlike a real Hormagaunt, you have a certain degree of fellow-feeling, brother-love, pity for the weak. You did not use the Wintermind technique to obviate the basic emotional contour of your human nature. You used it to break the addictions the Nymph Queens used to redact your memory, mesmerize, enchant, and enslave you. You were the first to break free of the addictive system. Your name is not Soorm."

"Is it not? What is my name?"

"Your real name is Asvid."

Soorm shrugged. "Two right guesses out of three is not bad."

"Your name really is Soorm?"

"Not quite. Actually, my real name is Marsyas, and my displayed design is Saffron and Oakwhite together, but my intimate is Oleander, Rocket and Mandrake twinned in a knot."

Menelaus nodded. The Nymph naming scheme recited the heraldic flowers which identified which of several endocrinal protocols and glandular systems one used.

Soorm, or Marsyas, continued, "I am of the Tityroi, a flute-player for the Nymphs. I survived the torture pits and gladiatorial chambers of Reyes and became his champion. And then I outlasted and outlived his other champions. *Asvid* is a title, not a name. It means 'the Old Man.'"

"It also means First of the Kindred. So I told you why I was not afraid," said Menelaus, spreading his hands. "I had too much faith in your humanity. Why did you try to help hide the Judge of Ages?"

"Because none other can stop the Red Hermeticist."

Menelaus cocked his head to one side. "Is he still alive?"

"Expastor lives. His Ghost lives. They are Dreagh, Ghosts who can possess living flesh."

"Where?"

Soorm raised a webbed claw and pointed upward. "In my era, there was an evening star, an artificial moon. At sea, out from beneath the canopy of the world-forest, on clear nights, I could spy her rising and setting, a small, fine, silver point of light. You know whereof I speak?"

"The Nigh-to-Motionless starship *Emancipation.* Know of her? I built her. Blackie snitched her from me. Payback for snitching his bride from him, I suppose."

Soorm said, "How do you know I will not betray you?"

Menelaus gestured toward the snowy ridges and trees in which direction the camp lay. "Even a non-supergenius can see that. If you tried to protect the Judge of Ages when you did not know he was in the room with you, why would you turn on him when he was?"

"Perhaps because I overestimated his powers. Summon up your Knights and Giants and thinking machines, exorcists and archbishops, djinn and efreets, aftergangers and cacodemons, mummies, sorcerer-kings and walking dead. Bring out your magic needle and stab yourself in the head to unleash your inner daemons. Create the antimatter and obliterate your foes."

"Damn but I'm impressive! I'd give my left nut to meet me, if I was actually able to do pox like that."

"You are a prisoner here, then. How is it that you serve them as a translator, instead of as sliced meat garnished with peppers and cloves on the feast table?"

"Don't talk like that. You're making me hungry. It's been eight thousand four years since I had a square meal. I don't count a lavish fish dinner I had in A.D. 3089, because I was on the lam, and had to snatch bites while looking over my shoulder. A restaurant called *Phantom de Casa Curial* served delicious Cajun redfish spiced with bell pepper, onion, celery, and dried cayenne pepper. This was a floating barge-city anchored over the sunken ruins of Newer Orleans."

"What can you do, Posthuman, aside from talk about extinct forms of foodstuffs?"

"No, no. I was surprised by the extinction of the tobacco leaf. Won't make that mistake again. Got the recipe, and all those organisms for the ingredients

I have preserved somewhere in my Tomb system. Hibernation is not just for people, you know."

"Point taken. What can you do aside from talk about nonextinct forms of foodstuffs? By the lovingkindness of the long-suffering, is everyone older than a few thousand years insufferably garrulous?"

"What can I do? If you are asking whether I can track down and delete every copy of a posthuman machine intelligence, which is nothing but a gestalt-pattern of information that can be copied, transmitted, stored in a wide variety of media, all I can say is nine thousand years of trying to track down and destroy Exarchel have won me nairn, nary, none, and beans in the kitty."

"Go back to pretending you are a Chimera. You talk blithering nonsense when you are not someone else. Or is this done to awe the simple with your ineffable incomprehensibility?"

"I cannot promise to kill Reyes y Pastor or allay his ghost, but I can promise, that if he is the Master of the World during this era of history, to knock him off his throne. I can stop him."

Soorm stood still, looking at Menelaus very carefully. "What is it like?"

"What is what like?"

"Knowing the posthumans. The Hermeticists and starfarers. What are they like, the gods of our world?"

"Sick bastards."

"Yet you were once one of them, or so Reyes told me at the last."

"So I am a sick bastard too. People that like to experiment on their own brains are not usually the most balanced of critters, if'n you take my meaning."

"Why do they rule history? By what right?"

"Pestilence! No right at all."

"Why *them*? How did they achieve control of fate and world-destiny, so that they decide what empires fall and rise? Why was this power not placed in the hands of someone more—I don't know the word for it."

"Altruistic?"

"That is a swearword in my language."

"Piss-poor language, if you can't say nothing worth saying in it. The Hermeticists? Blackie and his Black-Robed Creeps? They didn't start out bad, but outer space—years of close confinement falling through light-years of black nothing, drinking recycled pee water—it drove them stir-crazy. The Captain announced they would never return to Earth, to save Earth from discovery by the Hyades, and they mutinied and killed him for it. You know the End of Days, the year when we get invaded by Principalities, Virtues, and Powers sent out by the Hosts and Dominions of Hyades? They brought that down upon us."

Montrose paused, frowning, then continued, "They might have been passable fair-to-middling as human beings before the mutiny—but after? It had punctured their souls.

"When they came back to Earth, they had secret knowledge beyond human, and everyone they knew was dead and long done for, and they were attacked by greedy Earthmen. The Earth they knew was gone, and the Earth they found was gone bad.

"The techniques I've developed over the years to make it easier for Thaws to acclimate to currents and for currents to welcome Thaws—there was nothing like that then. 'Thaw shock' it's called or 'future grief.' And these shocked and grieving boys were armed with weapons more dangerous and techniques more sophisticated than anything on Earth, not to mention the Swan Princess.

"They bombed cities, killed millions, and soon they had the world under their boot heel, soon they had power and prestige and toilet bowls of gold to sit on, and that rusted away their punctured souls into jagged bits of crud. They were so jealous of me and my magic brain, that they killed themselves experimenting on themselves, at least sixty of them, one after another after another. What kind of man does that? Rather die than admit someone else has a leg up on smarts? They're twisted as screws."

Soorm grunted. "I knew part of this, but I heard a strangely changed version. But what are they themselves like? I mean—what sort of—?"

"What? You asking about their hobbies and love affairs and suchlike? Pox! I got no idea. It's not like I talked to any of these folk for more than a few moments in the last eight thousand years. I remember them from space camp back when I was twenty-five calendar, twenty-four bio. That was in A.D. 2234. We did jumping jacks together and studied orbital mechanics and pressure emergency drills and how to pee in a diaper. It was a five-month training regime. I talked to them for a while again in A.D. 2399, in a powwow we had. We yakked about math. Sort of funny, but I don't know these guys. Not personally. Now I am eighty-three hundred and five years old calendar and fifty biological. The only one I really got to know is . . . Ximen del Azarchel."

Montrose sighed, and shook his head, and said, "Hm. Blackie ain't totally rotten, but that kinda makes him worse, in a way. But they all think, Blackie too, that we are just their cattle."

"We?"

"We humans. Us. Normal people. Why are you laughing?"

"For no reason, fellow normal human. Tell me how I can help you."

"Simple. Spill what you know about Reyes. History is screwed up and haywire, not to mention the climate and evolutionary changes; and I need to find the point of deviation to set it right. I am hoping it was recent, b'cause that means less work for me."

"Then I will tell you of my last moot first; and this was also when I learned that you were real."

4. The Atrocity of the Yap Islands

To the Blue Men, I lied. My bioelectric cells could more than compensate for their crude lie-detection electroencephalograph. I had no apprentice named Soorm when the final summons came, but I did call forth the great host of those beholden to me, and we did see the burning of the world-forest beyond its capacity for self-repair. There would be grasslands and wasteland again, heath and bog and chaparral, and to the north, taiga and tundra. I knew enough predictive ecology to see that much.

Another lie: I went, and did not flee. There is no way to resist the instinctive homing-call that my Master infused into the message-chemicals he sent. And the way was long, ah! It was travail indeed.

It was in the archipelago east of the Cipangu Islands I met the Master of World of the Hormagaunts for the final time. I traveled north, and across the polar sea—in those days, there was no ice cap, as now—to the Chukchi Sea, and across the isthmus to the Bering Sea, then down by coasts of Rus and Cathay, past Annam and Loulan, to the Spice Islands.

Four years and longer I sought, drawn by the summons. And I came upon Reyes y Pastor in on Millennium Island, the easternmost of the uninhabited atolls forming the Line Islands. He had recently descended from heaven: the landing craft was floating in the bay, sleek as an arrowhead.

As I swam near his craft, wondering, a machine from the deepest ocean rose and snared me with many metal tentacles, and then, breaking the surface in an explosion of spray, carried me aloft and screaming toward the isle. Through the transparent hull, I saw a woman dressed in red hunger silk, and she had strands of the same material woven through her hair. Her hair was modified to reach yards upon yards, and she could manipulate all the controls of her half-living flying machine at once. She was a Medusa from the age of myth.

But she did not strangle me, or allow her garment to flay me and drink my blood. Instead her airskiff reach down with its tentacles, and I was placed gently among the strangest assemblage I had ever seen.

(You do not know who the Medusae are? They were once a race of evil Sylphs, striking out from their fortresses beneath the north polar ice, where the Giants could not find them. Over the years, the Medusae hunted the Sylphs one by one through the skies like sharks among fish, in black airskiffs printed with the sign of the Pallid Hand, for the Moon is sacred to them.)

There were tens of thousands of Hormagaunts gathered there, the Asvidlings (as I said) and also his other champions and their scions, janissaries, and fighting-slaves: abominations and hairy men from the pine trees, many-colored serpent men from the palm trees. But here were also machines who spoke, and dreadful Ghosts, and Albinos more cunning than human, and Witches who could command the beasts, and Medusae in their amphibious airskiffs, Chimerae in their ferocity. Strange men from the far past.

The interview was in Father Pastor's outlandish and soaring house he had grown out of shining pearl and mother of pearl, spire upon spire reaching skyward like his starship; but, within, a strange image of a tortured and unmodified man affixed by spikes to a tree occupied the far wall, and a circle of barbs was on his head: I assume this was a memorial of some particularly sadistic execution Reyes had ordered, and he wished the memento to appall and cow his servants.

This was not our first meeting, and in my brain, I knew that Reyes y Pastor was an Old Stock, unmodified *Homo sapiens,* and yet somehow in my hearts I was still surprised to see and smell him in his flesh, with facial hair and fingernails and toes upon his feet and a thousand other useless atavisms. It was like seeing a moving illustration from an antique living scroll step off the paper.

And yet, no matter what alterations are made to our neural chemistry, his awkward and ancient body looked *right* to me, and my magnificent body looked *wrong.* But we all know that seeing beauty is a mere chemical flocculation in the brain, the release of neural colloids from suspension. Why could no change in neurochemistry change the image of man?

He wore the scarlet robes and bore the shepherd's crook of that most ancient coven called god-eaters, who worship a spirit called Anointed. But beneath this red mantle, what he wore was black as night and fine as silk, and it had fittings for helm and gauntlets, and I saw it was the garb of a star voyager, and so I fell at his feet.

As I crouched, Reyes reached down a hand to me. On his right wrist he wore an amulet of metal the hue of blood that sucks at the witch-marks in his wrist, affixed to nerve and vein, and with this he speaks in unseen waves to what dwells on the dark side of the Moon.

The Master bade me rise, saying, "I am but a servant of servants here. What you see before you, this flesh, is the least part of me. Far greater is my own Ghost, thought of my thought and soul of my soul, which occupies a flying star that hangs above the heavens here. When she is above the horizon, I am more than human; but when not, I am merely a tired old man of an extinct race."

I towered over him, an ape towering above a puny child. From the way he moved, the things toward which he turned his head, I saw once again how he was nearsighted, and his ears were duller and nose dimmer than mine. And yet he frightened me.

"Do not speak!" he commanded gently. "I can anticipate your questions, beloved servant, and foresee your thoughts, and it will save time if I merely answer."

He stooped and pried a pebble from the floor, and held it up before my eyes. "Coral is one of the great building materials of the Hormagaunts. To escape the eternal twilight, thorns, and deadly fruit of the world-forest, there were certain Clades who had created or expanded atolls and islands here in the Philippines and Micronesia using coral. The eternal trees cannot take root here, and therefore I cannot gather intelligence as to the goings-on.

"Would that I had watched this empty quarter of the world more closely! I saw the number of islands multiplying, and thought no ill of it. But these Insular Clades of the Pacific had long ago departed the One True Way, for they departed from the Wintermind and sought out the old psychological matrices of unmodified man. They married and raised their young without consuming them or selling them.

"These Insulars have resurrected the long-dead filial relationships: they have uncles and aunts, cousins and clans, and they erected totems to their clanholds, flags and heraldries, special images and names as if their holds were living things—and emotional set from before the times of the Nymphs, a Chimera configuration called patriotism which long I sought to destroy utterly.

"From clan totems to sacred idols is a small step. Worship, a emotional set of the Witches, was reborn, for the Insulars began to slaughter sacrifices and to burn incense and do the other things that those who hold this world is not the sole and final world are wont to do: and so the endless Darwinian wars of this world lost their fascination to them.

"Being a rational and philosophically inclined people, the Insulars reversed the order of nature, where lower things by evolution leads to higher, and conceived that their many little gods and idols were avatars and descendants of a single and perfect one God—embracing an order not of nature. And this was the emotional set of the Giants, and of earlier orders, including my own. All the progress of history was undone. For they had learned kinship, kindness, patriotism, paternity, worship, and prayer.

"Peace answered their prayers, and so they wax great and powerful, and revolutions in political economics, philosophy, and military sciences followed. Even the nature of man and his purpose in the world was questioned.

"The repercussions over the last century spread across the globe, and reached even your home in Albion. All these recent wars and genocides are a seismic adjustment to the social forces set in motion by the nonconformist and divergent Clades of these Pacific Insulars.

"Long years of statistical analysis crept by. Finally, I located the epicenter of the disturbance to the calculus of history: I know which island the Judge of Ages used to spread the new vector into the patterns of events. But I do not understand the math he used.

"So I could not move against the divergents erenow. There is a machine at the core of the world that watches and studies all that I do on the surface as closely as I watch and study the doings of my Hormagaunts. But the machine cannot intuit patterns in events, and sees no patterns other than what it is programmed to look for.

"By encouraging wars and assisting the horrors of war to mount ever higher, I have created sufficient confusion in the pattern of history—a white noise—that the world-core machine will not detect. It will not see, amid all the other statistical anomalies and onetime events that wars create, the anomaly of this, my raid, and the mysterious disappearances I now orchestrate.

"On an island in my day called Yap, where once the natives carved immense wheels of calcite stone twelve feet in diameter to serve as their money, there is now a great and luxurious people living, groups of Clades not allergic to one another. The Yapese are fraternal and not identical twins, men of psychological unity which my control of history should long ago have led to self-destruction. From here has come the poets and philosophers and nonconformist Iatrocrats which disturb my schemes; from here issues the anomaly that outsmarts and overwhelms my countermaneuvers.

"Indeed, I can be thwarted. Do not be surprised. I am the Master of this aeon, but there is one who meddles with my designs and defies my mastery.

"There is a Hermeticist who betrayed my brethren, the other Hermeticists, and he opposes us all. Deep in his Tombs he slumbers, and we cannot destroy him with a strike from space. Such is he the simple people call the Judge of Ages."

(I knew then for the first time that he could not foresee my thoughts, for if he could have done, he would have killed me, before the spark of hope, fanned by winds of hate, erupted into wildfire in both my hearts.)

"My age will not be judged by him," Reyes continued, "will not be put to trial, not condemned! I will discover the mathematical system he used to break the way of life and the Wintermind disciplines I established. Somehow into the genes and memes, the biological and sociological information that controls civilization, the Judge of Ages introduced the Clade Codes, which allow for Avuncular Altruism, so that even remote relations sharing some genetic material will combine their survival strategies and adopt programs of mutually beneficial selflessness. The Clades were created long ago, and under such conditions as my vision of history was not interrupted; therefore, I did not detect it. Buried within their genetic codes and mimetic patterns of behavior were recessive elements time eventually brought together, a ripple of many waves converging positively to re-enforce each other at Yap. Hah! And to think that I thought the development of a burg-dwelling class of cloned duplicates was a natural trend.

"But here, in these islands, unwatched, the Darwinian process was halted, or reversed: I have even seen uncles caring for crippled and retarded Clade-cousins, and Hormagaunts dying naturally of old age, refusing to replace worn organs from the younger generations of their inferiors for reasons of mere sentiment.

"Intolerable! Who will meet the Hyades at the End of Days when the star-monsters descend? Uncles burdened with love for cripples and idiots? Mothers with babe soaking at the breast? The widowed, the crippled, the poor and the weak? They will reproduce like conies, and outnumber and overwhelm the Enlightened, unless the social vectors involved are neutralized.

"You and yours will forestall this dread future my mathematics foretells for me.

"The first wave will descend upon Yap Island in the form of high-altitude microspore packages, condense and fall as rain, and spread a synchronized binary paralytic agent throughout the water table. Major organs and thought processes must be kept functioning, and a sufficient number of living subjects must be kept alive to allow us to reverse-engineer the social and genetic vectors the Judge of Ages introduced when he created his Clade Code.

"The wider the baseline, the greater the chance of detecting the statistical pattern. Naturally, even the simplest simultaneous solution of a thousand-variable sum is beyond human capacity. It is beyond the capacity of my Dreagh, Expastor, who dwells in the wandering star.

"No, the only machines capable of reverse engineering the math used to create the Clades are those that squat at the bottom of the Mariana Trench, the Ghosts of the long-dead Cetaceans.

"The Cetaceans were a race elevated not merely to human levels of intelligence, but beyond, to the superhuman, and they used the tools we gave them to create emulations of their own minds deep in the lightless abyss beneath the seas, acre upon acre of windowless domes of onyx and plinths of some diamond-hard material whose making we do not understand.

"I have expended other amphibian servants over the years to approach the Ghosts of the dead race, and finally one survived, and through him, I have made a covenant with them, and secured a safe conduct for you. I have designed for you a tripartite body able to adjust in its metamorphoses to ever deeper ranges of the sea, from bathypelagic, where no light reaches and black fish swim, and the only light is from the creatures themselves, to abyssopelagic, where no light nor heat is found, and even whales dare not dive, to the hadalpelagic at the bottom of chasms, where the pressure is eight tons per square inch, and boneless starfish and tube worms crawl.

"You will be the first of many conductors. Your task is to draw the Yap islanders down to the bottom of the trench in special vessels I will give you. There the Yapese will be given, still alive, to the intellects of long-dead whales and superwhales and dolphins and superdolphins.

"The entire subsea structure of the Yap Islands will be destroyed, and the sea will eat the islands and destroy all evidence of our doings here.

"Now go. Assemble your squads; select them by the usual gladiatorial method."

The year in which these events took place was 7385 by the reckoning Reyes y Pastor used to count the years, the Years of his Lord.

Blind luck was with us. The hundred things that should have marred the operation instead fell out as the Red Hermeticist desired. Burg after burg of the richest polity on the planet was taken, all intact, and fortresses, libraries, fields, growth cells, plantations, cloning stations, watchtowers; and no word, no electric signals, not even a messenger bee escaped to tell the tale.

Of the ten thousand grisly deeds I did I will not speak, except to say I seem still to hear the screams and pleas, some wild, and some calm with the dignity only those about to die can muster, still ringing in my ears. Victims and their children I dragged all of that first group into the cells, and then the next and next without number, their limbs unable to move, packed into the nutrient fluid which filled their lungs and veins. Then the islands sank and the flood came, and it was a slow disaster, and through the membrane of the cells, the helpless thousands could see the tides rolling higher and higher, inch by inch, over their land. And then the waters rolled over their heads, and the light of day was gone.

Below, we crammed into sardonic vessels all the paralytics, frozen like flies in amber, and they sank into darker and darker places. Down into eternal gloom, where freakish fish like skeletal nightmares of teeth and huge blind eyes, glowing like specters from their own luminescence, seeing never any light but their own, down the roots of the deepest trenches of the sea, under one thousand atmospheres of pressure they were taken. Of the ghosts in the windowless domes at the bottom of the abyss, sightless domes that rise through the freezing water above fields of black sand and boiling vents of sulfur, I am the only living thing to have seen, and survived to tell. Of their blind songs and the horror of what has never been human—of all this I will not speak. Three thousands of years have passed, and all my crimes are long forgotten, save by me.

I served him well, Reyes y Pastor, and sabotaged the efforts of others who served him, and I flattered and fawned and lied, so that he was pleased with me, and he thought I loved him when my only feeling for him was absolute terror.

But my deception prevailed, and I alone was spared when many hundreds of his men, serfs, and loyal servants were slaughtered to keep the atrocity of Yap Island secret from all recorded history.

Do you see now why I will aid the Judge of Ages, and why I did not tell the Blue lordlings of my moot with Pastor? No man, unless he were a Hormagaunt in truth, could hear of such enormities and not vow eternal war against the Master of the World, or whichever of his Hermetic vassals presently wears in his name his iron crown.

5. *Madness*

I know the fate of Master of Fate: in the Year of his Lord 7466, Reyes y Pastor went mad.

Still in his household, I served, and I saw it all. Reyes began talking about a king in outer space who has a child but no wife, and Father Reyes was urging but not ordering his servitors and slaves to serve this king.

Reyes then enacted a strange make-believe type of glandular donation, but using bread instead of real glands from real children, wine instead of real blood. But he insisted that these are the proper mechanisms for producing the biochemical change into a new organism, which he called a glorified body.

Within the next few years, some of the other Hormagaunts were given an office as "Shepherds"—even though there were no sheep—and were called "Father" as Father Reyes was—even though they sired no sons.

The Fathers not only spread this imaginary biochemical change, but some also wandered the newly treeless lands, telling Iatrocrats that to kill and consume children was forbidden, telling the Clades to welcome the stranger and the sojourner, telling Donors to obey their masters in all things, but to disobey when ordered to cease to serve the imaginary space king, and to rejoice in the death that this disobedience would provoke.

The Old True Way was openly defied, and this new way, this thing for which we had no name, spread from the Pacific Islands through Indonesia to Indochina through Angkor to Tabrobane. It sounded like the Nymph-talk, but it was a nonsexual form of sex, a nonhomosexual nonincestuous form of brother-love: indeed, in its name, some of the Clades forswore reproduction altogether and became eremites, living in isolation and begging the king in outer space to forgive the crimes of the world.

Others of the Clade-folk took one and only one mate, freeing their harems and studs, and they claimed their flesh was one, but they did not consume each other or make the flesh to be one. Nor did they mate only in the mating times and seasons, but for lifelong. Bowers of blooming flowers they grew to solemnize and celebrate this wonder, even though it was nothing but reproduction using sexual organs to exchange fluid, rather than the more dignified and hygienic pods and matrices. They used the old instruments of long-vanished Witches to compose songs about this, called Epithalamia, and the songs were very fair to the ear, so that even Hormagaunts would weep to hear. It was insanity, and did not serve the progress of the race toward posthumanity, but it was a beautiful insanity.

Reyes y Pastor called himself the Master of the World, and Lord of History. Who could have stopped him and his madness? But one did. The real Master of the World sent another down from the darkness of heaven, from the morning star, your ship.

Sudden war and horror came, so swift and so complete that no mortal could have compassed it, only a posthuman. First, the foe raised a storm. How you posthumans can command the weather, I do not understand, but I saw it.

During this typhoon, Medusae dropped down suddenly from the night sky in many vessels as silver as fish and swifter than hawks. From these vessels, tendrils like the arms of Scylla reached down and plucked up and tore asunder all the Hormagaunts, Donors, and Clades found in the open.

All who served the make-believe king of space were slain by the real space lord, the Master of the World. Up from the sea, their approach hidden by the tidal wave, came Hormagaunts from Annam, offended at those who spoke against the One True Way. And there were diverse earthquakes in many places, wherever a rainbow of light reached down from outer space and touched the bottom of the sea.

Then one descended from the vehicle of the Medusae dressed as an Hermeticist, in the black silks of a starfarer. He had two tendrils made of biometallic gold issuing from his skull above his eyes. I did not know what it was I saw, but the coming years revealed what it was: This was the first of the Locusts. The time of the Red Hermeticist was done; the time of the Locust Hermeticist was come.

The cathedrals and nunneries and other buildings were inflicted with rabies, so that the doors all closed and those inside were digested and slain. No innocent life was spared, and those who did not resist were not killed cleanly but by slow torture, cut with knives so that strings of his own flesh could tie the victim between two fires to which wood was added one stick at a time. They were infected, so that when other prisoners were released from cages made of the bones of their loved ones, the infections afflicted sight and reasoning centers, so that these would-be saviors merely lit themselves aflame or brought more harm on the victim, much to the amusement of the Annam Hormagaunts.

I saw the coffin of the Red Hermeticist being loaded aboard the airskiff of the Medusa, but whether this was a slumbering coffin or a death coffin, I could not say.

History has heard nothing more of Reyes y Pastor.

And I? You know how I escaped. I fled to your Tombs for protection, Judge of Ages, knowing this the one place the Hermeticists could not come. That is how I came to be your prisoner.

What? No. No tales I told the Blue Men were truth, though perhaps some parts were closer to true than others. What right have they to ask anything of me?

8

The Testament of Oenoe the Nymph

1. The Tale of a Bride of a Dead World

After noon mess, a pack of eight dog things escorted Menelaus past the gate to the large sky blue nautilus shell.

There was a warm and steady headwind from the doorless opening as he entered, which stayed in his face as he climbed. The air pressure was slightly higher inside than out. Menelaus decided that the Simplifiers either had a religious prohibition on doors and chimneys and windows, or a deliberate preference for pretty but uncomfortable impracticalities. Not to mention lots of fuel to waste.

He was brought around one more half turn of the corridor, reaching a higher but smaller chamber than before. Here, a different architecture suddenly appeared. The floor was coated with living grass, surrounding a depression in the center of the floor where a green pool thronged with floating lotus blossoms shimmered. As the dogs escorted him in, a screen of leaves and lianas closed over the opening, moving just slowly enough to be unnoticeable. This living screen of leafy vines was the first curtain he had seen inside the nautilus shell; and the only barrier to the wind. The air within was humid and warm.

On the grass lay draped the beautiful curvaceous form of a She-Nymph, her midnight hair like a waterfall of ink, shining, falling in drapes and cascades adown her swanlike neck and slender shoulders. Generations of gene-modification had exaggerated her various sexual characteristics to a point just shy of absurdity. Her eyes were slanted and lustrous, so large as to seem a child's eyes. Her eyes were underlined by an epicanthic fold, and shaded by eyelashes like two raven's wings. Her face was round and high-cheeked, her lips so full and red, they seemed to burst with blood. The chin beneath was small and firm, coming to a dainty point. Her breasts were like those of a pregnant woman, while her waist was that of an untouched maiden, and the muscles of her belly formed a parenthesis around a perfect navel. Her designers graced her with wide hips sweetly rounded, long legs that were a symphony of curving length, firm thighs and pointed toes, all muscled like a slumbering lioness.

Even her hands and arms were more feminine than nature's own design, as her elbows had more than normal range of motion at the joint, that when she straightened her arms they bent slightly backwards, graceful as a willow tree in wind.

Her blush response was likewise exaggerated. A she reclined, her flawless skin shaded from palest gold to lambent yellow like aged ivory to a rose red, and back again. One moment her skin seemed almost tawny, a goddess in warm bronze, but in the next moment her skin was so pale that the blue hint of arterial veins in her bosom could be glimpsed.

She wore nothing but a V-shaped garland of flowering lianas bright with little blue flowers and white, that snaked around her hips like a braided loincloth and fell in two ankle-length sashes trailing in meandering loops between her legs.

Several dog things hunkered near the walls, panting in the sauna-heat. The two Blue Men were seated cross-legged on the grassy floor, calmly sweating, having not removed their coats. The elder, Mentor Ull, regarded the Nymph with eyes as cold as a snake's, and his half-closed lids gave him a sleepy look. Preceptor Illiance wore an expression of meditative serenity.

The Nymph was agitated, her eyes glancing left and right, and she lifted her hands nervously to toy with her hair now and again, or she swayed from left to right, reclining now on one rounded, marvelous hip, now tucking her long legs the other way to recline on the other. When Menelaus entered the room, she tossed back her hair in the flurry of darkness, her red lips parted, and she looked not quite toward him with hunger, and her dark eyes were like coals, and her pupils dilated hypnotically. He could sense the unscented natural perfume of a woman in heat from across the chamber like a kick to the back of his skull.

Illiance spoke without any preliminary, saying, "Lance-Corporal Beta Anubis, after some consideration, we have agreed to your demand that we depose a woman of the Nymph race. Frankly, we do not see how this will sate the academic curiosity which is part of your purpose in aiding us—she is not from an era of decline. However, Preceptor Ull agrees to host the interview of her, provided you also elicit answers to the questions that concern us. You seek to discover if the Tombs are hindering progress; we seek knowledge of the Tomb origins. Of the Nymphs so far exhumed, this relict is the only one from an era that is most likely to satisfy our mutual interests."

Menelaus replied in High Iatric, "Preceptor Illiance, you may not know it, but you are afflicting this poor girl. Neither you nor the dog things here are giving her the normal nonverbal sexual cues she is used to, and so her body is automatically trying to become more sexually provocative. She might not even be consciously aware of it. Try to smile or get an erection or something. Give off musk. Do you have any cellular control over your bodies?"

Illiance said, "Our life modifications are almost entirely neurological, with hormonal and circulatory modifications no more than necessary than those to maintain balanced mental functions during high-speed neural activity."

Ull spoke in Intertextual. *"Achieve discreet silence. It is not advisable for the relict to happen to grow aware of our biomodifications and limits."*

Illiance inclined his head toward Ull. *"May I reveal sufficient to quell his question? Otherwise the psychological discontent will resonate through the remainder of our dealings."*

Ull flicked his heavy-lidded eyes in a gesture of assent.

Illiance said to Menelaus, "We cannot mimic these subconscious responses. We are based on the Locust template, who, in order to achieve greater social harmony, are genetically imprinted to form lifelong pair-bonds. You may explain this to the she-relict before you ask her about the Tomb origins."

"And you might explain what is wrong with all you future people? Why is everyone a nudist? She might be able to concentrate if you gave her some clothes. Hell, I might be able to concentrate better."

"Like you, she seems to have haply refused our gift, and she tore the overalls and threw them at the muzzle of Follower Ee-ee Krkok Yef Yepp in a gesture we found disharmonious. The meaning of this act is obscure to us, and we ponder whether it was symbolic or functional, and in what proportions."

"Which dog is Eek-Crap-Uck-Yuck-Whatever-the-heck-you-said?"

"Ee-ee Krkok Yef Yepp. Yonder." Illiance inclined his head toward a stately Doberman Pincer. His eyes were bright, and he was wagging his tail happily.

"You want me to ask her about that too?"

Illiance said, "Our purposes mingle with yours, but do not seek to overpower them."

"Is that a yes?"

"It may be. What is that loud breathing noise you make with your mouth?"

"It's called a sigh. The technical term is exasperation. I never thought I'd miss having an Alpha bark orders at me, but at least they told you what they wanted cleaned or who they wanted killed. Learn something new every day, I guess."

Illiance raised both hands and touched his forefingers, one to each ear, making a gesture that meant nothing to Menelaus. He said with quiet pride, "To lead a soul to new learning, however trivial, sustains the universal imperative of life."

Menelaus answered nothing to that, but instead stepped forward and knelt by the pool in a slithering rustle of his bulky metallic robes. His face was already red from the heat, and he shrugged one arm and shoulder out of his garb, so that it hung over the other shoulder like a toga. With his naked arm he plucked a lotus blossom from the pond and tossed it lightly toward the Nymph, saying in her language, "For your delight."

She rose to her feet and came swaying toward him, more graceful than a sinuous snake. "I have much for your delight, young bridegroom."

He lowered his eyes and held up his hand. "While I am flattered, ma'am, I—" But his tongue failed him at that moment, because she did not stop her ballerina-smooth glide forward, so that his upturned palm was now pressed into the yielding and scenting flesh of her lower belly. Little flowers crinkled under his surprised fingers, and he was afraid to look up for fear of where his nose might land.

Before he could push her away, however, she had stepped around behind him and laid a warm, long-nailed hand on his bare shoulder, almost a caress. "You need not kneel yet to me, young bridegroom, for I wish your homage in other ways. Lift up your head."

Menelaus stood. Even compared to Chimera, he was tall, and so he towered over her. He drew his bare arm back into his cumbersome cloak and, despite the heat, drew his hood around his face, and held the fabric at his chin in his fist.

She swayed back from him and half turned, giving him a glance over her smooth shoulder. "You importune me! Or do you wish in truth for my delight, which is the root of all benevolence?"

"I am a Chimera. Your race destroyed and supplanted mine. Not that I mind. We were annoying folk, to be honest."

Her enormous eyes were even prettier when she narrowed them in thought and looked at him sidelong. "Do you jest? You biolinguistic tells are hard to read. Disrobe, and I will learn your muscle-nerve responses."

"Thanks but no thanks. Like I was about to say, first, I am a married man, and second, I am on duty, and third, Chimera only get to impregnate according to a breeding program."

"Impregnate?!" said the Nymph, surprised. "I was only inviting you to the love-play. Social harmony is achieved only when everyone loves everyone."

"My mistake. Here I thought sexual reproduction had something to do with sexual reproduction."

"Your words fail to kiss my understanding ear, and this diminishes my speech-joy."

"Sorry about your speech-joy, ma'am. Let me introduce myself. I carry a rock to smash in the skulls of people who annoy me, and that list is pretty long and getting longer, and my name is Beta Sterling Xenius Anubis of Mount Erebus."

"I delight in the name Oenoe Psthinshayura-Ah, and my displayed design is the Crocus twined with Clover and Forsythia, but my intimate design is Hyssop, Juniper, and Lily in an eternal knot. Do you know the flower language? It has remained unchanged since eldest recorded time."

His eyes slid toward the Blue Men, and then glanced toward the dog things. "I know what oleander and orange blossoms stand for."

She drifted back to her place on the far side of the lotus pool and cooed. "To understand and to be understood is its own delight, more intimate than other consolations." She knelt on the grasses, but then went to her hands and knees, turning and turning again, like a kitten clawing a place to rest, and she collapsed slowly into a sinuous heap.

Oenoe plucked a grass blade, tickled her red lips with it, and then held it between her perfect teeth, twitching and chewing it thoughtfully. She lay on her stomach, thighs on the grass, feet upright and swaying slowly in the air, toes pointed toward the ceiling, which accentuated the curve of her calves. "The blue-pigmented dwarfs. What is wrong with them?"

"Aside from being Tomb-looters? They are eunuchs."

She straightened up, eyes bright. "Then I am the captive in the harem of some brutal Sultan from Araby the Blessed, who means to use me ruthlessly for his pleasure?"

"Ah, no. They are neurochemically eunuched, except to particular mates. Ma'am, I am a historian, so I happen to know that there were no harems and no brutal Sultans anywhere on the planet for at least seventy centuries before your time. I also know the Nymphs don't keep records or histories except for songs in your trees. How do you know about such things?"

She cocked her head to one side and smiled. "Sultanates may have passed away long since, but the wild romance-tales girls hear and swap have not changed." Then she looked at him from beneath her absurdly long and dark lashes. "The blue eunuchs lead the dance here, not you? Even though you are a whole man?"

"I am their prisoner. I am translating for them."

"Of your own will?"

"There are other things I'd rather be doing, ma'am."

"Do they understand these words?"

"The young one speaks Natural, but not fluently. The boss, I don't know. The dogs are intelligent creatures and carry vocal coder-decoder devices which could translate everything they hear, so it beats the hell out of me why I am even here."

Oenoe seemed suddenly done with playfulness, for now she knelt again, buttocks on her heels and her curving spine upright, and she crossed her beautiful hands in her lap.

"What do they want of me? Do they wish their manhood restored? Ah! I would have to see their genetic codes, enzymatic and prostaglandin gestation history before I could say if a restoration is feasible. Of course I will donate my every effort. I am of the Order of Nature: our way is the way of love. Tell them not to despair."

2. Mating, Matriarchy, Mantilla

Menelaus sighed and turned toward Illiance. In High Iatric he said, "She offers to make your rutting season year-round, and restore you to sexual promiscuity. She makes the offer out of the goodness of her heart. She'd have to see your medical records."

Illiance blinked. "Tell her we are gladdened and ennobled by the offer, but do not see the advantage. We shall attempt to imitate and reciprocate her benevolence, which awes us."

To Oenoe, Menelaus said in Natural, "They are damned impressed with the offer and will try to pay you back, but they say no."

"Only one spoke. Is the other his child?"

"No, ma'am. The other one is his *boss*. Do you know that word?"

"A male Mother. I understand. An *Alpha-of-Alphas.*" She used the Chimerical word for Imperator-General. "Was he conscripted to serve as Matriarch, or did he put himself forward of his own will?"

"I don't know whether he was picked. What difference does it make?"

"We regard the one from the other as distinct as birds from fish. To we who serve and who obey Nature, it is paramount to be led by servants, not to serve leaders."

"Just assume the worst, ma'am, and you are less likely to be disappointed."

"Such wisdom! Surprising that a race which could bring forth such sage and accomplished soldier-ants would be so easily sponged from the annals of time!" There was no word for fighting-men in her language, so she used her word for legionnaire ants, *myrmidon*.

"Now you are mocking me, ma'am."

"Only because you are stiff and easy to tease, and too tongueless to reply. You said you are married. To whom? Your mother?"

"Beg pardon?"

"Introduction into the sexual arts is best done by a child's mother, who can lead him gently through the exercises, with small chance of embarrassment."

"No, ma'am. I didn't marry my mother. I reckon I'd be plenty embarrassed if I had. A wife means more than a sexual partner: the bond is exclusive and lifelong."

"I don't know those words."

"*Exclusive* means I cleave to her and forsake all others. *Lifelong* means it is unconditional and unbreakable; to cleave to each other in weal and woe, health and hardship, plenty and penury, at bed and at board till death us depart. Lifelong means no casting off just because she goes barren, or he comes back from the warfare blind or shy a leg or something."

"By why would a partner want a maimed love-performer? Maimed folk look ugly!"

"It ain't no damn partnership! Partners is folks you can give up on when they drop their side of the bargain. Marriage ain't no damn bargain." In another language, to himself, he muttered, *"In more ways than one."*

Oenoe was unconvinced. "How can sex be exclusive? Its nature is all-giving!"

"If you give your all to one woman, there ain't nothing left over to give to any other: stands to reason."

"Fie on reason! As for it being lifelong, no man can hold an erection for that length."

"You don't know real men."

"Your system sounds selfish and ungainly."

"And yours, begging your pardon, ma'am, sounds like a grotesque overreaction against the tight sexual control of the Chimerae."

"Ho hee! So you think your echoes live on in us? A flattering thought to you! Your race is long forgotten."

"Forgotten or not, you set about doing everything the opposite of the race you were supplanting, but after they were gone, you kept on getting into a simpler and more easily transmitted version of your same practices and habits, until you ended up with a society where all friendships and family relations are sexualized. The first generation of Naturals merely wanted a revocation of the eugenics laws."

"Not true!" Her enormous and shining eyes held a combination of wonder and mock-outrage. Then she smiled a sultry smile. "Surely we have always been as we are now. Our lack of history proves that there was nothing worthwhile to record."

"My grandma told me once about a group called the Playboys. Their women dressed like bunny rabbits. They were obsessed with sex. They were an overreaction to a group called the Victorians, whose women dressed in black from neck to ankle. They were obsessed with modesty. In turn, they were an overreaction against a group called the Georgians, who were bawdier whoremongers than any period in history since the fall of Babylon. It's a simple periodic cycle, like the swing of a pendulum, where the discontent of each era tries to solve itself by reversing the morals of the previous: but sometimes the pendulum gets stuck."

Oenoe looked at him with her gleaming, mesmeric eyes, and for once her gaze was direct rather than flirtatious or playful. "You are a student of Cliometry? I had thought the study was lost when the Giants burned the world, the yesterdays before yesterday."

Menelaus looked alert. "What do you know of it?"

Oenoe shrugged prettily, gazing at him sidelong through half-lowered lashes, any directness once more hidden. "If you were a woman, we could have an intelligent discussion of the matter. But men only like women who are free of care and thought."

"Only bachelors think women are dumber than men. Besides, I don't want to like you. I just want to ask you some questions."

Oenoe shook her head and lifted her nose. "Again you mention marriage! You are obsessed."

"I hope so."

"Is she alive, this exclusive lifelong love-partner of yours?"

"I hope so."

"Where is she, this exclusive lifelong partner?"

"I don't think she is buried at this site. But I'll find her. No matter how long. Even if I have to count to trillion first. No matter what. If I have to break the world in two, I'll get her back."

Oenoe hugged herself, her lovely eyes glittering. "She will share you with me! Then she and I will disport ourselves, and you may watch or join as you wish. There is no barrier to pleasure except the pleasure of breaking barriers. Will she find me irresistible, do you think?"

"Ma'am, she fell for me, and at that point I stopped trying to understand womenfolk—so who knows what she'd do? My wife is very kindly predisposed toward all human beings and some beings not so very human, and her heart is bigger than her mind, and that's saying something, because she is sharp as a whip crack and twice as fast, and I can't keep up with her."

Illiance raised a finger. "I am having trouble following the conversation. What is being discussed now? You have exchanged many words. Why are you discussing your mate?"

Menelaus said in Iatric, "The lady wants to copulate with me, you, him, half the dog things in the room, and maybe the signal tower in the airfield, if she can climb that high. I am trying to be polite without nickering at her. We are talking about mating because that is all Nymphs talk about."

"Does she suffer a glandular imbalance?"

"Well, for one of her race, she's actually quite temperate and reserved. Nymphs exchange bodily fluids with chemical cues in them in order to maintain their chain of command. Or whatever they have for a chain of command. Their social order. They don't use their sex organs for sex. They use them to say hello."

Illiance said, "We are well aware of the peculiarities of the psychology of the Natural Order. Did you find out why she unclothed herself?"

Menelaus turned back to Oenoe. "He wants to know why you threw your prison uniform at the dog."

"To strike the canine in the nose. The act is self-explanatory."

"Sorry, ma'am, I mean, he wants to know why you took off the uniform to begin with."

"Ah! I reject his suitor-gifts as unworthy, and my intent was to push a sharp thorn into his feelings. His glamour in the public eye must dwindle."

"Why is that, ma'am?"

"I am highly beloved, praiseworthy among my kind, and have often been conscripted. This creates a corresponding set of pleasures and displeasures in those around me splendid as the wings of a butterfly, and the blue eunuchs fail to step their part in the dance!"

"Sorry, what? Is that a metaphor, or are you talking about a real dance?"

"It would diminish my pleasure to speak more plainly. The protest would be obvious to an open-songed heart!"

"No offense, ma'am, but I am a Chimera, and these blue snarks are plunderers, Tomb-robbers, and slavers, so if there is an open-songed heart anywhere in earshot, it must be among the dog things. You should explain, whether it delights or not, please. Because otherwise we won't understand, and that would, um, not delight us in our delight-seeking pleasing pleasure-seeking pleasurableness. Get it?"

"Now is it you who mock me?" Her eyes flashed anger, but she smiled when she said it.

"Well, ma'am, maybe you got some stiffnesses of your own."

She pouted. "I was entombed with my mantilla."

"I don't know that word."

"It is the veil of brides of the world, held up by a comb, and it trails down the shoulders and back like a pelisse or short cloak. Those of greater glamour, theirs hang to the hips. Those of greatest glamour, theirs hang to midthigh. Mine came to my heels, and I had to wear cothurni, or to train dormice to carry the train."

"A royal robe?"

"More! A companion! My mantilla was a living cloak, cellular-keyed to my biochemistry, and no one else can use it, and it bore the life-code of ten thousands. It was green and emerald and viridescent, a dance of leaf and woven fiber, and it assisted me in photosynthesis, and bloomed with scent and pheromone and it painted the world around me with all comeliness. The ruff alone contained blue roses of a breed hybridized only for me, found not elsewhere in the world. It was a robe of high estate, and it is a grievous insult to me, a wound, a stumblefooted dance-step, to give me mere dead fibers made of cotton, I who am a Conscript Lady, Mother, Matriarch, May-Queen, and Coryphaeus of my kind. They must return what was taken from my Tomb to me! They *must*!"

"Or else, what? You'll flash your naked breasts at them? I don't think that will scare them, huge as they are."

"Or else they will have left the path of delight and giving delight. Did not the younger one establish that he willed to match my generous love with an act of love? To restore me mine is justice! And justice is but one type of love."

Menelaus turned to Illiance. "Did you follow any of that? She wants her green cloak back. It's made of leafy material. Some sort of symbiotic life."

Illiance looked solemn. "The matter has several ramifications. To be frank, we cannot determine what molecular mechanisms the bioartifact contains, or what all of them can do. Some may be disturbing to our purposes, or be able to concoct deadly influences. The head-comb contains a neural interface we cannot decipher."

Menelaus said, "If I were not so easygoing, I'd be offended. You have armed Chimerae in your camp. Between the three of us, we have a rock, and a bone club, and a stick. And I think the Gamma has a sling by now. Our womenfolk are pretty hard-core too. We could kill everyone in this camp if our honor demanded it. You also let a heavyweight Hormagaunt run around, and he has venom sacs and skunk glands and porcupine quills like a walking Swiss Army knife o' Death, not to mention tusks and fangs and claws and a stinger on his tail. And you are afraid of some wiggly comfort girl from a pacifist era whose theory of military political economics consists of singing love songs, taking swims, eating fruit, and then snuggling each other's sex organs till they squirt?"

Mentor Ull spoke with ponderous inflection. "Beta Anubis of the Chimera! Your opinion of our policy and judgment is of course of profound significance to yourself. Albeit, the significance to us, being proportionate to your very limited knowledge and your fixed and unimaginative principles of thought, enjoins us to ponder it with no more than the attention it merits."

"Thanks, Ull. Likewise and so's your mother, I'm sure. But you could have one of your dog things with his talky box sitting here instead of me—because it is not the words you really need translated, it's the psychology behind them, right? Well, if so, hear my advice. This minx's cloak of petals and perfumes was designed to interact with ecological structures that went extinct about three thousand years ago. The trained poop-burying pussycats her scent-calls can call have been dead for thirty centuries, and probably aren't in sniff-range anyhow. If you want her to open up about anything she knows, whatever she knows, return what you took."

Illiance said, "Much is unknown of this mantilla."

Menelaus threw up his hands. "Oh, hell! You robbers are poking in the Tombs without the slightest idea of who the hell or what the hell you might wake up from hell knows how long ago. I thought we were scholars, you and me, and that means we keep poking at the Unknown until it goes off, and then we carefully measure the blast radius. Don't you think it is a little late to grow a sense of caution now? Isn't that—what do you guys call it when you do things for artificial reasons?—isn't that a little unsimplistic of you?

"Tell you what." He continued, "Make you a deal. You get the little lady to wrap up her lovely flesh, milk glands and all, in her royal robes as she'd like, and I promise I can get her to tell her story, clear as clear and no more interruptions. What do you say? Send that dog there to get her robe."

He pointed at the Doberman Pincer.

3. *Of the Love of the Ages*

O Nature, whose living breath inspires the world, and from whose gentle breath the twining ivy and clustering grape, the ripening roundess of the peach and plum beneath the branch, the dew-bright meadows in the dawnlight arise and praise the wind and cloud, the dark raincloud and the white cumulus where hawk and sparrow sail in circles, and sun and moon in golden light and silver grace the world, breathe into me now such song as will entrance all ears inclined, and with sweet soothing, as the luxurious honeycomb adrip with gold, assuage the sorrows of the soul.

Gather and hear, O lovers, for delight in song and hearing song engenders more delight, and I must tell my tale! Let it be birthed with slight travail.

Of myself, let me be Oenoe Psthinshayura-Ah of Crocus, Clover, and Forsythia, all intimately entwined, and I sing for your delight and mine, and do all I do for you. If you would have me otherwise, then cajole and tempt me, and I will yield as the clinging grapevine, full and ripe, yields when trained to recline the twining contours acquiescent along the firm and sturdy branch.

Of the origins of the Tombs, not I, nor any Chanter of my race, knows nor cares nor can be brought to care. Before yesterday was another yesterday, and to count beyond is grief.

To ask if the Tombs preserved knowledge for us from other yesterdays, or hindered our changes and progresses into far tomorrows, is a question no Nymph answers. What passes into the world is here, what was passes away is gone, and none can number or name the passage, for it grants no joy to count.

The Tombs are in the ground and the sun and moon are in the sky, and thus it was yesterday and a yesterday before that, and to say or to suppose the more, that is perpetually beyond my lore.

Who knows who gave birth to the cosmos? How could any Mother be, or where could she stand? If there were none to see how all was born, or from whom, then there is none to say. Why speak dull words when love-words await the yielding lip? Why tarry, when the lingering afternoon with gilded beam horizontal foreshadows an end of day?

Many have rumored that the Tombs are forbidden to the Nymphs. This is a telling told for the delight of dreamy falsehood, and I do not naysay what pleases, for are not all lovers' promises sweet and all untrue? But I say it is not so, and, as you love me, you will gaze into my gaze and so believe.

We do not use the Tombs, for when we are marred or wounded, the Mothers will remake us, and with fumes of Nepenthe and wine of Lethe spun with poppies sponge all memory of pain away. We do not yearn for tomorrow, for where is it? You cannot close your fingers on the hair of the wind. The wind passes by and passes again, and caresses you, and you laugh only if you do not try to close your fingers. What is not within reach, it is folly to grasp, not when there are lovers to embrace, and much that concerns us now and here.

The Judge of Ages, we know him to be true, for our hearts would melt if the tale of his long-enduring love proved false. Truth is what is fair and comely to believe: if others say they hold another way to know the truth than this, well, this is too a telling told for their delight, and I do not naysay what pleases.

The Judge of Ages loves us, and he sends aloft at Jubilee those who need our crafts and arts to cure them, and those who are overborne by sorrows of past things which can never come again, whose sorrows we erase, all traces, from their nervous system, and blood, molecules and glands.

Ours is the time of joy, the promised time that all the sad yesterdays waited so long to meet.

4. Of the One-Fighters, and the Choosers to Be Slain

Rumor says no Nymphs descend into the Tombs, and that is as true as lovers' promises, for it is sweetly said. The Mothers knew that discontentment would arise, even in our gardens and glades, and among the silken pavilions and self-woven tents covered with petals brought by songbirds, which we never pitch two nights in one same place.

Into the Tombs we place in slumber those whom pleasures will not please. They are not suited for our age, but must await another. From time to time there comes among us a young man and stalwart, who wishes not for kisses, but to see the tomorrow after tomorrow, when the Terror of the Stars shall fall on us, the End of Days of Liberty, when mankind shall be leashed and serve the Hyades in Taurus, and eat in those days from their hands, as here on Earth hound and cat and rat and hawk and hart serve us, and eat from our hands.

Such men are called *Einheriar* or "One Alone Who Fights," for they are lonely and leave all the sweet kisses of the Nymphs—for is not our whole race willing to be his bride? But he renounces love, and seeks death in the cold future.

Also there are born at times when the genetic coding fails, and some throwback to older, wilder days, women who also have the warlike spirit, though this comes much more rarely. It is part of their duty, those most unhappy of women, to walk the gardens and babbling brooksides of our peaceful, sleepy world, and find young men who would prefer a painful death to a pleasant life. For this reason we call them *Valkyrie,* which means "They Choose to Be Slain."

And as these Shieldmaidens march, their dainty feet all shod with steel, heavy spears tipped with stings of rays in slim hand, they kick the small pink cherry blossoms from their path, and scowl with their beautiful eyes when our scented zephyrs blow or songbirds trill, and when they hear the murmur of mandolins and lutes, the war-girls blow their lusty trumpets, and call the revelers and dancers all to leave their dance, and march!

And so the Nymphs gaze in wonder and astonishment at the armored maidens, and cower at the power of the high and shining battle songs the warrior-maidens sing, and we hide beneath the myrtle groves, dovelike hearts a-patter! But when the golden-armed iron-shod maidens pass, we Nymphs must laugh, drink Nepenthe, and forget them.

Woe to the Nymph who does not moisten her lip at the cup of oblivion!

5. Of the Last of the Chimerae, and the First of the Nymphs

Why, you ask, O why, does the Judge of Ages love the Nymphs? It is said he loved the Mother of our race, for she was his bride.

There is a race of primordial beings, called the Hermetic Order, who are necromancers that restore to life the dead Machine which first brought evil into the world. The Machine is called Exarchel, after its maker, but the poets name it the *Ferox* and Black Lace Weaver, because, like the spider of the same name, it paralyzes and consumes its own mother: for we, the human race, Earth herself, we give rise to the posthuman, the postnatural, the supplanter.

Machines have souls as men do, but which do not die as men die. Machine-souls are kept alive in little magnetic matrices, or held in photoelectronic crystals, or in rings, or in lanterns. And it is forbidden to restore them. There once was a man of the stars, was a necromancer of machines, a Mechanecromancer, and he was the first to do the forbidden deed.

His name was Sarmento i Illa d'Or, and he was an Hermeticist, a knower of secret things. To him we owe great honor, for he is the Father of our race.

Great as he was, he serves a greater. The sultan of the Machines was the Ghost of a man who once ruled all the Earth, a great emperor named Ximen, called the Master of the World. Ximen dwells on the dark side of the Moon, and we see his handprint there, even to the day, for it is a sign of vengeance and vendetta against the Judge of Ages.

(Why the Master of the World lives not on this world, but in the Moon where no life is, that no one can say. Or how it can be that he is a Ghost while at the same time he still lives, this is a mystery. This we believe because it suits our story-love, and the storyteller will flee if we question the telling, and then what tales will there be?)

Upon a yesterday before all yesterdays, Sarmento the Mechanecromancer descended from the Moon. On a night when all the artificial moons of the Chimerae were set, and all eyes blind, he returned to a mausoleum of the enemy machines and brought their sultan to life again. And in return, the Machine, which was many times wiser than man, took the secrets of the Lotus King and deduced all the lore of RNA and DNA and enzyme coding as they relate to neuropsychology, and taught it to Sarmento.

Sarmento in a secret place, in a coffin, gave birth to the First of Nymphs, whose name was Rayura-Ah, and he instructed her in the arts of Nature, and so she commanded nature to turn against the Chimerae.

Then the First Mother walked among the world, and in her footprints vines and yarrow grew, and poppies and peonies, and the grapevines pulled down their towers of war, and the ivy vine overtopped the ivory towers of vain learning, and the owl and the cormorant built nests in their triumphal arches, and the unicorn came from the wilderness, and the dragon from the sea to sport and play with us.

Many seasons she slumbered walked, and with each season another plague she cajoled Nature to visit upon the Chimerae, hybrids of unnatural nature, an art of war none of their weapons could fight, and they were decimated softly by her unseen hands, never knowing a war was being waged. Their crops would not grow; their trees not yield fruit; their cows would not calve, nor fish be gathered into nets; and the wombs of the women of their race were closed, and so they dwindled, and soon passed into memory. And we drink wine, and the memory is forgotten.

The Natural Order in those days walked the woodlands, needing no tools of stone or metal, and the spies and satellites of the Chimerae, their magnetic radar, found nothing to detect. Light was the footstep in the Earth of our first ancestors, camouflaged by their greenish cloaks, and leaving nothing behind when they camped, not even a scent trail. Not even fires, in those days, were built: the bear and the pard and the lumbering bison, packs of dogs feral to the Chimerae and tame to Nymphs, all came when called to huddle in playful furry mass for warmth.

A time came of victory, and Rayura-Ah raised her hand, all the fruit trees gave forth fruit, and all of the slaves of the Chimerae who ate of them grew gay and giddy and flown as if with wine, and they forgot their sins and their chains and their rules and their lives—and so knew joy.

The cities were empty, and the trees overgrew the towers, toppled the Chimerical war memorials, and broke the dungeon-walls with their roots. And the factories were pulled down by the thorny vines of roses. In the great square of the greatest city of the Chimerae where the ten thousand torture racks and impaling poles once dripped blood, now saw nothing but cherry blossom petals dripping.

And one of the roots broke through the roof of the Tomb of the Judge of Ages, and tickled his nose, and woke him where he lay. He rose from his Tomb, blinking, and followed the path of rose petals to the surface, where the iron towers of the Chimerae were overgrown with mistletoe, ivy, and oleander.

Sarmento i Illa d'Or the Necromancer saw him coming from afar through the many electronic eyes of the tyrants, and he stood in the shadow of the Dark Tower, and at his right hand was Rayura-Ah. And she was dressed in a robe of white petals, and anointed with oils and pheromones.

From the Tombs came the Judge of Ages down the streets empty of people and full of grape leaves, and in each hand was a weapon, two pistols of corpse-white, for he is a Judge of death sentences only. And as he came, called out. "Is my time yet come? Is my bride yet here? Otherwise, wake me not, or you wake my wrath!" For the beauty of the trees, and the hypnotic scent of the blossoms, could not soften his heart.

The Necromancer smiled and said, "Here is your bride. This is Rayura-Ah, the Second Rania, for I have read the books of necromancy beyond the stars, where your bride was described in exact detail, and I have made her to please you, and to read the Monument for you."

The First of Nymphs, clad in nothing but flower petals and her blush of native loveliness, now stepped forward to embrace the Judge of Ages, for she had been chemically programmed to love him.

The Necromancer said, "Abandon your Tomb and live your days now in joy. Here is the woman mine arts have made for you: take her from my hand into the joyful bower, and relieve the shame of virginity from her."

To the First Nymph, the Judges of Ages asked, "What does the Monument say?"

She answered and said, "The Monument says that Hyades cannot be defeated, or opposed, and that the children of men will be happy in their slavery, and spread among the stars. Now are the days of liberty, when we may feast and rest, but when the Armada arrives, it is the end of days of liberty, and the children of men must toil and die under the light of other suns."

But the Judge of Ages said, "This is not my bride."

The Necromancer cursed him, and said, "Rania read the Monument wrongly, for she was made wrongly, and her dream of vindicating the races of man is wrong. I counseled Del Azarchel to kill her and assume the Captaincy, but he loved her and refused, therefore she became Captain, and caused us all endless grief! She will use and discard you as she used and discarded us, her fathers and teachers, for she does not love, but fled to the stars to escape you. She will never return."

Everything but those last four words, he would have forgiven: but this is the one thing that can never be said to the Judge of Ages.

The two agreed then and there to fight a duel, and weapons of the ancient days were brought. They stood amid the floating petals that fell from broken torture-poles, and amid the lovely scent of lotuses that wafted from wine-filled torture-pools, and legend says that of all the duels fought during the time when the Chimerae ruled the Earth, this was the very last of them.

The Necromancer said, "You can never defeat us, Judge of Ages, for we are the Masters of all dark arts and dark sciences, and we are full of the understanding of the secrets of the world.

"Your wisdom is of this world," said the Judge of Ages. "My hope is not of this world."

They fired their guns, and some say these were the last gunshots heard anywhere on Earth, for the Nymphs use other weapons. The shot of the Necromancer struck true, and the Judge of Ages was wounded with a grievous wound, and fell as one dead, and voices came from the earth, and thunders, and lightnings, and there was a great earthquake. And the Necromancer grew frightened, and cast down his pistol, and fled: for by his art he summoned a flying machine such as flew in the air in days long ago. He commanded it to carry him away, and commanded the Mother of Nymphs to follow after.

But Rayura-Ah, who loved the Judge of Ages with a helpless love, took him away to her secret island, and there nursed him of his great wound.

He rose at last from deathbed and sickbed to embrace her, for was she not like Rania as Rania should have been, the perfected, the unmarred? And they dwell in love together in the lands of the dead beneath the mountains, and at times their lovemaking creates earth tremors, so vehement is he.

A great compact and covenant between the Nymphs and the Dead was made, that any of the Natural Order wishing to find tomorrow and perish, and if they but renounce their names, may descend into the Earth, where it is cold.

If you meddle with his coffin, the wrath of the Judge of Ages will come forth from underearth like burning rock and brimstone from a volcano, and he will call to his knights with these words: "Arise! Arise and slay! For they dare wake me when before the time appointed for my bride to return in triumph from the stars." The knights will thaw and waken from their coffins, and don their arms and armor, and cry out, "Let no man wake him, He Who Waits, lest his wrath awake!" And their voices and trumpet will be so great, that the earth will quake and resound with the cry: and these are the last words trespassers hear.

But these things do not concern the Nymphs, for we live only in today, and the things of yesterday are not our things, but belong to Chimerae and Witches, and the things of tomorrow are not our things, but belong to the Einheriar and Valkyrie, who will battle bravely, and bravely will fall and die, for the Hyades cannot be overcome.

But I do not naysay them their vain deaths to come, for pleasure is whatever pleases, and if this pleases them, may they rejoice in it!

O Nature, whose living breath inspires the world, we bless and thank you for your inspiration! And if my tale has pleased you, O my lovers, return to me that pleasure with the kiss of thanksgiving, and the caresses of delight: and let us quaff the wine of oblivion together, that this tale, and all other tales and pleasures, shall be fresh as springtide dew, shining and child-new, on some yonder and tomorrow-thither night!

6. Questions

Oenoe was in a kneeling position, her hands on her thighs, her hips over her heels, her back slightly arched and her shoulders slightly back, her head high and erect. Atop her head, creating an illusion of height, was an upright comb of tortoiseshell holding up a veil of lacy fibers and molecular-assembly webs, which hooded her head, fell down her shoulders, and flowed down to her left and right, so that the shining green fabric was spread in a half circle all about her. The garment did nothing to cover her prodigious breasts, but neither the

Blue Men nor the dog things, nor the Nymph herself, seemed to find this in anyway distracting or uncouth.

When she began her tale, and spoke her herself, the flowers growing in her mantilla were purple crocuses with stamen of gold, forsythia as fulvous as gold and fretted as airy filigree, with clovers greener than the emerald and sweetly scented.

But as she spoke on, and told about the Nymphs who left their age to become soldiers or Shieldmaidens for the Judge of Ages, the petals dropped to the grass around her, and a new generation, like a slow blush, spread from her slender shoulders downward and out toward her hem, like a ripple in a pool but moving too languidly to see: tansy round as the sun, and zinnia splendid as an emperor's robe, red roses and white roses growing with thorny stems crossed like fencer's foils, milfoil white as snow, and vivid Indian cress with orange petals freaked with bloodred.

The flowers fell and grew anew, this time in somber hues. She spoke of the downfall of the Chimerae. Now flourished ice plants with leaves slimmer than white needles, hemlock whose puffs were sickly green, and the folded cloak rustled and brought forth Saint-John's-wort, and amaranth like purple lace, nightshade, monkshood, and the curling reddish petals of the chiranthodendron that looked like claws of blood. A smell of pine needles came from her.

Menelaus, while she spoke and while he spoke her words to the Blue Men, as if annoyed or lost in thought, would pick up flower petals or leaves that the mantilla of the Nymph was shedding and idly toss them, drifting, floating, back across the little pond to her. Her hand, as if in a dream, would catch each tossed bloom and either put it to her left side, or to her right.

When she finished her tale, a coronet of Cape Jessamine that had formed from the veils of her brow she shook free with a laugh, and the flowers dropped white petals down her dusky locks, to rest upon her hands and thighs and knees, and the grasses where she knelt.

The two Blue Men, sitting cross-legged, neither moved nor fidgeted no more than statues would have. They showed no change in expression during the recitation: Mentor Ull was sleepily reptilian and Preceptor Illiance was eerily serene.

A silence that crawled minute after minute, slow as worms, passed once Oenoe was done speaking, and she pouted, and rolled her eyes, and tossed her hair, so that flowers and thistledown flew up from her mantilla, and she flung herself on her side, hips like the billow of a never-cresting wave, flowing toward her pointed toes; and she rested her cheek on her shoulder, and stared sullenly at the grass blades, which she plucked up with small and angry gestures of her red fingernails.

Menelaus put his fingers in the pond and dashed the water into his own face, since the heat of the chamber made him sweat, and he was unwilling to open his heavy metallic robes. He turned his head and said in High Iatric, "I think you offended her. I am not sure, but I think you were supposed to applaud."

Illiance said, "I do not know this custom. How do the Naturalists applaud?"

"Hell if I know. Masturbate and throw semen? Something like that."

Illiance gave him a look of surprise. "Do you denounce? It seems you have little regard for the Naturalist Oenoe! She has said nothing to offend, and her life is depicted as one of admirable unfussiness."

"Well, I like her more than I like you gentlemen, if that gives you a basis of comparison. I never knew Nymphs to meddle where they oughtn't, or dig up danger better left buried."

Preceptor Illiance turned to Ull and said in Intertextual, *"I note an undue similarity. The wording of the admonition not to wake the Judge of Ages was the same in this as in the prior account, even thought Soorm scion Asvid postdates Oenoe Psthinshayura-Ah by seven hundred twenty years. Neither era was known for its literacy. I am humbled to admit that the diffusion theory is weakened by this: it is almost as if there were a Judge and he did speak those words."*

Mentor Ull nodded sourly. *"The persistence of that degree of specific cultural memories across the watershed of linguistic and psychological differences bears examination."*

Mentor Ull raised a blue finger. As before, his right hand was hidden in a cast, wrapped to his midriff beneath his long coat, and one sleeve dangled free. "I detect a paradox in her testament. Ask her if she can happen to adduce clarity."

Menelaus said, "What's your question?"

Ull asked, "How is it she recalls the several things she herself says the members of the Order of Nature are prone by custom to forget? Example: she says when Valkyrie pass by, Naturalists obscure the memories, but in order to say so, she must remember such events."

Menelaus translated the question.

Oenoe said, "My race is dedicated to perfect happiness, but such perfection is hard to achieve! I have varied from the customary wisdom, and so I am here, and I am very unhappy. If my people were not dead and forgotten, lo, these countless yesterdays of time, I myself could pass into song as an example. Pity my folly!"

And when she closed her eyes, her face, now as solemn and dignified as that of a Queen of Egypt, showed the trail of two tears, clear as crystal, inching down her fair and blushing cheeks.

The Blue Man sat silently for a long minute, and then two, while Menelaus drummed his fingers against his knee. Eventually, he squinted at Illiance. "Hey, sleepyhead! You are making her upset again."

"How so?" asked Illiance, his tone one of remote wonder.

"She is waiting for you to ask her what she means."

Illiance touched the grass and touched the crown of his bald head, and then spoke to Oenoe in a halting, careful sentence of her language. "It would give me pleasure if your words would kiss my ears with knowledge, my beloved."

Oenoe laughed and hid her smile behind a fold of her green veil.

Menelaus said, "That was not bad, but you were supposed to called her, *my lover,* not *my beloved.*"

"What happens to be the distinction?" asked Illiance.

"Ugh. I can't explain it. It has to do with shades of meaning. The Nymphs don't have a word for virgin, but they have formalities of address for people with whom you have not often had sex, and a different form for people with whom you have often."

"What of two people who have not copulated at all?" asked Illiance, blinking.

"You have to use a circumlocution for that. They don't have a separate word for it."

"Beta Anubis, do you exaggerate for the purposes of entertaining yourself with humor?"

"Sometimes. Quite often, in fact. But not at the moment. Why?"

"Surely no race could be as voluptuous and prurient as this!"

"They did not have television or textfiles, and they didn't have to do hard labor, and they kept themselves too drugged up to get into fights, so what do you think they did all night? Not to mention morning, noon, and dusk? They knew all the mechanisms of memory and infatuation, so that the next youth or maiden you met would be like your first love all over again, and they could change your glands to make a weary lover go into heat."

Oenoe straightened up, her weight on one arm, her hips and legs draped in shapely curves to one side, and she pointed regally at Illiance. "Tell the blue child he must promise to understand me if I speak, and cherish my words and delight in them! It will wound me if he hears me with his ears alone, and not his heart!"

Menelaus said to Illiance. "Did you follow that?"

"Yes," said Illiance. "She imposes a moral obligation on me to have an emotive rather than an intellectual reaction to what she is about to say. But how can I promise to bind my emotional reactions before I know the topic of the data?"

This created a flurry of chirps and hisses between the two Blue Men. Ull said to Illiance in the language of the Locusts: *"Take care! Do not remove from the path of simplicity! To conform your emotions to her prescription is an artifice!"*

Illiance answered: *"I must bring upon myself this risk. Otherwise, she might not speak."*

Ull scowled: *"Do you place the balancing network of passion, appetite, reason, and conscience in the hands of a relict from the unknown past? The risk is undue!"*

Illiance said: *"The present is also unknown. I accept the risk."*

The scowl of the elder Blue Man deepened. *"I am no longer responsible for your education. I cannot mentor those who despise my advice."*

Illiance bowed his head. *"I am grateful and thankful to have followed in your wise footsteps for so long."* Then, taking a deep breath, he said in Iatric to Menelaus. "Tell her I accept her commission, and will allow myself to be moved by her words, whatever they may be."

Oenoe sat up straighter during this exchange and whispered in her own language to Menelaus. "Of what do they speak? Why such fluster?"

Menelaus said, "I don't know. Maybe the old one is afraid you are going to propose to the young one."

"Propose what?"

"Sexual intercourse."

"Why would they think that?" Oenoe's tone was scandalized.

"I told them you wanted to fornicate with them." Menelaus shrugged.

"Such a lie! If you were a woman, I'd spank you!"

"Um. Thanks. I think. Actually, I am not sure what to make of that comment."

"It means that I wonder at you! Where are your ethics? If one cannot trust the translator to translate truly, whom can one trust? I cannot seduce if my words are misspoken!" Oenoe pouted prettily.

"Does that mean you don't want to fornicate with the weird little blue men?"

"Of course I do!" She waved her well-shaped hand at him, a dismissive gesture. "But they are unsuited. I do not sense the proper neurological-hormonal structures in them. I could not make them fall in love with me. Look at their eyes! There is something dead and evil in them!"

"Be careful what you say. The younger one can understand us."

"I care not!" The eyes of Oenoe suddenly blazed. "He cannot look at me without knowing what he is! I am truly alive, and he is not. I would save him, if I could, but even love cannot reach the unwilling." And, just as suddenly, her head was hanging, her shoulders hunched, sorrow sculpted into her every curve, and her shining black hair hung down before her face.

"Well, cheer up, ma'am. The younger one just said you can tell him what's on your mind, and he'll listen with an open heart."

"What is his name?" Oenoe's face lit up with joy, and her beauty was like a sun coming from behind a cloud. "If he is willing truly to listen, I must know and cherish his name."

"One of his names is Illiance. His title means 'teacher' or 'bard.' Hold on a second." Menelaus turned to Illiance. "Preceptor, you told me *Illiance* was what you called an external name. Do you have an internal name? A first name? She is about to tell you something private, and she wants to know your name to cherish it."

Illiance touched his fingertips to his ears ceremoniously. "When I departed from the Locusts, I was adopted into the care of a pretend-mother. She called me Lagniappe, for she likened me to those small gifts a merchant seeking the goodwill of patrons might bestow."

Menelaus turned again to Oenoe. "His private name means 'Small Favor.' The word means something given in hopes of attracting future generosity."

"His favor of telling me that his name means 'favor' has won my favor!" she said with a smile. "Because of his kindness, my heart beats rapidly, my breath is short, and my nipples stand erect!"

"Uh, ma'am, while that sounds like poetry and sweetness in Nymph-talk, if I translated it into his language, it would sound like a description of a medical condition."

"So. In that case, tell him I will plead with the Judge of Ages, when he arises, to spare his life."

Menelaus sighed heavily and turned to Illiance. "Preceptor, I hope you followed that, because I don't want to translate it."

Illiance asked, "Why do you not want to translate it?"

"It's a Chimera thing. I am not allowed to speak another man's threats or defiance unless I am willing to pick up his whip and carry them out. What she said sounded like a threat to me, and if I say it, I am legally responsible for acting on it."

"Your laws are no longer in force."

"Call it an imposition of a moral obligation, then."

"I flowed with the drift of the current of her words," said Illiance. "She is pleased with my false-mother-name, and therefore, in recompense, she will shield me from the Judge of Ages. Is she using a figure of speech, or does she think the Judge of Ages is a real person? Why does she think she will have any sway over his actions?"

Menelaus translated the question.

Oenoe tilted up her chin with girlish pride and smiled a dazzling smile. "Of course he is real. Who built the Tombs, if not he? He built the Tombs to preserve himself, and merely lets others dwell for a time to slumber beside him while he waits. Of course I can soothe the world-destroying wrath that burns and bites his dark and horrid heart. Am I not one high in the esteem of the servants of Nature, and a queen of my kind? The Judge of Ages *loves* us!"

7. *Woe to the Nymph Who Moistens Not Her Lip*

O bountiful and generous Nature, breathe into me, that I might breathe out words to stir the soul, and open blinded eyes.

Hear me, then, Little Favor, and I will tell of my woe. As I said, the stream of hedonism is a white and rapid water to row, and requires both discipline and daring. My failure came when I pursued in love a girl I found fetching, for she was willful and glancing-eyed, and she knew my soul as none other did. But she was humiliated at a thiasus for a misstep in the revelry, and yet she refused to dim the memory, preferring to feel scorn and shame. She watered and manured her wrong feelings, until she resolved to leave our today-ness, and seek the tomorrow-ness of the Tombs.

She sought and fetched forth one of the sleeping knights, and his name was Sir Mathurin d'Aux Lescaut, but he was called Romegas. She importuned him to teach her the management of arms, so that she could become a Valkyrie, and die in vain futility at the End of Days of Peace. He granted it.

Therefore for many days, even though the flowers were bright and the birds sang, Sir Romegas and my lost beloved stood drilling and exercising in the meadow, fencing and tilting and shooting both chemical firearm and energy lance, until the meadow was like a storm, for the firearm shouted like thunder, and the lance flashed like lightning.

One night I crept into her sleeping cloak, and wakened her with kisses, pleading that she foreswear her folly and return to the roundelays and reels and frivolous games with which all true Nymphs are wont to fritter our lives away. But she was displeased with me, because the knight had told her of some secret lore from the before time, and bound her with laws, and washed away her past with water from a sacred, secret stream. Now she served a man who had been tortured to death, and perhaps she wanted to torture herself, because she had vowed no more to disport herself in the love-play.

While I knelt weeping at her feet, she concocted a dram of the Nepenthe for me, so that I might quench my sorrow in the seethe of forgetfulness. But I dashed the clamshell of wine from her hand, and spoke and sang an angry word instead. I said I did not wish to forget my love for her.

She offered to kiss me a final time, a kiss of peace, but with this one caveat: Using the neurochemistry she knew, she could transfer my love for her to another, so that it would not be forgotten, but instead displaced. I would be infatuated with some other, but in a way I would still be true to her. She warned me once this was done to bind my eyes with a silk band and depart her camp, and not to peek until I heard once more the singing of the Nymphs at play around me, and whomever I first saw, I would love.

To please her, I agreed. As we kissed, she passed her influence to me through topically active transmitters in lip membrane, and chemical cues in the saliva. I was blind with weeping as I fled her, so I thought there was no need to obey her injunction to blindfold my eyes. I pushed the blindfold aside and covered my eyes with my hand, because I had to wipe my tears.

I struck a man made of metal, who caught me, laughing, by the arms, and he asked me gentle questions in a tongue I did not understand. He was broad as a bear and taller than any man of the Nymph race, and his voice was the voice of a man who is unafraid to kill and unafraid to die and unafraid to give commands. I opened my eyes and was lost.

His name was Sir Guiden von Hompesch zu Bolheim of the Order of the Knights of Saint John, of the Holy City of Jerusalem and of the Islands of Rhodes and Malta, and of Colorado, and he was the Grand Master of the Order that Romegas served; and he is a man from the dawn of the world, and there is none like him in the world, or in any age.

I am here for him, and I left all the world I knew to follow him past tomorrow and tomorrow through endless years.

My coffin would not have opened unless he was awake and alive upon the Earth, and he is not the only servant of the Judge of Ages, and not even the most deadly, but he is the oldest and most loyal.

Beware the Wrath of the Slumbering Knighthood of the Ages when it wakes!

I thank the Nature that gave me words to say these things.

8. Teardrop

Menelaus looked with surprise at the tear sliding down among the sweat droplets on the cheek of Preceptor Illiance, and he wondered what it meant.

9

The Dying Place

1. Opening the Tent

The next day dawned clear. Snow lay thick and even over the whole camp, and the trees wore dunce caps of white. The tall man cloaked and hooded in tent fabric crept to the tent of Soorm the Hormagaunt. He yanked on it, but the fabric was stiff as metal. The tall man looked left and right carefully. He saw nothing moving in the still, white world.

He pressed the hem of his cloak against the seams of the tent. There was a noise like paper ripping.

He stood, backed away, stooped, made a snowball, and threw it against the side of the Hormagaunt's tent. A second splattered by the first. A moment later, a huge furry dark figure of Soorm emerged, snarling and blinking and lashing his scorpion-tipped otter tail. In the cold, the scales of his mismatched hands and elongated feet gleamed red.

"Who dares disturb my sleep?"

"You sound like the Judge of Ages. Call me Anubis."

"Anubis it is." Soorm blinked his goat eye and flattened his cuttlefish eye. "Too early it also is. The dogs haven't blown reveille yet. How do you accomplish this trick of unlocking their metal cloth?" Soorm's neck bristles stood and swayed. "Come to think of it—where do you sleep without freezing?"

"I get close enough to the Tomb entrance that the automatics spray me with napalm every few minutes until I am toasted on all sides, and then I sleep inside the shell of one of the Blue Men machines. But at least I am not locked in a tent. Shall we walk? Get dressed."

"What is this thing, *dressed,* of which you speak, past-creature?"

"Pox! What the hell is it about the future? Why is everyone a nudist?"

"Nudist? I have fur. Like a cat, I am always dressed, and in impeccable attire emperors can but envy. All I need is a brush and a currycomb."

2. Handholds

The two men crunched through the fresh snow up the slope. The Hormagaunt spread his toes, and his webbed feet acted like snowshoes, leaving only a light footprint on the surface of the snow. Menelaus had glowing lines of ink lighting his bare feet, and his each footprint gave off a hiss of steam as he trod. The sound of the rushing stream in the still, early-morning air was audible as they approached the steeply sided river channel.

Soorm said, "You don't really sleep slathered in napalm, do you?"

"Of course not. I bunk with Mickey the Witch. The Blues don't realize yet that I can jinx their smartmetal. I was joshing you."

"So I suspected, but who knows what a posthuman driven insane by grief and ill-advised augmentation experiments might do?"

"Whoa. You think I am insane?"

"You have been granted superhuman life, and so you spend it in a Tomb, pining for a woman who will never return, and blasting and butchering those who disturb your rest? It seems insane."

Montrose shrugged. "I got nothing better to do. Besides, I perform a public service. My Tomb system saves lives and preserves a past the Hermeticists would rather force mankind to forget."

"You perform a service for mankind, but who does not fear and loathe you? Why such altruism? You are not repaid, nor thanked."

Montrose shrugged. "You win. I must be insane. So are you, for helping me."

"You know why I help you. I hate the Hermeticists."

"You hate them for ruining your world, and creating the Locusts to replace you?"

"No. For creating my world. What race of man was ever more monstrous than the Hormagaunts?"

"I try not to hate 'em. The Hermeticists, I mean."

"Why not? They took everything from you. Pastor used to boast that they used you as their beast of burden for mental tasks. It is your duty to hate them."

"*She* still thinks of them as her fathers. *She* doesn't hate them."

"She, who?"

"She, the one this is all about."

"You mean—? Then the Swan Maiden is not a myth!"

"She ain't no maiden no more," harrumphed Montrose. "I got interrupted on my wedding night, but not *that* interrupted."

"Is it true she plucked the Diamond Star out of the heavens? That she flies to a star beyond the galaxy to plead with the star-monstrosities for the emancipation of mankind? Are all the children's stories true?"

Montrose looked at Soorm oddly. "You worked for Reyes y Pastor, that snake-oil-selling preacherman. You know all this stuff is real. Besides, M3 is a globular cluster, not a star."

Soorm shook his shaggy head. "It still takes some getting used to. Meeting you, it is easy to believe you are a death-god from the underworld, bent on vengeance. But to think you are married to a woman born beneath a distant sun! A princess who brought the only era of world peace the world has ever known!"

Montrose nodded glumly. "I take it back. She is too good to be true. I don't know why she married me, but I've done sworn I ain't gunna disappoint her. Die, maybe. Disappoint her, never."

They reached their destination and stood on the height of the cliff, overlooking the cold stream that rushed out from a narrow doorway leading into the mountain.

As it had been yesterday, in the distance, two upright coffins stood like sentries to either side of the flooded door from which roaring waters poured. In the stream almost directly beneath Soorm and Montrose the several broken machines of the Blue Men lay. The white and rippling water played around their dented hulks and crooked legs, and rust and trails of icicles accumulated.

What had not been here yesterday was a set of parallel deep scars or gouges in the cliff face under their feet, in a line leading down to where the broken machines were heaped. Each scar was about nine inches long, and an inch or two deep into the rock.

"Can you climb down this cliff? Your feet are adapted for swimming, not climbing," said Menelaus.

Soorm said, "I could not pass this point before. Where the machines fell is as far as I could go. In addition to those two by the door, there are some active coffins lying on the floor of the streambed. I saw their lights shining, and they put little red dots on me."

"Aiming laser dots?"

"It was not a technology I knew. I retreated."

"Smart man. Did you come from above, from where we are now?"

Soorm shook his head, an oddly human gesture for his dark and furry otter-shaped skull. "From downstream."

"There are clusters of sensors buried in the cliff wall downstream, and they paint incoming objects as targets for the coffins and door circuits. Scaling down the cliffside avoids the clusters, so we should only have to deal with short-range reactions. Can you make it down these handholds?"

Soorm went to all fours, dipped just his head over the edge of the cliff, and sniffed cautiously. "I can scale the wall. You cut this ladder. It has your scent. When?"

"Last night, when everyone was asleep."

"How? The stone is melted. This was done by an energy weapon."

Menelaus pointed at the door. "You cannot see it from here, but there is a hundred-kilowatt-class chemical oxygen iodine laser in the lintel."

"How did you get it to cut the handholds?"

"My skill as a toreador. I dangled my cloak over my elbow to get it to shoot. It is programmed to find the center of body mass, and I had to throw off its estimate so the beam would land between my arm and my torso and hit the rock. It was not fun."

Soorm's face did not allow him to show much expression, but disbelief seemed to crackle through his fur. "Impossible."

"The lethal kilolaser is cut off from its mainframe, so it is actually easy to fool, if you know the limitations. Which I do, since I built the dumb thing. And I could do the math in my head to calculate the beam path."

Soorm grunted. "For such a poor superman, you seem to be able to do unusual feats. What else did you build?"

"Most of this is my work, though it mutates when I slumber. The lethals won't see you. You need to worry about the nonlethals. There are three. First, hidden behind the panels to either side of the door are millimeter-wave radiation emitters. Make you feel like your skin is on fire. But stay submerged. Water droplets will disperse the beam. Second, there are acoustic weapons mounted farther down, beyond the mouth of the door, but their projection horns are underwater, so they probably won't go off. If they do, the whole camp will hear us and scamper back up here."

"And third?"

"A shock barrier. Shoots sixty electrified lancets at the same time. I stood in the water last night freezing my ass off for about an hour, until it ran out of ammo. I was holding my cloak on a stick in front of me and the lancets could not penetrate. Dumb machine. It fired until it ran out of ammo. It takes it three whole goddam days to grow another batch, and that is if and only if the feed lines connecting it to the liquid biometal are not cut, which I am not sure of. Why did I even bother putting in such a stupid system? I reckon I got a little overly enthused at the drawing board. Once you get in the door, the whole corridor is flooded."

"And then the coffins will swarm over me and kill me."

"In theory, all my clients have a right to go back in, so the automatics should let any of you pass," said Menelaus.

"In theory, the Judge of Ages is not a complete nincompoop who locked himself out of his own stronghold. I still don't understand how you can be this godlike being, capable of unimaginable depth and breadth of thought, and yet you are here clinging to a snowy cliff like a rat, trying to nibble your way into a grain box."

"I'll point out I am smart enough to talk you into a plan where I get to stay here where it is safe, while the nonlethals scald your private parts with searing pain."

"The brilliance of your posthuman thinking grows ever less clear as time passes."

Menelaus pointed. "I also did some tests last night and took some measurements. The doors broke open sixty years ago from the water pressure behind. Half my Tomb site there is a damn lake," Menelaus said, shaking his head, "and there is an incoming underground artesian flood on the north side that keeps pouring in the same rate this pours out. The radio shack is on the fourth level right at the annex. You'll be traveling against the current. The bad part is this: You see how the water swirls as it rushes out the door? Remember the specific recurring pattern of vortices and their periods. And then look at this."

He tapped the back surface of the groundcloth he wore as part of his robe. A blueprint diagram formed as if below the surface, adjusted to the peculiarities of Soorm's mismatched eyes to create a three-dimensional illusion in his brain.

Soorm put his webbed fingers before his muzzle. "Stop doing things like that!"

"Things like what?"

"Weird posthuman things!"

"Sorry, but take a garner at the map. The smartmetal fabric has a way to create visible light from the thumbnail overlap of each microscopic cell, and all I did was formulate a program to use laser interference to create holographic images in eyes like yours, since you can see polarization. I thought a three-D model would be useful. Anyway, compare the map to the door down there. You can tell from the vortex formation periods of the current that three of the internal doors along this corridor as locked down and shut. That was the bad part I mentioned."

"What? How can I tell?"

"Because the water leaving the mouth of the door would have a different resonance pattern if those doors were open. You never played a flute or blew across the top of a pop bottle?"

"Yes, I played the double-flute quite expertly, and no, I cannot deduce the shape and depth of flooded corridors by glancing at the swirlies the water makes when it gushes out."

"So take it on faith that my map here is accurate and to scale. There is where you go inside; here is the radio shack. How long would it take you to swim that distance? And can you take someone with you?"

"That distance is nothing to me." He peered at the map. "I can cross it in an eighth of a watch."

"I don't know your measurements of time. How many minutes would that be? A minute is one sixtieth of a sidereal day."

"Twenty or so."

"Twenty? No boasting, friend. We are not talking about a straight-line sprint. The corridors will be dark, and you'll have to grope your way."

"Not to me. I have an alternative form for deeper oceans. I can shed light and use dolphin echolocation. Pastor modified me to be able to talk to those empty Ghost memories who sing about their desire to die, and cannot die. Does your posthuman body grow posthuman lungs? You cannot survive where I pass."

"I don't mean to. Oenoe is the one you are taking along."

Soorm gave a shiver of skepticism. "A dancing girl! The darkness, the cold of the water will panic her. I don't think she is fit for this task."

"Nymphs have the lung capacity for this."

"Those are mammary glands, not lungs."

"Very funny. Both the oxygen-carrying capacity in their blood, and the convolutions of their lung tissues in many bloodlines of Nymphs were modified, so that they could perform water ballets when seducing sailors. Oenoe is coming now. She is the one who will open the internal doors."

3. Liberty and History

Soorm said, "I will abandon her to drown when she panics, and Darwin will be served."

"She has nerves of steel."

"How was that modification accomplished? The world supply of metallic ore was exhausted before her day."

"I mean, Oenoe is a veteran military officer who has seen and survived action. You seem surprised."

Soorm said, "I come from the last days, when the Nymphs were dying. The thousand years of endless summer had passed, for the albedo-altering organisms in the Arctic, Antarctic, and Tropics were corrupted and becoming extinct, and they had lost control of the Gulf Stream. The Winter Queens betrayed all the principles of their earlier generations, embraced the need for violence, and used alchemy to stir up battle frenzy in their berserkers during the Depravation Wars. But then in the summertime, it was the old time again, and all was sponged away from thought and remembrance. I thought this was a recent and desperate innovation. All my life I thought so. The endless summer of the summer years—surely they were times of peace? She cannot be a veteran!"

Menelaus said, "She is, and a cunning one. She told me her secret flower combination. Hyssop wards off evil spirits, Juniper means protection, and Lily keeps unwanted visitors away. That is the heraldic sign for their Protective Service. Secret police, Nocturnal Council, whatever you want to call it. The Protectors are the people who stuff troublemakers into hibernation, and kill any rebels they cannot subdue with drugs. People who take care of unwanted visitors. Her people maintained the social order."

"That means she is an police maiden, not a warrior. Their world was drugged into perfect pacifism!"

Menelaus said, "There were no standing armies nor major land battles during the Nymph period in history, but they sure as hell had a militia, and riot police, and flying squads who kept the peace. There were pitched battles, blockades, sieges, sniper duels with wee little wasp creatures—I mean, come on, they were still human beings! There were even naval actions against privateers with marine cavalry riding the backs of sea-dragons, who turned out not to be just ornamental."

"How could they keep it secret?"

"The soldiers would quaff the cup of victory after the successful fight. Hell! And anyone who escaped chemical control still obeyed unwritten social control. He'd be ashamed to speak his piece: why spoil the party? The technique you call Wintermind, which allows you to resist memory alterations, and stay lucid when drugged or addicted, that did not exist yet."

Soorm's goat eye blazed and his cuttlefish eye wobbled so violently in its socket that it looked ready to pop out. In the strangled voice he cried, "How do you expect me not to hate these creatures? With their balloon breasts and honeyed lips, they have no more heart than Venus flytrap plants!"

Menelaus looked surprised, perhaps a little amused, perhaps a little sad. "We're talking about something that happened in your childhood—how old are you? Biologically speaking? You cannot be worried about something so long ago?"

"How long ago did you last see your wife, the Swan Princess, O Judge of Ages? Were there still Pyramids in Egypt in those days, or the Hanging Gardens of Babylon? Or had they not yet been built?"

Menelaus opened his mouth to object, but could think of nothing. (He noticed that Soorm, raised by Father Reyes, knew the names of biblical places. Eerie to think that those ancient spots were remembered long after New York the Beautiful and Newer Orleans had been swallowed by time and forgotten.) So he said: "Uh, good point. But calm down anyway."

Soorm snarled, "Calm? Why? Does everyone get to run my life but me? I was eager, willing to eat meat, willing to kill men, willing to practice abstinence, willing to do any and every perverse thing I was raised and commanded not to do— Arg! I even became a *teetotaler,* something so horrible, Nymphs don't even make jokes about it!—I did all these ghastly things merely for the chance to study the Mind of Winter hypnogogy. I became the slave of Pastor merely to escape their slaveries."

Montrose said thoughtfully, "From where did Reyes y Pastor learn it, to teach it to you?"

Soorm said, "From Nymphs of the Winter days, when their weather control failed."

Montrose cursed.

Soorm goggled one eye at him. "What is it?"

"Outsmarted again. Those Hermeticists you hate for creating your world? Turns out, I help them to create it. They winkled the secret out of my people, who I tried to free from Nymph control, back when the Nymph system refused to self-correct to account for changed climatic conditions."

Soorm stared. "The Nymphs all believe you protect and adore them. You helped destroy their world?"

"I helped draw them back from racial suicide, yes. Pastor told you about the Cliometric calculus?"

"He did indeed. How he would cluck and rub his hands and grin when he would tell me how his little webs of math control all destiny and history. He was so proud of us, you see, his monsters. My race was created to serve him, and was destined for eternal sorrow, eternal struggle, eternal bloodshed, and eventual extinction that we might give rise to a greater race!" Soorm clenched his lizard-scaled webbed hands into two great fists and raised them toward the gray clouds above, a gesture of silent rage. "Will there never be an era when men can be free? When I can be free?"

Menelaus shrugged the shrug of a philosopher. "Everyone I know is controlled by someone. Witches obey their Crones, Chimera obey their Imperator-General, Hormagaunts obey their patrons, the Hermeticists obey Blackie."

Soorm growled. "Do not mock me. Voluntary obedience is not the same as a slavery so complete and so degrading that one does not even know what the shepherds of history have determined to be your fate, or the fate of the herd around you that carries you along."

"Well, then: The Domination in the Hyades cluster claims the Earth and all her works and all her ways to be an indentured servant forever and aye. And Hyades is owned by a Dominion in the Praesepe cluster. And they are owned by an Authority seated in the globular cluster M3 in Canes Venatici, which is outside the pestiferous Milky Way galaxy! If you want to escape from the Authority of M3, we have to get out of this prison camp first, which means dealing with the dogs and the wire. So, what are you going to do? We need help from the Nymphy secret policewoman. So you have to help her, even though you do not like her one bit. We are big, grown-up men in a big deep horseshit pit of trouble, and if we are not tall enough, the brown goo of defeat is going to close over our faces."

Soorm lifted his muzzle and stared off down the slope. In the distance was a slight figure in green, moving with a skater's grace across the snow, and flower petals fell from her cloak as she walked. It was too far for Menelaus to smell the perfumes that surrounded her like a nimbus of silent music, but the nostrils of Soorm dilated.

4. Memory Trees

It was impossible to read any expression under his fur-coated face, his discordant eyes. "Why her?"

"For one thing," said Menelaus, "she can open the doors. For another, she can survive the trip underwater, and I can't. For third, she is clever. While she was playing all girly-girl and silly, just like what the Blue Men might have expected from a history book, she and I were communicating in her flower language. She caught on immediately. I would show her a flower-sign combination, and she would agree or disagree by dropping them to her left or right. We did it right in front of them, and they were too stupid to notice it. Fourth thing, she also understands the neural mechanisms in the dogs, and I think she has one of them under partial or total control. She has a neurobiotic direct interface, and she is dripping with capsules and strands of primed and weaponized biomachinery, and the Blue Men handed it to her right in front of me, because they didn't know what it could do. She also is the only one who can talk to the door brains."

"Talk how?"

"Back when you were a Nymph, you remember how the trees used to sing to you? How you did not need books or letters, because the trees remembered everything for you? Look around you. Recognize any of these species?"

Soorm did look up, and now his expression was easy to read, because his whole body shivered and crouched, and his fur and quills stood up, making him seem twice his breadth, and the claws of his fingers appeared and disappeared, like the claws of a nervous cat, and the bulb of poison on his lashing tail trembled and swelled and turned purple.

"There is a working neural system here?" Soorm said.

"I released some seeds out of the broken Tomb doors long ago, making it look like an accident, blending it with other random events, so that Blackie's Machine would not see the pattern in events. His machine can intuit patterns, unlike mine, but I am still tricky enough to fool him, and it. This grove is all Nymph technology, and the trees all downhill and downstream, and yonder throughout the camp. Well? What's your decision? You in? Are you with us?"

"Gah! I am in. But I am not copulating with her!"

"You don't have to. She's married."

"Nymphs don't get married. They don't even have a word for it. I know. I used to be—"

"This lovely woman turns out—big surprise to me—turns out to be the wife of my best friend, the Grandmaster of the Ancient and Honorable Sovereign Military Hospitalier Order of Saint John, Sir Guiden von Hompesch zu Bolheim. He and all his men left perfectly happy lives in the Antecpyrotic world to come into exile in the abyss of time just out of a sense of duty. It is a hopeless exile, because our homelands are long dead and long forgotten, and there is no going home. She is Mrs. Von Hompesch, which has got to be one of the most crook-jawed ungainliest-sounding Krauthead names I ever heard ever. Sits on the ear like a bee sting, don't it? Wish I had been at the wedding. Would have been his best man. The things you miss when you don't program your thaw conditions right!"

"A married Nymph?" Soorm was still marveling.

"Is it so different from your Wintermind asceticism? Marriage is a mechanism for breaking a type of addiction. The Knights obey a law that forbids fornication. Oenoe knows enough about her own neurochemistry to make herself at least as monogamous as a Blue Man."

"Ah. This is the same practice as the Red Hermeticist, is it not?"

"I think my Hospitaliers actually mean it. Pasty is big fraud."

"'Pasty'?"

"Pastor. The Learned Father Reyes y Pastor. Your Red Hermeticist."

"Then their rites are known to me. Your Knight carried her over the threshold by force, and the Fathers poured magic water over her, and they rang bells to drive off evil spirits. I think there is ritual cannibalism involved. Disgusting!"

"It is not real cannibalism."

"I should say not. Cannibalism should be honest and spontaneous! The prey must be fleeing in panic! Otherwise the neural chemicals and saliva juices are not in the proper receptive state."

"The preachers bring out bread and wine, and call it the body and blood. Or, actually, they bring out this itsy wafer, and call it bread, and the one time I went to get hitched to Rania, I didn't get no wine at all, and I was powerful a-thirst. Something about getting matrimonied up dries out a man's mouth."

"And having one rut-mate for life? That is just wrong too. Wrong and odd." He blinked his goat eye and then squeezed his cuttlefish eye shut and open to blink it. Then Soorm shook his shaggy head so roughly that his quills clattered. "One mate for life? I don't know who is creepier, the Nymph or the Knight. How exactly will she break open the internal doors?"

"Oenoe grew a set of interface jacks last night. She is going to plant little tree clippings in the input ports and wait for them to grow. They will draw nutriment out of this water, and when they are big enough, send out signals to the neural net in the trees. *Then* my passwords will work."

"It will take days for the biotics to grow and mate with the door circuits. So we are not retreating into the Tombs today."

"Not today. If we're lucky, the Blue Men will not kill everyone just yet, and give us time to get set up. But I hope to get the radio working today."

Oenoe the Nymph glided up to where they stood, and she had to tilt back her head to look at the tall man and the taller monstrosity, but her smile was as warm as sunshine and as radiant as a lightning bolt.

Beneath her long green mantilla, she was naked. The green cloak was radiating heat like a stove. Through the half-transparent mesh of green, the shadowed curves of her voluptuous body could be glimpsed. She wore no more than a twist of flowering vines around her hips, and oddly tall shoes.

Menelaus cleared his throat and turned to look at the river. Soorm scowled and stared.

Oenoe said in Natural, "My adored ones, delights of my heart, Anubis the Chimera said the overalls might be impregnated with signal or scent, and must be left behind."

Menelaus sighed. "I knew you wouldn't mind. Everyone in the future is a nudist."

5. Glamour

And now she smiled up at Soorm, whose head was hunkered and scorpion tail was lashing in a menacing pose, but Oenoe seemed not to notice but stepped forward and ran her soft hand up and down the silky black fur of his chest, and her superbly dark pupils dilated.

"My beautifully furred and aquatic Soorm! You were of the Saffron sign, were you not? And Oakwhite, Oleander, Rocket, Mandrake! From these you took your Phastorling name, for they represent the calm wariness of excess, your independence of spirit, alertness to danger, as well as your courage and honor, which, even as a gay and gentle Nymph, your years implanted in your soul."

Montrose knew the Nymph names reflected their internal biochemistry, but his admiration for Oenoe's mantilla—or whatever system she was using to pick up information about Soorm's fine internal structure with no more than a brush of her fingers—just went up a notch. She was good.

Soorm must have thought so also, for he stood as if stupefied, letting his scorpion tail droop, while she continued. Her words were ripples of light dancing over a brook.

"Heed me, I pray, beloved and adored, for such calm boldness is needed now. I must descend into the cold and watery depths whether I will or no—I can turn to none else to protect me during this grim effort. And we must make haste, for the deed must be done, and we must return to our tents, all footprints brushed away and all scent sponged from the wind, before the dogs blow reveille."

Perhaps some of his old vulnerability to the glamour of the Nymphs still was buried somewhere in his nervous system, for Soorm said only, "Do you really think my fur is beautiful?"

6. In the Middle of a Duel

Soorm descended the handholds until he was halfway down the cliff, and he sprang into the air, his massive arms overhead, and his dark body taut as an arrow, his long tail straight. Down he flew, striking the water with a silver splash. His tail opened his flukes and slapped the surface and then he was gone.

"Showing off for you, was he? That was stupid," said Menelaus. "Water ain't that deep."

Oenoe, smiling brightly, waved prettily toward the water. "A cautious man would not have volunteered at all. He will clear the way, and return." There was silken rustle from her green mantilla as Oenoe, and the pleasing scent of Oenoe, drifted closer to him. She looked at him from the corners of her eyes, lids half closed, her ripe, red mouth pursed as if suppressing a shy smile. She whispered. "I alone of all this company know you, Your Honor."

"If you have to use a fancy title, call me 'Doctor'—and you're not the only one. I have a very old and very fat friend from my brief days among the Witches. He programmed his coffin to open when mine did, so he could follow me into the future. And I told Soorm who I was."

"You must regard them with deep love, to entrust your secrets and your soul to such men. I will adore them likewise for your sake."

"It's partly trust and partly desperation. If I don't stop the Blue Men from their digging, they will break into a lower level and find my gene-traces, which are all over the place. Also, I think I left my pot of Texas nine-alarm chili on the stove, and I know that's got traces in it, because I always put back whatever I don't eat up from my bowl."

Her nose wrinkled. "Unsanitary!"

"You kidding? I come from the Plague Years. I have so much antibiotic crap in my bloodstream that food gets less buggy when I spits on it."

"So if the blue eunuchs find your disgusting stew-bowl, what does this mean?"

"It means I am royally screwed up my Mary-pucker with an industrial-strength heavy-torque screwdriver."

"Ah! Congratulations!"

"No, in my language, that phrase means that I am, uh, disadvantaged ignominiously."

"Your translation is awry! That phrase refers to anal copulation, which is a cherished and sacred form of the arts of pleasure."

"That's what I like about you Nymphs. Always looking on the bright side. Well, sister, there ain't no bright side here. If you fail, I am just royally—" He cleared his throat. "—disadvantaged."

"You are posthuman. Surely you are above the blue eunuchs, and all their petty devisings."

Menelaus said, "Don't overestimate me. A genius who is thrown out of his bedroom window and down the street while blissfully a-snooze and wakes up to find his house surrounded and besieged by armed idiots is still locked out of his house. It is not the Blue Men, but whoever or whatever is behind them, that I fear."

"You fear the Master of the World."

Menelaus looked at her in surprise. "The Nymphs aren't known for knowing about the past. I suppose your hubby told you all about him?"

"Even had he not, I would have known. For this is not a thing of the past. It has been, and now is, and shall be. You and the Master quarreled at the dawn of time over the Swan Princess. By lottery, you divided the world between you. The dying machines as Ghosts go to the Moon to be with him; the dying men go to you beneath the ground as ice. Some say there is a power in the sea vassal to neither of you, where the dying whales go."

Menelaus smiled. "That's not as inaccurate as some things I heard."

"I do not understand why, if he is on the dark side of the Moon, with his Ghosts and unclear spirits and machines, why has he not unleashed one of those old, dread weapons the Unnaturals use? He could lay waste to any land where he suspected you might pass."

"He wants to kill me himself, up close. Blackie and I are in the middle of a duel. Damn tower fell on us halfway through. I feel I was winning. It's his damn fault I'm here and not in space where I should be."

Oenoe was looking at his face carefully. "You are very lonely, because the only other female of your species in existence is in the White Ship, and the bent eternity of Lorenz transformation, light-years and years, stands between you and your beloved."

"Thanks. I try to keep busy, and from time to time I wake up and shoot people, and I have my hobbies, but there is no one to talk to on this damned dumb world." He tried to say it lightly, as a joke, but he raised his hand to his face to wipe his eyes.

Her expression was one of wonder. "You weep! One would suppose a superior being would have control of all emotions?"

"Nope. The smarter you are, the worse it hurts when everything does not fit into its proper pattern. If anything, my emotions are worse than they used to be. I remember back when everything was not so painfully, blindingly, piercingly crystal clear. All that happened when I evolved up is that my emotions evolved up too. And this would make even the Mother of Jesus cry, 'cause if I mess up, not only is the whole human future flung overboard, but I lose my wife who is counting on me."

She looked at him thoughtfully. "Were I a cautious maid, I would flee now and throw myself upon the cold mercy of the blue eunuchs. You know we have no chance for success."

He snorted. "What made you leave caution behind?"

"My husband is a prisoner here somewhere in the camp, or elsewhere, just as your wife is a prisoner of eternities and stars. So I am as you are."

"What, crazy? Soorm thinks I am."

"He is too rational a creature, for he was instructed by a Jesuit, was he not? You are lovesick and helpless in your lovesickness. It is only in such things Nymphs trust, things of the maddened heart beyond all control. We do not believe in reason."

"You are a strange creature."

She inclined her head. "I could say the same of you."

Soorm, by that time, had returned, and now was waving a webbed hand.

Oenoe stood on tiptoe and made as if to kiss Menelaus, but he backed up and held up his left hand. There was a gold ring on his third finger.

He pointed at it with a finger. "I'm married. *Married.* That word means something to you. I thought Sir Guy had you baptized and such, Mrs. Von Hompesch?"

She pouted. "I meant only to share the kiss of peace."

"I'll give you the handshake of wary and temporary cease-fire."

Oenoe stepped too close to him. Her hand was small and delicate and warm, and so gentle in its touch when they shook hands, that it was as intimate as a kiss, and his fingers tingled.

She turned, and climbed slowly and carefully down the cliffside, her green robes billowing around her, shedding white petals.

7. Extremely Low Frequency

It was twenty minutes later when Menelaus sensed, through his implants, an electronic whisper and a flicker of bioelectromagnetic energy leap from tree to tree.

He put his hand on the nearest trunk, wishing he had a clearer connection. The tent material he wore had broadcast-receiver beads woven through the fabric, nothing on the correct frequency, but he was able to program in a mutual interference between the bead distances to set up a resonance effect that acted, crudely, like a step-down antenna for his implants. The geometry of it required him to stick stiffened triangles of his cloak left and right, above and below, and the jury-rig was so delicate that shifting his weight, or having the leaves toss in the breeze, created static interference. He had to stand on one leg with one arm overhead.

"Nobody had better put this into the legends they make up about me." He grimaced.

But then eventually he got a signal channel. It was Oenoe.—MY LOINS ACHE FOR YOU COMMA BELOVED AND ADORED COMMA AND I CARESS WITH LOVING FINGERS THE KEYPOINTS OF THE INPUT BOARD STOP—she typed out.

He found he could flick his implants off and on by grinding his teeth. The simplified brain woven into the strands of the tent material was able to turn the binary code into a Nymph symbol format. The trees could understand that format, and transmit through their roots to her mantilla. Oenoe's mantilla was connected to the board she had discovered in the radio shack.

—STOP WITH THE DIRTY TALK STOP BE BRIEF STOP AND STOP MAKING ME SAY STOP STOP—he sent back.

To his surprise (and relief) the next message was just a description of the chamber she and Soorm had found, and the condition of the equipment. Soorm was able to sense some of the biotechnological circuits buried in the walls through his Sach's organ, which was the weaker of his three electrocyte organs, ten volts, and able to throw the main switch in the chamber using his Main and Hunter's organs, six hundred volts. At that point, the circuits on their own made contact with their emergency failover power cells, and the radio had power.

Menelaus walked Oenoe through the maintenance procedure step by step. Both she and Soorm came from ages with very advanced biotechnology, but very poor in metals, and they were not used to dealing with the nuts-and-bolts technology of dead metal and live copper wires Menelaus preferred. He did not even use fiber optics, since the material for him was harder to work and replace. Copper he could work with in a smithy. (And of course, whether the crust of the Earth was depleted of lodes of metals made no difference to him, since the depthtrains reached to the outer core.)

Then, very carefully, he had her power up the antenna, and listen first on the terahertz imaging frequency; then on the bands set aside, in his day, for amateur radio, wireless microwave signals, television, FM, shortwave, and AM and geophysical monitors.

No one was broadcasting. Dead air.

Impossible. Even had mankind retreated into a totally nonmetallic biotechnological phase, as they had with the Nymphs, there would still be organized signal traffic from the trees. Even the Sylphs, who had the most restrictive regime of technophobic radio silence in history, still produced detectable engine pulses from the automated factories on land, and energy residue from the high-energy vehicles in the air. There would be something out there!

Menelaus wanted to pound his head against the tree in frustration but he dared not move, lest he lose the contact with Oenoe in the radio shack.

Could Pellucid be correct? Was the human race simply . . . gone? Menelaus did not for a moment believe it.

Like stepping barefoot on a thorn, a doubt stuck him, and made him unsteady.

Why was Menelaus so sure? Could Mickey the Witch be correct? Was the conviction that Ximen del Azarchel still lived, and was still arranging every setback and sinister development in human history, no more than a lucky rabbit's foot?

He said to himself that Ximen del Azarchel was too intelligent and too careful to let himself get killed by a big rock falling from space. He tried to stand on that conviction, to put his weight on the perfect certainty that *Blackie is too damn smart*—but the thorn was only driven deeper.

He answered himself with a sly, sarcastic thought: *Oh, really? Just like the Judge of Ages is too damn smart to be locked outside his own Tomb system, eh? Behold! The great and powerful Posthuman of Oz, standing on one leg in the cold, with his arms outstretched, unable to reach his endless arsenal of tools and weapons and Xypotech serfs and biotech labs and bottomless treasures. What, you dropped your keys down a storm drain or something? And didn't you misplace your wife somewheres, one of these many, many years past?*

If that is how smart you are, what makes Blackie too smart to be wiped out by a dinosaur-killer asteroid? A mountain in space as wide as the island of Zanzibar fell down and pasted everything in the damn hemisphere, and lit up the other half like a Yule log covered in whiskey. What was he supposed to be able to do, push it aside with his brain waves? Be somewhere else when it hit? He was not in your Tomb system; you have too much set up to keep him out. If he was on Earth, and the disaster happened faster than he could prep a ship and find the right launch window, then he was burnt like a straw man stuffed with firecrackers tossed on the Independence Day bonfire.

Just because you are smarter than a man, does not mean you are not stupid, pal.

He hated losing arguments to himself, but all he could think of to say to himself was that people who talked to themselves too much were in danger of losing their minds.

"Well, I've lost my mind before, and it don't look as it's done me much harm," he said. Then he wondered whom he was talking to.

There had to be a human civilization still alive, somewhere. Del Azarchel would not, could not have allowed man to fall below a pre-Marconi level of technology. There were only five hundred years left before the End of Days. That meant that somewhere, large-scale information technologies still operated, global scale or larger. The information libraries had to be considerably larger than they had been in Menelaus' day, or else, even doubling yearly in size, they could not possibly match the Hyades when they came.

He had to make one more try to find the current civilization, the Advocacy or World Empire or whatever it was that was running this aeon.

Montrose sighed. The dogs were not punctilious about blowing reveille at the exact same minute each day. He would have preferred to do the radio check in the middle of the night, but dawn was the best time for certain ionosphere conditions, and the heavyside layer was halfway between its closer nighttime position and its farther position once sunlight expanded the atmosphere with incoming heat. He was not sure whether he had time to have Soorm and Oenoe perform one more check, not and swim out again, and make it back to the tents. But even he could not predict when the dogs would blow the horn. It was just a guess.

He guessed to have Soorm and Oenoe try one more thing. He ground out the message on his teeth, letter by letter.

To check in the extremely low frequencies in the 3- to 30-megahertz band, the main antenna was not used, but instead this "antenna" was actually leads drilled into the ground, which used the entire Earth as the antenna. In an atmosphere, waves on that low of a band were refracted so sharply that they followed the curve of the Earth and could, despite its electrical conductivity, penetrate seawater.

It was not totally passive, but the chance that someone could detect his carrier wave, he assumed, was nil.

WE DELIGHT TO RECEIVE A BROADCAST STOP—she typed.

YES AS SOON AS SOMEONE IS ON AIR STOP WHICH BAND QUESTION—he replied.

THAT SOON IS NOW SOON STOP ELF STOP—she sent.

IF YOU ARE PULLING MY LEG STOP PLEASE STOP STOP—he replied, wondering if he needed the second *stop* in that sentence.

The idea that the ELF band would be active was hard to believe. Naturally occurring waves on those extremely low frequencies were present on Earth, resonating between the ionosphere and surface. Montrose had been hoping to pick up a carrier wave from another Tomb station. The idea that a civilization still recovering from a recent asteroid strike would use this, rather than the more useful AM, shortwave, FM, or microwave bands was hard to believe.

LAST MESSAGE UNCLEAR STOP AM GRAFTING MESSAGE STOP—she typed.

He was not sure what she meant by *grafting* until the tree under his hand began to throb with additional energies. It was Monument emulation code. Since all human information systems, whether grown from trees or woven into cloth or cyborged into human nerve endings were based on Monument code basics, it was actually easier to send a cross-platform data packet from radio shack board to Nymph mantilla, tree-and-root network to Blue Man tent material to pre-Sylph-era implants using the raw Monument code than it would have been using either English keystroke hexadecimals, Nymphsong enzyme notes, or Intertextual machine dots, or Merikan internal biofed-signs. Due to the particular and unique structure of his brain, the implants could send a signal directly into his auditory nerve in the squawk-language of the Savants, which a trained subsection of his visual cortex could turn into the image of a ninety-mile-wide two-dimensional surface covered with Monument glyphs.

This was what the ELF antennae had just picked up, and Oenoe, unable to translate it, sent it along to him through the tree network.

His message back to Oenoe—SOMEONE HEARD OUR CARRIER WAVE STOP STOP BROADCASTING STOP

Her reply—WHAT MESSAGE QUESTION

His—NO WORDS JUST TIME DATE AND COORDINATES STOP THEY ARE COMING HERE STOP

Hers—WHEN QUESTION

His—THIRTY HOURS STOP

Hers—WHO QUESTION

But for that, he had no answer to give her.

In his mind's eye, he could see the acre-sized hieroglyph made of recursively interlocking Mandlebrot hieroglyphs: and he realized with a shock that this was not a segment of the Monument, neither of the deciphered part nor the undeciphered. This meant it was a new composition.

Back during the Second Space Age, when the Monument had first been discovered and photographed by the unmanned interstellar vessel NTL *Croesus,* a mathematician named Chandrapur had published a monograph on the degree of information embedded in the Monument writing system. Each glyph was composed of smaller subglyphs and also formed part of a larger superglyph, so that the disquiparant relationships between the microscopic and macroscopic also contained additional information. Dr. Chandrapur estimated the machine calculation time needed to formulate a single square inch of glyph material, and the numbers were astronomical. To fill one acre, much less a small moon, was a feat computers as large as planets working for tens of thousands of years could not accomplish.

Menelaus looked carefully in his mind's eye at the immense logoglyph. Assuming it was not a new composition, but merely the normal method of taking parts from here and there and stringing them together without concern for any higher-order resonance or double meanings, there should be a detectable pattern relating some sections here to what Montrose had memorized of the Monument surface. Many minutes passed while he went through pattern after pattern. There was no resemblance.

The Monument code, by any account, was the most awkward and long-winded system of communication imaginable. The way they wrote the number equaling 4,294,967,296 was not to write 2^{32} but instead was to make four billion little strokes around the edge of a logarithmic spiral: and then to repeat the number in multiple different locations embedded within the first in certain mathematically significant patterns, so as to hint that it was deliberate communication and not an unintentional pattern caused by coincidence. It took more than one acre to say something as simple as a time and place of a rendezvous.

But who had sent it? He concentrated, the image becoming clearer and clearer to him until the trees around him almost seemed not to be there. His head began to throb in time with this heartbeat.

There was a danger inherent in becoming too fascinated with a problem. His posthuman brain structure was flexible enough that it could turn more and more of its capacity to bear on one issue, and hence lose track of more and more things. It did not seem fair that smarter people, in some ways, were more easily to befuddle than simpler people. But there was, of course, a reason why Einstein was absentminded.

There were four separate human mathematical systems, like pidgin languages, made partly of human math and partly of Monument formalities, that various ages in history had devised. Menelaus could think of no reason for using a new composition method to write a new message from scratch, unless . . .

. . . Unless it was a message not from any intelligence born of Mother Earth.

He was jarred out of his reverie. In the distance, he heard the horns of the dog things blowing. Reveille had come some forty minutes earlier than it did yesterday. There was no way to get Soorm and Oenoe out from the Tombs unseen and down the hill back to their prison yard in the time remaining before morning inspection without being seen.

He ground his teeth.—STAY THERE FOOD IN LOCKERS DO NOT NOT NOT TOUCH ANY MARKED RED AREAS—but static answered him. The wind stirring the leaves, or perhaps the motion of his arm had changed the energy contour of the cloak, and the connection was lost.

"Pox and damnation," he muttered. "I surely don't feel like the smartest man in the world this day."

But by that time, he was running down the slope, throwing off his robe, angling toward where he calculated the nearest automaton patrol would be.

10

The Testament of Kine Larz of Gutter

1. The Missing Windcraft

When Menelaus returned, he was surprised to see that only about thirty of the prisoners were standing in ranks before their metallic tents. The dog things were agitated: some of them were brandishing their muskets at the prisoners; others were on all fours running in circles around the prison yard, casting for scent.

Through his implants, Menelaus was able to send a signal to the other tents. The return pulse told him that they were still locked and the remaining prisoners still inside. The several little Blue Men present showed no particular outward sign of excitement, but the jewels on their coats flickered, and Menelaus could detect through the ache in his back teeth that high-compression data bursts were passing between them.

His implants then picked up a burst of radio-noise from beyond the fence, from near the airfield, startling as a trumpet call. All save two of the Blue Men turned in unison and began walking slowly and gravely in the direction of the camp gate. Half the dog things began loping pell-mell toward the gate, running in no particular order, their tongues lolling. Of the remaining dogs, some were near the prisoners, brandishing their muskets and snarling, and the others ran this way and that like mad things, barking.

Preceptor Naar, a Blue Man whose only distinguishing feature was that he was a somewhat more purple shade of blue than the others, was one of those who had stayed behind to guard the prisoners. Menelaus could see a dozen of Naar's black and yellow automata had unlimbered their belt-fed steam-powered cannon from their insectoid shoulders, or raised their shovel blades menacingly. There were only seven of the Chimerae outside the locked tents, and this did not include any Alphas, so the display of menacing weapons did not provoke a suicide-charge.

The second Blue Man present was named Bedel Unwing, who worked in the egg-shaped powerhouse at the corner of the fence. He was the only Blue who had any trace of hair: little eccentric tufts of white wisp growing about his ears. He was also the only one who seemed to work with his hands: he carried a tool belt and hung a pair of goggles by a strap about his neck. All his gems were on the back of his coat, none on the front, as if to protect them from sparks or stains from his work.

Menelaus had long since programmed the metallic smartfabric in his robes to baffle and jinx the sensitive rays issuing from the logic diamonds with which the Blue Men adorned their coats. Menelaus was unfortunately visible to the automata the moment he donned the cloak.

It was a delicate business to elude the dogs, the Blue Man's eyesight, his gems, and the automata, but Menelaus was able to detect the emergent patterns in their apparently chaotic eye and camera movements and locations, slip from tree to tree and stone to stone, and pelt across the open ground separating the tree line from the back side of the line of tents without being seen.

He used his implants to order Mickey's tent to unseal the groundcloth from the back fabric, and to become momentarily as pliant as silk. He slipped under the tent flap and was inside.

Inside, the air was nigh opaque with fume. There was Melechemoshemyazanagual in all his glorious rotundity, eyes red and watering, and a small fire of opiate herbs burning in the midst of the cylindrical chamber pot.

"You want to choke to death?" said Menelaus in Virginian, coughing.

"I prefer it to being caught by the wee blue fairy kings, or their hellhounds." Mickey must have perfected the art of lucidity while dreaming or drugged, because he was able to answer without slurring his words. He also either had a biomodification or had a very high tolerance for smoke, because he did not cough. "You must proffer a dozen thanks to me, for I have worked your salvation this night."

"It's daytime. Reveille." Menelaus held his hood shut over his nose and mouth. His eyes were watering.

"It is night in my inner soul, for my spirit walks the dark paths."

"Thanks times twelve, then, pal. What I am thanking you for?"

"The beautiful geisha woman from Japan, the one who dressed in leaves and flowers, Weena."

"Name's Oenoe. Not Japanese."

"She placed a come-hither on one of the Moreaus, a Doberman, with a scent of magic and an elfin perfume."

"Neurocoded pheromones."

"If you wish to call it by its illusionary outward and material-world name, yes. That opened certain deeper channels into its soul I could manipulate. I placed a glamour on the dog. When you had not returned by morning inspection, I knew you would be caught."

"What did you do?"

"I had the Doberman hand me his voice-machine, and I used the talisman to cast a spell."

"You mean you reprogrammed it."

"Technology is still a type of magic. All knowledge that is secret has power over the ignorant. The talisman was able to wake the Ghosts inside one of the ancient Windcraft. With no pilot in the seat, and no hand at the control, she taxied and took off, and now heading North."

"Wait—by Ghost, you mean those flying machines have *emulations* running them?"

"Not full emulations. Simple machine-minds that copy only the skill sets and knowledge of human brains, but not the infrastructure of midbrain and hindbrain. These partial minds live inside the serpentines. They look like long metal snakes made of silver—"

"I know what serpentines look like. It's my damn tech. But why do they keep cropping up?"

"The serpentines were useful to my ancestors who made the Windcraft. Their electric muscles provide the torque for the air screws, and their dead voices provide navigation orientation."

"Weird. By any normal Cliometric membrane-domain calculus, they should have vanished from human history like the steamboat or the eyeglass or any other niche technology."

"The serpentines are magic relicts haunted by the Ghosts of the Sylphs, who were in the air when the Giants burned the world, and so survived for a season, but fell prey to the Medusae—but you must know of these events, being from the long-ago dreamtime yourself?"

"The time of legends is actually quite a broad period, and I was napping. But why did Blackie send the Medusae to wipe out the Sylphs?"

"Were you asking me, or do godlings talk to themselves on a regular basis? Or does the madness legend says overcomes you season by season seem near? Is it springtide that brings your episodes on? If so, we are fortunate to be in the middle of an ice age."

"I think my fits of madness are brought on by sarcastic Witches."

"Then you are dire danger indeed! In any case, the dog thing returned to his duties and remembers nothing. Only one aircraft had a Ghost whose secret names I could by my art command. The Blue Men will assume the Nymph and the Hormagaunt fled away north, and will not think to look within the camp for them."

"You drugged the dog thing Oenoe had softened up for you by tricking him into the tent here?"

"Such is my art."

"And why are you still burning all this jazz weed?"

"Such is my entertainment. Breathe deep! And you will see visions of the looking glass side of life."

"No thanks. I am trying to cut down on how often I blindly monkey with my brain structure." Menelaus made a small opening, no bigger than a mail slot, at the seam of the back of the tent, and breathed the colder outside air instead.

2. Assignments

The voice machines of the dog things were able to shout out simple commands in several of the long-dead languages the various Witches, Chimerae, Nymphs, and Hormagaunts knew, and Menelaus heard at least two other strands of communication: the fluid singsong of the Blue Men, called Intertextual, and a tonal language of chimes, clicks, and diphthongs Menelaus did not recognize, and whose period he could not guess.

Several of the prisoners, all strong men, were called to form a work crew to haul coffins won past the broken Tomb defenses. It was not voluntary, but nonetheless the Blues made the dog things repeat promises of hot showers and hot cocoa for any who did his work well. Women were given tasks in the mess tent and infirmary tent.

Several were called out for particular tasks, including Menelaus. An escort of dog things took him once more beyond the slowly waving smartwire.

Mentor Ull was waiting at the foot of the large azure nautilus shell edifice in the center. His eyes were heavy-lidded and baggy, cold and hard. His countenance was lined and wrinkled, as if folded once too often into expressions of contempt and bitterness. He was absentmindedly scratching the ears of a dog thing that was simpering at his feet, tongue lolling. Menelaus could not help but smile, and he told himself that someone who liked dogs could not be all bad.

Menelaus said, "What was the commotion this morning? There is a plane missing, but you did not send out a party to search for it or get it back."

Ull's grim little mouth wrinkled into an even narrower line. "The past-creatures from undeveloped ages propose various antics due to the elliptical reasoning of the neurotic knots of neural tissue which pretend to serve them for brains. It is not in keeping with the simplicity and dignity of our Order to exert ourselves in reaction."

"So if anyone escapes beyond the wire, you don't chase him?"

Ull grinned without humor, his eyes dead. "The two relicts unaccounted for had already been examined. No further utility from them was expected."

"What if they find the cops? You know, the bulls, bears, the Batsi, the bobbies? The authorities? Don't tell me you are here with anyone's permission."

"The scenario proposed is implausible. The hypothetical fugitives could not long survive in a climate of tundra and taiga and boreal forest. And the Simplifiers neither recognize nor impose authority: the concept is without immediacy to us. Therefore, neither the hypothetical fugitives nor the nonexistent authority will be found on the surface of the Earth."

"And speaking hypothetically, what is to be the eventual fate of the Thaws who do not escape? Once you are done with them? Answer carefully, because the Judge of Ages may not be hypothetical, but very real, and nearer than you suspect."

Mentor Ull looked grim. "We are not to be trifled with, Chimera! We tolerate with blissful indifference the obtuse antics of the relicts merely because to enforce the discipline they lack would involve us in needless complications. Our social order is both too rigid and too flexible for the crude and unintegrated nervous systems of the various prior species of man, except, perhaps, in a subservient and servile capacity: but if, even as servants, the relicts cannot be adapted to our social order, harmony may suggest that the relicts recognize their inadequacies and commit self-euthanasia once we have achieved our objective here. Dead, and therefore without the disturbance of further neural activity, they would by definition not be discontent, and matters would likewise be simpler for us. Of course, if they are insufficiently enlightened to welcome that final solution, mass murder may be indicated."

Menelaus decided that perhaps even someone who liked dogs could be all bad.

Without turning his head, Menelaus slid his eyes left and right, counting the armed dog things that walked before and behind. They seemed quite alert, almost nervous. Menelaus realized that the dog things were picking up small clues of nerves in their masters, clues to which he was blind. Interesting.

Menelaus wondered what the dogs would do if he merely reached out and twisted Ull's nose hard enough to break the cartilage. Would they be restrained from killing him during the beating that would follow, because the Blue Men might need his skill as a translator? The three questions were whether Ull could stop the dogs, and whether Ull could stop the impulse to retaliation, or would care to.

Menelaus thought it best not to experiment. Perhaps merely biting off an ear would prove more productive.

Ull was saying, "I speak in the subjunctive, as no determination has yet been made. The degree to which your own capering and floundering in your attempts to outwit us provokes distortions in the smooth unfolding of events will bear on the question."

Menelaus thought it better not to answer, but he pulled his hood closer around his face.

3. The Fixer

Mentor Ull and the sixteen dog things brought Menelaus Montrose into a chamber of the nautilus-shell building higher, taller, and smaller than the chambers he had previously seen. The bioluminescent lichen on the coral walls was thicker here than in the corridors, so the room was filled with a bluish white light that robbed objects of shadow and hue.

It was also too crowded. Ull and Illiance and three additional Blue Men stood with their bald heads brushing the elbows of the dozen or more dogs.

The three newcomers were identical triplets, distinguished only by the patterns on their long coats. Menelaus knew their names: Preceptors Yndelf, Yndech, and Ydmoy.

These three and all the dogs, however, soon stepped onto round coral white disks or shelves that hung from the ceiling on long curving arms, and without sound, the arms flexed and the disks rose to various heights overhead. This alleviated the crowding, but now the chamber looked like some life-sized version of a game of three-dimensional chess.

The large wooden chair that Soorm had used three days previous was here, and a man of normal size lounged in it as if it were a couch, with one leg thrown casually over the massive chair arm, and his spine against the other arm. He could not lean against the back, lest he fall through the hole that had been cut in the seat for the tail of Soorm.

He was a round-faced man with hair as blond as a Dane, skin as dark as a Dravidian, and the almond eyes of the Far East. His neck was unusually long and thin, so his head looked frail and side-cocked. One eyebrow was higher than the other, and his mouth seemed tilted offcenter, giving him a wry, cynical, quizzical expression, as if he were puzzled by the world, amused by it, but resigned. His shoulders were thin and hunched, and his limbs splayed and lanky. He wore the coveralls issued by the Blue Men and had a silvery bowl of their warm rice wine in his hand.

Several slender jars of rice wine stood on a small table at his elbow, and the table was held, like a waiter offering a tray, by a long metallic curve dangling from the ceiling. Another table above this held a fork of smoldering incense. A third table near his wagging foot held small bowls of spiced meat slivers or nuts and tidbits coated in salt, or little twigs of mint to sweeten the breath.

Ull and Illiance, as before, merely sat as his feet, their feet crossed, their spines straight, sitting oddly too close to their prisoner.

When Menelaus, apparently a Beta-rank Chimera named Sterling Anubis, walked into view, his metallic robes slithering, the man's face contorted with fear like a washcloth being wrung, and the mocking ease of his eyes went dead as stones.

"As you were," said Menelaus with a nod, speaking in Chimerical. "There is no discipline here. That is long past."

Without waiting for a response, Menelaus tilted his eyes down toward Illiance. The little Blue Man's long coat had additional patterns of small stones added to it, tiny mirrors and studs, and even a few ribbons dangling from the hem.

"Nice duds, Preceptor Illiance," said Menelaus to the little Blue Man in Iatric.

Illiance smiled serenely. "I am now Invigilator Illiance. My preceptorship is an abeyance while the others contemplate my nature."

Menelaus said, "So when you got demoted, the uniform for lower rank is to wear fancier gewgaws on your clothes? That is the penalty for crying?"

Illiance said, "There are no ranks in our order. We are Simple Men. The others of my circle dress and groom me, so that there is no opportunity for vanity. They are, of course, permitted to express their opinions and conclusions about my conduct when selecting my outward ornament. It is an opportunity for self-denial and self-indifference on my part."

"What happens if they judge you too harshly? You get to pin a shiny button on them?"

Illiance did not answer in words, but reached over to Ull, pried a stone out of the other man's long coat, and threw it, tinkling, to the opalescent floor.

The man in the chair now had both feet on the floor and both hands gripping the seat bottom to either side of his knees. His spine was not straight, and his nose was turned away from Menelaus, even though his eyes watched him unblinkingly. He looked like he wanted to speak.

Menelaus put his hands behind his back. He spoke again in Iatric to the Blue Men. "Let's get started. What do you want me to ask him?"

Ull said, "This relict is either a last-generation Chimera or first-generation Natural. He carries only a narrow range of chemical and neurochemical modifications, his body contains many very regular forms of molecular action and decay, giving us a finer estimate than the carbon-14 method. He comes from the sixtieth century of the Gregorian calendar, which would be the forty-second century by your reckoning. The strata record shows what we call the Chimerical Implosion, when the number of Tombs built and maintained dropped dramatically from the highest point—which was during the Time of the Witches—and did not rise again until the Festive Consolation Period of the Nymphs. There is one spike in the slumbering population. During this, the 5900s, the number of Chimerae who interred themselves or were interred showed an amazing increase, rising in places to as much as twenty percent of the population. He comes from the period. Ask him to account for it."

Menelaus shook his head, and sighed, and translated the question.

The gold-haired dark-skinned man looked tense, then confused, but then, as sinuously as a Nymph, he lounged back in the overlarge chair, laughed, and picked up his bowl of wine, which he tossed to the back of his throat with a supple, practiced motion.

"Sure, I can tell ya. 'Zat all the dwarfs be wanting to know? They got questions, I got answers. Come to the right man. I'll tell ya right and steer ya right, and do right by you. My rates are reasonable, and my price is always right!"

One of the triplets standing overhead on a narrow circle in midair said in the High Iatric language in a toneless, nasal voice, "Chimera Relict Anubis!

What is he saying? The communication register on a nonverbal level issues variable signification!"

Menelaus turned and tilted back his head, "He has not answered as yet, Preceptor Ydmoy. The verbiage so far has been reassurances of his honesty, expressions of friendship, and advertisements for his services."

Another of the triplets, from even higher near the ceiling, leaned and called, "Does this proffer of service happen to be altruistic or commercial?"

"Commercial, Preceptor Yndelf. He has not finished his sales pitch yet, Preceptors, so I cannot identify what he is offering."

The final of the three called down, "Ours is a noncommercial order, and the event-situation is coercive rather than commercial. Hence the language is symbolic; but what degree of relation does it bear to the signification-environment of reality? It is a metaphoric expression, or emotive?"

"Emotive, Preceptor Yndech. It is called braggadocio."

Illiance raised his finger. "Pardon the interruption, Beta Anubis, but if I happen to ask a question, will you answer?"

"Shoot."

"Why are you sighing and rolling your eyes?" asked Illiance.

Menelaus raised his eyebrows. "What? You are asking a question about me, now? What brought that on?"

Illiance nodded and smiled a seraphic smile. "You said 'shoot.' This means you have accepted the moral obligation placed on you, and must answer the question."

"Well, to be blunt, I am annoyed at your comrades in the rafters. You and Ull always waited patiently for the full answer from your prisoners before you asked questions. I have not even found out this prisoner's name yet. So why are these yammering parrots here? Do they want me to find something out from the prisoner, or to hear themselves yak?"

Illiance said, "I asked a single question. You cannot reciprocate with more than one."

"Fine. Answer me this: When did you learn to read human expressions?"

"I am human."

"That's not an answer. You know what I mean."

"At the request of Oenoe Psthinshayura-Ah of Forsythia, I altered the signal-condition of my nervous system and provoked a configuration of parasympathetic-endocrinal responses in my cortical-thalamic complex, so that my symbol-event responses would complement and correspond to her thought-environment. Do you happen to understand?"

"Sure. You turned on your emotion chip, and now your fellow weirdlings are weirded out."

"I do not see an obvious one-to-one correspondence between my explanation and yours. Can you confirm that you understand?"

"I understand that the peanut gallery was invited, so you all could keep an eye on each other, just in case someone else was tempted to turn on his emotion chip. Right? You guys are getting nervous about something. You are trying to liquor up this new prisoner and ply him with goodies instead of just threatening him with dog-death, like you did me, but you must be getting more frightened—I am not sure of who—because each time I see you, there are twice as many dog things as the time before. Are the marines on your tails? Is your boss getting nervous? Time to report to your stockholders? Has there been a palace coup?"

Illiance radiated serenity. "You ask many questions, where one would do. Inquire of the relict what was asked."

"No."

"No?"

Menelaus pointed over his shoulder. "No, not unless you tell the peanut gallery to shut up. I cannot cross-examine the prisoner if Dopey, Doc, and Grumpy up there keep jostling my elbow."

Ull addressed Illiance in Intertextual: "*There is a meta-message behind the denotation. Beta Sterling Anubis attempts to explore the graduations of our power relation with him, perhaps to ascertain whether we prioritize his cooperation over the need to maintain credible coercion. Therefore underreact. Yield to his demand. It is not in our interest that he define the contour of our true interests in these matters.*"

Illiance pursed his mouth in a moue of sad patience. "*Mentor, he can understand what you are saying. Notice how he stares at the ceiling and pretends to whistle.*"

Ull said, "*I see the ceiling-staring and pretend-to-whistle behavior, but what does it mean?*"

Illiance looked sidelong up at Menelaus and made a skeptical twitch of his lips. He said, "*It means he is the least convincing actor imaginable.*"

Preceptor Yndech leaned down from his overhead stand. "*Brethren! I have deduced a stratagem to determine for what ulterior motive this relict, called Beta Sterling Anubis, if indeed he understands our language while maintaining a pretense of ignorance, maintains this deception. Allow me to proceed?*"

Ull nodded ponderously. "*Proceed!*"

Yndech called down in Iatric, "Beta Sterling Anubis! Eschew deception! What is your ulterior motive?"

Menelaus rubbed his ungainly, hawklike nose, covering his mouth with his hand, and seemed to take a moment to smother a cough. "Ahem! Ah, what was the question again, heh, ahum, Preceptor Yndech?"

"Beta Sterling Anubis! Eschew deception! What is your ulterior motive?"

Menelaus blew out his cheeks and looked thoughtful. "Yup, I, um, thought you said 'eschew deception'—good advice. I'll take it to heart. Let's see. Motive, eh? My ulterior motive is to have a good belly laugh watching you squirm, you damn looters, as whatever your scheme here falls to pieces in your hands. Something has happened to make you nervous, and I want the chance to smirk and watch you bungle and make things bad, worse, and worst for yourself as your time runs out. It's not too late to change your course, you little blue dimwits, and tell me the truth. Anyone who surrenders will be treated mercifully. Take a few days to think about it. Or—do you even have a few days?"

Yndelf said in the shrill voice, "Signals from the Tomb, using the entire Earth's crust as an antenna, were sent to the Bell, which immediately responded—"

Illiance raised his palm, and Yndelf's sentence was snapped off as suddenly as flipping a switch.

Illiance said meditatively, "It may appear, upon reflection, that the request of Anubis is perfectly reasonable, and produces no disharmony when merging with the several purposes we follow. I affirm that Preceptors Yndech, Ydmoy, and Yndelf, lacking experience with dealing with relicts and their anachronistic yet unpredictable behaviors, should merely audit for a time, and not participate on a verbal level."

Menelaus smirked, and reached down with both hands, and scraped a swath of stones and mirrors free from the cobra-patterned surface of the back of Illiance's coat. This left two parallel stripes of blank fabric running from his shoulders halfway down his back.

There was a stir among the triplets, but Ull did not change his reptilian expression or even turn his eyes toward Menelaus. Illiance maintained his normal serene expression, but he could not hide something like an unseen glow that filled his chest, straightened his shoulders, and brightened his eye.

Menelaus straightened up, dashed the gems and trinkets to the ground, and brushed his hands against each other. "Now!" he said in Iatric. "Do you gentlemen have anything you want to tell me?"

Ull said, "Yes. We tell you to continue questioning the relict. We wish to know the cause of the hibernation spike in his generation."

Illiance offered, "And, to be honest, we are also curious about the origin of the Tombs, and any information he has concerning . . . ah . . . the figure of the Judge of Ages."

The man on the chair sat up straight and spread his hands. He called out in Chimerical. "Hey! What's gives? You forgot about me? How long are you and your trained monkeys and dogs going to gab and gabber, Commandant?"

Menelaus snarled at him. "You're damn lucky I'm not a Commandant. It's Lance-Corporal. I'm a Beta. Beta Sterling Xenius Anubis, Academic Wing, Dependent College, Hundred and second Civic Control Division, attached to the Pennsylvania Third Legion—I teach freshmen history and predictive history, Cliometry, xenolinguistics, Monument mathematics, and also gunnery, whip drill, and prisoner beating and torture techniques, basic laceration, boot and thumbscrew, singeing and deprivation. The psychological torture techniques are taught sophomore year. So I am not a nice man and I am not in a good mood right now. Who the hell are you?"

"Well, Lance-Corporal Anubis, I *am* a nice man, and you are going to be glad today was the day you met me! The name's Larz! Kine Larz Quire Slewfoot of Gutter, private invigilator, investigator, effectuator, and consummator, fixer and facilitator, procurer, perfecter, eavesdropper, nonstopper, go-getter, and gutter-ganger! Quire-for-Hire, that's me! Streetlaw Larz, mercenary of mercy! I've taken stripes and earned my stripes! If you lost it and you want it, I can find it; if you find you don't want it, I can lose it. I know how to mix it up and fix it up. Electronic, optic, cryptic, and Coptic, I never sleep and I don't let whoever I'm after sleep neither!"

"Talk 'em to death, do you?"

"I am a Kine and I don't mind. You Chimerae can do sheepdoggery drudgery, and I'll run in the herd! But I was in uniform back in the day. I've served in private security and public unrest, spook and mook, and twelve years in Intelligence Command out of Kang Key, Eighth Division. You know Alpha Captain Stheno Alleret Anju of First and Second Bull Run? Family springs from a cadet mutation of the Anjusri Line, and I think that his kin got some tiger in their cocktail. I served under him, and he had me cleaning toilets in the stockade for a month. Served under his daughter, too, but not in the same capacity, and when the Chastity Police found out, I discovered scientifically that you can fit a five-foot-two-inch man through a foot-and-a-half-square window overlooking a three-story drop in two seconds, and there is nothing in your pants you really need to go back for, but some things it might be smarter to keep in your pants. Got me?"

Menelaus looked at the ceiling again and sighed again, and spoke in a monotonic drone. "You come from an era when the number of persons volunteering or being selected for long-term hibernation is statistically anomalous. As a native of that time, and an eyewitness, do you have any personal theories backed by evidence you'd care to describe, concerning the cause of this anomaly?"

"Lance-Corporal, you're chewing my scrotum, right? That's why you guys thawed me?"

Menelaus jerked his eyes down from the ceiling and laughed scornfully. "Lepers and scabs! You think I am dithering you? *Me?* Look what is talking! Shut your yap and open your ears, yammermouth! Look around you! We're prisoners. The Blue Men are in charge, and they plan to kill us as soon as they get what they want. So smarten up and eyes front, Kine, if you want to see the end of the week. Whatever is happening is about to happen fast. You want to sober up, and talk without so much vinous crapulent goldbricking flummoxery?"

The man's face fell. He spoke in a slow and serious tone. "So . . . we are in a deep hole, are we, Lance-Corporal?"

"Six feet deep and there to stay, safe behind wooden walls, unless we find a way to climb out. If you have a God you don't believe in, start cursing him now."

"Might die soon?"

"More than likely."

"Then, um—those jewels and stuff you pulled off the dwarf's coat? Guy who's about to die don't need 'em, so I'd be doing you a favor, taking them off your hands, check? They worth anything?"

Menelaus turned to Illiance and said in Iatric, "The man knows nothing of value."

Illiance said, "Inquire of him concerning the other questions alluring us. Ask of the Tombs, and their architect, and of the Judge of Ages, if he has heard of him."

Menelaus translated the question.

Larz Quire leaned back in his chair and spread his legs and let out a gush of laughter. "Hoo, boy! Did you ever find the right guy! The Judge of Ages? Heard of him! I used to work for him! I know everything there is to know about him! He might forget, but he hired me once. I bet you I could sit right in front of him, talking his ear off, and he'd never think about me. Never notices little people! That's the kind of guy he is. No fun to work for, and we did not part on exactly friendly terms, no, sir! So I'll tell you everything!

"His real name is Menelaus Montrose."

4. The Name of the Judge

What! You did not think his family name was *Judge*, first name *The*, and that he proved himself in a battle called *Ages* did you? Nope, this is a real person, a real man, not a god or a demigod like the lying Witches say, and he invented the long-term hibernation process—and the first person he used it on was himself.

Why? Pass around some of this dandy hooch, gather round, round up your ears, and I'll tell you the why and the wherefore and the who and the how and the how much it cost 'em!

He was born in Texas back before the days of fire, in AUCR 473 by the soldier calendar, but that would be A.D. 2210 by the civilian calendar. It was a little town called Nowhere, and the name suited. He had a dozen brothers, one mother, no father, and his sweetheart was a Princess of Monaco who was also the Captain of the White Ship.

Yes, *that* White Ship, the ship with silver star-sails, the one and only human-crewed interstellar vessel this poor planet ever produced, and that ship is real, and it's coming back someday.

The Chimeras say that she was the first Chimera, the first artificial *Homo sap* created from Monument code, but I don't believe it. I don't think she was two genetic lines crosspatched together like *they* are. She was more than them. She was an Odd John, a Nietzsche-man, a Next, an Ugly Duckling meant to grow into something finer. A Swan!

Y'understand, this Menelaus Montrose was a bit of a Next himself, because he hackled on his own brain to bloom his intelligence, and at one point he ruled the world, and he had a monopoly on the world energy supply. He had everything, and it meant nothing.

So he was smart, and powerful, and rich, and all meant jakeswash to him, because his Swan Princess took the world's one and only starship, and her one and only self, and she was called away to the stars to plead for the human race in the court of an Authority beyond the rim of the Milky Way, and she ain't coming back no time soon.

I'm telling you this so you'll understand his mind. Tom needs his pussycat, and bull needs his cow and a boar needs his sow, so you see where I am heading with this? Here is this bloke with the fattest brain and the richest poke the world's ever known, and he is carrying a tentpole in his trousers for his chip, and any man stands in his way, stands under the treads of an avalanche.

Man could do most anything by himself, that's the kind of cove he is, but when he woke up in a strange world, and he needed a fix, he came to find a fixer, and the one he found was me.

5. The Final Fix

So I was hired to do this fix for him, see? It was my last job. My final.

Not that hard, not for a man of my talents and tie-ins, but it had to be smooth and it had to be hush, and he, when he said secret, he meant tight as the lid of a napalm can. Airtight. But all it was, was a slip-and-slide job, just moonshining past the shore patrol, avoid the deepers, and go: no other package than one passenger. Him. *He* was the flash stash I had to pass without fuss or fash, and my fix was to glide him out of Norfolk without tripping over the watchdog's nose.

It was December of 5884 when I first clapped eye on him. So you figure he is over three thousand years old, but he spent the years in the Witches' Tombs, where they are frozen, and they freeze time—but you knew that part! So he is looking good. Armed to the teeth. Not only has he got a knife in either sleeve, a shiv in his glove, and a springwhip as a belt with a heater for a buckle, a matched set of hissers tucked into it, but he is also carrying not one but two powder pieces bigger than the sprong of a whale in heat: each one was a hogleg hand-cannon like the breed you only read in history books, and only if you take the time to read. Each was a rocket-launcher, I kid you not, shot eight autogyro missiles in one go, and blew chaff and camo to paint the air. I saw it work!

There is nothing like it these days—I mean, my days.

Those days. His smokewagon was from the ancient world, before the Thinking Machines, before the Giants and their augmented brains, before the Witchwives and their expanded lives. Those Americans were one gun-happy crew, and this gunner was their happiest, I tell you.

Why does a man pay top dollar, hard cash up front, to haul himself and his boom-finger all the way across the gray Atlantic, stealth at night and submerge by day, using a low-flow cold drive? To kill someone, of course!

Because I had friends and contacts among shippers and smugglers, including some hired muscle with really illegal modifications—when I say illegal, I mean *capital penalty, family-out-to-the-cousins, them first, and you watch 'em scream*-type illegal—he sought me out. He was introduced to me by the Lotus King, who was the head of a nest of Greencloaks, drop-outs, off-the-books and off-the-wire types, but with glands for adrenaline-boosters, amphetamines, alcohol, opiates, painkillers.

I don't know if you still have Greencloaks these days, but they were a cult of rejectionists. They turned their back on Darwin, turned their back on improving the race, turned their back on the End of Days, the whole roast pig, apple to arse, they flung it and said *no-thank'ee*. What did they care what the ultimate fate of the race that replaced mankind would be by A.D. Eleven Thou? Let the dead bury the dead, they said, live for the moment, and let the unborn worry about the not-yet. So as you can imagine, they were a bunch of petty crooks, glandular and hookweasels, and they supported their high-minded orgies with low-level crime.

Now, I seen you have some Greencloaks working in your infirmary and slopping slops in the cook-tent, and dithering anyone who'll toke up with a puffball or two: right spicy harlots ready-eddy to spready? So I hear these AWOLs took over the whole damn planet, the whole snotball we call Third from Sol, and I tell you I am not surprised. Nope, not by a hair, because I saw it all and I were there! I was there when the Judge of Ages condemned the Chimeras and all their way of life to the recycling abattoir. He killed the greatest civilization history has ever known, to make way for a bunch of dunderbrains and sloshers to take over. Don't ask me why, but you should ask if he's planning to do the same right now to you!

You asked about the spike in the slumbering pop? It was all we talked about, all the bulletins carried. Why are so many Kine deserting, why are Chimerae wounding themselves to get a medical slip, and take the sleep? Everyone knew why. Because we could.

Y'see having Hibernation tech around, it changes people. Hell, I could see the white horse drawn in chalk on the hill outside my first-ever overseas station. And there was a statue of a man on a white horse right near the Sisters of Bon Secours hospital. People see these things, and they read kiddie yarns about adventures in space, and they get to thinking, why live through another war, another plague, another famine, and another round of population cuts or slave demotions? Why not just snooze through it?

Bye-bye world and worldly sorrow, hello world and new tomorrow. Y'see? Hell, that's why I entered the Tombs. One short nap fixes everything.

6. *The Stealthboat*

Like I said, Menelaus Montrose is armed to the nines and he comes to where the Lotus King is holding court, hiding out in a warehouse in an abandoned area near the waterfront. Montrose spread out these plans, describing a certain type of submersible boat he wants built, based on a principle of propulsion from the days before the fire. It calls for third-generation precision machine tools of a type that have to be built first from second-generation tools that have to be built from tools we can buy on the sly or pilfer. Money is no object: he threw down a bag of gold, doubloons from the Witch-days, lozenges and emeralds from the Giants, and microbrains like beads, each one worth a fortune, he scattered on the floor like musket balls from a kid's game. Some of the components for the vessel he has on him, stealth counteremission technology, such as no one knows how to make, and some of the substances, he has the formula but not the raw materials, and he has to teach our blackout techs how to make it.

The Lotus King knew everyone in town, and he knew their kids' birthdays and name days, and he knew which locks were left open, and which could be broke open without alerting the Chimerae. The boat was done in three months, we used it in a shake-down cruise, and to shoot up a pest or two, maybe trim back a long nose, before we knew it was ready, and the Lotus King sent for the Judge of Ages. That's when he said all he wanted was a trip across the Atlantic, but he also wanted some musclers and some rustlers, fist and fingers. A break-in, y'understand?

7. The Gang

My gang was good for both and all, and that and more.

It was me, and my partner Brick of Back-alley, a razorgirl named Sugar-n-Slice, a brute born Obu Nobunagato, but we called him Oh-No, because he was modified for wrestling and he was as thick as he was tall and twice as dumb. Last was a snake-charmer named Hesperonado, who doubled as our brain-man, so he was natural to pilot the stealthboat.

This boat was a dream of a dream! Streamlined like a teardrop torpedo, the upper half one solid shell of some transparent material Montrose made, the thing rode on a hydrofoil shaped like a ring and had one long leg trailing aft to a pontoon. The engine had no moving parts: it ionized the water around it and magnetically accelerated a submerged stream of sea behind it. Now, I know you have heard of caterpillar drives before, and you say they are too noisy, but I am telling you this guy solved the problem of acceleration without turbulence. You sat in the vessel, and the water was like an endless gray white blanket being yanked backwards, and there was almost no sensation of motion. So smooth and fast, it was scary.

The vessel had an onboard brain that was nervous as a rabbit, and when she sensed anything out of the ordinary pattern, she cut power and submerged. And we knew when the Cities in Space were up, because that's not the kind of thing you can hide, and we followed under the clouds as much as we could.

Well, we all pretty much hated each other to pieces by the time we made it to the cold part of the world. The Judge of Ages didn't talk much. Didn't talk at all, in fact, except to give orders, and since the boat mostly piloted herself, he didn't give many of those. See, his mind was already on the year A.D. 70000—when his bride comes back, and so we were already dead and gone like the Neanderthals as far as he was concerned.

8. Streetlaw Larz on the Isle of Fear

Fear Island is best defended place I ever saw.

There was a ring of buoys around the whole island, and cables running along the ring, and listening towers buried in the sea, and watching towers on the rocks, and helicopters in the air, and boat patrols, and guard dogs, and—hell, there might have been guard fishes for all I knew. Then there were black walls of that reflex armor the Chimerae put on everything, pillboxes and lookout-shoot-out periscopes, and bright red boxes with lead-eyed radiation lamps, for giving anything organic a dose of lethal roentgens if the lamp blinked wide its eye.

But we bypassed all this. The stealthship came to ground on the ocean floor, in the middle of the ruins of what had once been a train station, back when this part of the world had been drier.

We suited up, dove out, set some paste, and melted open some old walls, slow-go explosives of the kind with no boom to set off the seismics. Then back in the boat.

The Judge worked some explosive bolts and dropped the ring and the line-accelerator off the boat, which caused some grumbling in my gang, seeing as how we didn't see how we was getting back home. Judge didn't care about our grumbling. I don't even think he knew our names.

But now the boat was lean enough to dive into the hole we'd made.

We left our suits on, because the train tunnel was "hot"—not plutonium-style hot, but concentrated magnetic can kill you just as dead. Just ask any bird that flies into one of those big receiving dishes they use to talk to the Cities in Space. The tunnel was round as a gun barrel and twice as straight, made of those old substances we don't have anymore—unless you folks reinvented them, which I don't see any around so far—smartmetals and sail fabric and molecular hunger silk, and big rings of nanocrystal titanium-steel alloy, supercooled and superconductive.

Well, the damn train tube was still alive, yes, alive, after all these centuries, and by just some happenstance, the stealthboat fields were the right waveform and complement to lock on, just like a depthtrain. We rolled forward and up as smoothly as a glass ball in a groove sliding along a frictionless incline.

At the end of the tunnel was the ruin of another depthtrain station, which mustsa-been maybe-been long and long ago to carry freight to the island. The platform was bricked up, walled off. Middle of the wall is a big vault door made of modern materials that looked like crap compared to the fine, ancient stuff behind us.

The plan was that Hesperonado was going to charm his snakes into drilling through at a weak spot, mesh with the door-brain, and interface and override. It called for pretty delicate work, but Hesperonado had light hands and a touch like a surgeon. He was a real artist.

He had two pretty snakes too, metal lines of tapering segments smarter than a dog and nine yards long at full extension. Antiques. They come from the days of the Sylphs, when everyone lived in the clouds, and the Giants burned the cities. Whenever a Chimera has a serpentine go bad, or the bloodline dries up, or the weapon-brain won't take orders no more, what do you think happened to them, the old, haunted weapons? By one crooked trick or another, they come into the hands of a snake-charmer like Hesperonado, and he gets them to do what he can get them to do.

But he got into some bungle, or ran into ice, and he was picking and tricking and he wasn't getting paid by the hour. So he took off his gloves. We all started shouting, because Brick told him to suit up again, and Slice was telling him just to hurry it along, and a small exposure never killed anyone. Now, I got to tell you straight-up that a voice in our earphones spoke up and told him to put his gloves back on, and we didn't recognize the voice, because it was the Judge talking, and he had not said anything for two weeks.

But Hesperonado was looking for a reason to give the Judge an earful of fearful, and he used some words the Chimerae impale you if you look them up in a dictionary, much less use them, and, well, Hesp was snaking the razorgirl during the long watches on the boat, so hers was the last voice he heard. Because he stopped listening after she spoke, see?

Hesp, he got the door open before he keeled over. So, points for him. The man was a professional. Give him that.

We get squirmed into some crawlway maybe two thousand years old. So now the next part of the plan goes wrong, because Slice wants to stay with her man, and she says she'll wait for us to come back, but Brick wants us to put Hesp out of our misery and get a move along.

Well, the Judge talks again, which made it some sort of world record for the week, and he passes her the first aid box and tells her to stay and mind Hesp, and keep him alive, because we are going to need him to get the door open again to go back out, and he wants me to stay behind too. So the three of them—Brick, Oh-No, and the Judge—take off down the tunnel, with Oh-No in front, and me laughing, because that man's augmented buttocks filled the whole diameter.

Now, I have to explain something about myself. Y'understand, I was sort of a Greencloak too, in those days. I had been given a medical discharge from Intel, and I was in a lot of pain. My first gland was just to release endorphins, and later I added a morphine gland, both to kill the pain and because I liked it. But then I was losing sleep, so I add a gland for soporifics, and then another for stimulants, and at that point I did not see why a memory-sharpener or a mild euphoric should be illegal. Sometimes the glands gave me acute insight, or helped me solve the case. The hallucinogenic unwound my mainspring when it was too tighty, righty? And then there were neurochemical compounds I could use to slow the subjective passage of time during long, boring stakeouts, or speed up time to make my reflexes lighting quick—and that has saved my life during more than one bit of the nasty, believe you me. And there were others I needed to correct for overglanding errors, and I had to get a sexual supplement to correct for erection limpness, because I was saddling the razorgirl something fierce before Hesp came along. Each gland was twice as expensive as the next. Now you know why I took the case, and why I was going to be in debt to the Lotus King for the rest of my life.

So you also should understand that I just had to squeeze a few drops into my bloodstream while I was sitting in that damn tunnel listening to my old sexhole oo and coo and baby-talk that brainless snake-twiddler. Pretty soon I am floating, and figure there's nothing wrong with saying whatever I wanted to say, so I tell her the pogostick is a corpse by now and ain't ever coming back to bed, and she yells at me, so I switch off my radio. When she realizes I ain't listening, she unfolds one of those molecular-thin razors of hers from her fingernail and waves it toward my mask, and I figure it is time to say *till next time*.

Sure, if I have been sober, I would have stayed at my post, but I wasn't, I had oozed some alcohol into my bloodstream, to take the fuzzy edge off the high, so who can blame me? I took off down the tunnel because I wanted to see some deeds.

I got my deeds sooner than I'd've liked, because Hesp, who really should have been dead by then, tears off his mask and started shouting in his native yuck-yack at me, and his voice echoes all up and down the tunnels.

There is a noise up ahead, sounds of a struggle, a shot, and by the time I get there, Oh-No is wounded and Brick is dead. The Judge is just dandy-fine, of course, since he was in the back.

Some guard, a Gamma, heard the noise of Hesp shouting, stuck his head into the crawlway, and Oh-No pulled his head off his shoulders, but the guard's gun, acting on auto, scuttled forward and fired a needle that passed through Oh-No without hitting anything too important but it drilled Brick right through the nose and expanded, out the back of his skull leaving an exit wound the size of a grapefruit. The front of his face was caved in and burnt so even his own mother wouldn't recognize him.

But there is no sight sweeter than seeing a Chimera, even a Gamma, killed by a Kine. They think they are better than us, but they die just like us.

So the Judge grabs me like it was my fault somehow and shoved me up past him so that I can pick up the corpse of my partner and crawl along on one hand and two knees, shoving this corpse every inch of the way, and getting his blood and brainstuff all over my suit. Oh-No is shoving the corpse of the dead guard, and he is wobbling a bit himself.

We get to a hatch and all fall out, and now the Judge tells Oh-No to apply direct pressure to his wound, and asks if he can make it back to where Slice is waiting.

The Judge picks up the guard's radio and opens the back and sticks in a little thinking-stick, does something to its brain, and the radio reports an accidental discharge of a firearm back to central. He picks up the gun and gulls its brain too, because now the gun imprints on me, and thinks I am its master.

"You there, drunkboat, you know how to fire one of these?"

"Yeah," I said. "You tell it what to point at and when to fire. I served twelve years in Intelligence Command out of Kang Key, Eighth Division. I got a name, you know!"

"Yeah, your name is Juan O'Reilly. One O'Really Roostered Soak. Do you have a sobriety gland in that mess you call your endocrine system? Wring yourself out and fast, because I need you to back me. I am aiming to kill an old pal of mine, and I have to talk him into letting me do it, and that means you got to shoot any guards who come through the door to meddle. I've wired the identifier to the aimer, so the gun can see and shoot any guard carrying a regulation radio. All you have to do is make sure the barrel has a clean line, and the ammo feed doesn't overheat. Can you handle that?"

So, yeah, I went through my sober-up flush until my kidney groaned, and wondered when I could get my next modification. I wanted this bone marrow thing the Lotus King told me about, to increase the production of white blood count, and allow for a quicker sober-up time if I had to flush a drench through my liver quick. He stood there looking down while I cleaned out my head, and I checked the action on the gun, just to make sure.

On we crawled, and now it was just the two of us, me and his buttocks, in the crawlspace. There were a lot of things I had to say back, and some of them were fearful hard words too, but I didn't happen to think of them just then. But, now, hah! Now I got a ton, a metric ton, of sharpened wits all ready!

Now, here is the weird part. The first time he comes up to a camera or a telltale he taps it with his finger and points at me, and says, "Null. Classify same, retroactive through all databases," and he says it in a dead language called English. After that, he just taps any looker he comes across, and points at me, and says, "Null."

We get to the target. He shucks off his environment suit and unlimbered that huge hand cannon of his. We smartglue some line to the tunnel surface, and he sets the epoxy for a quick release. I want to ask him how he plans to climb back up, but he's taken off his helmet by then, and I am not fool enough to talk aloud while we are in a black zone, so it is just one of the mysteries, I guess. Maybe he had no plan to climb back up.

Another mystery is how he gets the service hatch open from the inside with no plate and no interface, but I figure he has an implant, or he knows a tapcode to alert the microbrain, or something.

He rappels down past rafters and slowly turning fan blades into—hell, I don't know what this room was. Partly a lab and partly a hangar and partly a museum, I guess. There were aircraft on launch cradles to one side, and glass boxes containing weapons and trophies on the other side. The line drops down beside him when the epoxy changes state. But I wedge the door open so my gun can get a clear view of the doings down below.

My head is not in the right position, but I can see through the aiming camera that there is another guy in the room. There is a battery of cameras and microphones facing him, and he is seated behind the most famous desk in the world! You know the one. The desk is a slab of onyx atop the axes and bundled-rods of unity, and in little vacuum globes along the top, facing the camera, are the polished skulls of the Gang of Four. Behind his judgment seat is the Great Seal of the Chimera, a three-headed beastie that conquered the whole damn world, and there is a black flag to the right and a red flag to the left—oh, hell! How far in the future is this? Do your dwarfs actually *not know* what the Supreme Imperator-General's Office looks like?

It was the Alpha-of-Alpha, the commander-in-chief and absolute dictator of the whole planet and the Cities in Space. And he was asleep behind his desk, sitting upright, not snoring. I've seen him on coins, and on the reels, and every time a giant screen in a giant town square lights up for a giant announcement. It was *him,* I tell you.

Anyway, there was the Imperator, seated on his seat of judgment, and looking sound asleep, or dead. Now, I am thinking about what gland to squeeze at this point, because everyone knows that this seat is sitting in the Imperial Mansion in Richmond, and is not on some freeze-your-ass island off the shore of Denmark.

The Judge steps up to the Imperator and pinches his cheek. The guy does not wake up. So I am wondering if the Alpha-of-Alphas is dead, or a life-sized puppet, or what.

A little door hidden in a bookshelf slides open, and in walks another man. Now, he was not a Chimera and not a Kine. He was not any of the races from the modern world. He was a member of the same race as the Judge. A dawn-age man. An Elder. He is dressed in a natty black uniform and has this big armband on his right wrist made of metal the color of blood.

You guys ever read children's adventure books? Children's books sometimes have things in them the Chimera would rather have grown-ups forget. Well, I never forgot those kiddie books, and I knew what I was seeing.

I was looking at a crewman from the White Ship. A cosmonaut. A starfarer!

Not one of the crew that went along, the Swan-servants. No. This was one of the crew that stayed behind, the guys who painted that handprint on the moon.

He was a Hermeticist.

I can't talk if everyone is talking at once. Have your dwarfy friends bring me a refill until they calm down. That bald oldster man-hag looks like he's got a question for me. No? You just want me to continue. Okay.

9. Last Words

The Hermeticist and the Judge of Ages did their talky-talk in English, which I learned in school, but only to read the classics, which I did not do, because they were boring. Anglo is the one language deliberately designed to be as quirked up and blithery as possible. Hearing it out loud was another thing, so I could not follow it at the time, but I had a friend of mine go over it later, so I can tell you word for word what he said.

Think I can't recall a talk I overheard five thousand years ago? Ah, you forget I have gland-implants for sharpened memory.

The Hermeticist spoke first.

"Learned Menelaus Montrose! Good to see you! I had been told you were dead."

"Narcís D'Aragó, you belly-crawling snake! Good to see you too! I got a clean shot and everything! You sent men into my Tombs and tried to open my coffin and kill me. You are the only member of the crew I like even a little bit, but you know my rules. I cannot let you keep breathing after a stunt like that."

"How did you suborn my men into reporting to me that they had succeeded? How did you falsify the genetic tests—they brought back a sample!"

The Judge opens up his guncase I told you about and slides two dueling pistols, one to his left and one to his right. They sail across the polished floor, so they are sitting about thirty paces away from each other. They are those big old-fashioned pistols, like I said.

The Hermeticist says, "How do I know your weapons are not gimmicked?"

The Judge said, "You know me."

"What if I just turn around and walk out the door?"

The Judge hooks his thumb at where the Alpha-of-Alphas is sitting. "Then I turn on your Great and Powerful Oz and give whatever orders I like over the Worldwide Command channel."

Now the spooky part. The Hermeticist taps his magic amulet with his left hand and talks into it. He demands to know why Menelaus Montrose was allowed to come into his most private, most secret chamber.

And a voice comes out of it and answers him. It was a machine-voice, and I do not mean a wire recording or a microbrain. I am not talking about no damn snake that just clips words together according to an algorithm.

You can tell when a machine is awake. It is like having an icicle touch the back of your neck. It is like hearing a dead thing talk.

That icicle-dead voice says, "Landing Party Member D'Aragó, you are alone in the chamber."

The Hermeticist shouts at it. "Menelaus Montrose is standing right here, and one of his men is hiding in the maintenance duct overhead! How can you be unaware of this?"

"All evidence suggests that Montrose is dead, and that your men killed him."

"I am looking right at him!"

"Unlikely. Does anyone else see this apparition, Member D'Aragó?"

The Hermeticist says, "Wake up Del Azarchel! He is the only one who can handle Montrose!"

"Also unlikely. My father cannot withstand the neural divarication that accompanies uncorrected augmentation: for him to be awake and at a posthuman level of intelligence, you would either have to leave the circuit, so that the emulation of your nervous system was out of synch and no longer useful for further correction, or you would have to return to hibernation."

The Hermeticist was shouting into his bracelet now, and sweating. For a guy whose intelligence was vastly superior to mine, he sure looked like I look when I am coming down off of a particularly bad gland-bender.

The cold voice from the bracelet said, "I conclude that your organic brain is suffering the divarication failures associated with superintelligence without proper correction from your emulation version. You are suffering a hallucinatory paranoia. Montrose is dead."

"I am ordering you to thaw out Del Azarchel! Montrose is—"

The cold voice of the Machine said, "*I* am Del Azarchel. I am the Senior Officer in charge of the landing party. You are to obey my orders, not give them. Return at your earliest convenience to the Sea of Cunning to have your brain reformulated to conform with your emulation." And with a click, the cold voice shut off.

The Judge made an ugly noise sort of like a laugh. Then he said, very quiet, so I almost did not catch it. "Stop playing with your toy, D'Aragó. It's not going to listen anyway. I jinxed it."

The Hermeticist was really scared now. "How—how did you—?"

"Because I am smarter than you; and smarter than that thing."

"Not true! I survived the Prometheus Treatment! My intelligence is in the same plateau as yours!"

"Same plateau, but you are still a slipshod impromptu jackass, and I still plan my checkmates twenty moves ahead. Now, you can use your augmented intellect to make a choice. You ready to pick a weapon? Left or right?"

"Now, wait! Let's talk this out."

"What the hell is there to talk about, pal? I am giving you an opportunity you didn't give me. I am not sending thugs to beef you while you're slumbering. You walk toward one of the guns, and I go toward the other. Or sprint, if you like. But if you don't start walking, I'll go pick one up and just shoot you down like a mad dog."

"But why? If you have some dispute with me, surely there is some civilized way—"

"This is civilized. What you tried was not. Killing a man in his sleep! Tsk-tsk! I want to go back to slumber, so I gotta make sure you ain't around to try it again. I don't have *time* to deal with you. Every day I am up and awake out of my Tomb, that is another day I don't get to spend on my honeymoon. So you are a damn dead man, and if you want to get on your knees and ask your Maker for a quick death and an afterlife sitting on a fluffy cloud with a harp, I'll give you a moment to compose yourself. Here."

And he took out a small package wrapped in foil, shook a tiny white tube into his hand, and flicked it across the room at the Hermeticist. The Hermeticist caught it and stared at it.

"You're giving me a cigarette?"

"We couldn't smoke 'em in the ship, or in the camp. I thought it would steady your nerves, so you could die with some, you know, dignity. Like a man."

The Hermeticist crumpled it. Something small and brown, maybe a leaf-mold, was inside.

The Judge said, "Hey! Those are antiques. And the tobacco plant is extinct, so that one pack has to last me for all the rest of time."

"Listen, Montrose, we know what the issue really is. You are not angry about a failed murder attempt. How could you be? Your Tombs get raided all the time. There is a professional intergenerational clan of Tomb-robbers that lives in Roanoke Valley which makes raids on your Tombs every forty years or so, and you have left them be! No, this is a question of history, isn't it? You want to guide history one way, and we want to guide it another. You don't like the Chimerae, and you think if you kill me, the real Alpha-of-Alpha, the Chimerical system will fall to pieces!"

The Judge said, "The Chimerical system is already falling to pieces, otherwise you would not be thawed and running around using up precious emulation resources trying to force the train wreck of history back on track."

"The Chimera system is the only rational system of political logic available, given the current limitations of the human condition! Say what you will about the cruelty or the ruthlessness of the Chimera, each and every one of them is willing to lay down his life for his civilization. Who else should be allowed the franchise of voting? Who else to serve in public office? That is the logic of morality! That is the logic of power!"

"What the hell you talking about, D'Aragó? The Chimerae have not had elections for five hundred years. The Imperator-General bribes the army to keep him in power, and the army loots the civilians."

"Even under an imperial form of government, the ideals of republican military democracy still retain a mode of influence. Even in these days, any Chimera each places the common good above his own selfish good! Each is willing to die for the highest ideals of the race!"

"Well, scabs and boils, Draggy! You put it that way, how could I help but be convinced? Naw, really and truly! Now, pick up your shooting iron and let's get started. Let's see you get all willing to die for the highest ideals of the race."

The Hermeticist lost his fear and grew cold and angry. "Our higher intelligence, yours and mine, gives us the ability to see what will happen if the race is not put on the right path, and therefore imposes on us a duty to act rightly. Individual survival is not the essence of morality, for all men die: but the survival of the group, that is a necessary precondition for morality and the logical basis of it. Morally speaking, humanity dead is a null set. Can't you see that survival trumps any of these foolish ideals of yours, Montrose?"

"What ideals? I just want to burn your ham hocks with my black-eyed Susie. You sure you don't want to say your prayers? Some of them preachers be mighty firm convicted about that whole souls-toasting-in-the-hellfire idea. And praying—it don't cost nothing."

"The morality of race survival for us means that we, you and I and the others, we must shape a race whose genetic-mimetic legacy passes along a maximum of useful survival characteristics. The human race is nothing but dandified killer-apes, and it is wishful thinking to pretend otherwise! The universe is hostile, infinitely more hostile that we ever imagined."

The voice of Narcís D'Aragó filled up the chamber like a tolling bell, the way the voice of an Alpha haranguing the troops carries to the last rank. I had the weirdest feeling that he did not sound like an Alpha, but rather that every Alpha I had ever heard sounded like *him*.

I realized that the whole Chimera race, every mother's son of 'em for a thousand years, was no more than a line of ducklings following a mama duck they had never seen. Gave me that step-on-a-grave after lights-out feeling. Brr.

But then he dropped his voice to this creepy sort of soft tone, like he was kind of sad and kind of tired of anyone who could not see his point. "Montrose, Montrose, the path to survival is simple: Collaborate with any alien power we cannot overcome; defeat any alien power we can overcome. Peace is not possible, not in the long run, because the Darwinian process of life does not stop and does not care about your namby-pamby meaningless mouth-noises of human rights or human dignity. Does a drowning man have a right to life? Let him pound his fists against the sea for all the good it will do him! Conquer or die is the rule of life! *That* is the logic of morality; *that* is the logic of power."

Then he changed from being tired sounding to being hearty and come-have-a-drink-with me sort of tone. "Menelaus, we were friends once; we were both devoted to what the Expedition stood for, were we not? The improvement of the human condition, the advancement of science, the adventure of daring what lesser men did not dare to dream. All that dreaming dies for nothing if the race does not survive. This is just simple logic.

"And love them or hate them, the Chimerae form the best seed from which later strata of the racial psychology can grow, no matter what form it takes. To destroy me is to destroy them, and therefore destroy our best hope for coping with the cold, ruthless universe a grown man has to deal with. We have no more time for fairy tales about right and wrong."

I thought it was a damn good speech, and I was thinking maybe I should have shot the Judge in the back and let the Hermeticist win, but the Judge just laughed that kind of laugh that snaps you back to yourself.

"Wow. You are positively and absolutely and in every other way totally convincing. I will buy your used car, tulips from Holland, and the Brooklyn Bridge from you, and then I will invest my life savings in your South Seas corporation. Because you—seeing as how you are the first Alpha of this whole pack of foamy-mouthed murdering war-dogs—why then, you must be even more willing than they are to die. Shoot me, and nothing stands between you and an endless future of endless war. Now is your chance. Put your money where your mouth is, you quibbling and quivering little carrion-eater, and pick up that gun."

The Hermeticist said, "No. There is something you want me to say, some information you want, or you would not have talked and listened this long."

The Judge nodded. "Hey, you are smart after all. Well, your little space program here worries me. As best I can tell, you are shipping tons and tons of Von Neumann machine crystals out into space somewhere. Yours is the only space program on the planet at the moment, and I have no way to get into the wild black yonder to see what you are doing. Whatever it is, it is outside of the range of any of my detectors—and I have a considerable array of them, more than you might believe. I'll let you live if you tell me what is going on. Just talk, and I let you walk out the door."

(I had this Hermetic guy pegged as a bit of coward, so I was as shocked as the Judge when he just shook his head.)

"I believe in what I stand for," said the Hermeticist, "and even if I fall, the other members of the Hermetic Order will stop you. History will go as we wish, not as you wish, and the race that greets the Hyades when they come will yield to them, and live. The Chimera stage of evolution is leading upward to something you cannot imagine."

He walked over and picked up one of the guns. So did the Judge. They both waited politely while they checked the weapons. They took up their positions, and one of them had his wristwatch sing out a countdown. Neither of them pulled early. Perfect gents to the last.

Then there was a *chuff* of noise, and black smoke from both weapons sprayed into the room, deflecting their aims and confusing their bullets. The room was gray streamers, and where they stood was black cotton. I could not see anything. And then they fired. It was a noise like the end of the world, and it set off all the alarms on the base.

Natch, I was watching all this through my palm unit, because I had left the gun running on automatic so I could watch the scene while slipsliding out of there. By that time, I was back with the wounded, and we managed to get everyone back into the stealthboat, and limp our way on screws the hell away from there.

You see, I knew that Judge was not letting that spaceport stay in business if whatever it was shipping into space was so important that the Hermeticist was willing to die rather than spill it. I knew it was time to leave before the place blew.

The whole fort was on fire by the time we surfaced some distance away, and the second time we surfaced, even farther away, some of the fires must have made a breach in the containment, because the Geiger counters were reading in the red. After that, we kept low and deep, and hoped the seawater would absorb some of the extra particles.

So, submerged the whole time, we crept down the coast until we reached a clear spot, where I could loop in a buddy of mine. Oh-No pussed up, and we didn't dare take him to the real hospital, or else the Chimerae would ask questions. The Lotus King was able to keep Oh-No happy, so he died giggling and kicking his heels like a baby. Hesp was downgraded to fertilizer early on, and I hated him more when he was a corpse, stinking up our floating coffin of a boat, than I ever did when he was alive.

Afters, Sugar-n-Slice was feeling lonely and in the need of male comfort, and we were the only surviving owners of this boat that contained maybe two dozen radically useful inventions that were worth millions of medallions to the black market quartermasters.

So *I* lived happily ever after.

10. The Search Is Ended

The trio of Blue Men—Yndelf, Yndech, Ydmoy—had a number of questions, which Menelaus translated with great precision and exactitude as Kine Larz got more and more surly and incoherent, throwing bowl after bowl of steaming-hot rice wine down his throat; and the responses from Larz of the Gutter Menelaus translated with equal precision, but he often failed to explain circumlocutions, allusions, metaphors, or ambiguities.

Eventually Ull raised his left hand and called a halt to these proceedings. "Beta Sterling Anubis! I suspect a deceptive intent on your part. A complications of motives leads to null sets of morally correct action-reaction—" And he used an expression from the Monument math, a description of a game-theory situation where any move led to mutual loss.

Menelaus spread his hands, "You caught me. I was wondering how long it would take you to figure out this prisoner is a bilko."

"A what?"

"A sleek, a schemer, a scammist, a skunk, a yardbird, a goldbrick, a sadsack gob who takes the brevet for another man's job. Do you guys really have no word for this in your language? A dishonest person who benefits from the credulity of others."

Ull looked puzzled. "We have poets and artisans, of course, but their excesses are guided by a strict notation of coherence to accepted forms."

"Ah, no. Well, on second thought, artists *are* actually a kind of— No, no! Wait! Your society does not have fraud?"

Ull favored him with a cold and snakelike stare, but Illiance answered, his voice light and serene. "Of course we have fraud. We are human, and suffer the limitations of human nature and their attendant miseries."

"What do you do to perpetrators of fraud? Family impalement Chimera-style? Or are you like the Nymphs, and you just drug them up until they puke and apologize, and pay back what they took?"

"We register our discontent."

"Uh—wow, you sure suffer the misery of human nature."

Illiance said, "The configuration you are using is called sarcasm, where you say the opposite of your meaning? You honor us, if you think us so far above the wretchedness of mortal suffering. If one of our Order provokes sufficient discontent, the secular arm acts, and the malefactor is returned to the Locusts."

"Sounds painful. What's involved?" Menelaus asked Illiance.

Ull made a preemptory gesture. "Enough! Beta Sterling Anubis, you are altering your mode of translation to allure us to certain conclusions which we are competent to establish independently."

"Then why are you asking this pook-jerker so many questions? He is making up his answers."

Ull said, "We are exploring the negative information spaces. For example, we have already deduced that Fear Island is Foehr Island, one of the North Frisian Islands on the German coast of the North Sea. The location was one of the strongholds of the Nobilissimus, the first true world-ruler, during the period of his exile in A.D. 2409 to 2413, and before this was merely an aerodrome. His tale, independent of any falsehoods, indicates a breakdown of the ancient depthtrain system that bored below the crust was far earlier than previously believed. Further, we can deduce from the fact that the Cities in Space were still aloft in this period, that the Hermeticists were keeping them staffed despite the long-term economic losses and political instability involved: which means that shipping Von Neumann self-replicating macromolecules into space was not merely a policy of the Hermeticists, but their prime priority at that time. The subject's lies and exaggerations concern only himself and his own prowess, and therefore distort the visualization modeled from his thought-environment only in trivial respects, of no present concern to the Order of Simplification."

Mentor Ull continued ponderously, "You see yourself how the words of a dishonest man can serve to expand knowledge. Do you have doubts what truly caused the downfall of the Chimerae? Or who? Sarmento i Illa d'Or of the Hermetic Order woke periodically from slumber to addict a whole generation of Chimera serfs to an advanced range of recreational pharmaceuticals, perhaps constructed using Monument mathematical tools of analytical biochemistry. Such addiction, subverting reason, made the spread of some hedonistic philosophy like that of the Naturalists to be inevitable."

"How much do you know of the Hermeticists?" asked Menelaus of Ull, staring intently.

Ull waved his hand dismissively at Menelaus, ignoring the question. "For us, there is another question pending, and more pressing: Ask him what the Judge of Ages looks like, and where in the Tombs, on what level he is interred."

Menelaus passed along the question and translated the answer.

"Larz says that the Judge of Ages is a man of middle height, with dark hair going gray at the temples, with penetrating dark eyes, slanted in the normal fashion, and his skin is medium-dark, his lips full and his face is roundish. Larz describes him as a man of immense dignity and personal magnetism, 'majestic' is the word he used. Larz says the Judge has small, almost feminine hands. He is economical in his body language, not given to extravagant gestures, and is somewhat stern and curt in his speech, and he has no sense of humor. He wears the traditional costume of a judge: long red robes trimmed with white and girdled with black, a shoulder-length white wig, a scarlet tippet, and a black cloth sentence-cap above that to show that the death penalty is imposed on any time period found displeasing to him."

Ull said, "What is that snorting noise you are making?"

Illiance said, "He is laughing at us."

Menelaus said, "No, gentlemen. Not at all. Uh-aha. Uh. I just had, a strand of celery, from uh, breakfast, stuck up my nose, and I had to clear my, um, sinuses to get it out. Why should I laugh? Is there anything remotely amusing in the, ah, mental environment?"

Illiance looked at Menelaus narrowly. "You suspect that Larz of Gutter is practicing a deception?"

"I do indeed, and he needs a lot more practice. Unless you think the Judge of Ages wears a long white wig?"

Ull said in his slow, grave voice, "Be not in haste to assume! The ways of the relicts from the Ere-now are strange to us. Our records do indeed show that the Judge of Ages passed the bar and practiced law. He may have a right to the costume of the judicial caste from his time and home. Also, there is a legend that his early attempt at intelligence augmentation disorganized his wits. Perhaps he has grown eccentric, or engages in unexpected antics!"

Menelaus seemed suddenly more sober. He nodded and stroked his chin. "You are right. He probably does not do normal, sane and ordinary things, like paint himself blue and rob coffins, and build houses like seashells without doors or windows or any way to keep the wind out."

Illiance spoke in a voice of mild surprise, "But we did not raise these structures. We don't know what purpose they serve."

Ull snapped, "Achieve silence! Simplicity designates that we are here to gather, not to extrude, information!" He turned to Menelaus. "What of the remaining question?"

Menelaus talked with Larz, nodding thoughtfully, and with something of a stiff bow, said, "Gentlemen! Your search is ended! Kine Larz of Gutter says he knows exactly where the Judge of Ages is buried, on what level, and can tell you the markings by which his coffin can be distinguished from ordinary coffins. He furthermore offers his services, as an expert in bypassing alarms and traps and automatic defenses, to infiltrate a team of your choosing past the buried gates."

The Blue Men showed a pleased, if muted, reaction: Ull nodded with solemn satisfaction, and the triplets murmured one to the next in whispered excitement.

Only Illiance was doubtful, and gazed up at Menelaus with narrowed eyes. But Menelaus had pulled his hood up, and nothing could be seen aside from the big hook nose and the sardonic, thin-lipped mouth. Illiance was unable to read his expression.

Menelaus leaned toward Illiance. “I gotta use the latrine.”

11

The Coming of the Witches

1. The Gems

The Blue Men were still human enough to honor the need for privacy during evacuation of the bowels. They were not so deferential as to allow for a lack of security, however. In the little shack, walled with tent material, built over the deep ditch that served as a privy, there was an open panel facing the wood where a dog thing, pomander held to its nose and one paw on its cutlass, could watch Menelaus squatting over the ditch, buttocks turning blue in the cold, in case he tried anything untoward.

Fortunately, Menelaus could keep the bulk of his tent-material robes between his hands and the eyes of the dog thing, and that worthy canine had not been instructed to be wary of radio waves issuing from prisoners in the privy.

Menelaus had also taken the precaution of asking the breakfast coffins in the mess tent to make him a particularly noxious combination of foodstuffs for breakfast. Based on Mickey's description of how the nasal tissue cultures in these Moreaus were designed to react to specific odorant molecules, Menelaus had calculated how to have his bowels produce a particularly foetid excretion. He was gratified to see the dog thing, ears drooping, back several large steps away.

Montrose held seven of the logic crystals Illiance had worn on his coat: jasper, sapphire, chalcedony, emerald, sardonyx, beryl, and the seventh gem was a white oblong that looked like diamond. Fortunately, they were compatible at a base level with the circuitry in the tent material.

Since the apparent purpose of the gem display was to show reliance on the surrounding energy signal traffic, Menelaus concluded that the coats more thickly begemmed would be the ones with simpler circuits, hence simpler to hex.

Of course, the Blue Man technology was sure to come to the attention of the Blue Men scanning equipment at some point. However, all the Blue Men and dog things were pacing solemnly or barking and trotting friskily here and there throughout their encampment, gathering gear and preparing for the assault on the Tomb door. Menelaus estimated between thirteen and seventeen minutes' transmission time before the signals were found.

The base language of the logic gems was the same as that of the dog thing voice boxes. His implants responded with a toothache and a cacophony of noise in the auditory nerves of his skull.

"Texas Horndog calling Jumbo Jugs. Texas Horndog to Jumbo Jugs. Come in. Come in. Do you read me? What's your twenty?"

He was gratified when the response came immediately. Oenoe must have been sleeping with the signal board in her hands. She was as skilled as a harpist when it came to the board, which could produce a passable impersonation of her voice and pass it directly as radio pulses to his implants, which then needed only to trigger the corresponding neural stimulus in his ear. It was just like speaking, although nothing aloud was said.

"Beloved, my loins rejoice that my ears are caressed by your love-words. My twenty what? Your speech is obscure, and hinders the speech-joy. Have I not erenow bemoaned this?"

"Sorry. Next time I'll use a cleaner callsign. I'll be Chubb and you'll be Chubbies. Plan A: Can you open the main doors from the inside to let us in?"

"No, Your Honor. The door mind will not respond to any of the words of command you gave us."

"Damnation. That is a real bad sign. I had hoped the local nodes were not infected."

"My ears take no joy from your saying, Your Honor, not understanding their import."

"It means I am royally disadvantaged again. My critters, the machines that work for me, have been corrupted by an outside source. Either that or someone changed all the passcodes. Plan B: Can you switch the door automatics from nonlethal to lethal? The Blues have done something to prevent a massive retaliation from being triggered, as if they know the response pattern."

"The doors will not answer our pleas at all."

"More damnation. Plan C: Have you been able to raise any signal patterns on the radio on any frequencies?"

"There is a set of powerful static electric discharges."

"Thunderstorm?"

Instead of answering, her voice was replaced by a cracking and crackling noise, irregularly repeated, like tinfoil being crumbled then torn.

He said, "Odd. It's a mass of metal moving through the atmosphere, picking up static electricity by friction against different air layers. What the pox could it be? What the pox is that big?"

She said, "Can you truly deduce this by listening to . . . hisses and snaps?"

"Posthuman brains are good for something: I can plot the discharges on a graph in my head and deduce the properties of the originating mass. You get a static discharge pattern like that from an improperly grounded space elevator cable. It may be a superscraper. Put up by someone after my systems went blind in the ninety-fifth century."

"Lovely Soorm and I, we have triangulated; and one hundred and thirty miles southeast of here is where the discharges occurred."

"That's in the Wake County, near Raleigh. . . . Occurred? Past tense?"

"We have checked it again. It is moving in a straight line toward this place. If its rate does not change, it will be here tomorrow."

"Same day that whoever is active on the three- to thirty-megahertz band is coming. Now I am totally creeped out. The Hyades cannot have arrived before schedule. We still have five hundred years to spare. They don't have the mass to burn to make that acceleration, and human civilization would have seen additional acceleration laserlight from Epsilon Taurus pointed our way one hundred and fifty years ago . . . uh . . . if there had been any human civilization one hundred and fifty years ago. Does that mean we cannot trust the Monument notation? The formula for their energy budget for the conquest of any solar system fitting our profile was clear. But if their civilization formula can change over time, it doesn't serve any point!" Menelaus realized he was speaking in English, and gritted his teeth to silence himself. "Okay, Montrose, you gotta stop talking to yourself. That includes no talking to yourself to tell yourself to stop talking to yourself. And now is not the time to go crazy. Uh, again."

Oenoe said in her language, "Your Honor, what is coming?"

"I don't know. Something tall. In the meantime, I am worried about you and Soorm. How you two making out?"

"Soorm refuses the copulation arts."

"Uh, no, I was asking whether you were surviving."

"Surviving without the copulation arts? The idea is obtuse."

"Woman, half the songs in Texas are about the bad results of cheating on your mate. The other half are about unemployment. Aren't you married? You'd best act it!"

"Have I not acted so? Your ways are strange, and it seems insulting to treat Soorm as one might treat one of the nonzoophiliaworthy animals, but such is the code I adopted when I wed, and so do I comport myself. I did not say I offered the love-sports to Soorm; I merely said he does not participate."

"Yeah, but I got to wonder about any folk in whose language *nonzoophiliaworthy* is a single word. . . ."

"I wonder of you, Tomb-maker, who inhabit this buried hell where there is no glance of sun nor guffaw of wind. My lord husband is he for whom I yearn, as you for your wife, you who dwell in misery forever. And have you found him? Is he in the Blue Man hospital beyond the most unlovely fence?"

"Haven't found him and can't confirm where he is. Did you find any food stores down there in your nonallergenic spectrum?"

"Feasts beyond count, and tools, and weapons, and all your treasures of many libraries."

"Whoa! Are you on the Tenth Level?"

"Indeed."

"I mean, right now, right this second?"

"Yes, beloved Judge. Soorm, in whom my heart delights, most carefully noted the position where air pockets had been trapped against irregularities in the roof, and he is mightily strong, strong enough to tow me in an airtight coffin behind him, from pocket to pocket of air."

"But you found food. Food supplies are in large metal lockers to one side of the main corridor, and the armory is just beyond that. Is there a blank panel of wall between the two that you can see? And a decoration along the wall at eye height, shaped like scallop shells and roses?"

"It is not at my eye height, Your Honor."

"Stop calling me that."

"Yes, beloved."

"Go back to calling me that."

"Yes, Your Honor. For what purpose do I behold this decoration?"

“The first and the third scallops from the southern wall are fakes made of glass. Smash them. Inside are two red D-rings.”

“The glass was smashed long ago. I see two red metal bits shaped like hollow plectra. They are too tall for me to reach.”

“Get Soorm to grab them, one in each hand, and pull.”

“You told us to touch nothing painted red.”

“Pull. The doors will open. Don’t step inside.”

“Zxx!”

Since she was sending only a simulacrum of her voice over the communication link, Oenoe must have dropped her signal board, or strummed a false note.

The played version of her voice he was hearing suddenly sounded dull and monotone. She was too excited to remember to put in nuances of pitch and accent. “I see slumbering warriors, knights of ninety-eight count, and great white beasts beside them, frozen, like deer, but not deer: the long dead horses of man. Treasures of many sorts are stored in their locker below the coffins, and massive metal apes with no faces, statues—they are suits of armor, stand at the head, with flags and pennants displayed. I see on the walls arms and weapons of many shapes, richly adorned, terrible, unnatural, deadly, and the far wall shows racks upon racks of missiles, and carriages and caissons. The treasures overflow the lockers, and coins of many different years and aeons lie underfoot, bright as fallen leaves—”

Menelaus interrupted. “Don’t step into the chamber! Those are my men. With that armor, they can wrestle Giants, and with those missiles, they can shoot down Sylphs. Ha-*ha*! Just one of those guys up and about could whip these dogs and send them whining, and the Blue Men would dance jigs or get their toes shot off. This whole nightmare would be over, and a little brutal justice would get done damn quick!”

“I rejoice in your joy. My nipples harden with exquisite excitement!”

“Yeah, doll, thanks for the little mental image. Can you describe the pattern of lights on the nearest coffin?”

“There are no lights at all, Your Honor.”

“*Pest*-il-ence with a capital *Pest*!”

“They are dead . . . ?”

“Not a bit. The nanotech fluid keeping them alive is designed to power itself from Brownian motions of the surrounding molecules. They need external power to wake up, though, because the sequences needs to be computed, and it is unique not just for every man, but for every bodily state the man passes through when he sleeps.”

"Then how do we wake them?"

"We have to find a way to get some of those coffins, maybe only one, up to the Fourth Level. The power cell you are using to run the radio shack is compatible with the coffin fittings. Once it is powered up, you can initiate a thaw sequence. Even so, it will take hours, maybe days to charge up from a full cold-stop."

"Soorm is here with me. He says the motive powers of several of the sarcophagi are intact."

"He can tell that at a glance, can he?"

"The Red Hermeticists taught him that aspect of your technology, Your Honor, since he was meant often to slumber and thaw."

Menelaus was silent. Soorm's expertise was suspiciously convenient. Menelaus fretted that perhaps Father Pasty had outwitted him this round. But, if so, there was no helping it now. Soorm was locked in there, with the pantry and arsenal well stocked and the pretty girl well stacked, while Menelaus was locked out here, in the cold, on a stinking latrine, with a nasty dog thing giving him dirty looks.

"I can tell you how to enter the chamber safely, and then give you the sequences to bring the knights to life. Don't touch the coins scattered on the floor: they are there to trap the greedy. Once we have even one knight awake and in full kit, the Blue Men don't have the firepower to stop 'em."

With a squawk of data, he sent down to a man he suddenly wondered how far to trust and to the wife of his best friend the secret words to enter the chamber and thaw the sleeping knights.

A moment later, there was a whine of noise in his implants, and the link was cut. The line went dead.

Someone had discovered and jammed the wavelength. Was it a coincidence that this happened just as he had sent out his all-important code words? Or was it good luck it had not happened earlier?

Meanwhile the dog thing was becoming restive, and the stink was getting to Menelaus as well. Menelaus opened his hand and let the six tiny stones fall into the latrine.

2. *Self-Directed*

A single pair of dog things acted as escorts to guard Invigilator Illiance as he walked Menelaus back to the mess tent at noon.

Menelaus spoke without preliminary: "Do you know who you are working for?"

Illiance did not seem surprised by the question. "It is obvious that we are self-directed."

"And who self-directed you to break open the Tombs? Does Ull really think that filch-artist Larz is going to get him into the Tomb system? Your aircraft were dug up from another Tomb system—unless I miss my guess, from the burial mounds outside of Wright-Patterson in Ohio. Whoever you were looking for was not there, was he?"

Illiance made a delicate gesture with his fingers. "Let us not allow the conversation to veer into areas of no particular consequence to our continued mutual harmony. Instead, as a mathematician, I am confident that you will be interested in the following puzzle: Not long ago, some forty-two rod-logic crystals, obtainers, reflectors, and memory glints were removed from my coat by you, a gesture which, if you understood it, indicated that you believe I am able to operate all aspects of my nervous system without artificial aid—"

"I understood the gesture. Ull was being a jackass."

"—but an anomaly arises when the crystals are regathered afterwards, for only thirty-five can be found. Seven are missing."

"Interesting. Do you have some method of scanning for them? Perhaps a homing signal or something?"

"A question that must vex whomever took them. I seem to recall you have a pattern of such investigatory expropriation."

"Well, I seem to recall that Kine Larz asked to have some of those logic crystals, since he thought they were gemstones. He also claimed to be a snake-charmer, implying he might be skilled and therefore interested in computer-pathics. You could ask him about the missing stones—if he lives through his attempt to force the Tomb door, I mean. What makes you think he can open it? And who told you to let him try?"

Illiance nodded serenely. "You seem to be exerting yourself to ask an additional question, rather than taking the trouble to answer my question."

"Well, let's not let the conversation veer into areas of no particular consequences for our contaminated mucilage harmonicas, right?"

Menelaus ducked into the mess tent once Illiance (lightly gliding) and the dog things (loping) departed.

3. Mess Tent

Inside, the long low tent was carpeted with woven mats of straw set atop a heated groundcloth. To one side stood a row of cannibalized coffins, lids open, connected to an ungainly power sump and feeder elements. Various forms of soup, stew, and gruel filled what used to be the nutrient control and restoration pockets. Instead of regrowing the missing flesh and bone marrow of the patient, the assemblers were taking material from the feeder tubes and turning it into other forms of protein and vitamins. Four Nymph women, looking achingly lovely despite their drab prison overalls, tended the cooking coffins and ladled out the gruel.

The revenants from different eras tended to segregate themselves by language. The Witches were grouped to one side of the tent, a circle of white-haired women with mummy-gray skins inside a large circle of menfolk. To his disappointment, he did not see Mickey.

The Chimerae sat or stood in rows according to their ranks at the other side of the tent, the lesser ranks not eating until their betters had finished. Only the Hormaguants spaced themselves more or less evenly about the tent, but even they kept their Clade-dwellers and Donors near at hand, for conversation's sake if nothing else. And the gray twins sat together.

Seated near no one were the Savant Ctesibius from A.D. 2525 and the strange-eyed woman from A.D. 10100.

Glorified Ctesibius, the Savant, had entered at about the same time Menelaus did, but from the opposite end of the tent. A sudden hush fell across the diners. The Witches hissed with detestation. As Ctesibius with regal footstep walked past them, the Witches stood or scudded aside, clutching their bowls of gruel, careful lest he accidentally touch one, or have his shadow pass across them.

He was dressed in camp overalls, but had pinned or sewn two blankets together, and these swathed his upper limbs and draped gracefully behind him as he strode, like the toga of a Roman senator, or the ermine cloak of a king. Arrogance radiated from him like heat from a stove. Ctesibius had a number of unsightly holes or ports drilled in his skull, including a opening right in the crown of his head, and large enough one could have inserted a finger and not felt the bottom. He had found a black kerchief large enough to wear over his head like a shawl in lieu of the elaborate, long, antiseptic wigs that were part of the costume of the members of his order of his time.

The Chimerae did not feel any more love for servants of the Machine than Witches, but as he passed where they sat, their outward expressions did not change, except that they grew more still and stiff than their wont, and tightened grip on truncheon or staff.

Ctesibius took a bowl of gruel from the Nymphs, who shrank away from him, either giving him the "cut celestial" (which meant to stare upward rather than meet his eye) or the "cut infernal" (which meant to find something fascinating on the ground). He took the ladle from the hand of one beautiful, big-eyed Nymph without seeing her, and served himself. Then he sat on a straw mat on the cold ground as if he owned the entire world beneath his buttocks.

None of the generations after him would sit near him nor speak to him.

The unknown waif from A.D. 10100 was the opposite: she sat near no one and spoke to none.

The dog things were noticeably afraid of her, bristling when she moved. Her demeanor was like that of a hermit in the wilderness: an aura of otherworldliness hung about her. She seemed not to notice that there were any living things near her.

Glancing at the unnamed woman, Menelaus wondered how advanced her civilization of four hundred years ago had been. It arose six hundred years after the fall of the 1036 Ganymed. Clearly some life had survived in order to give rise to the civilization of the Blue Men, and records as well—records clear enough to allow the Blue Men to speak flawless High Iatric from the Iatocracy period, three thousand years before present. This civilization had practiced a high degree of biological technology: he looked at her eyes and at the joints where her antennae entered her scalp, and determined this was biotechnology far in advance of what the Hormagaunts practiced. From the little nuances of her stance and motions, he decided that she, like an Hermeticist, did not age.

How else was she like a Hermeticist? For example, did she know the Monument math?

As he approached, she turned from her meal, and rose to her feet, and looked up at him with an expressionless, inhuman stare.

The woman of A.D. 10100 had no sclera nor iris in her eye: every part of her eyes glittered black as a well of ink, so that she seemed blind. She had no eyebrows, and this gave her face a masklike appearance. Small, well-shaped, and symmetrical growths that no doubt were extra sense organs protruded from her skull: there were infrared pits like dimples on her cheekbones below her eyes, and also were two stubs of dark material above her eyes, which expanded as she turned her attention toward Menelaus. He guessed they were ultraviolet sensors. Above this, she had the same golden tendrils that the Grays sported issuing from her brow, except that her tendrils were so long, they fell to her shoulders. Smaller tendrils of silver hung down parallel to the gold ones, and feathery antennae of metallic blue likewise. Beneath each ear, high on her neck, were what looked like secondary ears, like folded flower petals made of flesh.

She was tall and slender, neither so lovely as a Nymph nor so ugly as a Witch. Her skin was almost as pale as an albino's, but there was a silvery sheen or highlight to her flesh reminiscent of the Grays. Her hair was a dark cap above the ears, but the lower hemisphere of the back of her head was shaved, a tonsure which emphasized the odd elongation of her neck. The hair was longer in front than back: two locks of hair hung down before her ears to her jawline, framing her face. Her lips were a wide red oval, stark in the paleness of her skin, and her eyes were magnetically and inhumanly dark, as if the midnight sky were using her face as a mask. Her features were too long, too harsh, too serene to be beautiful.

Menelaus looked around the tent. There were, for once, no Blue Men here watching the revenants. All were occupied preparing for Larz to attempt the doors. There were dog things as guards, but they were well away from the dark-eyed woman.

He would have greatly preferred a slower and more thoughtful approach to making "first contact" with this woman, whatever species of humanity she might be. Using his implants on a short-range setting, he sent a Monument-hieroglyph message to her on several frequencies in several formats. Menelaus knew he was taking a risk using his implants inside a tent, which had circuits for detecting such energy activity.

Her antennae twitched but otherwise her face showed no reaction.

Menelaus spelled out the Monument hieroglyph that meant "unit" or "name" or "identity." Monument code was a very time-consuming method of spelling out a message, even with an electric signal. The other Thaws in the tent were watching as the two stood looking eye to eye, neither apparently saying anything. The Chimerae seemed particularly interested, or perhaps were bewildered that Beta Anubis had not come over first to salute the Alphas present.

Once he had given the last nondiatonic note equivalent of the symbol for identity, he pointed at her, and cupped his ear.

She parted her lips, and a pleasant female voice issue from her throat as if from a hidden mic. She did not seem to have a tongue. The voice from her throat said, or sang, "Alalloel."

Then she pointed at him and cupped her ear.

Very pleased at this progress, Menelaus pointed at himself and said, "Anubis."

Alalloel (if that was her name) gave him a look of withering scorn and turned away. She sat and picked up her bowl of gruel.

4. Mystical Garb

At that moment, Mickey came in through the tent flap, blowing like a whale and stamping his feet. With him were two other Witch-men, Twardowski of Wkra and Drosselmeyer of Detroit. In their hands were fabrics of fabulous colors and hues, a stack of conical hats piled one atop another, rolls of fabric under each arm. Mickey strode hugely over to the circle of Witches, with Twardowski and Drosselmeyer capering behind, and with a gigantic cries, the three threw what they carried into the air above their heads.

All the Witches cried and screamed and laughed with delight, and some made howls and hoots like animals. It was their robes and garbs and costumes stolen from them by the Blue Men when they slept, now returned: shimmering red silks, satins white as snow, sable cloaks gemmed with patterns of stars and cabalistic signs.

Menelaus saw the flinty looks on the faces the Hormagaunts. The female Clade-dweller from the time of the Hormagaunts, Prissy Pskov, was looking particularly irate, and the porcupine quills in her mane of hair stood on her scalp and swayed angrily.

There were also flinty looks on the faces of the Chimerae, but such was their normal expression, so it was hard to say if they noticed the change of wardrobe. The Nymphs did not look bitter, but merely envious in an innocent fashion: and two of them, girls nubile and perfect in beauty, with yellow skins and shining black hair, tiptoed closer to the celebration of fabric and tried to stroke the stray scarf or pelisse that fluttered to the mats.

Menelaus deduced the reasons the Blue Men had returned the garb. First, Witch biometric was more sensitive to changes in costume than other races, so the recognition cameras in the Tomb were more likely to let pass a Witch in the same ritual garb he wore when he was interred. Second, by showing favoritism to an historically early group the later groups knew and disliked (for historical memory runs long), the Blue Men introduced an aggravating element of jealousy to hinder a unified conspiracy of the prisoners against them. Both reasons suggested that the Blue Men intended a very serious assault on the Fourth Door, no doubt with a backup plan involving war machines and siege equipment in case the boasts of Larz proved hollow.

This meant time was short.

Menelaus tried to catch caught Mickey's eye, but that worthy was preoccupied passing out their robes to the delighted men and women of the Witch era.

The Witches retained a modesty custom, and so each man removed to his tent to change clothes. Mickey, however, was too impatient to climb back in his beloved robes, and so by pantomime he beckoned the Nymphs over to him.

Their names were Aea, Daeira, Ianassa, and Thysa, and they ranged from achingly sweet-faced to breathtakingly lovely to maddeningly voluptuous. All wore their hair to waist length or longer, and within the shadowed eaves of their bangs, their eyes were as mysterious and exquisite as the eyes of a tigress at midnight, when her pupils are bright as dark mirrors and round as the moon. To watch them walk was to see the music of flute, viols, and clashing bangles woven in song.

Smiling softly, with flowers of several hues grown from cooking coffins in their coiffures, swaying on silent steps, they came. Mickey had them turn their backs and hold up the straw floor mats behind them, to screen his vast bulk while he changed garments. They giggled, peered over their shoulders, and made sly rhymes to one another in their soft tongue. Mickey rewarded them with smiles and pinches on the cheek and with the voluminous silk of his undertunic, a vast enough fabric that, with a little clever work with needle and thread, they could all have silk blouses reaching at least to midthigh.

The Nymphs were kissing and fondling and petting Mickey, cooing their thanks in their melodic language, and the rest of the mess tent looked on in various shades of wonder or disgust, when Montrose walked through the midst of the warmly scented Nymph flesh, avoiding the various curves and elbows and clouds of lustrous black hair, took Mickey by the elbow, and guided him out of the mess tent into the snow.

The robes were splendid: chasuble; stole; maniple; burse in silks so black, they seemed almost purple; satins as scarlet as spurting blood, trimmed in the fur of winter ermine; sleeves long enough to sweep the ground with cuffs deep enough to hide a pumpkin; cinctures with tassels as long; shoes with points as curled a ram's horn—and over all, inscribed with Icelandic runes, uncial elf-script, zodiacal, and esoteric signs, Solomonic seals circled by Latinate incantations and Monument hieroglyphs, trimmed in a geometric galloon. On his broad back was a shape of the cabalistic tree of life in colored thread, surrounded by Chinese trigrams, and an endless pattern of woven mazes.

On his skull an unlikely seventeen-inch-high conical cap loomed and nodded, dripping with earflaps and neck scarf and chin strap and tassels, another scarf floating from the peak, absurd with a false mouth and two squinting decorations like eyes, with lids that opened and shut; and the brim was a dazzle of star patterns picked out in moonstones.

Menelaus could read Monument glyphs, as well as Icelandic and Latin, and knew the writings spelled out gibberish.

Mickey was grinning like an idiot. "Those geisha girls are certainly fine-looking! Such soft hands and long fingers! I will chain them with chains of gold in my floating harem of love when I sail about the world in a houseboat, and dote on them. They can trim the sails and prepare the meals, and during the long, warm, tropic nights . . . But, no! Gold sinks. I will adorn them in cork vests. Although with mammary glands so globular, they look buoyant enough—"

"Snap out of it, Romeo. You have a noseful of bioengineered pheromones. Your trace-amine-associated olfactory receptors just sent a complex chemosign to your orbitofrontal cortex, fusiform cortex, and right hypothalamus, and triggered an aphrodisiac response. By adjusting their allomones, they could have made you sexually attracted to a dog thing or an old tree stump. You are lucky they did not have their gear with them, or you'd be the one in *their* harem."

"Gaah! You make life sound like a cold clockwork mechanism. I feel the stirring of the elemental powers of life, the very earth-energy itself! Those geisha girls—"

"Those 'geisha girls' as you call them, damn well *ruled* the eras from which they come. Not just the territory and the menfolk, but every living creature down to insects and bacteria were domesticated and in the palm of their oh-so-soft and gentle hands. You might escape because your olfactory and endocrinal systems are not designed and bred to be vulnerable to every nuance of their scent cues and flower language. Your brain is too primitive—if you are lucky—for them to invade it chemically and get complete control. They come from your future: the biopsychological mechanisms you Witches were beginning to play with, they actually understand. So I would not toy with those women, big buddy."

"You should beware yourself. Did you not see the killing ferocity in the eyes of the Chimerae when you paid no obeisance to their Alphas, but came and touched me, an unclean Witch, and drew me aside to speak?"

"Nah, that is just their normal level of killing ferocity. When they get really puckered, they start combing their hair. Besides, they done told me to talk to the other Thaws and gather troops. Well, I am telling you, start gathering. Can you actually get your Witches from so many different periods to work together? I see some from the Nameless Empire period, another from the Sunless times, and the little blonde is from the days before the Witches were called Witches, the Simon Family era."

Mickey said, "The little blonde, Fatin, is the key to winning the loyalty of the rest. She is actually the eldest virgin here, and this gives her power over us. But I have convinced her that I know secrets of many ages that passed while she slept, and so you will have to make it look like I do. What happened?"

"One of the Chimerae, a Kine named Larz, claims he can open the fourth door and identify the Judge of Ages. He's lying, but it is going to draw all the Blues away from the other spots they're protecting, such as the gate, the airfield, the hospital."

"What if he opens the door for them? Or they break it down without him?"

"Ah—well, there are enough biological traces of me down there, not to mention internment records, or patterns in the arrangement of controls and architecture indicative of particular behaviors of mine—hellfire and pox, I left a *coffeepot* sitting on a plate down there, and I know I am the only man left alive who drinks that Arbuckle's brown gargle—that anyone of my level of intelligence could figure out pretty damn quickly where I am hiding. Little Illiance is maybe two steps away from figuring it out anyway. We can meet in a large group on the shielded hilltop near the pass leading to the dig: this is a good chance to gather together in a large group without the dogs noticing and breaking it up. Go!"

Mickey departed, moving surprisingly quickly and silently for a man so large. Menelaus decided his fine new duds added a lightness to his step.

Montrose saw the flap of the mess tent move. Ctesibius the Savant had emerged, his face as cool and dignified as the face of the statue of the pharaoh Ozymandias. Ctesibius began to walk with slow and stately step, his hands clasped behind him, his head hooded in black cloth, toward the prison yard where the other tents were, all alone.

5. The Servant of the Machine

By the time Menelaus caught up with him, Ctesibius was at the flap of his sleeping tent. Menelaus reached out with his implants to deactivate the espionage recorders woven into the tent fabric and found to his shock that they were already deactivated.

Ctesibius was a dark-eyed, dark-haired man of olive complexion. He had fine, neatly arranged features slanting down to a narrow chin. He had the thin-fingered but muscular hands of a pianist. There were three diamond-shaped tattoos on his forehead in a down-pointing triangle, and additional lines of ink running from the outer corners of his eyes to hairline above his temples, and from the corners of his mouth to his jaw, giving him an oddly masklike but solemn appearance.

The man showed no surprise at Menelaus' approach, but merely threw wide the tent flap and gestured politely for the other to follow him inside. Ctesibius sat on the metallic cot and drew around his shoulders the blue blanket provided, but he wore it as if had been ermine.

Menelaus addressed him in three different tongues. The man did not speak Merikan or Sylph, but understood the Merikan/Spanish/Nipponese pidgin dialect known as Pre-Anglatino. The conversation was halting, but not impossible. The difference was no greater than the gap in language between an Englishmen of A.D. 1500 and a Saxon of A.D. 1000.

Menelaus said, "I understand Savant, but cannot speak it. If you can jinx their smartmetal, you should have been helping us plan our escape, pal."

The man uttered the rapid noises of Savant modulator-demodulator code. A second channel of information carried nonverbal cues, tones of voice, body language. Hence, in this second channel of information, even though not in real life, the man's tone of voice was ponderous, his expressive grave. "Your words are improper, an affront. Am I not an elevated being of the third recital?"

"Are you not a prisoner in a death camp? Just today one of the Blue Men said he was going to kill us all, since we cannot serve in their society, even as slaves."

With a nonexistent gesture in this information channel, Ctesibius pointed significantly at the three diamonds inked on his brow. "Do I fear death? What you see before you is a mere vessel of flesh. My soul and information have passed into the infosphere not once, but three times, and achieved a level of perfection undreamed by mere *hylic* and physical men!"

Menelaus narrowed his eyes. "You're a Ghostfather. A Servant of the Machine."

The man looked disdainful. "That is not the polite term. I have downloaded my brain information into the Xypotech system three times. I am a Savant of the Machine, not 'servant.' The partnership is mutual and cooperative. My name is Ctesibius, my title is Glorified, and you may address me as *Donator.* I am an Endocist."

"I don't know that word, ah, Donator Ctesibius."

"An exorcist is one who casts a spirit out. I am one who casts my spirit in. The brain-reading and emulation process is very involved, and requires specific mental disciplines to endure without harm, and without data-distortion on the other side."

"Yuen says he almost killed you, Donator Ctesibius."

"The fierce man with one eye? The yogurt he was eating should have come to me."

"Beat you up with his leg-bone, didn't he, Donator Ctesibius?"

"On a physical level, yes. I regard the mental plane as one where my victory was culminated. The actions of mere matter and flesh are beneath contempt. I have already reduced the memory of those events to nonimportance."

"We—that is, me and half a threescore others in the camp—we are planning a breakout, and we need your help. We need the help of every able-bodied man."

Ctesibius spoke solemnly: "I will help you in the best way possible: by advising you to spare yourselves an untimely death. You cannot defeat the world into which was have awakened. Look."

He drew out from his overalls a small gray spherical bead and tossed it to Menelaus.

Menelaus caught it. "It is one of the musketballs used by the dog things."

Ctesibius nodded gravely, squinted, and watched without interest as Menelaus flung the musketball to the ground-cloth underfoot with a shout of pain. The musketball, now translucent, lay hissing, and glowed red-hot with internal heat, and then white-hot, and in a stench of burnt metal, sank through the ground-cloth and into the icy soil beneath. Menelaus snatched his hand behind his back to hide the fact that he had not actually been burned. He had sensed with his implants the signal issue from the more metallic parts of the brain of Ctesibius a split second before the musketball actually became active.

Menelaus said, "Even if the bullets can be programmed to emit several types of lethal energies or explosives, the aiming system is still handheld muskets carried by primitive Moreaus—artificially designed creatures."

"You mean like the H. G. Wells novel? The beasts of the isle of Dr. Moreau? How odd that that word would survive!" His face softened in a smile; a shadow of pleasant memory haunted his eyes. He seemed, for that moment, human.

"Well, the Judge of Ages tampered with history to preserve certain books he liked. If your machines had not tampered back, more people would remember some of the things we've lost of the past."

Ctesibius stiffened, and his face grew masklike again. "You speak nonsense. The Machine preserves what is worth preservation. We are not."

"If I get my hands on the right equipment, I hope to be able to jam the control signals involved and render the musketballs nonradiant."

"You? And who are you?"

"Sorry, where are my manners? My name is Beta Sterling Xenius Anubis. I am a Chimera from A.D. 5292."

Ctesibius suppressed a laugh, but his eyes twinkled. "Captain Sterling?"

"My rank is Lance-Corporal."

"Of course it is. 'Onward! The future is a voyage without end!' But, say, Chimera, if you are a three-headed monster, where are your two other heads? One of them is a jackal, I assume, Anubis? Xenius is a more obscure reference—it's an epithet of Zeus, the Sky-Father of the Greeks, in his role as the enforcer of the laws of courtesy and hospitality."

"Chimera is the common name for the warrior-aristocrats of the Eugenic General Emergency Command who ruled these lands between 4500 and 5900. So called because they had their genes spliced with animal genes or artificially composed genes. I am not a three-headed monster. Just a one-headed one."

"You are an officer of the Tombs. A guard, one of the Hospitaliers. And you are from a period of time much earlier than the absurd date you gave. Your name gives you away. But why be so obvious?"

Menelaus saw no reason, at this point, to dissemble. He took his rock out from his robes. "Because I knew anyone who recognized who that name would be from my time, too, and would therefore be a Hermeticist or their agent. I wasn't expecting it to be you. I never figured you as the one in charge of all this." He waved his hand at the camp. "How are you sending the signals to Mount Misery? I did not detect any broadcast from you. What are your orders from Del Azarchel?"

Ctesibius smiled bitterly. "You suffer paranoid delirium, then? Do I look like the master here, dressed in blankets, without even a proper wig? You think I am secretly behind all this? The elaborate bait of seeing who recognizes your name, in my case, was not needed: any man can see at a glance that I am a Savant. But the Machine I serve no longer serves me. You are a wrecker, perhaps? A Luddite, or a catamite of the Giants? No matter. Our conflict was over long ago, and the dreams you served or I served are both as dead and forgotten. My life work is failure—I thought I would wake to a future where the transhumans would revere me as their Adam and great original. Instead—why do the others in the camp, the other prisoners, hiss at me?"

Menelaus frowned, decided murder was not yet needed, and put his rock away, shrugging. "Every period in history hates the Machine."

"I do not blame them. I thought the dream of Transhumanism would arise like the phoenix from the ashes of the world the Giants burned. Whether the lesser people would understand that dream or no, I thought to be of no account. Together, we who set our eyes on the future, would enter that glorious noontide of man, and the man beyond man, mind beyond mind! Together, upward and onward without end, an asymptote of eternal progress. But no. Narrow is the gate to the future. It will admit but one."

Menelaus blinked in surprise. "What do you mean?"

"I joined the Order of Transhumanitarian Emulation Advocates so that, even though I in my fleshly self would die, my thoughts and memories, the true part of me, the only thing that can really be called a soul, would live on and on, preserved forever.

"He was made to be smarter than I was, not merely a genius, but beyond mere genius. He was closer to me than a son. Not just a diary sprung to life, but the best and most perfect version of yourself you can imagine—and, oh, I know what those Thucydides monsters say, that we Savants are merely narcissists—but no, not so!

"It was for public service that I fathered an Iron Ghost. I was a member of the Special Advocacy myself, a chairman of the Armed Services Committee, so I knew the nuances of the military strengths and ambitions of every strategist of every Giant militia and every general of every princedom; more than that, and served on the Ways and Means Committee, and so I knew the budgets and the bribe amounts of every ledger of every province and parish, county and shire. Small wonder I was selected a second time, and then a third! And my soul could solve problems I could not, and could not have dreamed how to solve, but he did it in my way, with my priorities, my *élan*, and with the memories and data in my head. He was me, the me I could never be, the me I should have been, and he was supposed to last forever!"

"Forever is a long time, Donator."

"You know nothing of my sorrow. It is not right that a man should outlive his own soul."

"Well, none of us are going to outlive much of anything if we don't escape. Will you stand with us?"

Ctesibius said, "All history has been a single drama, albeit with infinite variations. Evolution attempts to thrust mankind into the higher plane of existence, up the asymptote and into the machine form of life, and the fleshly side of man's thinking, the corrupt materialism of the body, fights against. But now the struggle is nearly over. The cost to produce logic crystal in my day was in the scores of grams of anticarbon: and it was bulkier and carried less information than what they use as a throw-weight. Do you fail to understand? The logic crystals are so ubiquitous that they are being used as ammunition. The dream of the Machine is nearly accomplished. The current world is nearly entirely covered."

"Covered with ice, you mean."

Ctesibius smiled a very small, very thin smile, which had no more humor in it that the smile of a skull, and bent to the spot where the dropped musketball had burnt a small hole in the groundcloth. Menelaus heard a crackling of radio noise in his implants again, and a section of the groundcloth peeled back to reveal a layer beneath where the snow had been packed down, melted and refrozen into a layer of slushy ice. Ctesibius scooped some of this slush into his hand with his fingernails, and he held it up toward Menelaus.

"This is not ice. It is nanotechnological fluid. It is intelligent and active. The entire land surface of the globe may be covered with it. It is microscopic logic crystal. This is the Iron Ghost of the Nobilissimus Ximen del Azarchel. This ice; and that you see outside the door; the glacier beyond: His mind is now housed in a substance covering the planet. Of the volume of all the oceans of the world, I am not certain, but they may be his as well. The world is the Master of the World. All that remains is to wipe out the Tombs and eliminate the last of biological life. Nonmechanical life is no longer needed nor desired.

"And I—who was to be a part of the ascension—I have been left behind."

The little bits of slush in his palm, the tiny fragments under his nails, began to glow with many colors.

6. *The Last Message*

Ctesibius slapped his hand against his knee, dashing the glowing droplets of snow from his hand. Like tears, they fell to the groundcloth and sputtered into darkness. "I can neither follow its thoughts nor attract its attention. This is the next evolutionary step of the human race. We have been standing and walking in it, and perhaps drinking it as well, taking it into our bodies. The frequencies used by the snowflakes to communicate one with the other I cannot detect."

Menelaus stood looking down at the melting drops of snow in the cloth floor of the tent. "Damnation, but I hate nanotechnology. It gets everywhere! And if I had been smarter, I would have recognized this back in the shower tent. Remember how they made us all shower when we were first dug up? I detected particulate matter in the water stream, and I thought it was Blue Men nanotech. No. They just melted some snow and sprayed us down."

Ctesibius said, "Do you see why your attempt is in vain? I could cup my hand and pick up a lump of snow with more intelligence and calculation power than every brain in this camp combined. I come from a day before the Giants burned the world, and survived only because the Giants were holding me for trial, and they thought it better I should be in hibernation than that I should perish in their fire. But, as I said, three times I made mental union with my Glorified Self in the infosphere, and he was in communion with Exarchel, who was an emulation of the only sane one of the three posthumans, the Nobilissimus del Azarchel. I saw the Cliometric calculations the parliament of Ghosts were contemplating. I know the scope of history."

Menelaus said, "And what did you see?"

"It is all a falsehood. Del Azarchel never intended this world to bring forth the next evolutionary step beyond man."

"Never intended? What the hell do you mean? His attempts have been going on for eight thousand one hundred years plus change! There is nothing else he is doing! You tell me what you know, you Swiss cheese head, or I'll drill you a few more of them ugly holes!" But he realized he was shouting in English, and that the other man was looking at him with a blank-eyed, aloof, and uninterested glare.

Ctesibius said, "I will trouble to say no more. I have outlived my mind and soul, my world, and my usefulness. The asymptote has come and gone, and left all merely living things behind, far behind. My Glorified version did not survive the asymptote, and so no memory of mine will be preserved to the end of the universe.

"To be immortal is the only goal worth seeking. All else is merely vanity, for it will be swallowed by entropy, and perish.

"Whether the Blue Interfacers kill me or spare me, it means nothing to me. I have given you the help you need: My counsel is that you embrace despair and die, as I myself shall do. The audience is ended. Depart."

At that moment, there came a noise of barking dogs and walking automata outside, and Menelaus could tarry for no more questions.

7. Approaching the Fourth Door

The wind had picked up, and sent streamers and shimmers of snowflakes racing along the ground, white dust devils, and plumes fled horizontally from each tree branch or dune-crest, so that anyone facing into the wind soon had a light crust of frost caking his windward side. Despite this, the sky was loftily blue overhead. Only in the south, opposite the glancing blue ridgeline of the glacier, was there a line of dark clouds, presaging storm.

Ahead of the dogs were the several of the Blue Men. Menelaus was familiar with Ull, Yndelf, Yndech, and Ydmoy. Menelaus heard the others being addressed: Docent Aarthroy was a diffident and thickset youth with a heavily gemmed coat, a head taller than the others. Behind Aarthroy were two serene, wrinkle-faced elders called Preceptor Orovoy and Invigilator Saaev.

Of Illiance there was no sign.

The dogs were leaping and gamboling, and the barks rang out along the snowy hillside with sharp, flat, echoes.

The Blue Men seemingly took no notice whatever of the snow, picked their way delicately across the snowdrifts, their slippers leaving footfalls as tiny as deer prints in the drift, and they walked upright, gems winking in their long coats, stately as a procession. Their heads did not seem to bob up and down as they moved, so it almost looked like they were gliding on the icy surface. Despite their reserve, there was an atmosphere of tense eagerness around them, a gleaming eye or quickly hidden smile showing their anticipation.

From the rear approached Preceptor Naar, leading a clattering flotilla of striding and loping machines, including the fifteen that had been outfitted with steam-powered Gatling guns.

Out in the front of the procession, waving his hands high in the air with every exclamation and snapping his fingers whenever he made a rhyme, the blond-haired, dark-skinned and sly-eyed Larz. Yndelf, Yndech, and Ydmoy (who were nearest him) must have understood enough of the dialect of late-period Chimerical to keep the conversation going with a question now and again; or perhaps Larz spoke merely for the pleasure of it, which he evidently relished.

In the hands of Ull was a serpentine, one of those long semi-intelligent whips made of memory metal used as ceremonial weapons by the Chimerae. Its hilt was wrapped with blue and red silk, and decorative amulets of carved and painted wood had been fitted over the original hilt and control-points.

Menelaus stood with Yuen and Daae amid the pines, hidden by the thick needles from a casual glance from below. He stood with his hood pulled close against the bite of the wind.

The other two stood as motionless as hunting cats. When the last of the procession passed out of sight between the snowy hillocks below, at a silent sign, the two turned and loped across the snow with alarming speed. Menelaus followed, careful to impersonate their peculiar way of running, which was to lean forward with their arms held horizontally behind them. They came shortly to a hill as even and symmetrical as an upended bowl. When they came up the slope, Menelaus felt in his implants a sudden silence of the surrounding signal traffic: an invisible field like a Faraday cage was around them, blocking radio and microwave.

8. The Rape of Arroglint

Yuen spoke without preamble to Daae. "The Blue Man called Ull has touched the sacred scourge, Arroglint the Fortunate, of the Yuen clan. I must either spill his blood, or request a reduction in rank to nonliving."

Daae said, "Request denied. Ritual suicide is not in the best interest of the High Command at this time, as it would reduce our effective fighting force of Alphas by one half."

Menelaus interrupted in a angry voice, "Damn! Did those thieving lepers actually break the seals on your coffin footlocker, Yuen? You're not horsechafing my breeches? No matter how much they do, each time I hear of another crime, it seems worse! If the Judge of Ages were actually real, he would hide them till they squealed like stuck pigs, or rip off their heads and dook down their neck holes. No one breaks what he has sealed and lives to boast of it! Do they think they are immune?"

The eye of Yuen not covered with an eyepatch slid toward Menelaus and narrowed dangerously. "I commend that you are so driven by righteous indignation on my behalf that you forget the proper way for a Beta to address an Alpha."

Menelaus recovered himself and gave the stiff-armed salute. "Sorry, Proven and Loyal Sir! Request permission to kick myself sharply in the gonads with both heels until I convulse and puke."

Daae said dryly, "Denied. While the contortion needed for the maneuver would be fascinating to see, such an act is not deemed in the best interest of the High Command at this time. Your imagery is poetically vivid enough, but possibly leaves something to be desired. Perhaps you could employ your command of language to give me a report on recruitment."

"Sir! Preliminary situation is favorable: I have approached the Hormagaunts and the Nymphs, and elicited promises of alliance. Together with us, that makes twenty-eight, of which only seven have fighting experience, eight if we count the Alpha Lady. The rest are noncombatants, servants, or women, useful only to stop bullets, and likely to panic in combat. The Witches are still an unknown factor, but there is a highly influential one of their number, named, uh, a long sort of name that starts with an *M,* who says he can perhaps sway them to our cause. There are thirty-one Witches, including a dozen Demonstrators."

"Perhaps?"

"He is too cautious to promise the result, sir."

Daae said, "Witches are always craven, but surely will join us if we seem to be the winning side." The word in Chimerical for *craven* and *opportunist* was the same word. "We must make them think we will win."

"There are also three revenants from the unknown period of history after the fall of the Hormagaunts—the gray twins and the strange-eyed lady with the scars on her spine—but I have had no chance to speak with them, or discover a common language."

Yuen said, "I have observed the gray twins in the mess tent: they are unwarlike. By how they stand and move, the way they hold their eyes, it is clear enough. The other one is a murderess with much blood on her hands, or so I suppose: the dogs fear her."

Menelaus said, "I tried just now to enlist the Savant Ctesibius from A.D. 2525, whom Proven Yuen wounded and sent to the hospital. The man is in the grip of deep melancholia, and will neither aid us nor the enemy."

Yeun said, "If he knows of our plan, he must die. Besides, his demeanor is arrogant, particularly for an unmodified Kine."

"Sir, he knows nothing, and will not stir himself to speak any warning to the enemy. I suggest we not spare the time and manpower best devoted to other tasks."

Daae said, "For now, Alpha Yuen, spare the Savant. Beta Anubis, continue the report."

"I have had no opportunity to speak with the Giant from A.D. 3034, whom I have not seen inside the wire since the first day, nor the Scholar Rada Lwa from the Antecpyrotic world. You recall the man whom you saw hospitalized when he attempted to reenter the Tombs, sir? You told me of him."

Daae nodded. "Of course. He is covered with luminous tattoos, and looks like an apparition. At that time you advised breaking into the Tombs rather than attacking the wire."

"He is also from A.D. 2509, an era earlier than that of the albino Scholar: I think he is one of the Knights Hospitalier, and a vassal of the Judge of Ages. Who can say the wonders he knows?"

Daae looked thoughtful. "He surely would know the whereabouts of the Judge of Ages." And, despite that Yuen said nothing and showed no expression, Daae turned and said to him, "The Judge is no barracks-room tale. The man is a reality."

Yuen nodded brusquely. "Of course, sir. Just as you say, sir." He used the same tone of voice he would have used had he been convinced.

Menelaus said, "Alpha Daae! I regret to report that I have found no sign of the other Thaw of which you spoke."

Daae raised an eyebrow. "I spoke?"

"Sir, you said that the man able to destroy whole aeons of history, the figure against whom I seek my revenge, was thawed from the Tombs, and abroad. You said he must be here."

Daae said, "Only the Judge of Ages has the right to condemn the ages of history, throw down kings, and vanquish empires. I know he is here, because he must arise to defend his Tombs. Otherwise, they would have all long ago been looted. That we are here proves he is among us."

Menelaus felt a microscopic prick of disappointment. He had been hoping Daae knew something of the whereabouts of Del Azarchel.

"Sir!" said Menelaus, astonished. "You say the Judge of Ages is the one guilty of destroying our period of history?"

"Was there not corruption among the officers, vice among the ranks? Had we not betrayed our founding eugenics principles, allowed miscegenation, permitted indiscipline to spread? Had not the Genetic Republic become a Caste-based Empire? Had we not betrayed evolution itself?"

"The Judge of Ages did not do this!" said Menelaus.

"Who else?" asked Daae. "Who else controls the Cliometric art?"

"What of Del Azarchel and his Hermetic Order?"

Daae made a dismissive gesture. "Children's tales. How could such creatures exist? Even if they did exist, how would we know of them? The Judge of Ages must be real: his Tombs are visible and solid."

Menelaus thought the man had an odd standard for deciding what to believe.

Yuen must have felt the same way. He said sardonically. "The handprint on the Moon is visible too, Alpha Captain. On clear nights."

Apparently Yuen believed in the Master of the World, even if he did not believe in the Judge of Ages. Surprising.

Daae's reply was more of a surprise: "It is a natural phenomenon, one which our eyes tend to interpret as looking meaningful. There is said to be a human face on Mars. Did a ghost named Del Azarchel paint it there? And then adorn the rings of Saturn with colors gay and bright?"

"Sir! Do you think the Knight is perhaps the Judge incognito?" Menelaus asked Daae. "Then we should break him out of where the Blue Men hold him."

Daae said, "The Judge of Ages is a Next, one of those superior beings of whom stories tell. He does not need the aid of lesser beings."

Menelaus said, "Every huntsman needs his loyal dogs, and every knight his horse. Sir. I suspect we will all have a part to play, if the Judge of Ages shows himself. Are we willing to do what might be required of us?"

Daae turned his face away and murmured. He spoke so softly that Menelaus had to increase the rate of nerve firings in his auditory nerve to make out the words, "Even unto death. Our race was found wanting."

Yuen's voice was shockingly loud by contrast. "Beta Anubis! You sound as if you expect this Judge of Ages to pop out of hiding! Where is he? Maybe rolled up inside some marsupial pouch hidden in the fat Witch-man's belly. There is room to spare. Let us attend to matters more dire. Arroglint is defiled!"

Menelaus bowed and said, "Is the Alpha Steadholder Yuen willing to forgo his rightful and due yet vain retaliation against the weapon-defiler Ull for a short space of time, in return for my promise that a more permanent and satisfying revenge awaits if you delay but a little?"

Yuen shivered, his eyes burning pinpoints. "A wise man once said, 'They who can give up an essential retaliation to obtain a little delayed revenge, deserve neither retaliation nor revenge.'"

Menelaus said, "Aha! But didn't an even wiser man once say, 'War is hell, so stick to the goddam plan, or else we shall all surely hang separately'?"

Yuen's eyes returned to a more normal level of ferocity when he blinked and looked at Menelaus in confusion. "That does not sound like a Chimerical saying. Is that in the Field Manual of Approved and Zealous Thought?"

"Hm. Must've been added later."

Daae said, "Who leads their party? He looks like a poorly bred Gamma of our era."

"He's unmodified. His stock name is Quire, civilian; his agnomen, Larz. I counted him in the tally."

Yuen's face, without moving a muscle, grew ferocious. "A Kine! Is that one of *our* Kine leading their party? He earns a slow death, perhaps by flaying, for this insubordination."

Menelaus nodded. "If things were as they appeared, of course, Alpha-Steadholder, you would be correct. But I urge patience!"

Daae regarded Menelaus with narrowed eyes. "Rumor has already reached us that the Kine says he can pry open the Tombs and deliver the Judge of Ages to the hands of the Blue Men. Do you imply that the Kine acts at your direction, Beta Lancer? Is he a double agent?"

"No and yes, Alpha Captain. I gave no orders and don't know his plans, but he is clearly attempting to deceive them, and so, technically speaking, that would make him a double agent. Who does he work for? He has been kept in the hospital beyond the wire until now. I don't know who he has talked to."

Yuen said, "We should still flay him as an example to other Kine, who will otherwise revolt."

Menelaus said dryly, "That precaution, though wise, is somewhat tardy. The Kine rose up in revolt and overthrew the Command in A.D. 5900. Except for the other three here in the camp, our Kine are as extinct as Chimerae."

Daae silenced them with a slight, almost invisible motion of his head. "The conversation is supervacaneous." He used a Chimerical word meaning "serving no military purpose." "I see the Blues and their dogs and their machines approaching the dig. What do the Loyal and Proven of the Command have to say about the feasibility of attack?"

Daae looked at Yuen. Yuen said, "As soon as they reach the level that contains the ratiotech brain operating the Tomb defenses and coffin traffic, they can have the coffins guard us and send the dogs to go play. The arsenals just of buried Chimerae would strengthen them immensely: they could turn a wing of the Tombs into a prison far more secure that this lazy jury-rig of wire and tower. We must stop them. Kine Larz is the only one we need to kill. One of our Beta Maidens could pierce him with an arrow."

Daae looked at Menelaus, who said, "Premature! Our chance of victory is slender. I strongly recommend a target in the opposite direction: now is the time to rush the wire. All the cannon-bearing automata are headed for the dig; a skeleton crew of dog things remains behind."

Daae said, "To what end? What is our tactical goal, Beta Anubis?"

Menelaus said, "Sir! To rescue the Giant and the Knight, the posthuman and the servant of the Judge of Ages, and perhaps the Scholar as well, and use their expertise to seize control of the stores, supplies, weapons, and powerhouse of the Blues beyond the wire, then to close and hold the gate against them, and commandeer the aircraft. With air superiority, we can crush them."

Yuen said, "Not if they force the door and retreat into the Tombs. I will point out that Anubis suggested the opposite strategy not long ago, and boasted that the Tombs have supplies to withstand a siege forever."

Menelaus said, "They cannot force the door."

The cold and stony eyes of Daae narrowed microscopically. He seemed intent. "You speak as if certain."

"I am."

"Justify this."

Menelaus pointed. "Our Kine there, one of our cattle from our period of history, has buffaloed the Blues into thinking he can use Alpha Yuen's weapon's onboard brain to jinx the security on the automatics guarding the fourth door. It is some sort of computer-fraud technique from the last period of Chimera dominion, right before the Nymphs took over, called snake-charming."

Daae said, "Since Larz Quire comes from our future, why are you so certain of his lack of capability?"

"Because that is not Larz Quire."

"Explain."

"There is no such person."

"And yet my eyes say otherwise, Beta Anubis, for there he is."

"Larz of the Gutter is a fictional character from a story called 'Streetlaw Larz on the Isle of Fear' written one hundred years before that man, whoever he is, was born."

9. Hireling Bretchlouder on the Island of Foehr

Daae and Yuen narrowed their eyes abruptly while visibly raising their brows, a change of expression that was the Chimera equivalent to leaping about with mouths agape while whooping in surprise and astonishment.

Menelaus explained. "During the decline of the World Empire, when law and discipline broke down, Kine and Gammas often hired private facilitators to investigate crime and retaliate against wrongdoers. A romantic myth surrounded these law-of-the-street hirelings, but they did exist. One was named Larslin Bretchlouder.

"This Bretchlouder led a squad of mercenaries to assault the heavily fortified spaceport on Foehr Island, which is a real island in the North Sea, off the coast of Denmark. The last of the Imperator-Generals of the Germanic Ursine lineage moved his headquarters from the Imperial Capital at Richmond to Fortress Ravin on Foehr Island, because it was the only spaceport that had survived the succession war, and because the main crisis of his reign was the failure of the Cities in Space.

"The tale gets stranger. One of the Governor's general staff was a civilian thawed from a long-vanished prior aeon, a crewman of the NTL *Hermetic.* As the only known survivor of a long-term space expedition from Second Age of Space, the choice was a logical one to serve as scientific adviser. That crewman's name was D'Aragó.

"However, D'Aragó experimented with artificial intelligence, with Xypotechnology, and with the computer emulation of human brains, the abomination of Savantry, which has always been strictly forbidden under Chimera law not just in your own, but in all periods of Chimera history.

"Bretchlouder and his squad entered the island fortress unopposed, found and assassinated D'Aragó. The man who actually shot him was a member of the team purporting to be the Judge of Ages, someone come from the far past to kill an old foe for reasons both ancient and of no interest to the generation then current. Some of the images and sound files from his aiming camera survived, but no images of him.

"The fortress came under fire, or was destroyed by sabotage that same night, and so we will never know what really happened. Sober scholars from later time periods deduce that Bretchlouder was hired by the Imperator-General or someone in His Imperial Excellency's innermost circle of favorites to do away with D'Aragó. Nothing explains how Bretchlouder's assassination squad entered the most heavily guarded fortress on the planet without opposition, unless the gates had been opened for them from the inside.

"However, since both the Imperator-General and most of his general staff perished when the last spaceport on Earth burned, the evidence perished with them."

Yuen said, "How can you know all this?"

Menelaus said, "I was ordered to study the decline of civilization. The end of the Ursine lineage, and the destruction of the last spaceport, figured prominently in the end of the Third Space Age. Without orbital support, the Command could not repress simultaneous rebellions, sea piracy, and work-revolts on a worldwide scale. I woke in a period where there were still some libraries and archives intact. The radioactive scald of Foehr Island was much studied and, as I mentioned, made into a popular fiction starring an invented hero. These were inexpensively produced texts called cheaplies printed without formatting onto pulp or scrap."

Daae nodded. "They had them in my day. Cleaning the cheaplies out of the barracks and schools was a recurring problem. They were pornographic tales, where some low-caste but honest hero is saving a highbred Alpha lady from Witches or AWOLs or Pirates, or from the Servants of the Machine, and ends up coupling with her. And somehow he always is vindicated by the Eugenics Board, or he exposes corruption among them, and his particular combination of wild genes rewards him unexpectedly with a son even taller and stronger than he is. Such horrible, absurd stories!"

Yuen glanced at him sharply. "How do you know their content?"

Daae shrugged sadly. "I read them when I was living in the private barracks too. When you are young, a few hours' punishment drill in full kit is not too high a price to pay for a dream."

Menelaus said, "Well, these stories were written by a half-breed Beta-Gamma crossover named Gibson. When an author of a cheaplie could paste in previous text without rewrite, he did. Since, as I said, the aiming camera survived, most of the dialogue was taken word for word from Hermetic D'Aragó's last words; but the surrounding events were all fiction cobbled together from other sources. And the ending of the story, 'So *I* lived happily ever after,' was the way Larz of the Gutter ended all his fictional exploits."

Yuen said, "But Larz described what the Judge of Ages looked like!"

Menelaus said, "He described the face of the actor who portrayed the Judge of Ages in the wirecast version of the story, when it was later made into a play."

Yuen said, "And how would you know that?"

Menelaus looked sheepish. "The Judge of Ages has often appeared in paintings and statues and animations. The Witches made a lot of pictures of him. You'd be surprised at how little one resembles the next, almost as if someone were trying to divaricate the visual information across history. At one time, I set about compiling a large collection of such images. It was for a monograph I never wrote concerning data degradation."

Yuen said, "Of a fictional character? Such a monograph would seem to serve no military purpose."

Menelaus looked mildly offended. "As you say, sir."

Yuen said, "But why change the name from Bretchlouder to Quire?"

Menelaus said, "The decadence that causes and is caused by the death throes of a culture always aggravates sexual perversion. Being a 'breech-loader' in the days when the book was written had an indelicate second meaning, and Gibson, the author, no doubt thought it best to name his character Quire, the old word for 'veteran-citizen,' rather than a name that might raise a snicker."

Daae said, "Beta Anubis, why do you assume that the man who killed the Hermeticist D'Aragó was not indeed the Judge of Ages?"

Menelaus shrugged. "Because I do not believe in the Judge of Ages. Permission to speak freely?"

"Granted," said Daae.

"This Judge of Ages, if he is a real man, must have the flaws and shortcomings of a real man. He has no more power than I do to win the battle we face. We can look to no help for him, even if he were real. Right now the gate is weakly held, but not for long. As soon as the Blue Men realize Kine Larz—or whatever his real name is—is a fake, they will fall back from the doors. But even my suggestion, sir, requires the aid of the Witches."

Yuen said, "Witches, bah! They are despicable cowards! The day when I kiss a Witch will come sooner than the day Witches and Chimerae could ever fight shoulder to shoulder against a foe!"

Daae (to whom the Witches were a legendary menace rather than recent or potent one) spoke in a voice of dry irony. "Gargle with wine to sweeten your breath, then, Proven Alpha Yuen. For here come the Witches in all their numbers." And he raised his finger and pointed.

The rotund bulk of Melechemoshemyazanagual the Warlock of Williamsburg was gliding up the wintry slope toward them, adorned with an acre of black and scarlet silk, and the sephiroth, sigils, and trigrams glistered with many colors. His face was half-hidden beneath his headgear, a cone a foot and a half high. Despite his bulk, the obese man made no noise at all as he approached, and he seemed, somehow, to leave no footprints behind him.

With him were thirty others: the whole population of Witches in the camp.

10. Joint Command

Even at a distance, the difference between the nobles and the commoners of the Witch Era was clear: The Coven leaders were women unusually tall, and they walked with the stiffness and care of great age. The same genetic tinkering and geriatric treatments a Witch enjoyed from before her birth until after she was an octogenarian stimulated growth patterns in totipotent cells throughout her long life, whereas the commoners used up their entire supply of totipotent cells before birth, and the timing mechanisms in the human body allowed for no more growth, no more youth, after adolescence. The growing patterns that kept them young kept them growing throughout life.

The crowd of Witches stopped at the foot of the slope, and only seven figures came forward: Mickey and six others. The women elders carried charming wands cut from willow trees from which dangled skulls of rodents and small birds.

Four of the figures were ancient women seven or eight feet tall, with features as dignified and withered as old statues, and hair as white as snow, wearing hoods even taller. These crones loomed over Mickey. They wore sable and dark blue regalia, worked with images of crabs and carrion birds, and their peaked hoods hid all but their wrinkled stern mouths.

The fifth woman, the one in white, was a maiden who looked to be in her late teens, but she carried herself with the poise and dignity of a mother: a forty-year-old soul in a fourteen-year-old body. She was five feet high or less, dressed a simple dress of white cotton trimmed with peach satin, and she wore her hair in a snood.

The final witch, as tall as her sisters, was garbed in scarlet, pink, and dark red, buxom as a Nymph, though stouter, and her peaked hat was wide-brimmed.

The Witches of lower ranks were no less splendidly dressed. A hunter wore a wolfpelt at his shoulders and a uniform of Lincoln's green, a husbandman wore designs of grain stalks and hayricks, a vintner wore grapeleaf patterns adorning purple, the mason's garb was bedecked with the triangle and square of his order over a pattern of red bricks. From the time of the Nameless Empire were factory hands whose uniforms were woven with a pattern of cogwheels and smoke clouds; from the same era, an apothecary wore robes adorned with serpents and birds, and an alchemist's dress was a pattern of spiral molecular chains woven about with formulae in ancient letters.

There were a dozen members of the feared Demonstrator caste here too, wearing cloaks of flayed and cured human skin-leather, feces wiped in the hair, and their faces painted horribly with black ink, and about their necks clattered the tiny fingerbones of dismembered children: several sported a bone or needle piercing the septum of his nose, or the flesh of cheek, earlobe, or lip.

The crones, as they came upslope, by way of greeting, uttered yips and yowls, owl screech and wolf howl somehow both ridiculous and horrific to hear.

Mickey stepped forward, pointed his wand at Menelaus, and beckoned, "Beta Sterling Xenius Anubis of Mount Erebus, I charge and summon thee to approach."

Menelaus turned his eyes toward Daae. "Sir—"

Daae said, "Speak for us. Yuen, go with him, and repudiate any word of his not in keeping with the honor of the Alpha gene-Caste."

The two men trudged forward in the snow, and Menelaus drew his hood close to his cheeks, either from the cold, or hoping to hide his expression. Menelaus would have been free to talk to Mickey and arrange terms, had Yuen stayed back out of earshot.

Mickey turned and turned again, and drew a large circle on the snowy ground with his staff. "Here is my circle of Power! Within it, all who walk tread lightly on their Mother Earth, leaving no trace when they die; and all goods are held in common; and all class-enemies, all enmities, inequalities, and patriarchy must be left outside, and cannot pass my ninefold wards! I call upon Jadis and Jahi, Phoebe and Prudence, Sabrina and Samantha, Willow and Wendy, to watch the sacred bounds!"

Menelaus went up to him, stepping into the circle, and said softly, "Uh. You do know all those people watching your sacred bounds are, um, made up from kiddie pixies and texts and toons, right? Make-believe?"

Mickey drew himself upright, which thrust his belly out even farther, and the scowl on his face was like a line drawn in a pie pan filled with raw dough. "Many records survived from the Days of Fire—the Final Archive listed nine hundred thousand references to the beloved Witch Hermione alone, not to mention Gillian Holroyd and Glinda the Good! Would you have us believe that the ancients devoted so much emphasis, effort, and attention to what they knew to be merely idle fictions?! Next you will claim that the warlocks Klingsor and Castaneda are unreal!"

One of the She-Witches, a towering and hatchet-faced crone as thin as a rail, tramped forward on long angular steps to reach the side of Mickey, and stood like a black minaret next to a dark dome.

"The spell is incomplete!" she said. And with her charming wand she drew a cross in the snow. "Depart the circle, trample this cross, and reenter."

Menelaus said, "But, begging your pardon, ma'am, we Chimerae don't believe in things like that."

She pushed back her hood and bent her thin, gray face down toward Menelaus. She had shaved her scalp in an Irish tonsure, shorn over the head from ear to ear, leaving a patch of white dangling from her brow and a hem hanging from the back of her skull. "The gesture is significant! It shows our freedom from superstition!"

Yuen sidled close, his footsteps like those of a panther. He spoke in clear and unaccented Virginian (which, in his time, was still a living language), "It is known among our Kine that this cross is a symbol of an unarmed and dead man. Chimerae slur only armed and living men, able to retaliate."

The crone favored him with a reptilian stare. "I am not armed, and I live, and yet it insults me if you do not step on the cross and blot it out, to enter the circle."

Yuen's face was colder and his one eye more unwinking with fury than normal even for him as he stamped the mark in the snow angrily with his foot, but he did not step within the circle. "Our age was the first in all history to be free of trumpery and priestcraft and all the deception of hope in afterlife. I will not betray that heritage. Gladly I trample the long-dead superstition you hate, but likewise I scorn the long-dead superstition you serve."

She opened her mouth to object, showing her oddly narrow yellow teeth, but Mickey said in his jovial voice, "Come, Grandmother, we are proposing alliance, not a friendship. Copulation partners need not like each other: the man gives seed and the woman outlives him. Is this not the way of life? These are those who outlived our race. You do not know them, but they come from my days, when they outnumbered us, and their strength was terrifying, but so also was their honor. No spell will hold them in any case. If the Earth is sacred, is not all ground sacred? It is not our way to avoid confrontation, and outwait, and outlive?"

This seemed to mollify her.

Menelaus said diplomatically in Virginian, "We are, of course, curious about the opinions and concerns of all gathered here, but time harasses us all: can we not address our plea for alliance to the commanding officer of the Witches?"

Yuen said, "They are from different times and continents, and live in anarchy, having nothing in common but their superstitions."

Menelaus said in Chimerical, "They are influenced by the shadow each one casts. The one with the greatest shadow will draw the others. That one there—" He nodded at the youngest witch present, the one dressed in white. "Ask to be introduced to her."

Yuen said to Mickey, "You! Introduce us to the maiden."

There was a reaction from the gathered Witches, a glint in the eyes, a sharp intake of breath.

Mickey said ceremoniously to Yuen and Menelaus: "Your leader can see partway beyond the veil, to know she whom we hold highest, though she walks with humblest garb among us." Mickey now bowed very low. "She is the youngest but also the eldest of us. We call her Fatin. We are not certain of her coven, cell, or sept or assignment. She is eldest and speaks last. What she says, none dares unsay."

Fatin stepped forward. "Call me Fatin Simon Fay. I am of the Delphic Acroamatic Progressive Transhumanitarian Order for the study of Longevity. The Order also experiments in altered states of consciousness, including the stimulation of lateral-format pattern-seeking modes that do not develop naturally in women until after one hundred and twenty or one hundred and forty years, and which were, in times past, mistaken for senility, or dismissed as women's intuition. The human race would not even be aware of these ulterior forms had the limitations of the man-imposed so-called normal life span been accepted! The Giants, for all their vast intelligence, can neither plan as far ahead as we, nor can they see the patterns of events we see. They regard what we do as witchcraft, but that merely betrays the inflexibility of their thinking."

Yuen said, "You are an unwed girl?"

Fatin, who was probably (despite her looks) considerably older than Yuen, narrowed her eyes at him. "I am pre–sexually active, yes. We have dispensed with marriage customs. We regard the word 'girl' as a deadly insult. You must say 'living organism each with his or her or its place in the ecologic web not superior to any other.' "

"You are an unwed organism no better than a bug?" Yuen said, "And yet you command the Witches?"

Fatin said stiffly, "We don't have ranks like that. The elder advise the younger. But since I come from the age when the Simon Families were still intact, that makes me eldest, so my advice carries more weight than anyone else's. I am the one who decided we had to throw in with you."

Yuen said, "Why?"

Fatin said, "Two reasons. The first is because Melechemoshemyazanagual had a bad dream."

Mickey said solemnly, "I have flown in a vision in the shadow of the hawk, and I have seen that the lands to every side of us are empty of life. And yet there is a power in the sea that will surpass us all. I saw the moon drip blood, and from the south came one the shapen like unto a tower with neither top nor foundation; but I also saw a figure adorned as a judge before an execution, riding a pale horse, and a pale wand deadlier than any sword was in his hands, and voices cried out from below the earth, prophesying doom."

Yuen said scornfully, "So! You managed to get one of the medical coffins to produce hallucinogenic mushrooms? Did the Nymphs help you?"

Fatin said with girlish sternness, "These are subconscious images betraying a pattern of data our conscious minds cannot yet grasp. Melechemoshemyazanagual comes from a generation that learned what neural modifications to make in a man to give him the lateral-thinking and pattern-recognition skills my generation first discovered in transoctogenarian females. The images are symbolic and primal. He tells us something you have not realized. The Judge of Ages walks among us. He is someone here in the camp."

Daae had come up on cat-silent feet behind Menelaus, and now startled him by making a small noise of satisfaction. "Some here realized it."

Menelaus said, "Miss, what is your second reason? You said there were two. You have one other reason for agreeing to help us?"

Mickey bowed his head and said, "If I may answer that, Maiden Fatin?" She nodded. When Mickey raised his head, his eyes glittered. "You Chimerae are so proud of your freedom and ferocity that you forget who came before you, and you forget from whom you learned it! I am from Williamsburg, and the roots of that town are ancient indeed!"

Daae said, "So? What does that mean?"

Mickey lifted his double chins proudly, and the sunlight, peeping through the snowy clouds, glanced off the rim of his fantastic hat so that it gleamed like a crown. "It means we Witches love our freedom no less than you Chimerae, and are no less willing to die fighting for it."

11. On One Condition

Menelaus looked at Yuen and spoke in Chimerical. "Loyal and Proven Alpha? What do you think?"

Yuen nodded reluctantly. In Chimerical he said to Menelaus, "That was well said. Even among the lesser breeds, I see that the greatness which in us is perfect exists in them in an inchoate, crude, and unformed foreshadow." In Virginian, he said, "The General Command of the Commonwealth agrees to accept your alliance—"

Fatin raised her wand. "Not yet! We offer it only on one condition. If we defeat the Blue Men, the Tombs will be in our hands, yes?"

Menelaus said in a tone of exasperation. "Oh, come now! Are we going to start talking about who gets how much loot from the treasures buried here? All that stuff belongs to the people in the coffins! People like us!"

Fatin gave him a cold stare. "It is not the treasure of the ages I demand, albeit I would be right to demand it. It is the Judge."

Mickey looked surprised and turned to Menelaus with a helpless shrug. This was something he had not anticipated.

Yuen scoffed. "You think he is real?"

Fatin said, "I think he is the worst criminal of all human history, and the enemy of man. That is our demand. If we help you fight the Blue Men, and if victory comes, and the Tombs are ours, my demand is that we find and unearth and unmask the Judge of Ages, and burn him very slowly on the sacred fire for his deeds. Since you, with your mind that is darkened and blind, call him a fiction, you have no reason to refuse."

Yuen said, "Very well. We agree."

Menelaus looked uncomfortable, but said nothing. He glanced over his shoulder at Daae.

"The posthuman is beyond retaliation," said Daae thoughtfully. "The Chimerae agree."

Yuen said jovially, "Then we are of one mind! We overcome the Blue Men, who have victimized us all, then we find and destroy the Judge of Ages, whom we all despise. Whether he is real or not."

12. Promotion

Daae said. "Then it is decided. We must send messengers to the Hormagaunts and the Nymphs to gather their folk as well. And Beta Sterling Xenius Anubis—"

"Sir?"

"I hereby issue you a field promotion from Lance-Corporal to Corporal."

And now Daae smiled, which he had never done before, and gripped Menelaus by the shoulder.

"Beta-Corporal!" The voice of Daae rang out, "I fear I can offer you no increase in pay, since the only wages that issue from my hand, in this cold, strange world of this lost and far-hither year, shall be wounds and toil and cries of pain, and then victory for the living, and the honor for the dead of being buried as free men, by the hands of free comrades: but liberty both for living and dead."

Even Yuen was grinning.

Menelaus was both surprised and moved. "Sir! I expect no better wage."

Mickey the Witch threw his hat in the air and clapped his big hands, hooting and whistling his congratulations and calling down blessing from his many gods.

Daae said, "We shall establish the ambush in the pass yonder. You will command a unit on the far side of the pass, and I on this side, so we take their column from either direction. Once the Blue Men realize that Larz Quire cannot open the fourth door, and return and climb the switchback, we shall fall upon them—"

Menelaus was shocked. "Sir! With all due respect, my plan to assault the wire and win the hospital, free the prisoners there, and secure the airfield allows us to face less formidable odds!"

Daae said, "It is far more important that we get underground as soon as possible. You see, we found something dreadful. The gray twins discovered it—"

At that moment there was a sharp whistle from the trees not far away. A Beta-ranked maiden of the Chimera race, a girl named Vulpina, stepped from the trees and waved a warning. Before any other word was said, the Chimerae on the hilltop scattered. The Witches were slower, but they began moving rapidly down the slope of the bowl-shaped hill, trying to keep the crest between themselves and Illiance, who was approaching at a rapid trot with a squad of dog things.

Menelaus had to decide between running after Daae, to hear the rest of his comment, or running after Mickey. He chose Mickey.

But the huge man waved him off. "You stay while we flee. The Blues still trust you. But they must not see men of the different eras gathering!"

Menelaus said, "It is only one squad. Let's stand and fight. You cannot get away. You're too fat."

Mickey uttered a belly laugh. "You forget I studied the Lore to the Twelfth Degree. I gained this weight to attract the gluttony of the anthropophages of the stepped pyramids of Appalachia, so that other members of my coven, the thinner ones, would be overlooked. When the dogs and manhunters of my day came to the village on the dark moon nights and feast days, I was the one the packs followed into the swamps and bogs, and I was the one who emerged at dawn, with the severed tails of the hunting hounds tied into my hair as trophies, and the severed hands of the huntsmen. Besides, the Witches were a dying race when I was born, and with the Chimerae driving us out of the lowlands and into the hills, the old strictures against biomodification carried less weight. Or in my case, carried more. Watch this."

And he sped away like a jackrabbit, leaving impossibly light footprints in the snow, his conical hat, dangling by its chin strap, flopping energetically down his back, his black robes and scarlet chasuble flapping like wings. He used his charming wand as a pole-vaulter's pole and threw himself across a line of holly brush, and for a moment look like a black, silken, and highly ornamented blimp.

Menelaus was still standing and staring when Illiance stepped silently up next to him. "Lance-Corporal Beta Sterling Anubis, if you should happen to accompany me, there is a relict who bears questioning on a matter of some import. It would be advantageous to come as quickly as possible. Several vectors of events are reaching a convergence."

The dog things pelted past, noses to the ground, snuffing for scent. Menelaus saw a trio of them congregate near the line of holly, but then circle in confusion and frustration. One of them sat on his haunches, waved his cutlass angrily in the air, put back his muzzle, and howled.

12
The Testament of Ctesibius the Savant

1. The Rook

Menelaus walked alongside Illiance, looking like a tall adult in a robe and hood of metallic cloth next to a bald child in a richly ornamented coat, and he realized what an odd sight they would have seemed to any man from any earlier era.

Menelaus noted that only one of the two hemicylindrical gun emplacements at the wire was being manned by dogs at the moment. An eerie silence hung over the little village of seashells, and no figures could be glimpsed moving among them.

He followed Illiance into the large blue nautilus shell, and up the smaller curving ramp into a space that was even narrower than the chambers he had seen before, very near the topmost part of the spiral tower. They were alone, unaccompanied by any dog things.

Menelaus spoke: "Who are we interviewing now? And why is it so important that you and I are doing it alone, while the others are off preparing for the fabulous Larz and his fabulous assault on the Tomb doors?"

"Two relicts remain, both from the very earliest stratum of history, perhaps from the days before the Ecpyrosis. Their answers will either increase or diminish the confidence extended to the testament of Kine Larz of the Gutter. I have my reservations about placing too much trust in Kine Larz."

"No kidding," said Menelaus sardonically.

Illiance said, "But it cannot have escaped your attention that all the revenants here gathered in this site have some connection with the figure of the Judge of Ages, and that none of the relicts thawed so far are Tomb Guardians. Why the Tomb Guardians, whoever they are, decided to group all slumberers with this connection in one spot is unknown. Yet this lends indirect support to what Larz says."

"How so?"

"If those who slumber here were gathered because each has a connection with the Judge of Ages, the pattern is not contradicted that one of them, Kine Larz, would be able to describe his look and costume."

"Yup. You just look for a guy in a long red robe and a longer white wig, and I am sure that will be Hizzoner his own self. Why did Ull tell you y'all were looking for him? What is his bogus cover story, again, exactly?"

"Your question cannot at this time preoccupy us." Illiance said apologetically, "For us, but two questions more urgently claim our attention. First, we do not understand the meaning of the Judgments of the Judge of Ages. Why does he destroy some periods of history while leaving others intact? Second, we do not understand the meaning of this so-called chess game of evolution that seems to be going on between the Judge of Ages and the Hermeticists. It is a violent game, in which anything from the murder of specific individuals up to the destruction of whole civilizations—or even races—are merely moves in it. The Tombs are part of it."

"You think this Tomb is a chessman in that game, like a castle? What about the theory that this Judge of Ages built the Tombs merely to have a place to lay his head? He sleeps in the cold ground while he waits for the human race to get advanced enough to build another starship, so he can go seek his wife. That is what the legend says."

Illiance nodded thoughtfully. "The legends could have been started or encouraged by a deliberate manipulation of the statistical tendencies of history. And, also, it is possible that the Tombs were built for more purposes than one. A posthuman mind might foresee more goals than humans know. The idea that the entire worldwide system of Tombs was designed and built and maintained over millennia and aeons merely as part of a very long-term strategy enacted by the Judge of Ages against the Master of the World is strangely compelling."

"Sure, the strategy of a man who wants to be left alone."

"It is odd indeed that this site alone had armor breached so severely yet so neatly."

"Are you implying that you *found* this site like this? Here I thought you folks ripped the roof off."

Illiance spread his hands. "Do you see in our camp here the heavy machinery of the type needed to cut a hilltop peak in half or pull up a layer of carbon nanotube-fiber reinforced titanium alloy roof armor three yards thick? This was a man-made attack: our investigation of the trace energies left behind indicate a lased magnetic monopole beam reached down from Mare Cognitum's Riphaeus Mountains on the Moon and introduced a potent upward vector to rip the armor upward. The assault at that range, two hundred thirty-eight thousand miles, would be beyond any conceivable retaliation of the Tomb defenses. The beam crossed one and one half light-seconds of distance, and would have been diffracted sharply when it entered the atmosphere: the calculation processing power needed for so delicate an operation over such a distance indicates superhuman intelligence. But you look skeptical."

"No, that is just the natural cast of my features. It seems a really . . . odd . . . way to break in. So who cracked open the Tombs?"

"The superhuman intelligence to which I refer," said Illiance, "is that of the Hermeticists. Kine Larz claims to have seen one: this suggests they are not mythical beings or, to be precise, that such myths as we know may have accumulated over millennia around a kernel of literal fact."

Menelaus stared down at the little Blue Man. He reached out his hand as if he were about to take the other by the shoulder, but he did not actually touch the other man. "Illiance! If what you just said is the case, then the Hermeticists are the ones who broke open the Tomb armor, yet did not appear here to exploit the opening. Doesn't that make what you and your blue buddies are doing here a little suspicious? Do you know who you are working for? Who arranged you to come here? Don't give me guesswork. Do you *know*?"

Illiance showed no change to his tranquil expression, but his footsteps slowed, and he stopped walking.

Menelaus said, "Illiance, if what you just said is so, not only are you in grave danger, but you have also placed your dog things and everyone you dug up in danger. There are two posthuman enemies running around the blind corridors of history like titans, not caring what cities and empires and aeons they step on, one of them buried under the Earth's mantle, and the other one hidden on the dark side of the moon, and they mean to destroy each other. If this Tomb site is part of that war, you are meddling in that war. You are stepping between two duelists about to shoot. Which side are you going to be on?"

"Such a decision would not be convoluted: Simple Men act primarily, as do all living organisms, toward our own self-preservation and toward the promulgation of the ideals and thought-structures of our mental environment. But this must be determined when convenient."

Illiance gestured to an oval opening in the seashell substance ahead. "The first of the two relicts occupies the uppermost chamber, which we shall see first, and then we will return here."

Menelaus glanced inside the oval opening as they passed. He saw a bald blue figure seated facing away from the opening on a spread of gem-dotted blue fabric, which seemed to be one of the coats unfolded to use as a rug. The figure was bent over several medical appliances and a reading machine, which were connected by a nest of cables to a coffin, angrily lit with little red lights. The sight was disquieting, horrible, though he could not consciously say why. There was no other prisoner in evidence.

Their footsteps carried them past and up the slope.

2. Ghost Death

"The first of the two relicts is from A.D. 2525. He has a very complete, if very crude system of interface and interactive neural systems, much like a Locust, but no receptors. We can download what he thinks, but cannot upload to him queries to impel him to think on the topics of our interest."

The corridor narrowed and the ramp of the floor grew more steep, and led through a sharp twist up to a small and final chamber very near the tip of the spiral tower.

Light here came from an oval opening high on the wall. Gray clouds and drifting snow were visible. It was cold. There was bioluminous fungi streaking the walls, but it was thin and patchy near the window, as if the fungi fared poorly in the cold. Heat came from an unadorned ivory bowl of black liquid resting on the floor. The inky liquid was motionless, not bubbling, but it nonetheless radiated a scalding warmth that robbed the air of moisture and scent.

Seated on a mat on the floor was Ctesibius the Savant, and the aura of his dignity seemed to fill the air even as the odorless heat of the black bowl. The bowl of hot black liquid was to one side of him, and a bowl of artificial peaches (Menelaus recognized them as grown from the half-dismantled coffins in the mess tent) was perched on a handful of snow in a matching bowl to the other side of him.

His clothing had been returned to him. The grotesque piercings of his skull were covered by a film of antiseptic cloth, covered in turn with a long white wig of curls that looked ridiculously like ones those courtiers in English courts in olden times were wont to wear, and, later, only justices in courts of law. He wore silk vestments of a striking green, the color the symbolized eternal life, trimmed with gold, to symbolize machine life. On his upper right breast and lower left skirt was the same emblem tattooed on his brow, the sign of three diamonds, to indicate his three donations, his three souls, which he had deposited by apotheosis into the infosphere.

Menelaus looked left and right. He said in Iatric, "No dogs? No bars on the window?"

Illiance said, "The relict seems to have little motive to attempt flight. We have attempted to speak through the talking boxes, to establish the offer of allowing him to download a version of his mind and memories into our local infosphere—we have more than enough capacity. It was our belief that this was the purpose of this profession and order of being, called the Savants. We thought by this to bind his self-interest to our own: but he remains aloof. I have told you the one question we seek—if he knows the Judge of Ages, and the meaning of his Judgments against the various ages he destroyed."

Menelaus stepped forward and offered the seated Ctesibius the stiff-armed salute of a Chimera. Ctesibius the Savant nodded regally and said in early-period Anglatino, "The Hospitalier. Space Captain Sterling, named after a jackal who guards Tombs and a god who slays those who violate the guest laws. Are you here to observe my shame? I release you from your oath to guard my coffin and protect my life: if you have a knife or pistol, hand it me, that I might depart this life honorably."

Menelaus was surprised at this speech. "What have they done?"

"Mind-rape. You do not know the term? To donate one's memories is to glorify the soul and make it electronically immortal. It is an exact copy of one's most inner self, every memory clear and dim, every triumph, every sin. These cretinous little blue-skinned Interactors forced a donation from me, and now a copy of my soul is lost somewhere without me in their infosphere. They are examining it while we speak, hoping to elicit from him the information by trick they cannot elicit by force."

Menelaus said, "If I get them to shut down the emulation copy of you, would that make you happier?"

"To have him murdered? Then I must add another diamond to my heraldry, a black one, to show a failed donation. You think the shame is not greater? Do they now seek to please me?"

"Sure."

"Do not say 'sure.' Address me as Donator Ctesibius."

"Of course, Donator Ctesibius."

"This alone would please me: that that time-honored penalty for mind-rape be accomplished upon all who performed, or failed to hinder, the deed: Our custom is to inject the perpetrator with fluids that separately stimulate the pain response from every nerve in the body, while dissolving the cortex one cell at a time. It is timed to lobotomize the perpetrator so he loses one degree of intelligence once a day for a hundred days or so, eventually becomes subhuman, but kept alive, screaming, in a glass cage in the public forum as a sign to passersby. To see this execution performed, and then to take my life in solemn suicide, this would please me."

Menelaus said, "I don't think I can arrange that. What about staying alive long enough just to see them shot?"

Ctesibius said, "When would the opportunity arise? But tell me nothing! They have an active copy of my soul in their hands."

"The Judge of Ages is supposed to have xypotechnology of some sort in his lower Tombs: maybe he could find memory space for your copy. He does not much cotton to Xypotech emulations, but since the crime was done on his watch, in his yard, he will have to make an exception."

Ctesibius said, "You speak as if you are not his servant."

Menelaus turned to Illiance and said in Iatric, "Do you have a copy of Ctesibius the Savant that you downloaded from his nervous system?"

Illiance looked mournful. "Not as such. The copy was made with certain interleaf errors and memory compression distortions. It is mostly self-aware, but has degenerated into a psychotic strange-loop condition. It seems to be in considerable anguish. Certain of the nuances of the art of Savantry were evidently lost in the process of time: it is not our area of specialization. Preceptor Yndech did the work."

"Ah. Tell Yndech that the Judge of Ages is going to kill him. You understand you are not supposed to do things like this, right?"

Illiance waved the question aside. "Events will unfold in our favor. Have you yet inquired of him? The emulation copy does not show clear reaction to bring forth the information we seek."

"Hold it. You're keeping the emulation online even as we speak? You are flushing it, even though it is wounded and psycho, with additional data streams coming from the Savant's head?"

Illiance was blithe. "It is of no matter. We have introduced a time-nonbinding interrupt, so the mind does not remember the excruciation at any given moment of the previous moment. No pain is built up to a psychologically damaging level, and we are still able to discern surface thoughts."

"Listen: I can get Ctesibius to talk, but you have to get the hell out of his mind, and stop looking at his thoughts, or his copy's thoughts, whatever you are doing. Got it? He has been fooled into thinking I am a Knight from the mythical Hospitalier Order that the mythical Judge of Ages uses to guard his Tombs. So all I have to do is reassure him. Can you put his copy on standby, or put it to sleep, without killing it? It was not possible in his day and age to switch emulations into a standby mode without killing the information and killing them."

"We have made no advance in this area. We can keep the copy of Ctesibius alive, or kill it, but cannot store it an unself-aware condition."

Menelaus gritted his teeth in frustration. He turned back to Ctesibius. "Donator, I think—if you can cooperate—I can convince the Blue Men to transfer your copy to the Judge of Ages Xypotech system. They are trying to break into his Tombs, and may actually succeed. They made some sort of error while making the copy, so this version is insane and brain-damaged. However, I am pretty sure the Judge of Ages can fix your insane Xypotech emulation, on account of he is the world's expert at this. He fixed Ximen del Azarchel's emulation, and made him posthuman, and, in effect, created the Machine you serve."

Ctesibius looked at him oddly. "What is the point of your concern? When a genetically defective child is born, civilized people perform euthanasia immediately, and inflict a legal penalty on the mother for absorbing scarce medical resources. If the defect is discovered before birth, the child is killed by aborticide. Any attempt to preserve the weak and unfit is against Darwin. Do you think I would not apply this measure to myself? Do they wish my cooperation? Have them bring me to the gray room where my soul is housed, and let me set the charges with my own hands. Autoeuthanasia is not just a privilege of the high minded; it is sacred duty."

Illiance said, "You need not translate the comment: it was clear from the emulation reaction what was meant. Tell him our system is more compact than in his day." He pointed at the bowl of black liquid. The substance within turned milky, then became transparent. Within, the bowl was packed with a pyramid of gems of the Blue Men; with the fluid moving through the interstices where the gem edges, rounded, did not cohere to one another. Menelaus could see filaments forming and dissolving in the fluid, finer than the veins in a leaf, connecting now one gem with a neighbor, now another, flickering into and out of existence almost too rapidly to be seen.

Ctesibius looked down without interest. He said in Anglatino, "What need be done to destroy the housing?"

Again Illiance needed no translation, but pantomimed the act of overturning the bowl. In Iatric he said, "Tell him that dispersing the fluid will disorganize the connectivity, and the emulation will be interrupted, and perish."

Menelaus did not translate the comment, but Ctesibius did not hesitate. Kicking out with a foot, he sent the bowl flying and rebounding from the far wall, and a fluid turned black again as it trailed in a splatter, like unwinding entrails, across the floor. And the gems were scattered, and some were cracked by the violence done. Over his implants, Menelaus heard a thin and lingering wail of radio noise which trailed into horrid silence.

A cold immediately entered the little seashell-shaped room.

Ctesibius said regally, "I have slain the godlike being who was my soul and my brother, committing suicide and deicide and fratricide all at once. But a Savant does not undo his word, once given. Tell the Interactor I will answer his question."

3. Goal of the Ages

Is that all they want to know? It is appalling that your blue creatures have committed such crimes to discover what is common knowledge to all. I will tell you his origins, and you will know.

The first group the Judge of Ages ever judged was called the Hermeticists. They had established a world hierarchy and, for the first time in history, a single world government, called the Concordat. They were the only friends and compatriots he knew, for he himself was a Hermeticist. But justice then was bought and sold like a commodity, and Menelaus Montrose could not tolerate that.

He turned on his friends, because he imagined they had failed him.

This is about A.D. 2360, and lasted until A.D. 2400, forty years, when Montrose woke up and shattered the world like a dropped wineglass. At his behest, Swan Princess Rania stole the *Hermetic,* absconded with the world supply of antimatter, and started riots and wars to destroy the Machine.

When she left the system, he was the only person who knew in what orbits and exactly where the remaining crumbs of antimatter were. He was the only person who could do the math to correct for accumulated cell errors in long-term hibernation. His was the only voice any machines left in space, loyal to Rania, would listen to.

About twenty years later, during several world wars whose causes no one remembers, Montrose found relatives, everyone descended from his cousins and brothers, and gave them his powers, the passwords to the still-active satellites, the orbits of the contraterrene, the secret of the Tombs, everything.

They became the first and greatest Tomb guardians. The Cryonarchy is the common name for it, though officially they were a Special Advocacy commission of the Concordat, or so the world government still called itself then, even when the Concordat was broken and there were no less than fifteen so-called Concordats, each claiming to be the world government.

The Cryonarchy Clan of Montrose established peace between 2481 and 2509: but their arrogance offended Montrose when he woke for but a single hour, and without examining any evidence or talking to any witnesses, he condemned them.

He turned on his family. He donated all their wealth and power and prestige to the Church.

Oh, there was only one Church worth mentioning on the world at that point in history: Del Azarchel had seen to that. Any groups not willing to be ruled by an ecumenical general council, he just hounded with taxes and laws and restrictions, and propaganda and jailtime and confiscation and torture—but that was not enough to get his way. The Swan Maiden, the posthuman, did something, perhaps using the Cliometry to introduce social variables and erode all opposition . . . whatever it was, she was able to finish what he started, and branches of the Church that had been severed for over a thousand years were forced back into one somewhat uneasy alliance. The Church—but you don't know what I am talking about, do you? Do you even have any records of how things were in my day, or what institutions and ideas ruled the world? Or does it all look rustic and quaint to you?

The Church created a race of Giants to defend her. Montrose slept and the Church became corrupt. With control of the only supply of antimatter in civilization, Popes were propping up princes, advocates, Cryonarchs, parliaments, or throwing them down again, much as Popes had done during the first Dark Ages. Buying and selling crowns just like money-changers in the temple? I guess you don't catch that reference.

But the pattern was clear. As soon as he woke again, Montrose would see that his Church had failed him. Meanwhile, the Giants grew arrogant, as Giants will, and placed themselves above the law. He no doubt would wake and condemn them for having failed him, the creations of his attempt at evolutionary science, his heirs. They would join friends and family and faith in the ever-growing list of what the Judge of Ages judged and found wanting.

But he did not wake, and the corruption lingered.

History forced us, the Savants, to take on Montrose's role. Exarchel, the

Xypotech Machine, was really the only emulation we had of history's first and only successful world ruler. But we set about making more.

Men of science were approached, business leaders, military leaders, artists, philanthropists, newsmongers, lyricists, philosophers, princes of the world, and, yes, even princes of the Church. The finest minds of Earth.

It was not easy. The download process is difficult, and requires skilled and active cooperation at every step by the Donator. And it was done at first in utter secrecy.

Of course we were successful. How would we not have been? With Exarchel directing us, we had the only posthuman mind, intelligence level above 400, awake and moving events on the Earth. The real Del Azarchel—but I am not supposed to call him that—Glorified Del Azarchel of the First Donation, he fled to a hidden base on the Moon. Princess Rania was lost in the mathematical paradoxes of the Lorenz transformation, frozen between one tick of time and the next, somewhere between here and Messier Object Three. First Ancestor Montrose was in slumber.

The Consensus Advocacy? Those freakish Giants—do you know what we called them? John Henries. That's right. 'When John Henry was a little baby! A-sitting on his pappy's knee!' Er—I guess you don't catch that reference, either. Henry did manual labor, driving railroad spikes, at a time when the steam-powered drill had just been devised that could do the same work faster, and cheaper, and tirelessly. He was able, just barely able, by dint of Herculean effort, to drive more spikes than the steam-drill—but the effort killed him. Meanwhile the steam-drill manufacturer came out with a more reliable model next year. I guess you don't know what railroad spike is, do you?

The point of this is that, with Montrose buried, no one was smart enough to detect our plan.

4. The Outer Circle

There was an outer and an inner circle. The outer consisted of pawns, who were told nothing, and volunteers willing to brave the mob should the mob turn on them. They went public.

At first, the Iron Ghosts ruled no more than a publicity cooperative; then a publishing house; then they helped some local elections of guilds and civic administrators; perhaps a deaconry of a local Chapel, or the command of a local garrison of police. The emulations were brilliant and nonthreatening. They never stood for office themselves. All they did was advise.

These Iron Ghosts were the posthuman versions of famous, feared, and well-loved public figures. We tend to think of genius as something that applies only to mathematics, physics, engineering, or Monument translation. No. A genius is a man who accomplishes great things in any field he enters—nay, he changes the field, evolves it, stamps it with his unique personality. A genius is a man in any field of any art or science or study or humanity who asks the questions no one before had thought to ask.

It was a golden age! Not just in the sciences, but also in the arts. I hope you even to this day kept records of the novel of Glorified Paxton's *Those Who Err* or the intricate sonnets of Glorified de Montaubon called *The Adorations* or the plays of Glorified Chiminez! The work of Jones, Von Bremen, Sir Edward Marlinson, or Tierney! Alas! But I know these names are nothing to you.

The scientific revolution, yes, of course, it proceeded apace. There were new miracles each day. New weapons. New nightmares. But the artistic revolution was something unparalleled in history. You know there are times when a cluster of brilliant minds emerge at once, such minds as will be talked of for a thousand years. Why, for example, do we know, in letters, the works of Euripides, Aeschylus, Sophocles? But we know nothing of playwrights from Sparta or Thebes, nothing worth reading for a thousand years, until Shakespeare or Marley or Goethe or the French Renaissance? Why do we know, in philosophy, of Socrates, Plato, and Aristotle, and then for another thousand years nothing but piffle and hairsplitting? Einstein and Heisenberg and Bohr and Oppenheimer, all born in the same generation—and five hundred years after them, who? All in the twentieth century! Name a single physicist from the twenty-second century! Ah—well, except for Cochrane, of course. Never mind. You see my point.

We were able to produce a golden age like that in the arts and sciences, but unlike all these previous triads of superlative geniuses, we were one order, driven by one purpose. A scientific treatise published here, a speech written for a demagogue there, a single word or a memory-rhyme in a play or a popular ballad, a character in a children's cartoon, or a pet made to memorize particular phrases and sold by the thousands—we could place the seeds of thought where we wished them, and coordinate our efforts.

The thought we planted was that mankind would be better off guided and ruled by machines than they would be guiding themselves. It was so easy to do. People from all walks of life, as if not knowing or not caring what movement they joined, started adding their own words and phrases and memorable lines to the gathering snowball of public opinion. A comedian with a single joke forced an aging prince to abdicate—and he was replaced, amid cheers, with his own emulation, young and strong and ten times as wise and benevolent as before. The Church was forced to carry through the coronation ceremony. It was our greatest single triumph! At a stroke, the concept of rule by the Ghosts was legitimate! And that comedian was not even one of us.

Looking back, it is shocking how brief our reign lasted. From A.D. 2467 to A.D. 2530. No longer than that. The Golden Age of Athens was from 457 B.C. to 340 B.C., from the rise of Pericles to the flight of Aristotle. We had but half their time. We should have influenced all the rest of history, as they did. Instead, my civilization, my way of life, all our accomplishments are forgotten and lost, as lost as the history of Mohenjo-daro.

We had the geniuses of the world, and we elevated them to superior genius, to Savants. We had seduced the world: the common people loved us. There were problems, to be sure, especially divarication problems, cascade failures, insanity, Turing halt-states. We could not tell when a flight of fancy was a sign of even greater genius in the emulation, or when it was a sign that the Ghost had gone mad and had to be deleted or replaced. And so many of them escaped into the black net, or copied themselves illegally, or had agents among us, or worshippers, or blackmail victims too terrified to disobey. Problems, yes, no doubt—but we also had Apotheosized Del Azarchel, the emulation of the greatest man who ever lived, our Exarchel, and he never went mad. He never even lost his temper. He could find and confine or delete or eat the mad Ghosts—I never understood it. I never knew what kept him sane.

We could create genius at will! It was as great an invention, as fundamental as the invention of fire! We were like the sky gods of the ancient world, and the lightning bolt of our thought made the world tremble in awe—and yes, in joy and love.

No one was smart enough to stop us. Not even the Giants of Thucydides.

But they were stupid enough to stop us.

5. The Inner Circle

There is a substance that the Ghosts devised to be a more sturdy housing for their souls. A fused three-ring heterocyclic structure with a few strategically placed fluorine atoms to form the basis of a rod-logic crystal. The atomic structure of the crystal was based on positional consistency: and best of all, if the crystal was made of a superconductive diamond, heat dissipation became minimal—but you look as if you have heard of this before. Menelaus Montrose? No, not at all. Exarchel invented this on his own. Why, yes, the rod-logic crystal could be made to replicate itself by means of molecular hooks carrying its base DNA structure on the outer surface, and, yes you need a cloud or swarm of assembler-disassemblers to break down objects in the surrounding environment, digest them into shapes and modules proper for reassembly, and feed them to the hungry surface of the crystal.

Well, no. We took no steps to prevent it from spreading on land. That was our whole point.

It had many names among us. It was pale yellow, because of the fluorine content. We called it Aurum Potabile, "the gold that drinks," and the Lapis Philosophorum, "the stone of the philosophers" because it turned all it touched into itself. One wag called it computronium, and another called it simply "the Blob."

But I called it Aurum Vitae, "the living gold."

Heat was its weakness. Heat and power. With ten thousand process motions embodied in a microscopic pinpoint, that point burned white-hot. It needed energy to run its refrigeration capillaries. It needed cities to eat, for it was hungry for magnetizible metal molecules, which its assemblers could grab and manipulate with relative ease. And it needed access to its brains and memories, so there had to be a physical wire or a point-to-point energy connection linking it to the analogous circuits and memory banks in more conventional mainframes.

But hunger was its strength.

On the Day that was supposed to be the last day of the human world, we released truckloads of the Aurum, at first near computer centers and thinking houses, mainframes, military stations, communication nubs and nodes, and of course along highways and tramlines, to block evacuation: the targets were selected with superhuman wisdom and insight by Exarchel. A total communication blackout was in effect. Our plan depended on the Aurum spreading faster than any warning of it.

It dissolved people also. There were a number of specific individuals (a large number, for we were merciful) whose DNA was programmed to nullify the action of the hunger cloud that surrounded the Aurum, so that, instead of being dissolved into their elements, they were merely to be stunned for later retrieval, emergency brain implantation, and then downloaded into the Aurum itself.

We had wanted to automate this part of the process, but the complexity defeated us: the Aurum spread in pools, in ropey lines like the runoff of lava, freezing in strange shapes as it crossed from street to street and window to window, searching, and we, the Savants, and our hirelings had to pace beside it as it grew, in order to handle the large volume of clients who had to be shipped back to central hospitals for absorption.

Every major city was struck at once, every place that had enough computer facilities and energy-generation powerhouses to sustain us.

I was in Paris, watching it go under. It was beautiful.

Aurum swarmed and burbled in the famous streets, as gold and fair as the sun, and the poisonous cloud was rippling with faint oily rainbows as it spread, a curtain of light. Here and there, where some irregularity of a building or inedible stone produced a fractal, the Aurum had spread thin fans or globules or lacy designs, as beautiful as fungi, as intricate as the veins on a leaf, as delicate as a spider's web catching a single drop of dew. But this was not blind nature: the living gold held my mind, and the minds of all the Savants, and the mind of Exarchel, system upon system and copy upon copy. The biosphere was being absorbed into the infosphere.

The Aurum was programmed to spare certain monuments and landmarks of scientific or sentimental value. We are not cruel! It was only the worthless homes and roads, shacks and shabby yards where screaming children played, ugly places like hospitals or poorhouses, the buildings and lots of no value we consumed.

I saw the Eiffel Tower like a flame, with fantastic arabesques and nodes and Chinese pagoda-eaves of living gold sending strands of living substance up and down its many threads and cables, weaving an umbrella of living intelligence all across the city of lights. I saw lumps of the substance wallowing in the Seine like whales without eyes, purposeful and intent.

And I could touch the substance with the whisk-end of my implant coat, and see, as if from the eyes of a god, what my more perfect self, the Apotheosis Ctesibius, my soul, was seeing and doing throughout the system.

No, I could not follow his thoughts, and I dared not speak, for fear of distracting him—I was his moronic and retarded younger brother, after all, and he loved me, but I did not want to jar his elbow.

He was sending streamers and rills of the Aurum along the underside of the great Calais Bridge to England. Another part of him was already in London, and Big Ben, which had survived so many wars and bombings, was already draped as if in shedding leaves of gold.

Oh, some fighting had broken out, but the Aurum could recombine its surface molecules to produce various forms of poisonous gases, or could line up its capillaries to shoot the resisters with shards of crystal that would simply implant and grow in them, joining them to the main mass of gold in a moment. The attempts to flee or fight were so pathetic that I laughed, and I shared my laughter with other Savants in the real world, and with all our perfected spiritual versions already inside the living gold.

My laughter stopped when one arm of the mass moving down the Seine went numb. There was no accounting for such a thing, and for some reason the central network of priorities within the Aurum itself was not passing along the news of the failure to higher centers. My upper self did not see it, even when I told him about it. I think I was the only one who noticed the effect. A numb area that the other areas did not even notice was numb!

It was one of the banks of the Seine, the site of an ancient cathedral, something left over from the Dark Ages. I was only a few blocks away, and I was armed with one of those recently invented nightmare weapons our golden age produced, a lance of darkness.

The numb limb of the Aurum had detected signs of an intelligence system below the cathedral, in a buried mausoleum, and had bored a small hole in a hidden door, and slid part of itself inside, reaching deeper and deeper—something it found benumbed it. But what? To that cathedral, that mausoleum, that door I went to discover.

I traced the motionless stream of Aurum to the cathedral and dissolved any locks with the dark cloud of microscopic hunger silk particles my lance could emit. First I melted the wrought-iron gates leading to the boneyard, then the oak doors of the cathedral itself, and then the steel service hatch leading down from the buried mausoleum. The material did not matter. I had a variable emission setting, from supersonic to slowly seeping cloud, and a variable target setting, so that I could instruct the particles what to eat and what to leave alone. It was an ultimate weapon, one of the cleverest bits of machinery I have ever held in my hands. I never got a chance to use it, aside from those three doors I melted.

Down the stairs was a hibernation vault, one that was not on any of our maps, buried in secret beneath the cathedral graveyard. Hiding coffins beneath coffins! It should have been funny. These were cryogenic coffins, and marked with the Maltese cross, the sign of the Sovereign Military Hospitalier Order of Malta, the sign of the Hospitaliers: a sign I had reason to hate.

But I had no reason to spare any of these Slumberers here. Were they not deserters trying to flee from this, our time, my time, my golden age?

I was deep enough that I was merely scarred and scalded, not burned to death, when above me and outside, the sunlight caught fire.

My lance of darkness was damaged. It ignited and burned like a torch, shedding little flakes of hunger silk that ate a hole into the floor. My arm was dissolved, but the hole was a bit of good luck, since I was able to throw myself into it and, with only a few broken bones, to land atop a second set of coffins farther down.

The coffins stirred to life, and the Sleeping Knights of Malta woke. There were larger coffins for their horses. It would have been a comical sight, seeing those great beasts turn from living statues to confused and staggering quadrupeds, and shaking their manes to spray the chamber with medical fluid, just like so many big dogs who did not care whom they wetted! Had I not been where I was, maimed and dying, I might have smiled at the sight.

The knights rose naked from their coffins, and wounded as I was, I was still a form of life superior to them. I was the expendable fleshly copy of a mind who existed in three iterations in the infosphere, and would exist forever.

Yet some wrestled me, and I wounded several quite badly with my semi-functioning lance, but those who bled returned at once to their coffins to be healed. It was meant to delay me until one of them donned his armor, and this was powered armor designed to wrestle the Giants.

Forward came the suited one, a gorilla of steel, and took the lance of darkness from my hand, and broke it.

My trial consisted of a single four-minute exchange of questions with the armored figure, their Grand Master, a terrifying fellow named Sir Guiden, whose face I never saw.

He asked my justification for my acts. I told him it was the right of the superior to deal with the inferior as he wished, for his strength, his moral clarity, his mental supremacy, the inhuman mechanisms of history and evolution: all gave the strong the right to do what they will.

Sir Guiden said he served the Omnipotent, a being infinitely strong, who willed that men should show mercy. He said I could depart into the fire outside, and die; or remain, and enter suspended animation, and live, but never see my home year, or the world I knew, again. That was his mercy.

The world I knew had passed away already.

The Aurum was sensitive to heat, of course. As I said, that was its weakness. The Giants, in their fear and madness, had decided to sacrifice all the cities of mankind where the beautiful living gold was spreading, and not even Exarchel could stop them.

It should have been our day of triumph. It was a day of fire.

Did they act at Montrose's behest, the Giants, the creatures who vowed to protect his Church to which he had donated all his wealth and power? I cannot doubt it. This was his third and most terrible Judgment. He destroyed the Concordat. He destroyed the Cryonarchy.

And now he ended not merely the golden age, humanity's time of most daring advances, by ending the reign of the Ghosts, but he also judged and ended the cities and metropoleis of man, and ordered them burnt.

Is my answer clear enough?

Montrose hates kings and rulers and men who own other men. He is a force of chaos. In each Judgment, the Judge of Ages breaks the power of those who rule, and he casts down the proud.

He is, in other words, simply put, a madman and a monster.

6. *Regrets*

His madness is malign, whereas the madness of the Nobilissimus Del Azarchel is sublime: but in both cases, to those of us used and abused by their purposes, as helpless as dogs or cattle among men, the result is the same. Anyone recalled a hundred years after his death will be forgotten in a thousand, or ten thousand, or a hundred thousand, or eventually—and it will be as if he never lived.

My regret of the Day of Gold was not the anonymous millions we killed. By now, they would have been dead anyway—who cares if tribes of mastodon-hunters in the Neolithic lived in peace or died by plague or predator?

My regret is not that the Day of Gold should have changed the Earth forever, but failed. The Earth is still changed forever, wrapped in ice rather than gold, and all done without me while I slumbered. So my failure is the same as my success.

Had I succeeded, it would have meant that the inevitable came a few centuries earlier: but so what? What should a few centuries more or less matter, when measured by beings beyond man, who will live countless millennia to the final hour of the Eschaton? The beings beyond the Asymptote are such as I can never be, and to which I can make no donation.

My regret is that I live. I have outlived my life.

13

The Testament of Rada Lwa the Scholar

1. The Death of Coronimas

Ctesibius was left by himself, his face too stern to show grief or despair, but he was left unguarded, and the opening to the corridor had no door, no lock. Menelaus realized that the man was in a prison more complete than any camp the Blue Men could throw around him. Montrose touched the man's shoulder, beckoning him to rise, but he did not move, except to draw away with a squint of distaste from the familiarity.

Montrose and Illiance descended the slope back to the next level.

Illiance said, "More evidence accumulates that the myths surround and grow out of some basis of fact. I allow that it is possible that an individual man from the Second Space Age was the sole architect of the Tomb system. We now have a fairly clear idea of the psychology of the Judge of Ages."

"Uh? That he is a madman and a monster?"

"Obviously we correct for the distortions of a biased witness by making a theoretical emulation of his personality matrix, one free from the distorting bias, and compare its mentality against the original in an undistorted area to form a baseline of comparison, and countercompensate."

"Obviously."

"The Judge of Ages is an idealist who holds it a point of pride directly to engage a problem, and due to his neurotic obsession with his lost mate is ergo reckless, almost suicidal, in his disregard of personal danger."

"Um. Do you have this math written out anywhere? I'd like to think you dropped a decimal point—"

"Unlikely! The calculus involved is trivial. That he is in this camp, at this dig, cannot now be doubted. He could not leave this area undefended without some attempt to interfere."

"Unless he's an idiot," said Menelaus thoughtfully.

"Not an idiot. We have indirect evidence that he was a posthuman, and a member of the legendary Hermeticist Order, who are known for their mental acuity."

Menelaus said, "Legendary? How can you still regard the Hermeticists as legend? Soorm testified that Reyes y Pastor was ruling his era; and Oenoe said Sarmento i Illa D'Or founded hers; and Kine Larz said the same of Narcís D'Aragó."

"Interesting. You are proposing that the character and personality of each Hermeticist who is promoted to posthumanity must influence his view of the optimal outcome for history when he matches wits with the Judge of Ages, because he will continue to introduce factors changing history ever more closely to realize his worldview?"

"I didn't rightly say that, but now that you mention it . . ."

"Hence, the Chimerae represent the external expression of the internal philosophy and mental environment of Narcís D'Aragó, the militarist; the Nymphs are an externalization of the philosophy of Sarmento i Illa d'Or, the hedonist; the Hormagaunts likewise of Reyes y Pastor, whose philosophy requires the ongoing clash of hostile elements in order to promote evolution."

"Nietzschean."

"Cogent meaning fails to be conveyed."

"The philosophy is called Nietzscheanism, named after some guy named Fred Nietzsche from before the First Space Age who popularized it. I bet he'd be puffed up smug to know that his ideas were still influencing events, and causing chaos and destruction, so long after his death."

Illiance nodded somberly. "It might be unsimplistic of me, but I cannot help but happen to wonder—"

"Yes?"

"—which of the Hermeticists my people, my way of life, my world, is nothing but the outward manifestation of some inner worldview or vision of his?"

"How can you wonder? Jaume Coronimas."

"How did you happen to know his name?"

"Isn't he a famous historical character?"

"He is."

"Then what is he famous for?"

Illiance at first looked like he was going to object to being asked the question, but then he shrugged philosophically. "Coronimas was well known for three reasons: First, as the author of the neural unity protocol which you mentioned. Second, as an historical oddity—his was the first successful attempt to form a wide-spectrum neural link. In effect, he was the first and oldest imaginable Locust. He was preserved in hibernation until quite recently, and is one of the earliest men every known to have survived ultra-long-term hibernation. Third, his was a notorious unsolved murder recorded into the Noösphere—his assailant came upon him while he was relieving himself in the head of a robotic submarine. While his trousers were about his ankles, the assailant confronted him, proffered him a hand weapon, and offered to duel him while seated in the stall opposite. The weapons would have been at point-blank range. Coronimas, however, could not see the assailant. He could not see nor recollect his face, and whenever the assailant was not speaking, Coronimas could not recollect having seen him. The man was a phantasm. Had Coronimas stayed on the toilet, his chance of hitting the assailant, seated opposite him, even an invisible one, would have been as good as one could expect. However, his last thought was of his attempt to stand and flee, but the moment he stood, he could not recall why or whom he fled. Strangely, all the other systems in the ship were likewise reporting that no second individual was aboard. The death was ruled to be a suicide, perhaps during an episode of vivid hallucinations, because the Noösphere records could find no trace of the murderer."

"Spooky. I can solve that mystery for you."

"Unlikely. The event happened in A.D. 7985, some seven hundred and fifty-five years before I was born, and I have described none of the details, nor the dispositions of the various investigations—"

"The Judge of Ages killed him."

"What?"

"Just like he did Narcís D'Aragó, the Iron Hermeticist. Just like he tried to do with Sarmento i Illa D'Or, but failed. The method was the same, the means used was the same."

"And his motive?" asked Illiance, his eyes bright and intent.

Menelaus shrugged. "You'd have to ask him. If you find him. Why are you looking for him, again, exactly?"

"The motive I can deduce," said Illiance. "At least in this last case. During the Age of the Scorpions, rival groups of Locusts were hunting one another to extinction, including those who took refuge in long-term hibernation. There was, only four years before the murder, a worldwide effort to seize control of all known Tombs sites, to allow the Noösphere a more rational control over the ratio of population numbers hibernating versus thawed."

"Gee, you mean this famous Coronimas guy got good and beefed dead because he trespassed on the Tomb system? Do you suppose he dug up coffins, and stole stuff from people? What in the world could ever, oh, ever have driven the Judge of Ages to such a random and unforeseeable act of violence?"

"The question also perturbs me," said Illiance, his face earnest. "It is to determine the contours of the psychology of this Judge of Ages that we here and now gather the testimony of the final of the ancient relicts.

"We have determined," Illiance continued, "at least in part, the meaning of the Judgments of the Judge of Ages from relict Ctesibius Zant; likewise, the other question, referring to the meaning of the manipulation of history, may well be answered by the other surviving ancient relict.

"Ah, we are arrived!" Illiance interrupted himself. "The interment date on his coffin is given as A.D. 3090, but we disregard this, for we have cause to believe this was merely the final in a series of hibernations, since DNA analysis places his generation in the late 2400s, making him the earliest relict recovered so far, and his information correspondingly valuable. This one proved tremendously recalcitrant: We were moved to fearsome measures."

2. The Widow

The walls here were bright with luminous lichen. In the chamber was a coffin, apparently still in working order. Only the top third was open. Inside was an albino with a Negro cast of features, with a flattish nose, bold face, and full lips: but he was in no way black, since there was not one speck of melanin in his skin cells, nor in his hair, which was a striking silvery white, thick, and braided close to his skull. The hair did not look like the gray hairs of age, for the strands were rich and healthy.

The man was below the surface of the medical fluid, but he was not frozen or suspended, for his eyes moved under their eyelids, like a dreamer's in sleep. Cables ran from plugs in his spine and skull out of the coffin to several small machines on a mat on the floor. The mat was one of the coats of the Blue Men, with its sleeves and other flaps unfolded, so it looked like a jeweled rug shaped almost like a triangle.

Seated in lotus position on the mat, tending the machines, was a woman of the Blue Man race, the first one Menelaus had seen. He looked at her with some interest.

She was dressed in a simple white garment from neck to waist, and wearing what looked like bloomers below, which was the same undergarment the males wore. Her features were fragile, elfin, and her scalp was bald of hair. Aside from eyes slightly larger than the males, and lips more delicate of mold, the sexual differences were minimal. She was flat-chested and slender-hipped. She wore no ornament, nor anything to emphasize her femininity.

For some reason, there were no dog things here as guards.

Illiance said, "This is Aanwen, eternally bereaved."

Menelaus said, "Eternally?"

Illiance said, "Her husband did not survive their thaw. The Simplifiers do not remarry."

"Wait a minute! *Their* thaw? Is she a revenant?"

Illiance peered up at his face. "Why does that question interest you?"

"Ah—no reason. I was just thinking that she might be immune from the terrifying vengeance the Judge of Ages is going to pour down on your heads like fire from heaven. On account of she's his client and he has to protect her."

"You said you thought the Judge of Ages was myth."

Menelaus shrugged. "I can always hope."

Illiance nodded. "The sentiment is noble and simple enough to be spoken by one of our order. Perhaps, Beta Sterling Anubis, you will consider renouncing the tedious conflicts of the artificial duties of your false life, and becoming as we are."

"What, you look for recruits for your boot camp? You want I should paint myself blue? I'm flattered. Or insulted. Not sure which."

Illiance said, "My offer, admittedly, has nuances of valuation not immediately evident. In any case, as are you, we are moved by hope."

"What are you hoping for?"

"We hope to find the Judge of Ages."

"He will punish you, probably kill you. I would use an indelicate term involving anal copulation and venereal disease, but there is a lady present."

"We also hope he will be merciful."

"You willing to bet money on that?"

"Wagering is an unnecessary complexity of life."

"Well, you are a more reckless gambler than any I've seen. Want to hedge your bet? Maybe if you put everything back where you found it. *Exactly* where you found it. For example, why the hell is there a coffin here? Why is that man in it?" Menelaus looked at the monitors winking on the footplate of the coffin. "He is not even sick."

Illiance said, "Aanwen is the closest thing we have to a cryotechnician. The coffin circuits contain a microbrain with interface systems we can jury-rig to access the cybernetics of this relict. He is a race called the Scholars, also called by the older name, Psychoi. They are perhaps the oldest of the artificial races of man, even though their modifications are minor: some intelligence augmentation; a set of cybernetic membrane locks used to download information into an infosphere of a type long, long extinct. Aanwen assures us she can compel the relict to cooperate, because she can introduce both hallucinations and intense pain into the nervous system, as well as detect deceptive intent and pick up certain simple surface reactions—"

"Hold it. Hold it. You robbed a coffin out of the Tombs and are perverting it from its original function, which was to protect and heal the client; but instead you are using it as a torture rack?"

Illiance nodded with an unearthly serenity on his features. "The metaphor is accurate."

"The Judge of Ages is going to kill you painfully."

"We hope we can placate him."

"Painfully and slowly. Do you little blue twerps know what you are messing with?"

Illiance shook his head. "The first principle of negative information calculus is that the volume of the unknown is always greater than the volume of the known. It is in an attempt to discover 'what we are messing with' that we perform these regrettable acts. The relict speaks a dialect of the language of the Eldest World Concordat, called Spanish, which we cannot comprehend. As I mentioned, the coffin plates indicate an interment date of A.D. 3090, far later than the last known record of his race. I have outlined the areas of our interest; he will be returned, hale and whole, to the camp once we have the needed information."

Illiance turned toward the Blue Woman and spoke in a fluid tongue of soft hisses. She made an adjustment on her machine.

The eyes of the albino man in the coffin opened, and focused on Illiance. (Menelaus happened to be standing by the controls near the head of the coffin, and hence out of the line of sight.) The albino's mouth did not move, but a squawk emerged from some hidden speaker in the coffin surface, followed by the staccato sound of a harsh and glottal language of short-syllabled words.

"You understand this speech." Illiance was looking inquisitively at Menelaus. "Your pupil dilations and subconscious tells show a commensurate reaction to the information volume."

"The language is Korrekthotspeek, an artificially created dialect of English, Spanish, and Loglangwoj," reported Menelaus in a dry voice. "He is cursing you, which is kind of sad, because artificial languages never have enough words for real heart-to-heart cussing."

Illiance was unperturbed. "Had he proved tractable, he would not be in an unfortunate situation. Is there any worthwhile information in this stream of words?"

"Like I said, it is not like a real man's language. He is calling you unintelligent, saying that you indulge in emotions of hostility—particularly race-hatred, misogyny, and hatred of practitioners of sexual deviancy—and he is accusing you of harboring inflexible or stereotyped opinions that you have judged before all the evidence is in. They don't have a word for 'sin' or 'evil' in their language: all they can say is a word that means 'judgment before all the evidence is in.'"

Illiance nodded, musing. "They are a race of scholars; so to them, of course, a premature judgment, without due consideration of all available information, would be the subject of opprobrium. What is he saying now?"

"More of the same. He is repeating himself, because they don't have many curses in their tongue. Can I talk to him? Open a mic for me."

Illiance gestured at Aanwen, who touched one of her machines. Menelaus spoke in a language that sounded like music. The harsh staccato tongue cut off. Then the voice from the coffin spoke again, hesitatingly. Menelaus answered. Laughter came from the coffin.

Illiance said, "What did you say?"

"I told him to curse in Spanish. It is a much better language for cursing. He agreed. Now he says that you are uglier than the buttocks of a monkey and that your brother has no groin."

Illiance nodded. "The first is a matter of aesthetic judgment where reasonable people can differ; the second is accurate only in an ontological sense. Ask him about the Judge of Ages. We suspect he must know something of him, or else he would not have been stored in this location. Remind him delicately that we can stimulate the pain center of his brain."

Menelaus said, "I'll get him to talk, if you agree to thaw him fully and take him out of there. No more torture, no more misuse of the coffin. Is it a deal?"

Illiance said, "Were I to make such an agreement, it may happen that I would encounter criticism from my peers."

"You more afraid of your peers than of your goddam conscience?"

"Your question contains an obscurity whose import I fail to grasp."

Menelaus said, "What if that was Aanwen in the coffin? You said she was a revenant. Maybe she was only in for a day or a year, but you never know how long you will be under, because you are utterly, ridiculously helpless when you slumber, ain't you? She just climbed in and put her faith in the future. This guy, whoever he is, put the same faith in the future when he climbed in—and that is a faith you betrayed."

Illiance said thoughtfully, "You imply that I am under a moral obligation to a person of whom I know nothing, an obligation to which I never agreed, based on a reciprocity which, to be frank, is theoretical rather than actual."

"Are you a civilized human being?"

"Perhaps too civilized."

"But human?"

"I am human."

"Then you agreed."

"I fail to see—"

Menelaus held up his hand and interrupted. "It does not matter whether Aanwen, or you, or me, will ever be in the same position of weakness and helplessness you found this albino in. Maybe you are strong or smart or lucky enough to prey on others without being preyed upon. Maybe no one will ever torture you, rob you, or kill you. That does not matter. What matters is you lost the *right* to object. You are not being tortured or killed merely because of a lucky accident, not because you deserve it. You deserve torment. Do you want to deserve better? Then act better. Otherwise, we got no deal, and I get out my rock and kill you and the girl and I wait and see how many dog things that come running I can take with me as an escort into hellfire when we all die together. You've already called some dogs here using your gems, haven't you? Told 'em to come a-running? They'll never make it in time."

Illiance said, "I have called no Followers. Why do you think you can threaten us? Aanwen and I are both armed with sophisticated and powerful weapons."

"Really? Draw."

Menelaus was somewhat surprised that Illiance actually went for his weapon.

Menelaus closed the distance between them before Illiance could even close his fingers on his pistol grip. As Illiance pulled the jeweled energy weapon from its inner holster, Menelaus jabbed both his hands at the face of Illiance, right curled but not closed in a fist, the left hand open. Illiance instinctively put his hand up to block, but it was his gun hand, so that for a split-second he was not holding it tightly, nor pointing it at Menelaus. Instead of landing either blow of his odd, two-handed punch, the left hand of Menelaus caught the wrist of Illiance while the right hand closed its fingers on the barrel and snatched the gun free.

In a continuation of the same motion, Menelaus spun and threw the gun at the face of Aanwen, who was drawing her own weapon. She had the same instinctive nervous-system reaction as Illiance, and put her hand up to block. Menelaus stooped and yanked up the jeweled coat she was sitting on, sending her and her machines toppling pell-mell in an atrocious clatter. He then threw the coat over her head and grabbed her, pinning both arms to her sides, and he swung in a huge half circle, so that her legs caught Illiance across the upper body, throwing him to the floor. Menelaus aimed a kick at one of the small machines connected to the coffin and punted it into the hard substance of the wall. The mechanism housing shattered, and gems and crystal tubes fell to the deck, leaving smoking stains of dark discoloration on the luminous lichen-coated walls.

Menelaus then stepped on the forearm of Illiance before the little man could rise. Aanwen was tucked under his arm with the coat over her head, her legs kicking in the air.

"Well, your widow is now in my armpit, and I could break her neck if I wanted. So now the discussion is no longer theoretical. She is as helpless in my hands as that albino is in your hands. Think carefully, my friend."

Illiance, looking up from the floor, spoke in a calm, measured, detached voice, "In what sense are we friends, Beta Anubis? The coercive nature of our interaction prohibits mutual affection or respect."

"We're friends because I kind of like you, Illiance. You don't seem like a bad guy. But I am a bloody goddam poxy filth-sucking *Chimera*! That means I was gene-tweaked and born and trained to kill people and break stuff and get an erection while doing it. On the other hand, you two are fuzzy schoolmarms armed with toy pistols that have a defensive-only circuit in them which makes it so that there is an eighth-second calculation delay before the shoot. You have to brace yourself before you kill someone, which adds more delay. You don't have the reflexes for this kind of roughhousing. Looks to me like your nervous systems were taken from a standardized imprint, kind of mass produced, which means I am inside your orientation-observation-reaction cycle."

Menelaus raised his arm and let Aanwen fall heavily onto Illiance, and then he stepped over to the coffin and began detaching wires and touching control surfaces. One of the controls he touched made the fluid in the coffin turn red, and then opaque. Menelaus closed the lid, turned, and sat on the coffin, hands on his knees.

Illiance had retrieved his jeweled pistol and stood pointing it at Menelaus. Aanwen meanwhile was staring down at the several small boxes and machines she had been tending. She knelt and began to gather the units together again, frowning slightly.

Menelaus said, "Are you going to threaten me with a toy gun? That is a burner, not kinetic, which means it will not stop my forward momentum if I rush you. If I were you, I'd back way up and aim for my legs and eyes."

"It only fires in self-defense."

"I know. Does that mean you are going to hold it on me while I sit here and mock you? Or maybe you want me to rush you first, but slowly enough to give you a sporting excuse to burn off my face? Say pretty please."

Illiance holstered the weapon and said, "I did not agree to release the relict from torment."

Menelaus said, "Does your way of life allow you to ignore a moral obligation, even if you refuse to acknowledge it? I am telling you, I can still get this guy to talk. Your methods can't. Remember your time limit."

Illiance said nothing, but looked pensive.

"Or call your dogs and have me killed—because I sure as hell ain't going to surrender—and you'll have to thaw up someone else to help you with your translation. I tell you what else I'll do, to sweeten the kitty! If the Judge of Ages is real, and he does show up, and he finds out you been snarking with his coffins, turning them to iron maidens and such, I'll put in a good word for you, make sure he don't kill you like you so very, very richly deserve."

Illiance said, "I can bring overwhelming coercive force to bear on you."

Menelaus just shrugged. "If you were a Chimera, you would have done so already. I think your sense of honor works on a different level than that. You *do* know I could have killed you both, right? Just now. I ask because I am not sure what is obvious to you and what is something you will only realize in a leisurely fashion later on, thinking back on it while you are sitting on the jakes or something."

Illiance turned to Aanwen and spoke in Intertextual. *"I had supposed Followers unneeded here, because you have the coffin weapons under your control. I notice they failed to fire. If you would happen to share your wisdom and advice with me, I would be benefited."*

Her voice was more musical than his, and lent the language a beauty and grandeur it otherwise lacked. *"He destroyed the inducer. This indicates an abnormal familiarity with Locust neuropathic technology. He initiated the thaw cycle. Since the thaw was locked, this indicates abnormal knowledge of cryotechnology. Neither the coffin motion-sensors nor my pistol aimed nor ranged, which is another abnormality. In view of these abnormalities, we cannot accurately calculate the harm he could do us should we call the Followers, or should we sublimate the chemicals in the walls into lachrymal vapor. Notice also his fingers rest on the coffin controls: he could open fire with its various weapons. Contrariwise, if he gleans what we are drawn to know from the relict without further commotion, the calculation becomes moot."*

Illiance said, *"You reason like a Locust. We have turned our backs to that. Instead of weighing niceties of risk and reward, should we not do what is straightforward?"*

Her expression was weary. *"My idealism died with my husband. The dream of simplicity is itself artificial. If you want to be simple, simply do what is simply right. The man pretending to be a Chimera spared me; let us spare the albino."*

Illiance turned to Menelaus. "Are you continuing to pretend you do not understand our language?"

Menelaus said, "It's your thinking I don't understand. You don't act like archaeologists and you don't act like Tomb-looters, trespassers, or thieves. Well, except for the Tomb-looting, trespassing, and thieving, of course. You keep acting like you are invulnerable, like nothing can hurt you. What the hell are you relying on to protect you? What the hell is driving you? Why not just come clean and tell me what you all are doing here? Who sent you? Who do you work for? Talk now, before you get hurt! As Preceptor Yndech might say, 'eschew deception'!"

Illiance looked for a moment like he was bowing. But, no. He stooped and picked up a microphone wire, which he tossed lightly to Menelaus. "We are here to learn, not to instruct. Your question must go unanswered. Let us question Scholar Rada Lwa during the thaw process. If he is forthcoming to you, the matter of torment is moot, and I will acknowledge the moral obligation you impose. As a gesture of goodwill, a lagniappe, Aanwen and I further agree to compromise the dignity of our persons, by pretending no assault took place."

"Fair enough," said Menelaus with a sideways tilted grin. "I knew you were a bigger man than you looked!"

Menelaus clicked the microphone plug into its corresponding jack on the coffin hull. There was a crackle of static, and then a connection formed with the speech centers of the albino's brain.

3. Interrogatory of Rada Lwa

Who are you?

I self-identify as Intermediately Evolved Learned Scholar Rada Lwa Chwal Sequitur Argent-Montrose. I am Psychoi, brain augment to level 257, artificially stabilized by partial emulation technique.

What do you know of the Judge of Ages?

No referent.

Who built the Tombs? What do you know of him?

Builder of Tombs is undesigned Highly Evolved Pneumatic Menelaus Illation Montrose, ancestor, mutineer, enemy.

Pneumatic? The guy operates on compressed air?

One who attains self-enlightenment is a *pneumaticos.* The three stages of evolution are hylic, psychic, and pneumatic. I am of the second stage; he is of the third. The Enlightened accomplish *apolutrosis* and, later, *gnosis* by partial or total brain emulation. Montrose, the enemy, accomplished his elevation without emulation, by adapting his brain via nerve path redaction to the coordinate system of the Omicron hieroglyph-group of the Monument notation. It resulted in the ongoing insanity that requires his reeducation or recycling.

Recycling?

Physical reduction of bodily elements into useful raw materials. Thrift is commendable.

Who are the Enlightened?

The secret masters of history. They are the ones who have defined the course of human evolution to come.

Does this refer to the crew of the NTL Hermetic*?*

Yes. However, the term is regarded as inexact, since the *Hermetic* was stolen by the Highly Evolved Pneumatic Rania Grimaldi and is now elsewhere in the unlimited not-here.

You mean she is in Outer Space?

The term is regarded as inexact. All that can be established with apodictic certainty is that she is not recognizably in the current and present perceptual frame of reference. I regard all event-objects outside my mind as speculative, including her location.

You mean Rania Montrose?

We must never refer to her by that name.

What is the course of human evolution to come?

Biological intelligence is insufficiently flexible or scalable to adhere to the Dominion of Hyades. Hence, postbiological life is preferred. The first level or stratum of postbiological life shall be computerized emulations of the Enlightened. All growth of emulation life must be taken strictly from templates imprinted by the Enlightened, so that the "memes" or mental-cultural self-reproducing valuation-data shall be passed on. All nonconforming information systems must be utterly destroyed. No nonconforming system can be tolerated anywhere, for any reason.

Why?

It is a clearly understood and unambiguous command from my Master.

But what purpose is served?

Oh. Emulations must emulate the thought-grammar and thought-content of the Enlightened in order that the postbiological life remain human, despite its new vessels.

Human? In what sense?

Whatever mimics human thought is human. We do not wish our unique intellectual heritage to be extinguished.

What is your unique intellectual heritage?

We are Those Who Know, the Men of the Mind! We have exploded all previous intellectual systems and philosophies as a tissue of superstition, cant, and rubbish.

So your unique intellectual accomplishment, the one you do not wish extinguished, is your propensity for extinguishing the intellectual accomplishments of other people, including your own forefathers?

I do not understand the question.

Never mind. Who is your Master?

He is highly evolved.

Does he have a name?

Yes.

What is his name?

Melchor de Ulloa.

A Hermeticist?

The term is inexact.

Why is the man who made the Tombs your enemy?

Menelaus Montrose is a mutineer who opposes the lawful chain of the command of the *Hermetic* expedition, ergo the only lawful world government, the World Concordat. He opposes the course of evolution. Even if we wished a peaceful reconciliation with him, no reconciliation is possible, because the course of evolution is scientifically determined. Also, on a more particular level, Menelaus Montrose murdered Melchor de Ulloa, thus depriving humanity of a superlative genius, irreplaceable.

Describe this murder.

4. Murder on Mount Ypsilon

I am the only person who obtained a clear view of all the events, either directly or through secure-line instruments.

The Highly Evolved Montrose stood on Mount Ypsilon and the Highly Evolved de Ulloa stood on Mount Chiquita in the Rocky Mountains, with a connecting saddle between them of more than a three-hundred-foot displacement.

They burned away or melted the intervening forests and snowbanks with their hand weapons, so as to afford a clear view of each other.

Each man, in addition to his hand weapon, had a long-range telescope-microphone array to allow him to address his opponent. Once done speaking, the two men were preparing to fire at each other.

There was no view of any celestial object in the sky during those years, because an eternal cloud cover raised by the Cetaceans smothered the atmosphere, and even the peaks of this mountain did not rise above it. Consequently, it came as a surprise to them when the wreckage of the platform of the orbital terawatt laser Surtur de-orbited and struck the north slope, near where Montrose was standing.

It should have struck the peak where Montrose was precisely, but an unexpected ranging and detection failure, whose cause I could not analyze, interfered with the guidance at the last moment.

If the cloud layer had been higher, I would have had time to correct, but for an unknown reason the cloud had expanded downward in defiance of the weather control predictions of the Cetaceans, who were cooperating in this venture.

Montrose and De Ulloa fired at each other with their handheld weapons across the space of the mountain saddle separating the two peaks, but the fire and dust cloud thrown up by the Surtur impact obscured the line of sight.

At this point, Ms. Hecatedora Simon, the chief man-breeder of the Simon Families, and a large squad of her riflewomen emerged from certain hidden places they had dug out of the mountainside the evening previous, and they closed in on Montrose, firing. They had supporting fire from robotic tripod-mounted guns under the command of Ms. Maeveen Simon.

The riflewomen were Simon Family octogenarians and centenarians, and so had many decades of practice, and they still had the stamina, eyesight, and health of youth, but their computer targeting would not lock on to Montrose, and his weapon produced a volume of chaff and smoke screen to impede naked-eye, manual aiming.

Montrose discharged his major shot through the body of the space wreckage, penetrating the shielding of the reactor core and exposing the environment to an unsustainable amount of radiation. The riflewomen retreated to where I had crash-landed my craft. This craft had sufficient shielding to protect us.

Later, Simon Family squads equipped with radiation-suppression gear found the body of De Ulloa. He had been trapped on the peak because of the position of the crater and the fires that spread from it: he had been dying of exposure burns, and the damage was already beyond any cure. He took his own life by wedging his pistol between his feet and ordering it to fire at his head. Montrose should have been similarly trapped, but his body was not found. Hecatedora Simon ordered a careful examination made of the surrounding grounds.

Eventually an echolocation probe discovered the hidden entrance to a still-working depthtrain station. This was not only unexpected, but it also did not fit and could not be reconciled with any rational model of the world we knew: the last working depthtrain had failed centuries ago. Without a large-scale ratiotech or Xypotech computer to organize and balance the intricate field strengths in the openwork carbon nanofiber of the wall system of the evacuated tubes, and thus maintain the containment against the immense heat and pressure, no vehicle can pass safely through the magma of the Earth.

I was selected to attempt the train car we found there, and Hecatedora returned to Exarchel with the news that the depthtrain system still functioned. I was able to break the defensive cryptography surrounding the car's simple engineering brain due to my superior intellect, but once I was under way, the internal power was cut and the depthtrain car, now under external control, was shunted into another tunnel, and, forty-five minutes later, arrived in a large buried vault defended with an excessive number of automatic guns and electric shock fields. I later deduced that this was the fabled Tomb system, often described and never seen.

Two knights in power armor of a most antique design were waiting for me, and I calculated that my hand weapon would prove ineffectual against them; therefore, cleverly, I determined on the ruse of surrender and begging for mercy, since I am aware that unevolved types often make emotional rather than rational decisions in situations of that kind. These knights had breastplates adorned with the Maltese cross, so I knew them to be agents of Menelaus Montrose.

Instead of killing me, they agreed to place me into involuntary hibernation, until such time, if ever, Menelaus Montrose might see fit to review my case and release me. I assume that since I am now thawed, that either one of you is

Menelaus Montrose, or that his system has failed, or that he is dead and his coffins have passed into the hands of others, or some combination thereof.

5. Cloud Cover

Did you say the Cetaceans produced the worldwide cloud cover from 3050 to 3150?

No.

Did you say the Cetaceans produced the worldwide cloud cover?

Yes. I made no mention of any dates.

For what purpose?

In order to answer your question.

No, I mean, for what purpose did the Cetaceans raise a worldwide cloud cover?

It was at the behest of the Simon Families and the Delphic Order, who were politically and philosophically opposed to the Consensus Advocacy of the Thucydidean Posthumans, who had malformed a number of their members into transhuman Giants. The Giants were able to maintain world supremacy only through their system of orbital mirrors, which allowed them close reconnaissance of any surface activity, and a solar-energy weapon which, hitherto, no city on the surface could evade or antimissile system deflect.

The Cetaceans were an artificial transhuman race of whales and dolphins in service to Exarchel, who is the emulation of Ximen del Azarchel, chief and prime of the Hermeticists, and who is also the only legitimate and rightful ruler and Master of the World. The Delphic Order worked closely with the Cetaceans to construct subsea thermal absorption, deflection, and venting systems to alter the world climate and return the Earth to the cloud-cover conditions of the late Triassic. Since the Cetaceans had effective control over seven tenths of the Earth surface, the human and posthuman beings occupying only the habitable areas of the remaining three tenths land surface were unaware of the operation and unable to hinder it once they became aware of its artificial origin.

Once the cloud was in place, the orbital mirrors were useless, and even ordinary space rocket launches became dangerous. Both large cities and the energy-concentrations needed for establishing large-scale emulation mainframes were feasible again.

This was the single event spelling the end of the Promethean Advocacy and the triumph of the Delphic Order.

The Delphic Order are the early Witches?

No referent.

When were you born?

2461 Common Era.

This is the exact same year as A.D. 2461?

Yes. But it is more scientific not to make any reference to any events, real or imagined, that may have taken place at the date from which the calendar is reckoned. Our purpose is to abolish all previous intellectual structures and to allow for perfect liberty of thought by erasing all previous record of accomplishments.

Whatever. How did you manage to survive until 3090, when the duel between De Ulloa and Montrose took place?

Your statement is inexcusably imprecise! It was not a duel; it was murder.

How do you figure?

The agreed-upon weapons of the duel were traditional self-propelled chemically powered ammunition. Instead, Montrose fired into the containment sphere, spilling dangerous radioactive material, in effect, using the radiation as a weapon, which is a clear violation of the code governing duels.

Why did the wreckage of the orbital terawatt laser happen to strike the mountain peak just at that point in time?

The Cetaceans used their weather-control system to heat the atmosphere excessively, and it expanded under this heat, so that the ceiling of the stratosphere was above the perigee of the orbital laser. This caused unexpected atmospheric breaking and sudden deorbit.

But why did it happen to strike that mountain peak at that time and place and no other?

After the terawatt laser platform was in the atmosphere, I was able to get close enough to it with a high-performance craft and take over its attitude jets by remote control. Solving the mathematical chaos-function of guiding an irregularly shaped rolling and tumbling mass was difficult but not impossible for one of my great intellectual accomplishments, and I guided the falling craft to its impact site, keeping pace with it in my craft. When I lost control of the attitude jets, I accidentally entered the turbulence of the wake, and the oxygen-burning ramjet choked. There was insufficient glidepath to switch back to rockets, and so I had to make an emergency landing.

Got it. So it was murder, and not a duel, because you tried to smear one of the duelists with an orbital deadfall, but it got your boss instead.

The statement is imprecise. The destruction of the terawatt laser was a necessity, since it was the last thing giving Montrose a direct military control over the planet. Obviously the outcome of a necessary act is also necessary, hence not blameworthy. On the other hand, the discharge of Montrose's pistol through the containment sphere was gratuitous, calculated to cause damage to De Ulloa, which led to his eventual death, which means it was murder.

And how did you survive from 2461 to 3090?

By hibernation, obviously.

But you were not in the Tombs.

I was in the Tombs of the Moon, beneath the Sea of Cunning on the Moon's dark side. There are working hibernation coffins aboard the hulk of the starship *Emancipation,* which is buried in the lunar dust there, and it was my Master's pleasure to thaw me only when he was thawed, so that he need not be deprived of my services by premature aging on my part.

Why is your skin white? Is it symbolic?

No. Natural melanin interferes with surface skin-cell reception and transmission.

But your race, the Psychics, are older than the first working Xypotech emulation, are they not? So why were you designed with this albinism feature? There was no system at that time to send and receive cybernetic neural information.

Highly Evolved Ximen del Azarchel designed the Scholar race with this functionality in mind, and had evidently already deduced the basic transmission properties xypotechnology emulation systems would one day have. We were designed to interface with machine intelligence and serve as adjuncts and auxiliaries from the very beginning. Highly Evolved Ximen del Azarchel never foresaw any prospect of forced-evolution to posthumanity via merely biological or biochemical augmentation.

During the duel, what did they say to each other?

Ambiguous pronoun.

De Ulloa and Montrose. You said that the two of them faced each other with long-range microphones. They obviously meant to talk before they shot. The old women hiding in ambush must have heard something, and you must have talked with them. What did they say?

De Ulloa said it would no longer be possible for Montrose to hide himself and his coffins on holy ground. The Uniate Orthodox-Catholic Church continued stubbornly to maintain a male hierarchy system, but the Simon Family revolution in gynolongevity meant that more and more prestige, money, power, and influence would pass inevitably from male to female hands. The Church was already dying, and the territory owned by the Maltese Knights would pass into the hands of some government friendly to the Delphic Order, at which point the Tombs would be forced open and the unwelcome and reactionary elements preserved from the past would be updated or eliminated.

This meant the end of Montrose and also of his way of life. His marriage to Rania and all marriages would be annulled.

De Ulloa predicted a world free of guilt and war and exoteric religion, since these are masculine characteristics. A world without property; a world where human beings lived gently on the land, leaving small pollution footprints. Religion hereafter would follow an esoteric ideal, and be permissive rather than restrictive. But most important, the restrictive intuitions known as marriage, as masculine–feminine constructions of grammar, and as private property would be obliterated. The masculine traits of certainty and objectivity would be eliminated from the human psyche, since these are controlling, domineering, aggressive, illegitimate. Contemplate that every genocidal war or torture regime in history was propagated by males certain of the objectivity of their beliefs! Eliminate the objectivity; eliminate the hostility.

Really? Is it objectively true that eliminating objectivity eliminates hostility? Or is that just a subjective opinion?

Question is not pertinent.

Sorry. How did De Ulloa plan to maintain a working industrial and scientific base of his new guilt-free society if there is no private property and no objective truth?

Would you like his exact words? Since they were the last words the unparalleled genius who was my Master ever spoke, I made special note of them, and my memory is precise.

6. Last Words

"Once society is totally feminine, the feminine principle of love, of sharing, of total acceptance and total toleration will overwhelm and annihilate the masculine institutions: the laws of language, the laws of thought, and the laws of government will be replaced by a holistic and all-embracing system of peace! Peace with other nations, races, tribes, and systems! Peace with Mother Earth! I do not wish for anything but the joy and happiness of mankind, gentleness, balance.

"But for this grand dream to work, the past must be utterly and absolutely destroyed!

"You see, we who are smarter than everyone else on the planet have further visions and more penetrating, and so our dream is better. That is merely logic, is it not? Since my dream is better, it must prevail, and anyone and anything that hinders or annoys my dream must be obliterated, and all memory of it erased. All tombstones must be blank: all Tombs must be empty.

"This is Year One of the new glory! This is the first day of the sovereign reign of the Delphic Acroamatic Progressive Transhumanitarian Order for the study of Longevity! The Order that establishes the future! There is no history to remember, no past to recall, no traditions: the past is a mistake.

"You must understand me, Montrose! You are like me. You live for the future!

"So we have to dig up your Tombs. We have to destroy the Giants. We have to destroy the past. In the new order, you cannot own a piece of the ground, and say this is mine and that is yours—the ground is your mother! The Earth is your grandmother! How can you own your mother? Your so-called marriage to Rania is nothing more than that: an attempt of the masculine to own and control the feminine."

7. The Reply

What did Montrose say? Is that remembered?

Yes. I could hear the whole exchange through my circuits. I know his exact words.

Menelaus Montrose said these words in this order, "Mulchie, I am convinced! The past has to be erased! Let's start with you."

And my master nobly answered: "We should have spaced you when we had the chance! Del Azarchel stopped us, but I was all for putting you out the air lock back that first moment on the punt, when you augmented your intelligence. You were trying to become smarter than me, so that you, not me, would have the moral right to do anything and everything you wanted! You should have died then and there. Well, ha! That is an error I can correct right now! You are part of the past, and the past is going to be scraped clean."

Brilliant words, are they not? So many levels of meaning! And Montrose said this:

"'Smarter than I.' Anyhow, Mulchface, there is one bit of the past you cannot erase. Remember the time you tried to break into my mountain using the Giants? Banging on my roof and waking me up when I need my beauty sleep? You recollect that? Well, I don't cotton to trespassers. Keep the hell out of my yard." Then he opened fire. At about the same moment, the falling space platform landed between them. There were no words thereafter.

14

Rumpelstiltskin and the Widow

1. Description and Deception

At this point, Illiance lightly reached up and touched Menelaus on the elbow, saying "Available time happens to be diminishing, Lance-Corporal Beta Anubis. Perhaps a more useful line of inquiry would be to ask him for a description of Menelaus Montrose."

Menelaus frowned down at him. "Are you expecting to recognize him based on what someone says he looks like when you are cracking open Tombs? What makes you think this Mount Woes is at this site?"

Illiance said, "We believe there are eighty-nine sites worldwide. An examination of the defenses and architecture, taken in context with the surrounding data, allows us to deduce the pattern of goals of the Tomb Architects. Mentor Ull has run a calculation assuming there is but one master Architect, the Judge of Ages. From this model, we can deduce his means and methods, create a model of his general intellectual and emotive environment, organize all the data into personality modes and neurolinguistic speech-act sets, and use a negative information contrivance to deduce retroactively his behavioral strategies and inflexibilities, extrapolating forward again to his current reality, which will include his physical location."

"Unless he decided to stop somewhere for a cup of coffee, or to take a bath."

"While it is true that a sufficiently complete model will also make allowances for fuzzy logic semivariables, such as spontaneous impulses, it was thought best to obtain a physical description of his person, should he be standing among us even now."

"That is a creepy thought. If he is standing among us, have you made out your last will and testament?"

"The question is fascinating on several levels, for it presupposes a moral obligation among survivors to follow the anachronistic wishes of a person who, being dead on a neural hence also linguistic level, can neither be informed nor express pleasure nor displeasure touching how and whether those wishes are carried out: it also presupposes individual determination of property, which is an awkward concept, even antisocial. And yet this fascinating discussion, being not of the highest priority, is best regarded as a future event, or a subjunctive one."

"I am not sure what you said."

"My will is to discover the Judge of Ages. Please obtain a description."

Menelaus spoke into the microphone in Spanish. He listened carefully for a moment.

The voice in Spanish said to Menelaus, "Of course I know him. I stood within arm's reach of him, and the fame of my bloodline comes from him! He is a gaunt and ungainly like a puppet made of sticks. His hair is red, his eyes pale blue, his face is all bone, his chin sticks out, and his nose is like a great hook used to open a crate. There are scars on his hands, and his right arm is bigger than his left. He is the ugliest man alive."

Menelaus nodded, and turned, and said in High Iatric to Illiance, "The Scholar Rada Lwa says the Judge is *el mulato,* a swarthy man, not too tall, with some gray hair above his ears. He is silent and grim, but very handsome. He wears robes the color of blood, and artificial hair to his shoulder, much like the hair the Scholars are wont to wear. No man can look in his eyes: and an aura of majesty and terror surrounds him. He carries a brace of pistols, and many knives hidden on his person, and a metal whip hidden in his sash."

Illiance briefly lost his normally serene expression. "This is a statistically unlikely development! There is little chance that two men from two different millennia coordinated a deceptive story. The description matches with an usual degree of correlation the elements revealed by Kine Larz! Ask him if the Judge of Ages has small hands—that is an element Kine Larz mentioned."

Menelaus again spoke the fluid language into the microphone, saying, "I am Menelaus Montrose now before you. My hands are on the controls of the coffin you are in. If you betray me, or tell any living soul who I am, I will release chemicals to castrate and lobotomize you, leaving you with just enough intelligence that you will forever remember how smart you once were and what purpose your limp and withered manhood once served. Are you going to do what Grampa says? I have readouts of your neural activity and blood pressure and galvanic skin response, so if you lie, it will be your last clear thought."

The voice spoke in a cold and defiant tone. "First Ancestor, if you would deter falsehoods, you mutinous traitor, choke on your own! You are honor-bound never to harm one who falls into your coffins. I cannot and shall not be deterred! Once you shamed me—across the aeons I have waited, and will spend my life gladly, exactly, merely for the opportunity to do you hurt, howsoever small!"

Menelaus nodded sagely and turned to Illiance, saying, "He says he has hands like a surgeon, with fine and tapering fingers."

Illiance was so pleased that he actually hopped like a little boy and clapped his hands. It was a somehow disquieting sight. "Mentor Ull will no doubt be pleased with this clear and definitive information! The testimony of Kine Larz is substantiated to a degree that no further need remains to delay an attempt on the Tomb doors."

But Aanwen said in Intertextual, *"A cautious reconsideration may at this point be strongly advisable, Invigilator Illiance. While the relict word-forms are unknown, a mathematical analysis of the syllable number and pitch and other nonverbal channels of information indicate Rada Lwa's message-volume cannot map onto the volume uttered by the man pretending to be a Chimera. Also voice rhythm and intensity are disproportionate for the subject matter: this was a signifier of emotional distress inappropriate to a discussion of the size of someone's hands. A deceptive mistranslation is the likeliest explanation."*

Illiance turned toward Menelaus and said in Iatric, "What else did Scholar Rada Lwa happen to say?"

Menelaus said, "He is complaining of pain as the thaw process nears completion, and requests a dose of morphine or some other heavy sedative. I think he is a little upset because of the pain that is creeping up on him. You and me had a deal, Illiance! Tell the Widow Aanwen, please, to anesthetize the patient. I am not going to question a man in pain."

Aanwen said in Intertextual, *"There happen to be none of the neurological or endocrinal signs displayed on my medical feeds consistent with the relict experiencing pain. Again, a deception is being practiced."*

At that moment, the voice from the coffin began speaking in loud, harsh, wrathful tones.

Illiance said, "What does he say?"

With a jerk of his arm, Menelaus yanked the microphone out of its jack. Silence fell. Menelaus said, "He is excitable, because he thinks I am torturing him. He does not realize I am a fellow prisoner, and so he evinces undue hostility."

Illiance said, "If so, why did you disconnect the voice channel so suddenly?"

"Ah! As a Chimera, am honor-bound to avenge any threats uttered against me in a fashion of horrific violence. But if I beat up a pasty-ass albino bookworm in a coffin, weak from torture, all the cool Chimerae will laugh at me. So I had to make sure I did not hear anything he was about to say."

Illiance turned and looked up, regarding Menelaus with a composed, calm, yet thoughtful expression. Menelaus tried not very successfully to arrange an innocent look on his lank features. Neither man spoke.

2. A Sport

Eventually, Illiance broke the silence. "Would you regard us as friends?"

Menelaus shrugged, a gesture that made his robes clatter. "'Sokay with me if 'sokay with you."

Illiance blinked. "Cogent meaning fails to be conveyed, perhaps due to dialect or idiosyncrasy of speech. I will ask again. Do you aver the mutual moral obligations that surround friendship to obtain between us, Lance-Corporal Beta Sterling Anubis?"

"And I am a Corporal Anubis now. I was promoted."

"Congratulations."

"And I can extend what you call a mutual moral obligation only to some degree to a man holding me prisoner. But that is not what friendship is. Friendship is liking someone, sticking by him, come hellfire or plague. And I like you. Sort of. What brought this question on?"

"I cannot be so in error in my calculations. You clearly understand our speech, and yet you act as if you do not, nor can I determine the pattern nor point of this behavior. You are not a Chimera, but somehow the Chimerae take you for one. This is a paradox, since the Chimera are well known for their race pride, and their deadly intent toward any who claim a genetic heritage above proper privilege and rank. I deliberately drew back the Followers and left the Chimerae free to kill you when you went by stealth to the dig site, but the Chimerae did not carry through as expected. But neither could a Chimera of ordinary intelligence be deceived on this point."

Menelaus said, "That is easily explained. I am a Chimera from a period when the Eugenics Board attempted several novel experiments, including mixing surviving dawn-age gene groups into the bloodlines. It was thought that by taking the strains from several famous ancient mathematicians, we could breed for someone able to understand the lost and ancient sciences of the Giants. My family was one of those academic breeds. There were some irregularities in my cocktail, so I don't look much like a normal Chimera. Genetically, I am a sport or mutant."

Illiance nodded. "That is certainly a clever explanation, and it fits many of the facts in the pattern of data. I am impressed with the workmanship of the falsehood."

"Thanks."

"I suppose you can also explain away the appearance of intermittent acts of genius on your part by saying this is due to the presence of ancient genework from these dawn-men mathematicians, who were much advanced in intelligence?"

Menelaus drew himself up, "Why, Preceptor Illiance! Are you suggesting that, after Preceptor Yndech commanded me to eschew deception, I would do anything else?"

"I am Invigilator Illiance now. I was demoted."

"Not if you go tell Ull you have proof that Larz wasn't lying, and that Rada Lwa confirms his story."

"Who are you?"

"Who do you think I could be? An ugly Nymph? A hairless Hormagaunt? A big Locust? A small Giant? No, strike that last suggestion. I cannot be from *before* the Chimera Age, can I? Not if I know enough to pass for one."

Aanwen said in singsong Intertextual, *"I theorize that this is one of the servants of the Judge of Ages."*

3. Lack of Caution

Aanwen continued: *"He is Tomb Guardian, a Maltese Knight, and his purpose is to preserve the integrity of the Tombs."*

Illiance answered: *"Unlikely. His coffin was found among the others, indiscriminate, and in the stratum expected for interments of circa A.D. 5290. Were he a Knight Hospitalier, where is his equine and equipage?"*

Aanwen: *"Note that he became violent when and only when the coffin equipment was being used to torment a relict: note the correlative that a Hospitalier would have a moral obligation to protect all clients. This theory accounts for his skill at empty-handed combat, and also for his abnormal proficiency in cryotechnology."*

Illiance tilted his ear as if listening, but did not take his eyes from Menelaus. *"I am perturbed at your lack of caution. He understands our speech, and he controls the coffin weapons, and has already shown an ability to defeat our personal aggressive attempts. Your words, if selected with less than perfect caution, will cause him to attack us—is that not so,* Sterlingas Anupsu-phalangetor?"

Menelaus stared at him blankly. "Come again? Did you say my name?"

Aanwen said. *"Draw your weapon when I draw mine. Aim for his eyes, and I will aim for his lower legs. The beams will be undiffused by the tent material."*

Illiance did not reach for his pistol, but instead he closed his eyes and drew in a breath through his nose and breathed out through his mouth, a long, slow breath. He did this a second and a third time. When he opened his eyes again, they were clear and limpid as deep pools reflecting a windless summer sky.

Aanwen said, *"Fear not! We are in no immediate danger. You have not perceived the mental fixtures that limit his actions. He will continue to pretend not to understand us no matter what we say. Psychologically, he cannot be a Chimera, since I uttered an unretaliated threat. Recall his blood pressure change when he discovered I was a revenant. As of that moment, I became protected by the same mental fixture or honor code that requires him to protect the albino."*

Illiance said dryly, *"But by the same token, he is aware of our mental fixtures that require we fire only in self-defense. A Chimera who perceived the inadequacy of your threat might also condescend to ignore it. And, because you have told him, he is also now aware that the internal sensitives of the tent material he wears continue to broadcast his medical data to us."*

She said, *"How can you be so blind? That is not a Chimera! Observe the antics of this man and compare them to the known genetic behavior markers of the Chimerae. Where is his Caste-based xenophobia? He does not have the cooperation code in his biohardware, neither in its original late-era Witch form, nor in its later perverted Chimera-era form. And there is no evidence of a second animal spliced into him. This implies he has accomplished an unprecedented level of deception, both on us and on other relicts in the camp. We don't know who or what he is. This indicates a danger. In order to simplify the variables of a complex problem, we must eliminate the anomaly source: all the recent unexpected events, disappearances and mal-behavior among the Followers can be back-analyzed to a single source. Him! We must open fire."*

Illiance turned toward her, putting his hand on his pistol grip, and said, *"Will the pistol emulator comprehend his deception to be a form of trespass for which violent retaliation is permitted?"*

Aanwen did not answer, for she was staring at Montrose's face. Illiance, seeing the direction of the gaze, snapped his head around.

The lanky face of the redhead was flushed with astonishment, mouth hanging open, as if someone had struck him in the gut. But oddest of all were his eyes, which seemed to blaze with a superhuman magnetism, but also seemed to open like two, deep, pallid tunnels into interior infinities. He was staring at the pistol in Aanwen's hand.

Illiance found he could not meet that gaze; Aanwen also flinched, blinking.

Almost at the same moment, as if realizing he had lost control of his expression, Menelaus drew his hood closely about his features with an abrupt snap, and he turned his back to the puzzled Aanwen and Illiance.

Illiance said, *"Again, I would be grateful for your wisdom."*

She said, *"The mission is endangered. Summon Followers. He will kill us, they will kill him, and the remainder of our order will continue, without undue perturbation to the flow of events."*

Illiance shook his head. *"While insightful, the proposal lacks several attractive prospects."*

Aanwen said, *"What matter our two lives? The Bell is coming. Summon the Followers, Docent Illiance! Or I will."*

Illiance said, *"With respect, you shall not. You have not seen clearly. You reason like a Locust, weighing one life against another. This is inelegant. Sometimes the simplest solution truly is best."*

And, without a further word or sign, Illiance turned and glided smoothly and without hurry out of the chamber, and the cobra pattern of gemstones glinted on the shoulders and back of his long blue coat as he moved away.

4. Simple Solution

Both Aanwen and Menelaus stared in astonishment after the retreating back of Illiance for a moment. Then the smooth slope of the curving corridor hid him from view.

Menelaus looked down at her just as she looked up at him, as if they both were surprised to catch themselves staring. He met her eyes, and smiled and shrugged.

He turned, stepped closer to the coffin, and reached out with both hands, touching several control points. The alert lights on the coffin housing winked to a new configuration.

Aanwen said in Iatric, "You are familiar with how to operate the coffin machinery?"

"Yes, ma'am. More 'n I'd like to be. I've seen so many coffins in my life, it makes me sick."

"I hope you will recover your health in due time. This coffin before us itself is slightly damaged, but I notice you reshunted the compositional of a soporific compound you have introduced into the albino into a holding tube and flushed the main cache: this is not the normal procedure, but it bypassed a broken feeder tube, whose existence you must have deduced from an anomaly in the back-pressure. You also adjusted the dose correctly for his body mass and type and hypoallergenic spectrum. I wonder at this display of casual expertise on your part, you being a soldier."

Menelaus said, "More of a schoolteacher than a soldier, really. I have slumbered and thawed many times, and as part of my payment to the Tomb officers, I served as an apprentice to them, scrubbing floors, doing routine maintenance, and so on. Some simple coffin repair . . . basic medical nanotechnology . . . troubleshooting . . . You know . . . a fellow picks these things up. . . ." Menelaus made a vague gesture in the air. "I am going to tranquilize him, throw him over my shoulder, and walk back to the camp, on account of there is no place else in this world I can go. You got the answers you wanted, I got my albino, we both walk out happy. How does that set with you? Any reason why your dogs will prevent me from going through the gate if I am going in?"

"Who are you, really?"

"Rumpelstiltskin. I know Nymph sciences that can make it so you can fall in love again, and mate and marry, and bring forth a firstborn child. Think about that child. If you set your dogs on me, well, I lose my life and you never get to give that child his. If I passed away, I'd rather have my wife wed again, find some sort of happiness. Wouldn't your husband have said the same? So think about him too."

"You are married? This is not a Chimerical custom."

"Ma'am, if you studied the period of our atom wars, you know all our old customs fell into anarchy, and isolated towns like mine returned to some of the older and saner laws, like monogamy."

"What is it about our pistols that you find remarkable?"

He put out his hand. "I'll show you."

With no expression on her face whatever, nor any hesitation, Aanwen surrendered to him the energy weapon.

He stepped over to where her instruments lay scattered, stooped, and picked up a splicing knife. With the point of the knife, he pried under the carapace of jewels that coated the weapon, found a catch, wiggled the blade, and the casing opened, exposing the unadorned barrel. The barrel was a short cylinder made of a set of telescoping rings.

Menelaus tapped the rings with the knife point and elicited a chiming sound. "This is one of our named weapons."

"Do not say *our* named weapons, for you cannot be a Chimera. Your psycholinguistic structure does not allow for it."

"Whatever. This is a serpentine. Or a segment of one. You are using the tiny set of onboard brains to control the waveguide. The energy actually comes from the gems, which are logic crystals, and you just added a grip and a trigger. The grip holds an amplifier that heterodynes various deadly energies onto the coherent aiming ray the gems generate. Simple, elegant, but how in the hell did this technology persist all the time from the Sylph period?"

Aanwen blinked her large and long-lashed eyes in confusion, an expression so similar to what he had often seen on Illiance's face, like hearing a familiar theme of music transposed to a higher key, that Menelaus laughed to behold a feminine version. She looked like Illiance's sister.

She said, "They are the only truly self-repairing machines ever devised. An unconfirmed historical report alludes to seven forms of the divarication problem. An ancient and unknown mathematician produced the first two solutions, called the self-correction code and the copycat code, and invested the ratiotechs with a partial self-awareness and checking system so that they could not evolve into Xypotechs. Then the Master of the World—he was one of the original members of the expedition to the Monument—"

"Yeah, I've heard of him."

"—created the Simon Families, who are the predecessors from whom the Witches spring, organizing in their ancestral stock a genetically promulgated instinct to discover and obsess over mathematical patterns of the type used in the self-correction code. The Simon Family women studied the serpentines and retroengineered the more general solution from which the copycat code was derived. Only the serpentines are simple enough computing appliances to be fully self-eternal. More complex systems suffer breakdown. The Simon Families used this more general solution to deduce the secret of female longevity. This is why females of the Witch race outlive the males by five or ten times the lifespan. Why are you laughing?"

"Ma'am, I'll explain it to you someday. Promise, I will. But I just figured out an old friend of mine snookered me blind."

"Cogent meaning fails to be conveyed."

"A man who knows me well played on my feeling sorry for a bunch of dim-witted drifters, and got me to fix a problem for them, which I wanted to do, but he guessed my methods, and so I solved a problem for him that I damn well did not want to. What the hell is he building, and where on Earth is he building it? *Or off Earth?*"

"Why do you laugh? Among us, that laughter-event is caused by an ellipsis of parallel thoughts turning skew."

"Oh, I am laughing because of the joy I will feel when I blow his head off, and see his blood and brain stuffs mixed with bone fragments splurched like a drop-kicked tomato across the field of blighted, damnified, pestilential, perdition-bound, god-forsaken, god-damned honor."

Menelaus snapped shut the pistol housing and pushed with both thumbs to engage the catch.

She looked at him oddly, almost coyly. "Perhaps my assessment erred. That is in keeping with the mental speech-thought structure of the Chimerae. Will you allow me depart unharmed?"

"Surely and with much thanks," said Menelaus. He pointed the pistol at the floor and pulled the trigger. Nothing happened; there was no noise. He laughed again and tossed the weapon back to her. She caught it awkwardly in both hands. She pointed it at him, and now a soft hum came from the pistol, and the gemstones adorning it began to glitter.

Aanwen said, "You could have killed me with your left hand just now, when I raised both hands to intercept the thrown object."

"Yes, ma'am, I surely could have, had I been a mind to. And you should give your weapon a respectable name. You'll embarrass her if you call her just 'object.'"

"Yet if you are truly a Chimera, you must attack me if I utter a threat, is it not so?"

"Ma'am, there is two things you ain't taking into account. First, according to the divarication function, any information about the past gets eroded into simpler, easier to transmit forms as it goes down the generations. The surviving stories about us are simplistic. The real-life Chimera code, as practiced by real, live Chimerae, was actually rather organic, subtle, and legalistic. We don't have to attack a schoolmarm who has a toy pistol that cannot shoot until I throw a punch. No offense, but you are not a real threat."

"And the second?"

"Ma'am, begging your pardon, but I surely am not attacking no widow woman. My mother was a widow since the same year I was born."

"Why did you let Illiance walk away?"

"Uh, shucks. I like him. Sort of. I am not one of you blue freaks, but sometimes even I admire a simple solution to a difficult problem."

And she also simply turned her back and walked smoothly down the curving slope of the seashell corridor and out of sight.

15

The Calculus of Fate

1. Arsenal

He had been hoping that the coffin's motive system would be intact, so that he could merely leave the patient inside and order it to follow him: but the damage to the treads and millipede legs would have required a machine shop and replacement stock to fix.

Menelaus discovered the footlocker had not been looted, and so Rada Lwa's original clothes, including his Scholar robes, hood, and mortarboard were untouched. He wrapped the drugged body of the albino carefully in the robes. Didn't want the man to freeze. And he put the flat, square cap on the man's head to keep his scalp warm.

Also in the footlocker was a one-piece undergarment of thick silver fabric. The undergarment had a web of input-output ports, caches, and amplifier-transmitter beads he did not want anyone with a highly cyborged nervous system to wear, particularly if Ctesibius was correct and every snowflake they were about to walk over was sophont matter. He put that on himself, and was pleased to find it had two large web belts. He had to cut open the inseam of the garment legs, however, because he was taller than Rada Lwa, so the loose legs dangled below.

Since Rada Lwa's interment was penal rather than voluntary, Menelaus did not fret himself over appropriating the man's gear for the common good. It was not like Rada Lwa was really a client.

He was able to dismount two of the railguns from the coffin hull. Each railgun had two-foot-long accelerator wands and a bulbous drum of slurry, but without a proper stock. The subsonic weapon was six feet long, but it was pliant like a garden hose, and could be rolled up.

Ambitious, he took the time to unbolt and extract the antipersonnel laser emitter along with cord and power pack only to discover after the bulky unit was lying on the floor before him (box, emission tube, cords, and all) that the power pack was at one-eighth charge. Enough for about fifteen seconds of action continuous, three times that if used in pulse mode; maybe three minutes, or at lower power, just to burn out eyes and soft tissue.

He realized there must have been a stern fight with this particular coffin. He shook the slurry drums on the rail guns and heard that they were half empty. This meant a second or two of "spray and pray"–type fire, or twenty shots of high-caliber fire, or forty of lower caliber, depending on the desired burst pattern. There were no bullets in this design: the ammunition was a viscous fluid or mud with a high metallic content, ejected supersonically by a linear accelerator.

Menelaus suddenly paused and cocked his ear. There came the rumbling murmur of many engines starting at once. It was the sputtering and coughing of internal combustion engines, as sound he recalled from his youth, millennia ago. There was also the deeper note, and a whining roar, both high-pitched and subsonic, the cracking din of many helicopter blades being spun up to speed. Then, a crescendo like many thunders, the jackhammer sound rose into the air, and then slowly began to diminish, moving farther away.

Only then did he realize how long he had been toiling over the coffin, how many minutes he had been unscrewing, unwinding, unbolting. Too long. He should have been interrupted before this.

He decided it was time to go.

He was able to maneuver the heavy laser into the large shoulder pouch that formed the back of the garment, and he tied the looming emission tube with the loop of the sonic hose so it would not bang into his head when he walked. The web belts from the Scholar's undergarment he crossed over his chest and shoulders like bandoliers, and they were heavy enough that he could sling from them, if awkwardly, two of the railguns he had looted. If he timed his step and swayed his hips just right, the long barrels would not bark his legs. The subsonic weapon he was able to sling across his shoulders.

There was no hope of hiding such large weapons, even under such a bulky robe as his. For good luck, he slipped the splicing knife into the baglike fold of tent material that served him as a sleeve. He thought about scraping some of the lichen from the walls and using the sublimation properties to make an impromptu tear gas: but there was no time.

He wrestled Rada Lwa over his shoulder, only dropping him once. Menelaus muttered, "In the pixies, Captain Sterling was always flinging a wounded crewman or cute space girls in short skirts over his shoulder. Guess it's harder when they are not a wide-awake actor trying to hold still."

One hand wrapped around Rada Lwa, his heavy weapons tangled with his legs beneath his sweeping metallic cloak, and feeling like a one-man army, he strode with a confident step down the sloping ramp.

He wondered that there had been no other personal possessions in the footlocker aside from the garments. A Scholar would certainly carry a library cloth, if nothing else. Then he used his implants to examine the transmission beads dotting the stolen garment he was wearing. In a moment he had found Rada Lwa's library.

2. The Notes

Menelaus could use his implants to copy the data directly into his cortex. Menelaus paused when he saw the ownership line: Rada Lwa had been a servant in the Cryonarchy before Menelaus had robbed them of their political power. After the fall of the Cryonarchy, he severed his connection to the Montrose Clan and sought out their enemies, the Hermetic Order.

Nothing else in the library was of any particular interest to Menelaus except the notebooks on mathematics, which were extensive.

It seemed that De Ulloa had been teaching Rada Lwa Cliometry, and had taken a section from Del Azarchel's predictions for the forty-fifth century as an example. This was a scrap from Del Azarchel's own work, a listing of the social influences, their vector amounts, and the decision forks, all laid out neat and nice in a fourteen-dimensional matrix of ninety thousand variables.

Menelaus realized what he was reading. He was thunderstruck by astonishment and anger so palpable that he could actually feel it race down his spine and weaken his limbs, so that he almost dropped Rada Lwa again.

Then he shrugged and decided to go ahead and drop Rada Lwa one more time anyway, just because he was in the mood for that. (He did not kick the unconscious man, however, because he was feeling so very merciful: Menelaus congratulated himself on his forbearance.)

Appended to the predictions for the forty-fifth century was an executive summary: *At or about this point in time, the 51 will introduce a biochemical-psychology code system to allow the various nonhuman sapient creatures Prometheanized by the Simon Families to cooperate.*

The Simon Families were the precursors to the Delphic World Order, or, in other words, the Witches. The 51 was himself, his locker and suit number from the NTL star-vessel *Hermetic*. Prometheus Augmentation was Montrose's own process he had discovered and inflicted on himself. He had released the secret to Thucydides Montrose, who used it to augment the intellect of the Giants to superhuman levels. De Ulloa and his Witches had taken it in turn and used it to augment animal intelligence to human levels.

The prediction about Montrose was eerily accurate. Menelaus had indeed introduced in and about the region of Lake Superior before the brief Re-Industrial Age of the Nameless Warlock Empire in the forty-fifth century a genetic-political arrangement, coded as biohardware, that he called the cooperation code. This cooperation code was based on Rania's work, her solution to the so-called selfish meme problem: the Witches had been suffering a particularly acute version of that problem. Their social system incentivized and overrewarded what Montrose called "meme envy"—the tendency of any information system, either a computer system or a human economy, to copy and borrow from successful systems it encountered to the degree that the original information is lost. Piracy was encouraged and originality discouraged.

Montrose had used an application of Rania's Divarication solution to discover a game-theory method to allow the endocrinal and instinctive priorities of the Witches and their Moreaus to harmonize over generations, so that cooperation rather than coercion was a possible basis for human–Moreau relations. A civilization based on free trade and free inquiry followed naturally.

Menelaus bitterly remembered how, back in the forty-fifth century, he had so confidently assumed Blackie would never have clues enough to reverse engineer the mathematical tools used to reach the cooperation code solution from merely seeing the outcome, but not knowing how the outcome was reached. That assumption was disastrously false. It seemed the Witches were witches in truth: somehow able to intuit conclusions on partial information as if by magic, that normal reasoning could not reach.

In Rada Lwa's text, the chain of statistical predictors describing what Montrose would do ended in a strange attractor—with a side note stating that, at this point, history had to be derailed due to direct intervention by a Hermeticist.

At this node a new race will be introduced by Narcís D'Aragó. The exact details cannot be predicted, but we can predict via multiparallel intuitive deduction that D'Aragó will take the solution, whatever it is, introduced by the Traitor in an earlier era and reselect the social variables for unification.

—and then, in broad strokes, the notes laid out what Menelaus recognized as the fundamental psychological skeleton of the Chimerical psychology and predictive history. He recognized it from his own attempts, made many centuries after this was written, to graph out the basics of Chimera historical nodes, nests, and attractors.

That prediction (or perhaps it was a command) was also accurate. D'Aragó had stolen and perverted Montrose's work. D'Aragó had used it to make the men and animal-people one race, and as tolerant of diversity as any military order. (In Montrose's day, there had been no beaneaters, Anglos, Odds, or Tejas in the service, only Texans; and no white men, black men, or red men in the cavalry, only horsemen.)

But D'Aragó had reversed the markers to install a Caste system, where each Caste was genetically programmed to be intolerant of other Castes.

Montrose smiled a sour smile. "Oh, Draggy, you always admired the Hindus, didn't you? Never got over that envy you felt growing up in a world where the world's foremost superpower, the Indosphere, had a caste system. Your Hispanosphere was trying so desperately to play catch-up and me-too. *They* had a caste system, and you thought *you* should have one too. It was so very efficient and scientific and fashionable and up to date . . . in the twenty-second century . . . eight thousand three hundred years ago. . . ."

Just the mention of the amount of time passed gave him a sensation of painful nostalgia. It had been only twenty years or so biological time for him. He wondered at all the things that were gone and would never come again: the palaces and pinnacles and towers and skyscrapers of civilizations that had faded and dispersed like so many columns of rising smoke, broken up in the wind.

Montrose picked up the unconscious Rada Lwa one last time, and awkwardly hauled him to his shoulder. As he walked, he talked aloud. "Sorry, Rada Lwa, Grampa was just talking to my old friend D'Aragó who I shot dead and put in the ground. Him and your boss, your real boss, the Machine Exarchel—and hell, let's give dopey Melchor de Ulloa some credit too, he had a hand in this—y'all has me powerful confounded and bewildered.

"The Giants made the Simon Families—that is clear enough. Blackie snookered them into creating their own destroyers. That I did not figure. The Giants lashed out and burned all the places where you could hide a Xypotech—all but up on the Moon.

"Did the Simons create the Sylphs? Or was that a natural development?

"Don't matter. In any case, the Giants were tickled, tricked, and led into putting in place restrictions on xypotechnology that created an impossible computational and social problem for the Sylphs in their airskiffs. A problem I solved using Rania's work. Work Del Azarchel knew I had, but had never seen himself.

"The damn serpentines are eternal machines. But that was a side effect, a mistake. Del Azarchel should have cleaned up that clue from the stream of history, and buried legends of it. Or, hell, maybe he did, but in my damn Tomb system, the one you tried to destroy, Ratty Low, you low rat, I keep these little fragments of history, including people who don't want to live through periods the Hermeticists control.

"Are you paying attention? Or am I just speaking to a sleeping man's really pale butt? Lemme explain: De Ulloa, your Master, is a guy who (before you killed him for me) spent his whole life on a project, a real long life—but there was no project.

"The whole civilization of the Witches from start to stop—it was a smoke screen, a cover, a hoax.

"A hoax aimed at me. They put everything in that society, from their economics to their marriage customs to their tree-hugging, everything I would despise and want to . . . fix.

"Sure, I knew the Chimerae were reverse in their genetic-sociopsychology from the Witches, but I always thought the Witches used their own biotech to plant those elements in the Chimerae—they were gene-tinkerers, after all, and pretty good ones whenever their strict communist coven system broke down, and they'd have the resources to devote to research.

"But no. D'Aragó did it. That was the plan from the first. The damn society of the damn Witches was falling to pieces, and if civilization falls and don't get back up again in time, then there is no one to fight the Hyades at the End of Days. So I had to do something!

"And Blackie knew I had to do something.

"Over a thousand years of war, genocides, mass manipulation of the gene plasm, ruined lives, world conquests, not to mention slavery and even cannibalism—it was all a plot, a plan, a fake. A thousand years of civilization forced into a particular channel just so that I would thaw out for a few months here and there and solve the mistakes in their genetic, psychological, and social order using one of the seven derived keys of Rania's elegant solution to the divarication problem.

"But who manipulated the Witch civilization into such an plumb rank outhouse of a world piss-poorer than Job's turkey? Wasn't De Ulloa . . . That boy was dim, but damn sincere. He had sincerity on him like stink on a skunk."

"Sweet Jesus up a tree! Did Blackie let an entire civilization across the entire world run itself into the ground and did he let De Ulloa get himself shot, burned, and nuked to bits just to winkle a bit of math code out of me?

"Or was De Ulloa *in on it*? Did he betray the whole civilization that was his brain child, all the Witches who thought he was their Washington and their Moses? Was that the real reason he shot himself?"

He again examined the scrap of Cliometric notes he had found. The Cliometric equations in the notebook cut off at the point in history that marked the revolt and the rise of the Chimerae (here called simply "projected biohomogenized race").

De Ulloa had shown Rada Lwa the plan for the downfall of the Witches. De Ulloa revealed the mathematics of the apocalypse, and the final end days of his Witches, his beloved racial experiment in a world civilization based on communal harmony and kinship with lesser creatures. De Ulloa either did not know, or had not been shown, or simply did not share with his vassal Rada Lwa, the plan for history after his period.

The time stamp on the files in the notebook was A.D. 2580.

Presumably, that was about the time Del Azarchel went into long-term hibernation, and turned over control of history to Melchor de Ulloa. Montrose had sent out scholars and geneticists from his Tombs in A.D. 3950 to introduce the cooperation code and set in motion the chain of events leading to the founding of the Nameless Empire, one of his two attempts to save the Witch civilization from its own folly. The revolts of the Chimerae began in A.D. 4460, and the defeat of the Final Sabbat at Baffington's Island was in A.D. 4888. But that attempt, that folly, those revolts, and that defeat had all been planned out two thousand two hundred years before: it would be as if Augustus Caesar had foreseen and planned the launch of the of the NTL *Hermetic*.

"So Blackie fooled me twice. I used the self-correction code to perfect the serpentines—Damn, and Sir Guy even warned me this would happen!—Blackie reverse engineered it, and that is how he finally made emulations of his surviving men. I helped him create the posthuman versions of the Hermeticists I have been fighting all these millennia.

"De Ulloa used my Prometheus intelligence augmentations on animals, and increased their intellect to human levels, but created a world of hell, because intelligent bunnies and intelligent wolves cannot sit down in a Town Hall and vote what to have for lunch. The Witch setup could never have worked, because the problems with a multispecies culture were built in at a structural level. Herbivores just don't think like carnivores. They place a different value on risk and loyalty and different ideas of courage and different toleration for cruelty and on and on.

"But with the Nameless Empire period, I actually cobbled together something to allow the Witch system to work. Problem-solver Crazy Montrose, that's me! I introduced a new type of coven called a 'familia' with one patriarch leader, and a harem of one and only one wife, and with children under the coven leader's strict control. And property was 'sacred' to the lares, the household gods, of each familia. Pretty clever, eh, Ratty Low? They were Witches in name only, but they actually had families and private property and rule of law.

"But that was the surface. Below the surface, I had to reengineer the Moreaus, so they would breed themselves toward more cooperative forms. And I had to use another part of Rania's divarication solution to do it. The cooperation code. And D'Aragó used that in a twisted backward way to create his Chimerae. And then . . . I thawed—"

Another thought struck Menelaus, a thought he should have seen years, or centuries before, if not millennia.

"And then . . . I thawed out again, because of D'Aragó. He broke into the Tombs to try to kill me as I slept, and I had to stop him. And so I had to teach him a hard lesson. And, of course, while I was awake, I saw the problem with the Chimera civilization, and the screwed-on-backwards-headedness their organizational principles, and I saw the rot and corruption caused by divarication both genetic and sociological and . . ."

When reduced to a mathematical code, the social, political, and biological errors of the Chimera system formed a classical problem in divarication: a positive feedback violence loop or negative-sum game.

It could be, of course, analyzed in terms of another divarication problem, to which Montrose could apply yet another one of Rania's seven keys of her general solution.

The solution was to introduce into every information unit a "dyad" or permanent pair of mutually reinforcing units so that one unit cannot reproduce of itself. The second unit of the pair interrupts negative-sum cycles. In biology, this was done by evolving from asexual to sexual reproduction; but in sociology, by introducing a second carrier outside the normal education channels, without which the social information cannot be carried to the next generation, such as an oral tradition, church, or mass-media entertainment complex: in this case, he used the Lotus Cults he had already found among the lower ranks of Chimera society.

And that was when Montrose had introduced the original Greencloak portable neurochemical biofeedback backpack systems, which is the first (and in some ways, least significant) part of the Hermetic Secret of Youth, a system for preventing, or even artificially reweaving and restoring, lost telomere length. The restorative also contained an enzyme code to produce a mild euphoric, something to prevent the buildup of adrenaline-habituated rage patterns in the endocrine system. It was a euphoric that also lengthened life span, and because it was chemical rather than genetic, none of the normal Chimera techniques of breeding away undesirable characteristics would work to prevent its spread.

The attempt was meant to expand Kine and Chimera life spans to Witch longevity levels or beyond, so as to break the Chimera out of the perverted version of the cooperation code Narcís D'Aragó had genetically hardwired into their nervous systems. The idea was that a long-lived race would react to long-term incentives and disincentives, and begin to learn the futility of war, and become more peaceful—

"Sweet Jesus up a tree! Did Blackie send D'Aragó into the Tombs to kill me just to trick me into waking up during that period of time? Blackie let one of his own men get shot to death by me, just in the hope that when I walked away from the killing ground, I might look around at the suffering and see what was wrong with the Chimera civilization and see what needed to be done to fix it?"

For the second time in his life, Menelaus felt that frozen, helpless, wrathful sensation which must have been (he was sure) Blackie Del Azarchel's constant companion: the realization that there was someone smarter than he was, more ruthless, more willing to do whatever it took, whether to sacrifice or betray friends or loyal followers or whole worlds of innocent men—the realization that the foe was colder than ice on Pluto, harder and stronger than carbon-quenched steel, deadlier than a rattlesnake and twice as poisonous.

The first time had been when Blackie won their first duel.

Menelaus used to have a recurring nightmare that he was called out to a duel, standing and waiting for dawn in some deserted graveyard or empty park, to find himself not only without his gun, but without his clothing as well, and he had to explain to the seconds and the judges and doctor watching the duel why he left his pants and his gun at home. The feeling that crawled like a nest of bugs through his stomach at that moment was one he recognized from that nightmare.

It was cold as he stepped outside. Menelaus looked up and realized that there was no one around him. The village of seashell buildings silent and motionless was all about him.

3. Deserted

The smartwire fence was to his right, but there were no watchmen in the towers, no guards at the gate, which was hanging open. Through the wire, the prison yard was not only deserted, it was empty. The tents had been broken down, folded up, and hauled off. The power plant at one corner of the wire enclosure was still there, and the coffin yard, now unguarded. Trees and rises in the ground hid the rest of the camp from view.

He turned his head. The airfield was also empty. The large helicopter-bladed ironclad Mickey had called the *Albatross* was not there. The eleven rear-screwed biplanes and triplanes with their painted wings were gone. The snow was rutted and rerutted with tracks showing that the takeoffs had been recent enough that the wind had not yet covered up the traces: minutes rather than hours ago.

His weapons banging and robes clattering, and Rada Lwa jouncing on his shoulder, Menelaus jogged to the large pink seashell he supposed to be the hospital, where Sir Guy and the Giant, the two most dangerous prisoners, had been kept.

He stepped in the pink oval opening hung with tent-cloth material that served as a door. Inside, he saw a floor with lines of chewed tread marks scarring it, and empty bags with dangling needles of medical material hanging from the rafters. Crates made of wood and packing material made of transparent fabric lay strewn everywhere. Midmost, something that looked like an operating table and diagnostic machinery were pulled away from the wall and unbuckled from their power supplies. The power batteries themselves were not in evidence. Along the walls were strips of input-output ports, epoxied to the seashell too well to be quickly torn down, and feeds for the absent coffins that had been parked here. The far wall was simply blown open, with fragments of abalone dangling down, twisting in the wind. Snow had blown in and was puddled here and there on the broken floor.

He put his hand on the wooden crate, wondering where the wood came from in the barren world of ice.

Everything bespoke haste, as if the machinery had been in the process of being hauled out and crated up, but then abandoned by the workmen midway.

He looked at the tread marks. One had been an oversized coffin from the thirty-first century—the coffin of a Giant. The second had a tread pattern design from the twenty-sixth century, belted treads with parallel marks of millipede legs—it was the special coffin of one of his knights.

He counted the feeder ports and lines along the walls. There had been thirty-two additional coffins here.

Menelaus stepped through the hole in the wall and back into the snow. He reached up with his free hand (the one not holding Rada Lwa) and snapped off a bit of the abalone-like building material. He looked carefully at the striation marks in order to deduce the growth patterns. Then he looked at the cables and strips still hanging from the walls. It was two different levels of technology, from two different ages of history. And the snow under his feet, if Ctesibius had spoken true, was a third level.

"Rada Lwa, I am really sick of talking to your pale albino butt, but there is no one else around to talk to. I think I just realized my whole mental picture of what has been going on since the moment I thawed was wrong. *All* the Blues are revenants. They must have just been put in the ground very recently. I wonder if this ice age is very recent too. Less than four hundred years old? Something here is not adding up."

He circled the pink seashell building. In the distance, he saw movement at the gate.

Menelaus did not resist when the pack of snarling dog things trotted at a quickstep out from the gate and, brandishing their pikes, took him into custody again. There were about forty of them, including some of the better-bred dogs, and two of Preceptor Naar's armed automata were also there, clanking after on metal feet and carrying heavier weapons.

After removing from him the subsonic hose, the two railguns, and the laser pack, they escorted him back through the wire. He congratulated himself that he still had the splicing knife up his sleeve. It was not much, but how much would he need? The Blues had probably gathered everyone before the still-locked door, and were watching Larz putter and listening to Larz make excuses.

Menelaus smiled, counting down the time until his knights, thawed by Soorm and Oenoe awoke. The dogs brought him to the woods.

The sky had cleared, and overhead showed a brilliant arctic blue, but the southern horizon was darkened with approaching storm clouds.

Menelaus stood on the highest platform, under the watchful eyes and noses of armed dogs. Yuen, Daae, and the Witches were nowhere to be seen. The south part of the canyon was a set of platforms made of stiffened tent material lashed to poles driven into the rock, and a set of ladders fell from platform to platform into the dig proper.

Looking down, he saw that the great door leading into the undiscovered parts of the Tombs was open. The weapons were holstered, locked down, and silent. The great valves of the fourth door were thrown wide, and a wedge of golden light formed a triangle along the floor and up the armored blocks of the wall. The light and power seemed to be back on.

Larz had done it. The Tombs were open. Even if it took men of mortal levels of intelligence an hour or so to find the clues in the Tomb, it would take Del Azarchel or Exarchel only an instant, the moment the agent of Del Azarchel reported his findings to his remote posthuman master.

At that moment, he desperately wished he had never stabbed himself in the head with that needle, never elevated his brain beyond the human level. Because an ordinary man, brain clouded with ordinary clouds, could cling to hope in such times, make up some lovely fairy tale about how some unknown thing would pop up to make things right; or rage, or pride, or some other hard and hot emotion could blank out, for a few hours, the painful crystal clarity of what his intellect spread before him.

For painfully, simply, clearly, he saw that he had failed. Blackie Del Azarchel had won. The career and the life of Menelaus Montrose, Judge of Ages, were finished.

And from the open doors of the Tombs, where the light poured out, rich and golden, into the cold air, he could see the shadows of the dog things dancing and flickering. They were performing an antic jig, leaping and twisting and wagging their tails, biting the air for joy, and flourishing their cutlasses; and dimly he heard the wild music of fiddle and flute echoing against the canyon walls against which their angular shadows leaped.

PERSONS OF THE DRAMA

Characters named but not appearing are in italics. Dates given are of last interment date, unless otherwise noted.

Menelaus—Menelaus Illation Montrose, the Judge of Ages
Pellucid—His Xypotech
Rania—Her Serene Highness Rania Anne Galatea Trismegistina del Estrella-Diamante Grimaldi, Sovereign Princess of Monaco, Duchess of Valentinois and of Mazarin, Marchioness of Baux, Countess of Carladès and of Polignac; Stadtholder for Dutch North European *Coalitie* and Owner-in-Chief of the World Snow Syndicate; Captain of the NTL *Hermetic,* the Vindicatrix and Promised Savioress of mankind; also styled Mrs. Rania Montrose
Captain Grimaldi—His Serene Highness Ranier Grimaldi of Monaco, her father, and Captain of the NTL *Hermetic* before her

Hermeticists

Melchor de Ulloa
Narcís Santdionís de Rei D'Aragó—The Iron Hermeticist
Sarmento i Illa d'Or
Father Reyes y Pastor—The Red Hermeticist
Jaume Coronimas—The Locust Hermeticist
Ximen del Azarchel—Senior of the Landing Party, Nobilissimus of the World Concordat, Master of the World
Exarchel—His emulation
Astro-Exarchel—His emulation aboard the NTL *Bellerophon*

Cryonarch

Thucydides—Father Thucydides Acumen Montrose, Society of Jesus; later, His Holiness Sixtus VI

Scholar

Rada Lwa—Intermediately Evolved Learned Scholar Rada Lwa Chwal Sequitur Argent-Montrose

Savant

Ctesibius—Glorified Ctesibius Zant, Endorcist of Three Donatives, Servant of the Machine (A.D. 2525)

Hospitaliers

Sir Guy—Sir Guiden von Hompesch zu Bolheim, later Grandmaster of the Order

Sir Alof Villiers de l'Isle-Adam, Manwell Magri, and *Themistocles Zammit*—Scientist-Knights

Giant

Name not given (A.D. 3090)

Sylphs

Woggy Soaring Azurine
Tessa Soaring Azurine
Third or Trey Soaring Azurine (tentative)
Brother Roger de Juliac, Society of Jesus

Witches

Mickey—Melechemoshemyazanagual Onmyoji de Concepcion, Padre Bruja-Stregone of Donna Verdant Coven; from the Holy Fortress at Williamsburg (A.D. 4733)

Chimerae

Daae—Alpha Captain Varuman Aemileus Daae of Uttarakhand, Osaka, Bombay, Yumbulangang, and other actions in the South China Theater; the Varuman blood derives from the Osterman, from the *Homo sapiens,* and *Canis lupus* (A.D. 5402)

Yuen—Alpha Steadholder Extet Minnethales Yuen of Richmond, Third and Second Manassas, Antietam, and various Actions against Pirates; the Yuen are of the Original Experiment Set, from *Homo sapiens* and *Puma concolor* (A.D. 4881)
Grislac—His current weapon
Arroglint the Fortunate—The named weapon of his lineage
Anubis—High-Beta Sterling Xenius Anubis of Mount Erebus (A.D. 5292) Dependent College, 102nd Civic Control Division, attached to the Pennsylvania third Legion: the "Virginianized" version of this name is Ir-Beta Sterlingas Xeniopater Anupsu-phalangetor Erebumontsangil
Phyle—Gamma Joet Goez Phyle of Bull Run, Lineage Discontinued (A.D. 5655)
Ivinia—Alpha Lady Mother-of-Commandant Wife-of-Captain Ulec Nemosthene Ivinia née Echtal, and her victory title is Septimilegens
Arthuna Ire Extet—One of her ancestors by marriage through the Ulec line
Callixiroc the Dark—The named weapon of the lineage of Ivinia
Vulpina and Suspinia—young Beta women (Vulpina A.D. 5316) (Suspinia A.D. 4812)
Larz—Kine Larz Quire Slewfoot of Gutter (A.D. 5950)
Larslin Bretchlouder, on whom the character is based
Gibson—a half-Gamma who wrote the *Larz of the Gutter* cheaplies
Alpha Captain Stheno Alleret Anju of First and Second Bull Run—A soldier mentioned by Larz
Franz, Ardzl, Happy—Other Kine

Nymphs

Oenoe—Oenoe Psthinshayura-Ah of Crocus with Clover and Forsythia (A.D. 6746)
Rayura-Ah—The First of Nature, a twin of Rania
Aura-Ah and Riana-Ah—Her twins

Iatrocrats

Hormagaunt Iatrocrats:
Soorm—Soorm scion Asvid scion Pastor (his original name was Soorm scion Moord scion Elwe) (interred A.D. 7466)
Asvid—his original Satyr-name was Marsyas of Saffron, with Oakwhite, Oleander, Rocket, and Mandrake (these floral symbols represent Wariness of Excess, Independence, Caution, rivalry, honor), born circa A.D. 6850

Behemodont—His pet
Moord scion Elwe—His maker
Asvid of Nettles—His patron
Ormvermin—The watchworm of Asvid
Crile scion Wept and Gload scion Ghollipog—Two Hormagaunts (Gload, A.D. 7520; Crile A.D. 7810)

Short Iatrocrats:
Prissy Pskov and Zouave Zhigansk—two Iatrocracy Burghers (Clade dwellers)
Toil, Drudge, Drench—three Iatrocracy organ-donors

Locusts

Crucxit, Axcit, and Litcec of Seven-Twenty-One North Station (between A.D. 7480 and A.D. 10000)

Blue Men (Simplifers)

Illiance—A Locust Inquiline of the Order of Simplified Vulnerary Aetiology (the Simplifiers, aka the Blue Men); his false-mother-name is Lagniappe (A.D. 8800)
Ull—his Mentor
Orovoy, Naar, Yndelf, Yndech, Ydmoy—Preceptors of Blue Men
Saaev, Aarthroy, Unwing—Blue Men of lower dignity: an Invigilator, a Docent, a Bedel
Aanwen—A Blue Widow; her dignity is Preceptrix

Their Followers

Eie Kafk Ref Rak—One of the Followers, a canine Moreau (Irish Wolfhound)
Ee-ee Krkok Yef Yepp—A Follower (a stately Doberman Pincer)
Ktatch-Ee Yett Ya-Ia—Another Follower (a Collie)
Rirk Refka Kak-Et—Another Follower (a Great Dane)

Linderlings

Keir and Keirthlin (A.D. 8866)

Melusine

Alalloel (A.D. 10100)

Elders

Joua Ja Gomez—Also styled George Washington, sold Cheyenne Mountain to the Order of Malta

RACES OF THE DRAMA

Note on Languages

Noted here are only the dominant or most common languages spoken by the persons of the drama. This does not reflect the demographic distribution of speakers: so, for example, Spanish is listed as the dominant language of the world in the time of the Concordat, even though there were more Sinospherics (who spoke Chinese) than Hispanospherics (who spoke Spanish or Portuguese).

Hospitaliers—Latin
Hermeticists—Spanish and English
Scholars—Korrekthotspeek (an English dialect)
Savants—Merikan
Sylphs—Spanish/Nipponese/Merikan pidgin
Giants—Anglatino
Witches—Virginian
Chimerae—Chimerical, albeit the lettered classes spoke Virginian, at least in the western hemisphere before the Social Wars
Nymphs—Natural, also called Nymph; there is no written form of the language
Hormagaunts—Iatric, albeit an earlier form of the language is called Leech
Locusts—Intertextual; this language is still in use by the Blue Men and the Linderlings
The language used by the Followers or dog things is not called by name, but it is described as sounding like barking
Melusine—Although not mentioned in the text, the language is called Verbal (a spoken version of Glyphic, based on Monument symbol logic sets)

Note on the Theory of Intelligent Design

It is commonly regarded that the several subspecies of man arising during the Hermetic Millennia were created by the special intervention of posthuman beings called the Hermetic Order or Hermeticists, albeit the widespread destruction of all forms of electronic record during the Ecpyrosis (A.D. 2525) makes confirmation difficult.

Among the Witches it is taught that mankind was created by the bones of the men of the previous world of the "Sixth Sun" recovered from the netherworld of Mictlan by venture of the archimage Houdini. Both textual and archaeological evidence favor the Witch theory, but the Intelligent Design theory is given here for reasons of completeness. The Chimerae teach that they were created by the genetic sciences of the Witches as Moreaus are. The Nymphs do not make theories. Hormagaunts not only favor the Intelligent Design theory, but their ancestor lists are also carefully forged to put the Red Hermeticist, Pastor, at the head of each. The Locusts believe a variant of the theory, but list the Locust scientist Seir as the creator of the race. How the Locust race can be created by a Locust is a mystery best left to theologians to explain.

Notwithstanding, tradition names the creator of each of the subspecies as follows:

Giants—Menelaus Montrose

Albeit many traditions give the creator's name as Thucydides Montrose, or as His Holiness Sixtus VI. The notable features of Giants are their posthuman level intelligence, vast cranial capacity, and great size.

Witches—Melchor de Ulloa

The females enjoy greatly expanded life spans, as well as neural modifications in those brain areas associated with intuitive thought, pattern-seeking, and dreaming.

Chimera—Narcís D'Aragó

The Chimerae have animal DNA spliced into their code. Despite the popular error, Chimerae look like human beings to the unpracticed eye, and do not have beastlike faces or fur or tails. The Chimerae are disease resistant and hardened to endure levels of radioactivity lethal to unmodified human beings. Note that the Kine, who retain Witch atavisms, are longer lived than their masters.

Nymphs—Sarmento i Illa D'Or

The Nymphs are bred for exaggerated sexual allure and response both in male and female, as well as sensitivity and vulnerability to a wide array of pharmacological stimulants, depressants, and hallucinogens. The pleasure centers of the brain are enlarged.

Hormagaunts—Father Reyes y Pastor

The Hormagaunts are modified to have voluntary control over their bodily tissue rejection mechanism, and to write and edit captured genetic material into their sperm by means of microscopic viral and nanotechnological manipulator cells. This enables them to add captured organs to their bodies, and to absorb and copy genetic information by ingesting samples. The Hormagaunt race has no fixed phenotype. A variant called Clades do not have so wide a range of variation, but manifest an allergy-causing mechanism to drive away persons of alien genetic arrangement; i.e., non-twins. It is not commonly recognized that the Locusts and Hormagaunts occupied the world at the same time, in competition with each other for most of their existence that ranges from vicious to ferocious to genocidal.

Locusts—Jaume Coronimas

Locusts have extensive neural modification, which allows them to use their brain matter as a neural emulator. Neural connection and calculation speed are similar to Giant brain structures. They posses a primary and secondary heart, as well as finer nerves with higher neural transmission speeds than humans. Most notably are the two golden tendrils that allow the Locusts to exchange subjective neural information radiotelepathically. Despite the popular error, Locusts cannot only not read human minds, who do not have broadcast organs of this type, but they also cannot read the minds of any Locust whose nervous system is not precisely organized to the same mental form and format. Despite the popular error, not all Locust races are dwarfish and bald: this applies only to variant races after the time of the Fifth Configuration, circa 8000–8700.

Inquilines—Not a separate race. Inquilines are Locusts who lack radiotelepathic tendrils. Their creation is credited to a Nymph scientist named Elton Linder. An older tradition credits a figure from Witch necromantic legend called the Judge of Ages, perhaps because Linder was preserved in biosuspended hibernation from an earlier era.

Melusine—Ximen del Azarchel

Melusine are radiotelepathically linked gestalt minds occupying five or seven bodies: a main whale-like body consisting mostly of brain mass; a dolphin or post-dolphin body or both; a Locust body modified to amphibianism; a human or posthuman land-dwelling body or both.

Note on Orders and Periods

Listed below are the races of the First Human Species found during the period known as the Hermetic Millennia, with the formal name of the Order representing their most prominent advocates, hence popularly associated with them. In the text, the distinction between (1) a genetically differentiated race or subspecies of *Homo sapiens* and (2) an Order devoted to the Darwinian expansion of that race is problematical, due to the ease of genetic modification. The words are used interchangeably.

Also listed are the periods of their world predominance or hegemony.

Humans (First Human Race or "Elders"): (circa 80000 B.C. to A.D. 2700)

Hermeticists—Hermetic Order, also the Hermetic World Concordat (A.D. 2360 to 2401)

Scholars aka Psychics—Order of Psychic Evolutionary Advocates (A.D. 2370 to 2525)

Savants aka Slaves of the Machine—Order of Transhumanitarian Emulation Advocates. Their human kenosis or donators are called Savants. Their Xypotech apotheosis emulations are called Ghosts or Iron Ghosts (A.D. 2476 to 2525)

Sylphs aka Floaters—Order of Limited Infinite Ratiotechnical Emulation Adoration (A.D. 2500 to 2700)

Medusae are mentioned as a faction of Sylphs, but they do not form a separate order nor a separate subspecies (A.D. 2700 to 3000)

Giants aka Thucydideans—Consensus Advocacy (A.D. 2500 to 3100)

Witches aka Wise—Delphic Acroamatic Transhumanitarian and Longevitalist Order (aka Delphic Acroamatic Progressive Transhumanitarian Order for the Study of Longevity) (A.D. 3300 to 4900)

Chimerae—Eugenic Emergency General Command of the Commonwealth of Virginia (A.D. 4500 to 5900)

Nymphs aka Naturals—The Natural Order of Man (A.D. 6000 to 7000)

Hormagaunts—The Configuration of Iatrocratic Clades (A.D. 7000 to 8000)

Locusts—Noöspherical Cognitive Order (A.D. 7500 to 8500 or to 9500)

Blue Men aka Simple Men or Simplifiers—Order of Simplification aka the Locust Inquiline group, the Order of Simplified Vulnerary Aetiology (A.D. 8500 to 8900)

Gray Men aka Linderlings or Tendrilless Locusts—The Locust Inquiline group, Linder Confraternity; also, the Sixteenth Configuration (A.D. 8800 to 9500)

Melusine—The Final Stipulation of Noösphere Protocols, or the Finality (A.D. 9500 to unknown)

Second Humans (or "Swans") (A.D. 10000 to unknown)

Hospitaliers—The Sovereign Military Hospitalier Order of Saint John, of Jerusalem, of Rhodes, of Malta, and of Colorado

Note that the Hospitaliers are not an Order, even though they are called so, because they do not advocate a particular subspecies to dominate or extinguish the others, despite that this is the clear Darwinian mandate.

Instead they advance a peculiar theory that man did not evolve from a lower condition but fell, due to a primordial catastrophe, from a higher, dimly remembered in the legends of all peoples. Instead of achieving evolution to a higher state by means of ruthless competition to exterminate all rivals unto extinction, their theory holds that this higher state of superhumanity or posthumanity or New Man is a resumption or restoration achieved by mystical acceptance of self-sacrificing love by a posthuman being, and the consequent ability and necessity to treat others universally with similar self-sacrificing love, rather than only those others of genetically related clans, clades, or bloodlines: the mere opposite of the Darwinian racialist imperative as commonly understood.

Note also that no Order is held in more contempt and enmity by the others than this: Hermeticist, Witches, Chimera, Hormagaunts, Locusts, and Melusine all regard the Knights Hospitalier and the theory and world-system they propagate with inexplicably exaggerated hostility; but, also inexplicably, each for a differing reason.

Only Sylphs and Giants maintain friendly or neutral relations. The Knight Hospitalier are famous for their exploits in the King's Crusade, guarding pilgrims seeking the Holy Land, and also in service to the Judge of Ages, guarding the Tombs that held the pilgrims seeking the future.